Situationship

Situationship

E.M. WILSON

W wattpad books FRAYED PAGES

FRAYED PAGES

wattpad books

An imprint of Wattpad WEBTOON Book Group

Copyright © 2025 E.M. Wilson. All rights reserved.

Published in Canada by Wattpad WEBTOON Book Group, a division of Wattpad WEBTOON Studios, Inc. 36 Wellington Street E., Toronto, ON M5E 1C7

www.wattpad.com

First Frayed Pages x Wattpad Books edition: April 2025

www.frayedpagesmedia.com

ISBN 978-1-99834-119-1 (Trade Paperback)
ISBN 978-1-99834-160-3 (eBook)

Library and Archives Canada Cataloguing in Publication and US Library of Congress Cataloging in Publication information is available upon request.

Printed and bound in Canada

1 3 5 7 9 10 8 6 4 2

Cover design by Carina Guevara
Author Photo by Aigerim Donentay Rafael
Typesetting by Delaney Anderson

To the black sheep.
You're not the problem. You just need better friends.

AUTHOR'S NOTE

To my readers,

As the title implies, the two main characters' desire is to get into bed—quickly, and long before they admit to having an emotional connection—to avoid addressing the deeper issues they have with each other and in their lives. Like most works of fiction, this story was inspired by life. It contains mentions of mental health and disordered eating, which are handled with as soft and healing a touch as possible without minimizing the importance of such topics.

I hope you enjoy the story.

With love,
Em

ONE

Teagan

Holy shit, we have to break up.

"Oh, god. Teagan!" Lenny moans as he finishes. His body shudders the way it always does after a hard four minutes of work. His expression is one of pure bliss while he leaves me frustrated yet again.

No, we don't need to break up. This is fixable. Something that can be improved upon with proper time and training, I tell myself, not registering my solution is appropriate for dogs, not men. Lackluster performance aside, it's not worth overlooking all the positive traits he has. He's intelligent, ambitious, and that body . . .

Sweat glistens against the defined muscles of his chest, taunting me. I stroke my hands over them as he catches his breath. It wouldn't be fair if he was perfect in *every* way. He just can't seem to figure this out, even after five long months of trying. Five aggravating, vexatious, frustrating months.

He looks down at me, wetting his lips while he pants. "That was so good," he says. *Was it, Lenny? Was it?*

He collapses onto me and wraps me in a hug. When I'm not looking at him, I don't like him nearly as much. I stare up at the ceiling in annoyance, replacing my expression with a smile when he turns his head to look at me. "Did you . . . ?"

If you have to ask, the answer is no. "I . . . no, I didn't," I admit. "I was close, though." I wasn't close at all. The sun is closer to that orgasm than I was.

He looks rueful, as if realizing he's let me down. He has. "I'm sorry, I thought you had."

Bitch, where?

"No," I repeat in as gentle a tone as I can manage.

Lenny is a sensitive little lamb, but he has yet to figure out I'm a wolf, hungry for more than he gives me. Unfortunately for me, I *need* this relationship to work. I've been playing coy to keep from scaring him away, focusing on school and work while hoping this part would work itself out, and it gets harder every day that passes.

"It takes me a while to get there," I explain. He nods in understanding and presses an apologetic kiss on my cheek. "There are . . . other things we could do to help me along, you know."

"Like what?" he asks. He brushes his hand over my cheek. "I'll do anything you want."

"Well . . ." I tread lightly. "You could go down on me."

His gaze drops from mine and his mouth presses into a straight line.

"You love when I do it for you, so maybe you could try—?"

"I told you that makes me uncomfortable."

"I know you've had a bad experience with a partner before, but I'm very rigorous about my hygiene, it would never—"

"No, Teagan. I don't want to."

"Okay, okay," I coddle him. "Then would you let *me* do things to help me along?"

"You shouldn't need those things when you have me. I should be enough for you."

He pulls out and rolls over to sit on the edge of the bed. I stare at his back, watching his muscles flex as he fumbles with the condom. Big arms that can curl me like a pillow, wide shoulders that would be a great resting spot for my thighs if given the chance, and a nice, tight ass. Ugh, why does he have to look so good? Every part of my body wants him, only to get nothing when I have him.

He's the human equivalent of a bag of chips. The image on the front promises so much, but you open it up and find out it's mostly air and won't go down on you.

"This relationship isn't working," I blurt.

He turns to me with wide-eyed surprise. "What? Why?"

I sit up, holding the covers to my chest. "Because I'm not happy."

"Not happy?" He looks as if he wants to cry. It would break my heart if I had one. "How can you not be happy? I thought you loved me."

The L-word is far too strong to describe how I feel about him, but that's beside the point right now. "I care about you—obviously I do, Lenny. It's just . . . you . . ." Frustration sets in again. He can't see how selfish he is being. I don't need his money or his connections, things most women would use him for. I just want him to get me off. Why is that so much to ask? "You haven't given me a single orgasm the entire time we've been together, and it is driving me insane."

"I want to satisfy you. I've been trying."

"Have you, though?" I laugh out of frustration rather than humor, which I realize comes off as crazed as I'm about to seem. "It's been months of the same shit. You don't like it when I touch myself. You hate when I suggest toys. And what kind of straight dude doesn't want to eat pussy? Seriously!"

"Excuse me?" His eyebrows rise.

"If I didn't suck your dick or get you off, you would have dumped me months ago and you damn well know it. But here you are acting like it personally offends you to return the favor!" There goes my plan to play coy, but I feel so much better getting it off my chest.

He stares at me in disbelief. "Who are you right now?"

"Someone who is sexually frustrated," I say. "You are the most irritating person I have ever met. You have an amazing mind and an absolutely *ridiculous* body, but you have no idea how to use either. How can someone graduate law school with honors and not be able to figure out where the fucking clitoris is?"

"You'd throw away a future with me because you think I'm not good in bed?" He shakes his head. "I'm very disappointed."

"Well, now you know how I've felt every time you've been inside me."

There's an awkward silence as Lenny dresses. He grabs his wallet and keys from the top of my nightstand. He doesn't turn back to me when he walks out of the room. I listen for the sound of the front door closing before I flop back onto my pillow.

As I stare at the ceiling, I realize what I just did. A giggle bubbles up and breaks the silence. I cover my smiling mouth with a hand.

~

So, maybe breaking up at the start of summer wasn't the best idea.

For most people, the summer is a time to relax, enjoy the sun, and have a fling, but in my world, it's cuffing season. Just like the winter stretch of holidays that are much easier to navigate with an already established beau, my summertime is filled with event after event, none you want to show up to alone. Weddings, parties, banquets—one million places to see and be seen by the same circle of socialites and *Forbes* 500s, all ready to be neck-deep in your business for the sake of entertainment. It's worse when you're the one who already seems out of place.

Adoption has its ups and downs. One of the ups is getting wealthy parents who wanted me and my brothers more than anything. One of the downs is always having to explain yourself and your presence in a room you wouldn't be in if not for the parents who look nothing like you. Growing up, my parents always felt the need to prove we were a family—and a happy one—before anyone had the chance to ask. They brought us to all the summer social gatherings, always dressing us to the nines, making sure we were coordinated, on theme, and appropriate for the occasion so we wouldn't stick out for the wrong reasons. Now I have an irrational fear of showing up without meeting every ostentatious expectation.

I try to remind myself the operative word is *irrational*. I don't *need* a date for this party or the next. No one will even notice I'm alone. It'll be fine. Totally fine.

I pull my fingernail away from the absent-minded gnawing of my teeth.

My dress tickles the tops of my feet as I walk into the banquet hall. I feel confident that the floor length, high slit, and cowl neckline are up to par for this event, but I'm not feeling confident that my orgasmless sex hair is doing the same. I was too overwhelmed to tame my curls back into compliance. Swooping them up into a makeshift updo was the best I could achieve.

"Teags!"

I turn to find my best friend, Ryan, approaching, his fiancé, Mary, in one hand, a flute of champagne in the other. Mary's graduation is the reason he threw this soirée, but their short, six-month engagement has turned all of their big events into prewedding celebrations.

"Congratulations, Mary," I say before we kiss cheeks, careful not to touch my lacquered lips to her skin. She thanks me, her smile gleaming like the crystals on her dress and the massive diamond on her finger. The mermaid gown hugs every curve, its gold color flattering her tan skin and brown eyes. "You look beautiful, as always."

"Thank you! I'm just trying to get on your level." She flatters me.

Mary, unlike her common name, is a rare gem. Grounded and painfully kind, she makes it a point to ensure everyone around her is comfortable and included. In the four years they have been together, she has grown my bestie from a little prick into a semitolerable man. The only way I could be happier for them is if I wasn't the one responsible for planning their wedding and all the upcoming parties to celebrate it.

"The whole gang is here." Ryan gestures behind me. Sure enough, the rest of our friends stand in a circle along the edge of the crowd.

"Right," I say. "I better say hi, and you need to mingle. I'll catch you two later." I give them more kisses and wave goodbye.

The gang smiles when they see me approaching. There is a mandatory relationship that forms when you are stuck in the same places with the same people for fifteen years. Since elementary school we have been entwined in each other's lives. Our graduating class from high school was an intimate group of twenty, and out of that, only the six of us went to Columbia.

While I spend my school months with future groundbreakers, Divine Nines, and powerful women who inspire and challenge me, my summers are dictated by my family's curated network, leaving me with these fucking guys. Even with me being the glaring black sheep of the group—the only girl, only Black friend, only adoptee—we're all a bunch of nepo babies and trust fund kids. People most of the public would find intolerable. Whether we like it or not, we are inescapably enmeshed, a family, together for every milestone and every celebration.

"Teags!" the guys say in unison.

"Hey, guys." They're all here, and everyone has a date except me. *Great.* Brett and his wife, Jeremy and Ritchie with their long-term beaus, and . . . Heath. His gray eyes meet mine, and I ignore the ache in my chest.

He always cleans up well considering how he practically lives in athletic wear. His dark hair is freshly cut and styled, his tux impeccably tailored to his athletic build, his navy bow tie making his eyes pop. It's hard to appreciate his Calvin Klein–model perfection when it's hidden behind his glaring, douchebag persona, but for most women, it's the opposite. The Pilates-body blond he has wrapped around his arm proves my point. She's at a black-tie event in a cheap cocktail dress. He didn't even bother to tell her the dress code, and she doesn't care, because the man taking her home tonight is rich and fine as hell. I hate him. So much.

He lifts his chin to greet me, and we go back to ignoring each other.

"Didn't think you were going to make it," Jeremy, my other bestie and roomie jeers. We have lived together since sophomore year, but since he met his boyfriend, his little jabs have grown less playful and our time together less frequent.

"You try walking in these shoes," I say, swishing the end of my gown to the side to reveal them.

"Okay, Angelina Jolie. I see you working that high slit," Jeremy's boyfriend, Chet, compliments me. He is always the soothing balm after Jeremy's cutting remarks. The two of them have opposite per-sonalities but look so much alike—burly, kind brown eyes, the same groomed beards—it's weird.

"Where's your guy?" Brett asks me. Of course he does. By far the wealthiest in the group, he was and *is* the biggest fuckboy, yet somehow, he was the first of us to get married. He and his wife, Felicity, look like the generic brown-haired, blue-eyed wedding top-per, perfect and preppy, but we have all been trying to figure out how and *why* he got married at all. "I thought you were dating that buff lawyer dude?"

"Oh, we broke up," I say with a casual wave of my hand, even though the situation is *anything* but casual.

"Really? No way!" Ritchie jumps in, even though I know he doesn't care. While I will always despise Heath, Ritchie is a close second. The two finance bros, Ritchie is the Donnie Azoff to Brett's Jordan Belfort. From school to career to their new jobs, he copies whatever Brett does, but with half the money, half the charisma, and none of the common sense. He's five feet six inches of pure chaos.

"I thought you two were getting serious," Brett continues. "With your parents and everything, we had a bet going that you'd be the next to get engaged."

His reminder makes my stomach turn. "Yeah, well . . . apparently not."

A waiter walks by with a tray of champagne flutes. I grab one with a bit too much enthusiasm then down all of it in one go.

Thank god for open bars.

TWO
Heath

She wants me bad. I can tell.

My date has been stuck to me all night like sequin-covered Velcro. It was a risk bringing her a party like this as a first date, but nothing gets a girl to put out quicker than showing them how much money you have and making them think you're looking to get married like your friends. To my luck, she has been starry-eyed and entertained the whole time. The problem is it's taking forever to seal the deal. I'm three drinks in and starting to get impatient.

Her short dress rides up high on her thighs, and the top of it is cut low, both taunting me. It's enough to give me a sampling of the goods while still making me curious. She giggles at my joke as she licks the sugar from the rim of her lemon drop. Weak, sweet drinks like that always lead to midnight fun.

I glance at my watch and see it's 11:11. *Already? Damn.* What does a man have to do to get laid in Manhattan? "It's 11:11," I say in a flirtatious voice. "Make a wish."

She smiles and closes her eyes. She's either wishing for my dick or she's stupid.

When she opens her eyes again, her pouty lips turn up in a smile. I know what that means. "What did you wish for?"

"I can't tell you that, silly." She bats my arm playfully with her hand. A little touching? She *so* wants it.

I catch her hand and hold it in mine. She looks up at me from beneath long lashes. Her fake nails are shaped like claws and have about a million crystals glued on them. Girls who pay that much money for hand glitter are always down to fuck a guy like me, and I'm not complaining.

"I'll tell you what I wished for," I say. Pink appears on her cheeks. I lean a little closer and brush my lips over her ear as I whisper just one of the dirty, dirty things I want to do between her thighs. Her cheeks are a vibrant red when I lean away. "Make my wish come true?" I ask.

She slams down her glass. "You're a fucking pig." Then she stands up and grabs her purse.

"What? No, wait! I was kidding?" That last part probably shouldn't have been a question.

She glares at me over her shoulder as she walks away. Watching her ass move under that little skirt makes my balls ache with despair. *Fucking hell.*

A familiar chuckle sounds near me. I look over to find Teagan laughing at my misfortune from the end of the bar. "*What?*"

"Having a bad night?" She flashes a mischievous smile over her glass.

"Shut up." I know how bad I fucked up without her telling me about it too. "What are you still doing here?"

"Watching you crash and burn." She laughs. "'Make my wish come true?'" Her laugh turns into a cackle.

"Fuck off." I fight a smile. I'd take it personally, but Teagan never fails to throw a punch with any of the guys. It's needed with a group of misfits like ours. I slide onto the stool next to her and signal to the bartender. "What are you drinking?"

"My favorite drink after every breakup. What-the-fuck-ever."

"Having a bad night, too, I see."

"No. I'm great." The twist of her face illustrates her lack of sobriety. I wait for her lie to fall apart. "I mean, yeah, I just broke up with my boyfriend two hours before this party, but it's fine. His replacement is arriving tomorrow by nine p.m." She turns her phone and shows me her vibrator purchase on Amazon. The girl is a damn mess.

"Looks like we both need to make good use of these free drinks tonight."

She clinks her glass against mine. We down them and I signal to the bartender for another round.

"Hey," she starts again. "Weren't you dating that girl from NYU? The pretty redhead?"

"That ended months ago."

"Oh shit. Sorry."

"Don't be. I dodged a bullet with that one. Actually, I dodged a textbook and a lamp."

She snorts. "I just *know* you deserved the textbook, but I'll need more details to defend the lamp."

"I really fucked up. We went back to her place after going out and it looked oddly familiar." I shrugged. "When her roommate came home, I figured out why."

"Let me guess. Because you were fucking her a few months before?"

I give her a sheepish smile. "More like a few weeks."

Teagan bursts into laughter. She covers her mouth with a hand and tries to compose herself. "Yeah, you deserved the lamp too."

I join her, laughing at my expense, the alcohol loosening my shame. "I thought we were chilling, then she wanted more, so I ghosted her and started seeing someone else I met at the same party." Summarizing it makes me see the error of my ways. "Don't say it."

"What was I going to say?"

"That I'm practicing typical fuckboy behavior." Her raised eyebrows and slow sip show I'm right. I know her well. "Why do I always act like a piece of shit?"

"Maybe because you *are* a piece of shit?" she responds. I give her a sideways glance, but I can't kill my smile. When she's right, she's right.

The bartender sets down our drinks and we both take a swig. I steal a shameless look while she is distracted, hating how fucking hot she is. My eyes trace up those long, long legs, her deep-brown skin glistening like she's made of the same silk as her dress. One of her straps keeps slipping down her shoulder, her hair is falling out of her updo, and her shoes are already kicked off and lying on the floor next to her stool.

Teagan has always been zero or one hundred, and nothing in between. One minute she's obsessing over her image—an overachieving perfectionist, *looking* like a model while also being a model student and daughter—seemingly without a single stumble. Then the next she's laid out, wild, and giving us a run for our fuckboy money. She's a lot to handle.

Not that it ever stopped me.

"Why'd you break up with your boyfriend?"

"I couldn't take it anymore. He made me go five months without an orgasm."

I almost spit out my drink. *"Five months? How?"*

She shrugs. "He's the son of my dad's business partner." That's enough of an explanation. Teagan will do anything to maintain her perfect image with her parents, even if it means making herself miserable. "I *really* tried to make it work. He was great in every other way—intelligent, ambitious, great body . . ."

"But his stroke game was weak?"

"Try nonexistent," she slurs. I laugh, but that's just sad. "It was like he *refused* to let me come. I've never been with someone I liked that much but hated in bed. If I had some side dick, I probably would have married him. Well, he wouldn't have married me when he found out about the side dick, but you get it."

"I do."

"How can being in a relationship suck as much as being single?" she asks. "It's either you stay with someone you barely tolerate just so you can get laid on the regular, or you have freedom but waste all your time trying to convince someone to fuck you."

God, she's speaking my language. "Yes! It's like the in-between disappeared. Fuck dating. All I want is someone who'll be in my bed as often as possible without expecting a pet name in a month and a ring in a year."

"*Right?* All I want is someone who'll get me off and then get off me."

"Someone who'll suck my dick then fucking dip."

"Give me some P in V, then let me pee and leave."

Both of our drunk asses find that funnier than we should. We laugh so long we're in tears and gripping our stomachs before we manage to stop.

The bartender comes over and cuts into our fun. "Sorry, guys. We're closing up now."

We down the rest of our drinks and stumble away from the bar, still laughing to ourselves. Teagan can't figure out how to put her heels back on, and almost tumbles down the stairs when we make it out front. When I help her down the rest of the way, she doesn't let me go. Now *she's* the one stuck to me, and it gives me a very bad idea.

"I'll get us a cab," I say. Teagan nods in agreement.

~

The cab pulls up to my apartment a few minutes later. Teagan and I only live a few blocks from each other *and* go to the same school, yet we only see each other every few months. We have classes, internships. She's busy, I'm busy. We could still see each other if we really wanted to, but we don't. At least *she* doesn't.

We have history. Years of friendship tarnished by a moment we pretend we've forgotten over time, but Teagan never forgives. She hates me—when we're sober and clothed, at least. Two things I don't plan to be for much longer.

It takes us a full minute to climb the first flight of stairs up to my apartment. Teagan can't walk straight. I find it hilarious, and both of us keep keeling over while laughing about it. We make it to the last landing, and then she trips. I keep her vertical while she stumbles to the wall and leans against it for balance.

"Fuck, I haven't been this drunk since . . ."

She thinks for a moment but laughs when she can't remember. Her breath smells like tequila and her hair is a mess, but she looks beautiful when she laughs. That smile does things to me. A very specific, swelling part of me. Fruit is always better when it's forbidden, and I already know how sweet she tastes.

I press my hands to the wall, caging her between my arms. When she looks up at me, I step closer. "What's stopping us?"

"The walls and floor are moving a lot right now."

"No, what's stopping us from solving our mutual problem?" I give her all the smolder I can muster in my drunken state. She stares me down, a smirk on her plump lips challenging me to do more. I lean in even closer, my mouth hovering over hers, but she still won't give in.

"You want to fuck me so bad," she whispers.

I reach down and run my hand up her exposed thigh, loving the feel of her buttery-soft skin. "I don't *not* want to fuck you."

Her doe eyes look at me from beneath heavy lids. I watch the desire swim over her face as she tries to suppress it. She's too proud to go down without a fight and, oh, how I would enjoy that battle right now.

Her hand runs over the nape of my neck before she slides it down to my chest. In a sexy little voice, she whispers, "I hate you."

"I know." I smirk at her. "Come on."

Taking her by the hand, I lead her up the last few stairs and into my apartment.

THREE

Teagan

My eyes snap open to a room I don't recognize. *Where the fuck am I?*

Slate-colored walls and dark hardwood floors frame an expansive living space, only interrupted by velvet and leather furniture in coordinating shades of black and gray. White charmeuse curtains barely block the sun beaming through the tall windows into the otherwise dark space. It looks like a millennial bachelor gave up halfway through decorating and hired someone with taste to finish the rest. More importantly, I've spent a night and all morning in a place I don't know, doing god knows what.

When I sit up, my head screams at me. Open bars are only fun until the next day, a lesson I should have learned by now. Looking down, I find I'm on a couch with a faux fur blanket draped over me. I blink until my vision clears, my head throbbing, and find the naked man lying on the floor next to me.

My heart races when I see him. Recognizing the black tattoos on his shoulder and thighs makes it worse. *"Heath?"*

He groans as if telling me to shut up.

Oh shit. Oh shit, shit, shit. I sit up straight and cover myself with the blanket. "Heath!"

His head darts up from his pillow. "What? Am I late?"

"Late for what, shithead? It's Sunday."

He looks over at me, his hair twisted with day-old product. "Then what the hell, Teags? Stop yelling, my head hurts." He lays his head back down like nothing is out of place.

I nudge him with my foot. "What am I doing here? Why are you naked?"

He groans again. "Chill, dude. Seriously." He sits up, pulling the blanket from his bare buttocks onto his lap. "We didn't have sex, if that's what you're asking—not that you didn't want to."

When my head stops pounding, I realize I'm still partially dressed, my shapewear still squeezing the life out of my waist and pushing my tits as close to heaven as possible. Taking shapewear off is difficult enough, but putting it on? That's a task for someone who is much more sober and dedicated to a smooth silhouette than I was last night.

"Do you remember the party? Coming home in the cab?" he asks. "Do you remember telling me to take off my clothes, or laughing yourself to sleep when I had trouble getting it up?"

I stifle a laugh. "That does seem like something I'd do."

His eyes narrow with annoyance and the memories from last night begin to return. The bar, the many, many drinks that led to my inability to hold my tongue or walk a straight line. Classic Teagan behavior.

"I need to pee."

"Bathroom's through there. Knock yourself out," he says, flopping back onto his pillow.

With the blanket securely wrapped around me, I get up and scramble through the door of his bedroom. Inside is a king-sized bed with a jersey comforter the same color as the walls. *Why couldn't he let me sleep in here?* Not that it would be a good idea to be in Heath's bed. Again.

Sliding the pocket door closed behind me, I tear at my shape-wear. After minutes of struggle, I sit and sigh with relief. It makes me wonder why I put them on in the first place. No dress is worth that.

Wait. Where *is* my dress?

I clean up and leave the bathroom, shapewear in hand, blanket tight around me, and find Heath standing in the bedroom rummaging through the drawers of his dresser. He looks over at me with tired eyes and smirks.

"Can you let me borrow some clothes or something?" I ask. "There's no way in hell I'm going home looking like I'm doing a walk of shame."

"Sure." He chuckles, then tosses me a shirt and, after a moment of searching, some sweatpants.

"Thanks."

"Yep."

I try to keep myself covered with the blanket while I put them on, pretending I'm not embarrassed to be standing in my underwear in front of someone who could be a literal underwear model. Not that he hasn't seen it before.

Heath has a soccer body, but his mom's Samoan genes work overtime. I'm tall for a woman, but compared to him at six foot four, his pant legs bunch up on my ankles. I'll look like a kid wearing their older sibling's hand-me-downs, but it's better than trudging through the Upper West Side in what is clearly last night's ball gown.

I turn around, drop the blanket, and pull the shirt on. When I turn back, he's staring at me with a laughing expression. "What?" I snip.

"Why do you always act like you hate me?"

"Because I *do* hate you," I answer matter-of-factly.

"You didn't hate me last night. And you definitely didn't hate me after Brett's wedding," he says with a conniving grin. Of course he would bring that up. "You remember last summer, right? The hotel right off the beach. That humid night the AC went out and we couldn't sleep, so we stayed up and spent hours having hot, sweaty se—"

"Stop."

I try my hardest not to remember that night. Not to say that the sex wasn't good—it was amazing, actually. Mind-blowing, really. The kind of sex you think about while buzzing your clit off after your talentless boyfriend leaves you high and dry again. But it's Heath, the biggest douchebag on the planet. I'd rather kick a rat while wearing open-toed shoes again than pay him the compliment.

He steps closer to me, invading my personal space. My eyes trace down his defined chest and abs. The low ride of his pants provides a teasing view of the only dash of hair on his otherwise waxed body. It's frustrating how fine he is, but Heath won the genetic lottery. His dad was a heartthrob quarterback, his mom a Miss Universe contestant. Together they made one objectively stunning human. And he absolutely knows it.

"You rocked my world and then didn't talk to me for six months," he says. "I didn't see you until Ryan's Christmas party, and you acted like it never happened."

The memory makes my heartbeat quicken, but I play it cool. "So?"

"So . . ." He steps closer but I refuse to shy away. "It didn't feel nice to get brushed off like that."

"There are a few women who might call that karma, Heath."

He lets out a heavy sigh. "You hate me. I get it. Most of the time I hate you too. We both know we'd have nothing to do with each other if it wasn't for the guys and Levi."

My brick-wall façade cracks when Heath says Levi's name. My brothers are my everything. Levi and I are close, but he has always worshiped the ground Heath walks on, even before they trauma bonded over their injuries. We almost lost Levi after his accident. Heath was there the whole time, helping Levi through his recovery, and still helping with his physical therapy today. No matter how much I've wanted to be rid of Heath, he's always been in my life in one way or another.

Heath twists the drawstrings of my pants around his fingers and then tugs them. My eyes snap up to his, but I ignore the warmth igniting between my legs. "Why is it so hard for you to admit you want me?"

"I *don't* want you."

"You sure?" he asks. "You seem to want a certain part of me."

When he moves closer, I step back, hitting the wall. He reaches forward and places his hands on my hips, pulling them gently against his. I fight to ignore the pounding in my chest and somewhere much lower.

"You know and I know that under all your control freak bullshit is a regular old freak. Everything we talked about last night, your frustration over missing an orgasm you know I could give you in five minutes," he says with a cocky grin. His hands slide up my waist slowly, making me shiver. "You know what you really want, but then you waste time on some prick who can't get you off."

"You're saying I should waste my time on a prick who *can* get me off instead?"

"That's still an upgrade."

"Lord." The bar really is in hell.

He laughs and lets go of my waist. It irritates me when I feel colder after he does. "Think about it, Teags. You're busy with school, I have my internship at the ortho clinic taking up most of my time, and that doesn't include all the wedding party bullshit we have stacked up," he says. "We'll be stuck together all summer, and we're both too busy to be on dating apps swiping through randoms for the chance at occasional, mediocre sex."

Is he making a valid point? "What are you suggesting we do instead?"

"Why don't we make some kind of arrangement? You and me this summer."

"An arrangement? You and me?" I repeat with suspicion.

"It's not a relationship. At best it's like a . . . situationship."

My eyes narrow as I try to find a way to hate his idea. "In theory, that sounds great, but how would that ever work?"

"The only reason it doesn't work is because people can't be real with their expectations. We can fuck each other's brains out and still manage not to talk to each other afterward. It's pretty clear what we do and don't want from each other."

Arguments are my forte, but even I can't find a rebuttal to his claim. "If the guys even catch a whiff of this, we'll never hear the end of it."

"They didn't find out about last summer and it happened right next to them. Loudly." Again, he taunts me, making it worse when he steps away and crosses his arms, his biceps and abs flexing as he does. "You're the law student. If you need rules, think some up. See if we can agree on something for once."

All the possibilities of how this could end badly run through my mind. As much as I hate him, he presents a rather attractive offer. Maybe *he's* the attractive part. Even reeking of last night's alcohol, he still has me drooling.

A smile spreads across his face. "The way you're looking at me right now makes me think we have a deal."

I take a breath and steel myself back into my poker face. "I'll think about it."

FOUR
Teagan

I'm a smart person, I swear. Intelligent, worldly. But this? This is just stupid.

Five days after the breakup, I'm acknowledging I may have made an error. I don't want to be with Lenny—*definitely* don't want to be with him—but I picked the wrong weekend to come to that realization.

The bell jingles a familiar sound when I walk through the café door. The smell of freshly ground espresso and the sound of an acoustic guitar instantly annoy me. As much as being in a preppy coffee shop makes my skin crawl, this is where I've spent much of my free time over the last few months. Because this is where Lenny works.

He stands behind the counter, watching the musician while wiping down one of the espresso machines. The muscles of his back flex beneath his polo, his big biceps stretching the material to its limit. A distraction, one eclipsed by the ramifications of our breakup.

We didn't get together by chance. Lenny is the son of my father's law partner. They expect both of us to follow in their footsteps and become partners in the future. In my parents' minds, nothing could be better than us being partners in business *and* in life. So, like always, they decided what was best for me and set us up.

With the firm's party happening at my family's house this weekend, it won't be a good look to walk in with news that will piss them off. I can avoid the drama if I smooth things over with Lenny. Unfortunately, that's not something I'm great at.

Proving how spectacular Lenny is at his job, it takes an exaggerated clearing of my throat for him to notice me standing at the counter.

"Teagan," he says with surprise. "What are you doing here?"

"I came to talk to you."

"I'm a little busy right now." He turns away from me and focuses his attention on the machine again.

The son of a multimillionaire working as a barista is the quintessence of our fathers' hypocrisy. Both of our dads said they wanted us to learn what a hard day's work felt like, but I'm not sure they know what that means. Lenny's father still pays his rent and gives him a four-figure allowance each month, as long as he holds down a part-time job. I make sure I can cover my bills on my own, but my dad still gives me money each semester, lording it over my head as if I can't live without it.

My dad will go on thinking the hardest part of my life is not being able to fly to the Maldives to hang out with my friends over the weekend, and I wait every day for him to recognize that constantly placing a Black woman in white male spaces is *considerably* more of a struggle.

"Lenny, I came off a bit harsh last weekend. That wasn't my intent." I may have regrets, but I refuse to say the words *I'm sorry* to him. He doesn't turn my way. "I'm not asking you to forgive me for what I said, but . . . the party is this weekend."

"So?"

"We both have to be there."

He glances at me over his shoulder. "And what do you want me to do? Show up with you and pretend we're still together?"

"Preferably, yeah."

"You are unbelievable." He turns back to me and crosses his arms. "You're afraid to tell them we broke up. Our dads are going to be pissed when they find out—and imagine how your mom will react, seeing how excited she was that you finally got with someone who has career prospects and an IQ higher than ninety-five."

Well. "That's valid."

"Why don't you tell them why you did it? Tell them why I wasn't good enough for you. Tell them you're not interested in nice guys, you're just another typical female with daddy issues, on her way to having a body count higher than her annual salary."

My eyebrows rise. "Are you calling me a slut?"

"I don't know, Teagan. Would that *satisfy* you?"

I scoff, taken aback by his audacity. "Fuck you, Lenny. I was trying to apologize."

"No, you were trying to save face. Maybe you should learn the difference." He turns toward the machine, forcing my glare to fall on his back.

He hit a nerve he knew was there. Causing drama at the party will be so much worse for me than him. He'll continue to play the part of the good guy who had his heart broken, and I'll get the blame and the brunt of our parents' disappointment.

Sadly, I'm too petty to let him win. If he wants to throw me into the fire, I'm dragging his ass with me.

Unable to help myself, I push the large pitcher of cream off the counter, spilling it onto the floor behind him. "Damn it, Teagan!"

The music stops. In my peripheral vision, I can see people are staring. Why stop now that I have an audience? I put my palms on the counter and lean in.

"I'm not a slut, Lenny. Even if I was, it wouldn't make me less of a person. I didn't leave you because you were a 'nice guy.' I left because I deserve someone better than you," I correct him. "You are not the prize you think you are, you're just another privileged little boy who never had someone tell him he can't have everything he wants."

He fixes his lips to say something else but I don't give him the chance.

"I don't care what else you have to say. Learn how to make a woman come before you come for me."

I cast a glare in his direction and leave the store, storming all the way to my car.

When I get inside, I drop my forehead onto the steering wheel. *Fuck*. I know I've lost even though I've won.

The summer just started and I'm already neck-deep in shit. I have enough to wade through over the next few months without adding the depth of my parents' disappointment, but Lenny was doing nothing to help. I should have held out for one more week, but I was desperate for something to relieve my stress. Something distracting, mind numbing, toe curling . . .

My thought ends when visions of Heath come to mind. I open my eyes in an attempt to push the image of him naked out of my head, but it doesn't work.

He asked me to think about what he proposed, and I would be lying if I said I hadn't thought about it every moment since. As ridiculous as it sounds, all can think about *now* is running back to his apartment and riding him until I can't see straight.

It's just another stupid idea, but after everything I've done so far this summer maybe being smart is overrated.

I open my Notes app and begin typing up ideas. We can do this. I can do this. Just need a few guidelines first.

FIVE
Heath

The sun glares through the glass walls of the eleventh-floor gym, making it hard to focus on my workout. As I run on my machine, the golden-hour glow makes me want to sleep. My desire to sleep brings thoughts of being in bed. Thoughts of being in bed remind me of sex. At this point, what doesn't?

It has been too long. Four months since the accidental roommate altercation, and karma is taking its sweet time. But, if I'm being painfully honest, I haven't had *great* sex since last summer.

It was crazy. Teagan and I were complaining about the heat, bartering over a fan and a bucket of ice, then a few minutes later we were in my room, fucking on the cold bathroom floor, in the shower, and on the windowsill while catching the 2:00 a.m. breeze. It was a spur-of-the-moment thing that left me so fucked up I thought for sure we'd do it again. And then she ghosted me. Hard. Now I'm still thinking about it—*obsessing* over it—praying she gives me another chance to see her staring up at me with *that look*, hear her moan my name, and feel her nails dragging down my back while I—

"Heath!"

Surprise makes me trip and almost fall off the machine. I catch myself and stand on the sides, glaring at Ritchie. He leans over the arm of the treadmill beside me and smiles like an asshole. "What the hell, Rich?"

"What? I called your name like four times. Where is your head at?"

With a roll of my eyes, I hop back onto the belt. I lower the speed and grumble, "What do you want?"

"I was trying to ask you about the party last weekend."

Ritchie's tone always sounds like he's plotting something. I swear, every part of him screams *punch me*. Five-six max, he has a baby face that makes him look sixteen and a haircut that looks like it was done by a sous chef. Yet, somehow, he's getting laid more than me.

My breath picks up when I increase my speed back to what it was. "What do you mean?"

"Did you score with that girl you brought?"

"No."

"Damn, man. How long has it been?"

"Why don't you mind your own fucking business?"

"Yikes," Brett says when he magically appears in frame. "What crawled up your ass and didn't sleep with you?" His tongue hangs out when he laughs and slaps his palm against Ritchie's.

"Man, fuck both of you." I turn off my machine and head for the showers.

Ritchie follows me. "Chill, bro. We're only teasing."

I use my work perks to get them access to this bougie-ass fitness club, then they want to make fun of me? Nah. Fuck that.

"Heath, you know we're just messing with you. You're pent up," Brett says, hanging an arm over my shoulders. "You should fly out to Valencia with us this weekend and see the new boat before the wedding. Let off some steam."

"The boat" is his dad's new two-hundred-foot yacht docked somewhere in the Mediterranean. It would be a tempting offer if I wasn't tired of his shit right now. "We'll be there at the end of the summer. I'll see it then."

"Yeah, but all of Felicity's bridesmaids are coming with us too." He shakes my shoulders as if his drift wasn't easy to catch. "You had fun last time you were around them."

I was having fun with *Teagan*. They didn't know which bridesmaid I was talking about.

The spa makes the locker room smell like eucalyptus and chlorine. I can't wait to shower so they'll quit talking to me. "Both of you need to stop," I say. "I'm not doing as bad as you think. I fucked it up with my date, but I didn't go home alone."

"What?" Ritchie leans into my view and looks at me with a very punchable smirk. "Who?"

"It doesn't matter. Nothing happened." I unzip my pocket to find my key and to keep him from seeing my smile. "At least nothing yet."

"There's my Heath! You can come out this weekend with us, get laid, then come back and seal the deal with that girl right after," Ritchie says.

I swear they live vicariously through me, encouraging me to be more of a dog than I already am just to make up for the monotony of their monogamy. "Seriously, I'm good."

"Your loss, man. Let's go for a soak," Brett says.

The hot tubs just behind the doors call my name, but I don't want to be around the two of them any longer. "You go on, I need to get home."

"Suit yourself." Brett smacks a hand against my ass as they walk away.

When they're finally gone, I exhale a sigh of relief.

I rip off my shirt and toss it into my locker. Under my towel, my phone's screen lights up with a missed notification. When I see who it is, my day gets a lot better.

Teagan: Are you free tomorrow?

~

My knee bounces nervously under the table while I wait for Teagan to show up. She asked to meet at this café but never replied to say why. I stare at her text message again, hoping it will give me more information.

Maybe she's decided she's down to hook up for the summer, but there's no way to know for sure. All I *do* know is that she never texts me, especially not out of the blue. The last text I got from her was over a year ago when we were planning Brett's bachelor party. She suggested we go to a strip club *she* wanted to go to, which we did, and it was wild. We had fun but not nearly as much as her. She took all of our cash and made it rain on a stripper with the fattest ass I've ever seen, then took her back to her hotel room that night.

That's Teagan. You never know which side of her you'll get— neurotic or chaotic. She's got a few screws loose, but goddamn, that pussy is *tight*.

Her big ponytail catches my attention over the back of the booth. "Teags!"

She looks my way and heads over. Her perfect body is wrapped in a pair of tight yoga pants and a school hoodie. Maybe I'm getting chaotic Teags today. I can only hope.

Sliding into the booth next to me, she doesn't say anything and she doesn't smile. She's in business mode, avoiding eye contact like a parent who's about to give you The Talk.

"I got here earlier than you." I break the silence. "That's a first."

"I told you to meet me half an hour earlier so you'd actually be on time."

". . . oh."

A waitress walks over and cuts the awkwardness. "Can I get you something?" she asks Teagan.

"A latte with almond milk, please." She loves those things.

"Nothing for me," I say. The waitress nods and walks away. I turn back to Teagan, who still won't look at me. "Do you want to tell me why we're here?"

Finally, her big eyes find mine. "I thought about what you said."

"And?"

"There might be a way to make it work." *Fuck, yeah!* This is exactly the news I wanted. I lean on my elbows and smile at the possibilities.

She pulls out her tablet, keyboard attached and all. "I wrote something up."

"You *wrote* something?"

"Yes. Two parties doing business should be in agreement on the terms."

"Doing business?" I slide my hands over my face. "Wow, Teags. Can't wait."

"Just read it."

I take the tablet from her and ready myself for a whole lot of bullshit. What I see is less legalese than I expected. In fact, it almost makes sense.

Proposed Guidelines of the Hargrove-Reynolds Situationship:

This contract is to outline an agreement for scheduled sex. The Situationship is limited to June 1 through August 31.

Sex is defined as acts including but not limited to all forms of consensual physical contact with the intent of achieving orgasm or equitable satisfaction. Sex is always to be an equal exchange. An unequal exchange will provide grounds for the termination of this agreement. Sex is to be exclusively between the two parties through the duration of the contract except as defined in the terms below.

Both parties shall treat and keep the Situationship secret and confidential, and will not directly or indirectly communicate or disclose the existence of, or terms of, this agreement to any outside party.

Cessation of this agreement is allowed for any reason with proper notice by either party.

The terms are as follows;

1. Schedule is to be preapproved. Both parties must approve all changes.

2. No shared meals or public excursions generally defined as dates; any public appearances and events will be worked into the preapproved schedule, with notice.

3. Dramatic or emotionally based decisions are to be kept separate from the schedule and terms within the contract.

4. A sexual relationship with an outside party can be accommodated through the pausing or cessation of this agreement with proper notice by either party. Reinstatement of the agreement will require a negative STI test.

I lean back in the booth and nod. *That ain't half bad.*

"What do you think?" she asks.

"I like it."

"Great. We'll need to agree on a schedule."

She pulls out her phone and opens her Calendar app. Awkwardly, I do the same. She shows me her typical week and we compare it to mine. Her classes and work schedule almost align with my shifts.

"It looks like we have Wednesdays, Fridays, and Saturdays," she summarizes.

"Sundays would be good for me too," I say. "A little stress relief before Monday?"

"I have family dinner that day. You know that."

I *do* know that, but I don't know why she thinks she can't do both. "Even if we are free at the same time, we can't have sex because it's not on the schedule?"

"Spontaneity crosses into relationship territory. It's dick by appointment only, or I'm out."

"Okay. Damn."

She considers for a moment, then says, "We can add a twelve-hour notice for extra available times. Does that work?"

I take that as a win. "Yeah, that works."

She unfolds the tablet's cover to expose the keyboard. As she types, I close my eyes with a sigh and remind myself this will all be worth it when I can have her plump lips wrapped around my—

"My place weekdays, yours weekends?" she asks.

The throbbing in my pants makes me want to agree to anything. "Sure."

"That's three times per week, guaranteed, with the possibility of four. Sounds adequate."

Adequate? It sounds like a dream *cum* true. I'm glad I didn't say that out loud.

"What about the weeks when . . ."

"When what?"

"When it's your time of the month."

"You can say *period*, Heath, you work in health care. And it won't be an issue. I have an IUD."

I paid enough attention in the sexual wellness parts of my anatomy classes to know an IUD is a birth control device and not an STI, but that's about it. "Cool, but what does that mean?"

"It means I don't really have a 'time of the month' anymore."

"Really?"

"Yes, really. Congratulations to us both." She looks away from me again. "Are you still good to use condoms?"

I catch her true meaning but I let it roll off me. "Yeah, of course."

"Good." While she types, the awkwardness settles in again. "Any concerns for you?"

I scan the outline again and one thought pops into my head. "The last one." I peer at her, hoping to judge her expression. She sips her drink and raises an eyebrow. "You left room for us to be with other people."

"Isn't that the point?" she asks. "If we find someone we *want* to be with, a situationship is unnecessary."

"Then why a pause? Why not end it?"

She smirks. "With your track record? The chances of you keeping a girlfriend for more than two weeks is slim as hell."

I laugh at my own expense. "Okay, true. But if that's the case, maybe we should elaborate the 'no drama' rule? What does that mean to you?"

"The problem with situationships is that someone always catches feelings," she says. "I want sex and that's it. No cuddling, no sleepovers, no talking unless it's about the schedule. Nothing."

"And I don't want any fuckshit," I say, keeping my true intentions vague. "No drama, no emotions, and no ghosting either. We communicate like mature adults."

"When did *you* become a mature adult, exactly?" she asks, then takes a slow drink.

"Can we add a requirement for you to be nice to me?"

"Yeah, that's not gonna happen." She types, then scans her work. "Anything else?"

I stare at her with contempt. If we're being honest, I've done worse things for a blow job. "Nah, I'm good."

"Great." She finishes writing something then hands me the tablet. "Read it again before you sign."

I review the changes, shaking my head at the ridiculousness.

1. Scheduled times are between 7 p.m. and 11 p.m. on Wednesdays, Fridays, and Saturdays through the duration of the contract; both parties must approve all changes.

a. Additional days or times outside of the established schedule require 12 hours' notice.

3. Emotionally based decisions are to be kept separate from the schedule and terms within the contract, including but not limited to the following;

a. No drama, ghosting, or "general fuckshit";

b. Conversations are to be kept to a minimum and remain professional in nature;

c. No cuddling, no pillow talk, no sleepovers;

d. If either party is considered to be "catching feelings," cessation of the agreement will be rendered, effective immediately.

This has to be one of the top ten stupidest things I've done to get laid. Definitely not top five, but it's close. "You realize this is insane, right?" I ask.

"Do you want to fuck me all summer or not?" She holds the stylus out to me, challenging me to change my mind. I chuckle at the attempt. She knows she has me.

I scribble my signature and hand it back. "Signed. Now what?"

She takes a final sip of her coffee and throws the tablet into her bag. "It's Saturday. I'll see you at eight."

"Oh." *Shit, we're really doing this.* "Okay, see you then."

I watch her stand and leave without another word, as if nothing happened. "It's cool, I'll get the check," I murmur to myself.

SIX
Heath

Knowing how Teagan is, if she says she'll be over at eight, she'll be outside my door at 7:58. I'm not mad about it. This arrangement of ours has had my not-so-little man rubbing against my zipper all day.

The slowest nine hours of my life. Fuck, I want this bad—I want *her* bad. Dry spell aside, knowing the way dreams of last summer have made me wake up to sticky sheets more times than I'd like to admit, I rubbed one out in the shower the minute I got back from our meeting to make sure I wouldn't embarrass myself tonight. But even that barely took the edge off.

Reaching down to give it a little squeeze, I find I'm harder than I thought. I'm not sure I'll make it to 7:58 at all.

My phone vibrates against the kitchen counter and I snatch it immediately, thinking it's a message from her. It's not. Just my dad again. I ignore it like the last three I've gotten from him this week.

The quiet taps on my door catch my attention. *Finally.* I glance at the clock in the kitchen and smirk when I see it's 7:56. "You're early," I say when I open the door.

"I'm always early." Teagan walks past me and drops her things on the island countertop like she lives here.

Her outfit is different from before. Her hair too. The thin material of her white T-shirt dress hangs loosely while still tracing every curve of her waist, hips, and ass. Beneath it I can see the crisscrossing front of her black bra. I know she didn't just throw all that on just to walk around her house.

"I don't mean to rush you, but could we make this kind of quick?" she asks, turning around to lean back against the island. "I forgot I have a thing tonight."

Quick? I get to get in her sooner than I thought? My pants suddenly feel much tighter. "Yeah, sure. No problem."

When I step closer, her eyes flit around the room, avoiding mine. Her long lashes flutter down as I lean my hands onto the counter behind her, caging her like my prey. She brushes her straightened hair over her shoulder, pretending she's unfazed.

"You're nervous," I tease.

"I'm not nervous," she hisses. Her snippy demeanor makes her so edible. "I agreed to do this because you said you could give me an orgasm in five minutes. If you're going to be all talk, we can call this shit off and—"

She stops short when I reach up her dress and slide her panties down her thighs. Her mouth closes when I move my hands back up to grab two overflowing handfuls of her perfect ass. Her bottom lip catches between her teeth as I pull her body tight against mine, letting her feel my excitement. "Do you want to keep bitching at me or do you want me to make you come?"

Her glare remains, but her mouth stays shut.

"Yeah, that's what I thought."

As I kneel down, I rip her panties down the rest of the way, holding them while she clumsily steps out, the little piece of lace catching on the buckle of her shoe. In one quick motion I swing her leg onto my shoulder and lift her up to sit on the countertop. She murmurs something about me not needing to, but I'm not doing this for her. I'm hungry.

She smells like body wash, her warm honey scent hidden underneath. I slide the tip of my tongue up the full length of her, feeling the delicate petals against my tongue, tasting the sweetness waiting for me deeper inside. *Mmm* . . . I pull her other leg onto my shoulder, spreading her wide so I can get a better taste.

Taking my time, I appreciate the way her body can't hide her arousal from me. She feels warmer, tastes sweeter, smells better. She's melting for me. I press my tongue inside and back out to circle her sweet little bud before gently sucking it between my lips. Her fingers comb into my hair, tugging it as she moans, her thighs quivering in my hands while her hips swirl against my tongue. *How did I get this lucky?*

I pull her from the countertop to stand, then turn her around. She looks back at me over her shoulder but doesn't protest. Both of us know she likes it better from behind. The low light glistens against her pussy as it awaits my company. While I tear my shirt over my head, push my pants down my hips, and roll the condom on, she pulls her dress up higher and wiggles that tight ass, teasing me. Can't leave her waiting, can we?

Not wasting any more time, I grip her hip and push my way in, my mouth dropping open when I feel her stretch over my head. *Fuck.* She's as tight as I remember, wet and warm in a way that makes my mind quiet and my senses heighten. Spreading her feet wider, I slide in deeper, burying myself in her heat. When I press against her, her whimper is halfway between pleasure and pain, making my balls tug.

The second I start to move, it's already over for me. I love the tight friction when I pull myself from her, the small fight it takes to make my way back in. I pull back and thrust hard, my hips crashing against her ass. The way she squeezes around me when I'm deep drives me crazy. When I'm inside her, watching her ass shake with each impact, hearing her little moans while I'm stroking it . . . nothing compares.

For a few moments I'm lost, but before I get too carried away, I exhale and remind myself I have a point to prove. I slow my roll, running my hands up her sides, trailing them back down her spine and over the dimples on the small of her back. The feel of her soft skin against my palms, the taste of her still on my tongue—nothing else matters but the pleasure I'm about to give her.

Teagan thinks I'm beneath her, that she's doing me a favor by letting me have this. But she forgets I'm an athlete through and through.

Sex is a game. One I play very well.

A good stroke game is nothing on its own. It's just offense—important, yes, but it's not everything. Some men think you can win with just that, but women are complicated, multidimensional. Like any game, the strategy is in nuance; the upper hand is in the details. I listen to her, watch her, feel the subtle way her body responds to my touch. When I find what she wants, I keep it steady, even, and when she's getting close, *don't fucking stop*. I know I'm stroking it right, but she won't get there with only that.

I press a hand against her back, pushing her down against the countertop as I keep pumping away. "You like that?" I ask.

Her "Uh-huh" sounds more like elongated hums between her moans. *That's right.*

That's my defense—the shit that keeps things in line. A firm grip, some dirty talk, and maybe a little spank to let her know that I'm here, I'm in charge, and I have the stamina to keep it that way as long as she wants it.

A rush floods through me, making me groan when it catches me off guard. But I'm not alone. Every movement I make, she coos with delight. She arches up with a loud moan and looks back at me with surprise, her brow stitched, those plump lips parted. She's close, and I know the one surefire way to get her there.

Sliding my hand between her thighs, I find the slick bundle of nerves. She bucks beneath my hand.

"Ah!" Her grip tightens on my wrist, her pussy does the same around my cock. "Don't stop. Oh fuck, don't stop!" She yells my favorite phrase.

Rubbing my fingers faster, keeping to my rhythm, I train my focus on her skin under my grasp. I'm hot, hard as hell, my muscles wound tight. I'm barely hanging on when her legs start to shake and her head falls back with a cry. There it is.

I feel her slick grip tighten around me. Her body dances, her ass jumping as her pussy teases up and down my length. When it's game over for her, I let myself go.

Slamming my hips hard against her ass over and over and over, I take what I want. The feeling builds with every thrust, every whimper and moan I make her cry. I lose myself in the control, the pleasure, the power—until it slips from my grasp in the most satisfying way possible.

"Oh, *fuck.*" My balls feel like they're bursting when I start coming into the condom. Moans fall from my lips while the core of my being empties from me in rush after glorious rush.

As I enjoy the last few strokes, I feel high. All my stress and worry drain from me, leaving a blissful blank slate behind.

This is what we both wanted. The emptiness, the silence. We deal with our shit the same way—physically first, and emotionally, almost never. Whatever stress made her desperate enough to come back to *me* for relief, I'm thankful for it, as fucked up as that may seem.

When I'm finally empty, I breathe out a sigh of relief and slip from her warm embrace. She turns and leans back against the counter with a pleased grin on her lips. Her legs wobble when she puts her panties back on. The pleased grin on her lips and the glint in her dark eyes tells me all I need to know.

Like I said, sex is a game. Everyone can learn how to play, but few play as well as I do.

The clock on my oven reads 8:04. "That was a little more than five minutes, but I think I proved my point."

As annoyed as she would like to be, Teagan is too happy to give me shit. "Yeah, I guess you did."

I smile at my triumph.

While straightening her dress, she avoids looking at me, then grabs her bag and keys from the counter. "See you Wednesday?"

"Yeah," I agree while trying to catch my breath. "Your place, right?"

"Yeah." She walks to the door, still failing to hide the drunken haze of happiness. A glow, really. One I gave her. "Try to be on time, okay?"

She lets herself out and leaves me alone in my kitchen with a used condom and the smell of sex on my fingers. I breathe in her scent one more time and feel the smile pull at my cheeks. Five minutes with Teagan was worth a year of waiting.

My phone buzzes on the countertop again. I toss the condom in the trash and pick it up. The texts from my dad make my stomach turn.

Dad: We need to talk about your mother
Dad: It's happening again

This is what I didn't want to think about. *This* is the shit I wanted to fuck away.

Wednesday can't come soon enough.

SEVEN

Teagan

It's the day of my parents' garden party and I am not ready. I made it to the house ten minutes ago, but I'm still sitting in my car across the street, trying to work up the nerve to go in. Lenny might be there already, crying and lying about how awful I am. My parents' perfect child has egg on her face, and rather than helping me clean it off, they'll interrogate me about where it came from and why I hadn't thought to surround myself with less fragile food.

I pull my finger from my mouth. There is a spot of blood on my cuticle left by my nervous chewing.

Never again will I agree to do something as stupid as date someone in my inner circle. Sure, Heath is my inner circle, but a contractually obligated sex schedule is as far from dating as you can get.

A day after my dick appointment with him and I still smile when I think about it. I didn't "have a thing" afterward. I wanted to give myself time to spiral in case my anxiety took over or my emotions went awry, but everything about that night was perfection.

In only a few minutes—not much longer than my last time with Lenny—Heath had me seeing stars and gave me an orgasm so hard I wasn't sure I was on Earth anymore. It was the kind of sex that makes your head spin and your brain turn to mush. To someone like me, turning my brain off for a minute is almost better than the orgasm itself. Almost.

As nervous as I was to do it, Heath gave me a reminder of what Lenny could never do for me. I needed a little proof that I'd made the right decision to end things. Especially before this party.

Finally, I climb out of my car into the glaring sun. Manhattan becomes a humid hellhole in the summer, but the heat in Westchester is barely any better today.

My parents' house looks like it could fit on a college campus. A two-story brick behemoth with white-framed windows, dormers, and an interior clad floor to ceiling with mahogany. All it's missing are columns and Greek letters on the front.

In the backyard, fifty or so people mingle on the concrete patio, each group doing their best impression of a Ralph Lauren summer collection advertisement, holding glasses of wine and taking shade beneath the twelve-foot manicured Italian cypresses. I open the gate and, to my undeserved luck, find my two favorite people. I wave to my brothers and relief lights up their faces.

Levi wheels his chair over with excitement, Rowan following him. I lean down and squeeze Levi into a hug. He returns it with equal fervor.

"Finally, you're here," he says into my shoulder, and I can tell he is smiling. Levi has the same snarky personality I do, but sometimes we slip up and show our genuine affection for each other. When he leans away, he asks, "This is the best dress you could find?" *That's more like it.*

"Love you too." I press a kiss to his cheek, then reach out for Rowan. I wrap my arms around his narrow waist, stretching up to kiss his cheek as well. The six-foot-two timid baby of the family, he greets me with his smile rather than words.

No one sees a Black woman with two Asian men and thinks "siblings" first, but I'm the luckiest person alive to have them as family.

"How's the party going?"

"*So* good," Levi replies with as much sarcasm as humanly possible. He has his hair slicked back into a folded-over bun. His wrinkled white oxford is lacking the customary beige jacket Rowan has on. He wants to be here about as much as I do. "Mom and Dad have asked where you are like five million times. They want to show you off to everyone."

I close my eyes with a sigh. "How drunk do you think I can get before then?" I look over and find both of my parents waving us over. "Not drunk enough, I see."

We go to them and I cling to Rowan's arm for support.

"Teagan, there you are," Dad greets me. Confusion stitches his brow behind the wire frames of his glasses. The tilt of his mouth shows his disapproval even before he vocalizes it. "Where is Lenny?"

"Oh, um . . ."

I trail off when Mom turns to face me, placing her hand against Dad's back. "Hi, darling. Where's Lenny?"

Someone once told me that couples start to look more alike the longer they are together, and that is definitely true for my parents. Mom's glasses are a different shape than Dad's, but they still have the same wire frames that match their *perpetually in business casual* aesthetic. Over the years their faces and waistlines have grown a little rounder, and their medium-brown hair has grayed at the same pace. They may be older than the average parent, being in their midsixties when I am the oldest at twenty-three, but that is not the main reason for our disconnect.

They love a summer's day with a chardonnay. It's a reprieve to see them in a good mood, both smiling rather than scowling, and I don't want to ruin it with the answer to their question.

"We decided to come separately," I say, finding a blip of enjoyment in my double entendre.

Mom gives me a look of confusion before an unfamiliar woman
claims her attention. "Cheryl, I just wanted to say congratulations to you and your husband. Thirty years in business is a huge
achievement!"

"Thank you," my mother coos, much like she will the rest of the
night. "We're still having a blast, but we are excited about the future."
She pulls me against her side.

"You must be the famous Teagan," the woman says to me. I
wonder if I'm famous because Dad has a fondness for hyperbole or
because, as is true for most of the environments they force me into,
I'm one of the few—if not the *only*—women of color in the room. She
looks at my brothers and says, "And you must be . . ." Her eyes drop
to Levi's chair. "Levi and Rowan." She points between them as if it's
an accomplishment to get it right.

Most people use Levi's disability as a point of discernment
between him and Rowan—something that has always infuriated me.
But our family's diversity often overwhelms people.

After going through the struggle of adopting me from Ethiopia,
my parents pretended the process was too hard to go through again.
But all that changed when they saw Levi.

I was four when my parents went to the Philippines to meet him.
Two years old, wide-eyed and expressive, he was the cutest toddler,
even when he was tearing the house apart. They put him in every
sport possible to give him a channel for his abundance of energy.
The car accident his freshman year of high school left him without
the use of his legs, but he never let that stop his athleticism or stifle
his brash personality.

I was six when Mom and Dad found Rowan. The four of us flew
to Laos to meet him. He was still a baby—the first time I had been

around one. I spent so much of my time watching him, holding him, caring for him. That hasn't changed much either. Even though he's almost eighteen, I will always be protective of him.

Back before the Jolie-Pitts, and before most people were aware of how unethical transnational adoption can be, my parents always planned to grow their family in that way. They wanted to share their abundance of wealth and privilege with children who had none. The problem is that, while wealth can be shared, not all privilege can. I'm not sure they've learned that yet.

"Your mother tells me you're top of your class in law school," the woman continues.

I open my mouth to answer but my mother speaks for me. "Yes, she has always been a wonderful student. Valedictorian in undergrad, perfect LSAT score, and we expect the same when she takes the bar exam next summer." She gives me a little squeeze, so proud of the mountain of expectations she has placed upon me. "We can't wait to see where she takes the firm when she becomes a partner."

I look over and find Rowan fidgeting with discomfort. He hates this discourse as much as I do. "I'm going to grab a drink. Can I get you anything, Mom?" I ask as my excuse to leave.

She shakes her head before continuing her conversation. I gesture for Levi and Rowan to follow me, and they happily do so, sharing my desire to be literally anywhere else but here.

Weaving through the beige sea of affluence, we escape to a less populated area at the other end of the garden. I grab two glasses of champagne from the bar and hand one to Levi.

"Where's mine?" Rowan asks.

"Three years in the future," I quip before taking a drink. The crisp liquid slides down my throat, soothing me with its cool temperature and the thought of the alcohol kicking in soon. I drain half the glass then sigh.

"This party is ass," Levi says what we're both thinking. "I need some drama. Are you going to tell Mom and Dad that you broke up with Lenny?"

I shoot him a look. "Wasn't planning to throw myself into the fire to entertain you. Sorry."

"You broke up?" Rowan asks. "Why?"

Levi and I have no filter with each other, but Rowan is different. He is the quiet one, keeping most of his thoughts inside, even when we're away from our parents. An innocent lamb in a family of wolves.

I search for the most appropriate words. "He wouldn't . . . he couldn't . . . um . . ."

"He couldn't give her an orgasm," Levi finishes for me. I bat a hand against his arm.

"I'm not a baby anymore. I'm seventeen," Rowan reminds me. "I know all about sex and stuff."

"You do?" Levi and I say simultaneously.

"*Yes*," Rowan answers with a pout.

Levi and I exchange a knowing glance and take a slow sip.

"Oh shit, is that him?" Levi points through the gate as a car pulls into the driveway.

My jaw drops when Lenny climbs out of his Maserati. He adjusts the lapels of his tan blazer and then holds out his hand. A woman I have never seen before runs over and takes it like a well-trained puppy. Her curled balayage hangs to the middle of her back while her white minidress barely covers her ass.

"You've got to be fucking kidding me," I say to myself. I hide behind Rowan as they walk through the gate and into the party.

"Mom and Dad are going to have so many questions." Levi snickers.

"Shut up, I know."

Lenny and his date make their way through the crowd in the direction of our parents. I gnaw on the edge of my glass, wishing it was my finger instead.

"Chill, Teags," Levi says. "It won't be that bad."

I laugh. Through the crowd, I watch them turn their heads toward me and glare. "Sure it won't."

~

"You broke up?" my father asks me for the ninth time. Our postparty Sunday family dinner can't pass quickly enough.

We sit in the dining room just off the veranda, the caterers still in view while they finish the cleanup. Mom keeps herself busy packing away whatever leftover hors d'oeuvres she thinks will keep, while the only thing on Dad's mind is the one thing I don't want to talk about.

"Yes," I answer again.

"You broke up with him or he broke up with you?"

"Does it matter?"

"It does."

Levi is busy shoveling his food down like the bottomless pit he is, and Rowan sits with his face in a book at the end of the table. Sitting directly across the table from Dad, there's no escape from the intensity of his gaze or his line of questioning. In the case of *Teagan's Orgasms v. Lenny's Feelings*, my dad is the prosecutor and I am getting deposed without counsel.

I sigh, knowing he's not going to let it go until I answer. Invoking my Fifth Amendment right is sadly not an option right now. "Technically, I did, but it's not—"

"I can't believe this. He is my partner's son, the future of our firm, just like you, Teagan. You couldn't dream up a better partnership. I don't understand why you would break up," my father laments. "What was wrong with him?"

Levi snorts with laughter next to me and I shoot him a glare. "It just didn't work out, Dad," I say.

"How? He couldn't have been more right for you."

Right for me? Or right for the picture of me Dad has in his mind? There is no arguing with an attorney who believes they're correct. I stare down at my plate and chew on my finger rather than the actual food in front of me.

Mom returns to the table and uncorks the second bottle of wine. She has nothing to add, no disagreement with anything Dad says. My finger is bleeding by the time I pour my third glass, hoping they won't notice.

As the oldest sibling, I have always taken the brunt of my parents' nitpicking. It's hard to remember a time when my life wasn't dissected at every meal, but with Levi and Rowan still living at home while I'm away in the city all week, nothing is as exciting as diving into my business. If only they knew what I was actually up to.

Heath sent me a text this morning to give me notice for tonight. I left him on Read, even though I knew today would be a shit show. I peek at the message again to give myself some encouragement.

Heath: This is my 12-hour notice for Sunday. I'm available ;)

As much as he pisses me off, Heath is my saving grace right now. He ruined me in the best possible way. Sex every week? Chef's kiss. *Great* sex every week? A masterpiece—a *smash-terpiece*, if you will. The *penis* de résistance.

I'm so desperate, I'm starting to sound like him. The promise of sex is barely enough to keep me hanging on, but at least I have *something* to look forward to.

"Give her a break, Dad. She's allowed to choose who she wants to be with," Levi defends me. "You can't force her into some kind of arranged marriage. She didn't like the dude. Simple as that."

"It isn't as simple as that, Levi. It's a matter of the future of our firm. If the partners can't get along, the business is doomed."

"Oh my god, Dad. Stop being so dramatic. She doesn't have to *be* with the guy to get along with him."

"Judging from how they avoided each other all day, I find it hard to believe she can." Dad turns his focus to me again. "You need to patch things up with him."

His wide-eyed scowl tells me that is not a question, and it is not a time to rebut. "I will."

"Immediately."

"I will!"

He leaves the table to cool off and help Mom in the kitchen. With my stomach turning, I pick up my phone and type the text I've been sitting on all day.

Me: Are you free at 9?

It's only six but I don't know if I can wait much longer. Maybe I don't have to.

I retype my message and hit Send.

Me: Are you free in an hour?

The typing indicator appears right after. I watch the dots dance while holding my breath.

Heath: Hell yeah

EIGHT
Heath

Teagan is eight minutes early this time, not that I'm complaining. After spending all morning trying to get my dad to listen to me when it comes to my mom's treatment, Teagan's text was a godsend. Having sex two days in a row is the ultimate stress relief after butting heads with my father yet again. Sure, a professional might suggest it's better to *talk* about your feelings, but I'd rather be balls deep in Teagan than trudge through half the shit I'm dealing with right now.

She's waiting at the door when I open it, wrapped in a white sundress and tall sandals. There's a pissy look on her face, but it's not directed at me. A first.

"Hey."

"Hey," she says. Nothing else. Not that anything else is needed.

I step to the side and she walks in, immediately heading to my bedroom. "Let's do it in the bed this time," she says. So bossy.

"Okay, cool."

Once in the room, she kicks off her shoes and unzips her dress. Right into it again. *Badass*. I tear my shirt off over my head and resume my view at the perfect time.

Teagan adjusts the sides of her thong, the string lost in that perfect ass. When she pulls off her bra, it gets tangled in her hair. I chuckle to myself until she frees it and her curls tumble from her clip onto her back as effortlessly as a goddess. *Damn.* She shakes them out with her fingers and looks at me over her shoulder. My not-so-little man knocks hard against my fly.

Her eyes narrow into a glare when she catches me in my stupor. "Why are your pants still on?"

"Sorry."

Pulling a condom from my drawer, I toss it onto the sheets. Hastily unbuttoning and unzipping my fly, I barely get my pants off my hips before she takes over.

Teagan pushes me back to sit. "You're taking forever," she grumbles. When she drops to her knees beside the bed, I catch myself grinning like a jackal.

She inhales my cock like she hasn't eaten in days.

"*Jesus,*" I murmur as I pull my pants down a bit more. She sucks me so hard I get tunnel vision. I see nothing but her hollow cheeks, her plump lips wrapped around me, and her eyes when she gives me a teasing peek.

She looks at me like she can see all the filthy thoughts flying through my mind, then swallows me again, my head pressing against the back of her throat. *Fuuuck.*

You never forget good head. Teagan is one of the best I've had— top three at least. With that hard pull on my cock and her soft lips and tongue teasing the tip, I debate whether it would be worth pissing her off by spilling myself down her throat.

When she stands, my eyes drop to her chest. Like a magnet, her tits fall into my face and my mouth finds her nipple. I lick the little peak, sucking it into my mouth for just a few seconds until she pulls me away by my hair. She holds the condom in front of my face and I get the message. Speed it up.

I do my job, watching her strip off her tiny thong and drop it onto the floor next to her.

Her tongue traces her lips, her legs settling at either side of my hips while I roll on the last inch. Without time for a breath, she sinks onto me, her pussy snug, hot, and already so wet.

She slides herself up and down, her body gripping me like a fist. The slick sounds fuck me up. I don't know what got into her, but goddamn, I'm glad one of those things is me.

With her hands on my chest, she moves faster, humming her pleasure, stroking me with every swirl of her hips. I reach for them, an instinct to move her to the rhythm I want, but she's already there. My hands hover above her while I watch her work.

"Shit," I whisper with admiration.

Her eyes open and she looks down at me. Her parted lips curl into an evil grin.

Like a dance, her body rolls on top of my lap. All I can do is stare in awe. "You like that?"

My teeth dig into my lip to quiet my moan. "You know I do."

"I've wanted this all day," she says like a sigh of relief.

"Yeah?" My voice sounds as drunk as I feel. She nods and closes her eyes with a moan. Her hips shiver in my hands. "Me too."

She moves my hands to her ass. "Fuck me," she commands. I move my hips in time with hers, meeting her halfway on her descent. "Harder. I want it rough."

Yes, ma'am.

I thrust up, hard, fast, holding her hips tightly in place. She arches forward, her breasts hovering an inch above my chest. I spread her wider with a hand and push myself deeper than before, planting my feet to lift my hips and get her right where I know she wants it.

Her eyes snap open, her nails dig into my chest while she cries out. And there it is.

She grows slick, and when I slow, her pussy dances around me. Her orgasm keeps her rigid in that sex kitten position—back arched, hands on my chest, knees spread wide over my lap.

She whimpers and collapses onto me, her head dropping onto my shoulder. I watch the pleasure roll through her, loving the way she falls apart for me.

I brush my fingers over her mass of curls so I can get a better look. Her eyes are squeezed tight, her mouth dropped open. A little whine escapes her every time I push my way in. I want to hear that sound the rest of my fucking life.

When she opens her eyes, she stares into mine while ecstasy paints every detail of her beautiful face. My cock strains in response. I can't have her look at me like that and keep this up much longer.

I slide her off me to give myself a moment to calm down, but I need her to stay up. She starts to roll to her back, but I stop her, flipping her onto her stomach and pulling her hips up to me.

Her hands grab fistfuls of my sheets when I slip back inside. I thrust downward, hard and deep, one hand pushing my weight down onto her back, the other holding her hip in place while I fuck her senseless. Maybe *I'm* the senseless one. Every ounce of frustration, every emotion I have fades away with each violent impact of my hips against her ass.

"Fuck! Oh, *fuck-fuck-fuck*," she moans. Her eyes snap open. Her hips shudder and bounce as her pussy squeezes around my cock. *Again?* I know I'm good, but damn.

Rolling my hips to stroke it slower, I give her a few seconds to enjoy it, then pick up my pace again, nailing her to the bed until I feel it.

I pull out and rip off the condom just in time. Shot after ball-draining shot falls onto her back and her ass. My head drops back when the feeling overtakes me. As it slowly fades, relief replaces it.

I massage the last bit out and wipe my head against the base of her ass cheek. She looks back at me, breathless. Maybe she wants to scold me, but she doesn't say a word. She's spent, sweaty, and satisfied.

Teagan thinks she needs control, but she doesn't. The minute she lets me take over is when she gets what she really wants.

I sit back and smile at my work, smacking my hand on her ass and giving it a grateful squeeze. "You good?"

"Yeah."

Like a gentleman, I go to retrieve a towel from my bathroom. While I clean myself off, I catch a glimpse of my reflection. My breath is still short; my heart rate is up too. A little cardio with an orgasm at the end? Is there anything better than that?

I return to the bed and wipe my dirty work from her back, flopping onto the bed beside her.

A minute passes while I watch her, waiting. She seems to have no intention of leaving. "Are you chilling for a while, or . . . ?"

"Shut up, I had a long day. I just need a few minutes."

"I'm just sticking to the contract, and I'm pretty sure sleeping over isn't in it."

She opens her eyes to glare at me. "Giving me five minutes to rest doesn't constitute a sleepover, you ass. If you want me to go right now, just say that."

"I didn't want to be mean, but . . ."

With a huff, she gets up, walks to the bathroom, and locks herself inside. My postcoital glow is such a relief, but with every second that passes, I feel the stress of my family drama creeping back in. I want to be alone when reality hits me again.

She comes out of the bathroom and picks her clothes up from the floor. It looks like her shitty mood is back too.

"You sure you're good? Everything cool?"

"Yeah, Heath. Everything's sunshine and lollipops." I didn't need to hear her tone to catch the sarcasm. "Everything *cool* with you?"

No, I want to say.

Even though I don't want to admit what struggle my mom is going through or why I'm fighting with my dad again, I wish I had *someone* I could tell just to get it off my chest. Instead, I'll keep everything inside and try to make it through the summer without exploding. At least Teagan is letting me fuck some of my stress away, but I won't dare to fly too close to the sun by expecting anything else from her. Getting burned again is the last thing I need right now.

"Yep," I say. "Rainbows and popsicles, babe."

NINE
Teagan

Two weeks into my contract with Heath, I feel . . . *good*. A rare word for me to use when it comes to my general mood or outlook on life, but it's an apt one. I feel good.

At work, the smell of old books and fresh toner is like a scented candle to me, the whirr of the copier digitizing files in the background is my lo-fi playlist, the busy work of scouring through discovery is my reality TV. I'm neck-deep in my summer internship, scheduled for thirty-two hours every week at one of my parents' associate law offices in the city, with just enough time off to attend my summer semester course for four hours every Tuesday and Thursday. At 7:00 p.m., it's two hours past my shift—a good gesture to show I'm not the *worst* nepo baby to exist—and time to clock out. I highlight and tab the section about Married Boss Man having sexual relations with Also Married Client #33 and shove the rest into the folder. Class starts in an hour, then I will stay to study and prep with Ryan at the library until midnight at least. An easy day.

On my way to the elevator, my heels echo through the lobby. Our head secretary looks up from her phone and smiles.

"Hey, Teagan," Brooke greets me like a watchful auntie. "You should leave earlier on the days you have class."

I can't feel burnout when I bury my feelings beneath copious amounts of iced coffee and hot sex. "I'll be fine. I still have time to grab some caffeine on the way."

"Caffeine this late at night." She tuts. "Do you ever sleep?"

She knows my parents, their associates, and makes it a point to learn everything about my classes, my friends, and the wedding. I can never tell if she is just being nice to me because we're the only two Black women in the office or if she knows my connections to the partners provides her with job security. I don't mind either way. It's nice to have someone looking out for me.

"Occasionally," I say with a smirk.

"You can't let all those white boys run you in circles with no rest, Ms. Lady."

"I know. I promise I'll sleep next month. Have a good night!"

She laughs while shaking her head at me. "Have a good night."

~

Class was a great distraction. The more hours that pass bring me closer to the weekend—my two, possibly three days straight of getting busy in a much more enjoyable fashion.

"What's that face?" Ryan asks.

My eyes snap to his. "What face?"

"You're smiling. It's weird."

The sex last night was everything, and I get more tomorrow. What's not to smile about?

"It's weird for me to smile?" I ask.

"Uh, like *that*? Yeah."

Six-week courses are killer, but it will save me time and stress in my last year. My parents have a strict timeline they've laid out for my success. Graduating next spring and passing the bar exam on my first try next July is nonnegotiable. With an internship and full-time class schedule, it leaves little time for *life* to happen, but that's why I don't have one.

Ryan's engagement was a curve ball, and asking me to help with the wedding made me want to commit felonies against him, but here we are. Mary graduated with her bachelor's, and our next year will be consumed by classes and exam prep. It was either this summer or make her wait another year and a half while the Spanish side of her family shames her for "living in sin" with Ryan. Mary deserves the wedding of her dreams, but it is *very* inconvenient for me.

While I wish I was hooking up with someone other than Heath, the abundance of items on my to-do list feel less arduous when half of my days end with an orgasm or two. Sex is my Me Time this summer. Rough, sweaty Me Time.

"You're doing it again!" Ryan says.

Damn it.

"Can you focus, please? We need to get this done. I have work in the morning, remember?"

"Oh right. My bad."

Under the gothic arches of the law library's ceiling, next to our tired peers pouring over case studies for our class's mock trial, Ryan and I have one of the study tables to ourselves. Occasional laughter echoes through the designated no talking area, giving life to the usually somber space.

We're not worried about the trial. It's straightforward and we're great at filling in the gaps in each other's knowledge, no matter how large or small they may be. It's one of the joys of having been best friends *and* classmates for a decade and a half.

"I cannot believe I'm getting married in two months," Ryan says. His dreamish stare into space makes it hard to tell how long he has been thinking about it. He's a lovesick little douche.

"I can," I grumble.

"Oh, right. This is crunch time for you, huh?"

"You gave me six months. It's been 'crunch time' the *whole* time," I complain.

Ryan laughs at my misfortune, his blue eyes squinting. "I'm sorry. I do appreciate it, though. You're the best 'best ma'am' ever."

With Mary's only sibling being her brother, they went with the modern arrangement of a man of honor and best ma'am. As demanding as it has been, I can acknowledge that it *is* an honor, or whatever. "You're lucky to have me."

"I am." Ryan wobbles the pen he holds between his fingers. His nervous tic. "It's good, right?"

"What? The wedding?"

"Yeah."

I may be worried about schedules and florists, but Ryan is scared about the big M. *Marriage.* He won't say it, but he knew I would be the only one trustworthy enough not to stress him out more than the thought of lifetime commitment. He and Brett are close, especially now that they are the first ones to get married, but Brett is too out of touch with reality, humanity, and the concept of time to organize anything. "I've got this. Don't worry."

"I know. You always have it together." He moves from fiddling to tapping the pen against his book. "I can't comprehend how you manage to do it all."

"It's really not that bad. There are websites with superhelpful checklists and Mary's brother is basically—"

"No," he stops me. "I mean everything. All the time. Only you can balance school, a job, wedding planning, and wrangle the five of us jackasses. You're a freak of nature, and I mean that in the best way possible."

People say that so often. I'm anal-retentive, yes, obsessed with detail and control, but it isn't easy for me. Not that anyone notices. Or cares.

"Thanks, I think? Honestly, if you were marrying anyone but Mary I would have told you to go fuck yourself."

His tapping stops when he chuckles. "Why?"

"You don't remember how much of an asshole you used to be. You were as bad as Brett."

"That's why you moved in with Jeremy?"

"And because you were a horny little shit and I didn't want you humping my leg."

He acknowledges the truth with a grin. "I wasn't that bad."

Ryan is the dark-haired, blue-eyed love interest of every rom-com. The Bad Boy who turns into the Nice Guy after he meets The Girl. Clichéd, but much appreciated. "She brings out the best in you. You bring out the best in each other."

He looks down at his book, a smitten grin pulling at his lips. "Yeah?"

"Yes, idiot. Can we study now?" I go back to my book, finding where I left off at the same time his pen starts tapping again. I slam my hand onto it. "What, Ry?"

"Nothing." When I hold my glare he answers, "It's just . . . Mary's not the only person who helped me grow up, you know." His subtle way of complimenting me. Still, raising my friends isn't the heart-warming achievement he thinks it is.

Over his shoulder, a curvy woman approaches, her black hair wrapped into her signature loose top bun. "Speak of the devil."

Mary has a cup of coffee in each hand. "*Hola, mi amor.*" She leans down and kisses Ryan's cheek. "I brought you some coffee."

"You're the best, baby."

She hands him his cup and then extends the other to me. "Here you go, Teagan. An oat milk caffè latte, right?"

No, but her gesture is kind, nonetheless. "How did you know?" I look at Ryan. "You don't deserve her." Back to her. "You're settling, Mary."

She giggles. It's a cute sound. "Oh, that's not true," she coos, running a hand over Ryan's disheveled hair. "Good luck. I'll see you later tonight?"

"Maybe tomorrow morning?" Ryan asks permission with a grimace.

She forgives him with a knowing smile. "Just say hi whenever you get home."

"Okay."

They kiss and I want to gag. "Ew, ew, gross, stop," I tease them. Mary giggles again and walks away. "Your love is disgusting."

"Oh, stop. You act like you don't want to be in a relationship."

"I don't."

"Really? So you didn't spend five months trying to like Lenny because it was better than being single?"

"Excuse you! I mean, yes, probably, but excuse you."

"See? You must get lonely when you spend all your time here and then go home to an empty bed."

"Who says my bed is empty?"

He raises an eyebrow. "You have a new squeeze?"

He's not new. "No."

"You do! What's their name? When do I get to meet them?"

I laugh for reasons he doesn't need to know. "Okay, so what you're doing right now is getting in my business and—"

"Come on, Teags. Give me something."

I sigh, knowing he means well, but I added the nondisclosure clause to the contract for a reason. The second he finds out I'm with Heath the floodgates will burst open and I will never know another moment of peace. "It's not a thing. Just let me get some dick, okay?"

"Lenny didn't burn you out on men?"

"It's purely out of convenience," I quip. "I'm just trying to get through all the summer events without getting dry-spell rage, not to start something real. It's not that deep."

"Yeah, because no one ever falls for their rebound."

"He's not a rebound. It's just sex." I look at him for a response, but all he does is hum a sarcastic agreement. "You're rude."

"And you're naïve."

We exchange playful smiles and get back to reading.

~

It's two in the morning when I finally make it home. Jeremy left a note on the refrigerator like a boomer, saying he'll be at Chet's tonight. A shame he didn't think to text me like a normal person, but it doesn't make much of a difference. He already stays at Chet's half of the time.

Climbing into bed with my clothes on, I flop onto my pillow and stare through my window. I'm exhausted, but my body is still stirring with my all-nighter second wind. Pulling my phone from my pocket, I stare at my last message to Heath, contemplating sending him another, but that's not allowed.

Thursdays are not in our schedule, and though it's technically Friday, it's not within our agreed-upon window. I'd appreciate the chance to get it in after a long day, but it's better this way. Sticking to the contract keeps our secret safe. It keeps me safe from everything else that might happen with Heath.

Behind the whirring sound of my window AC unit, Ryan's words creep through my head. I'm not naïve. Heath is not a rebound—I have nothing to rebound from. But am I lonely? Did I stay with Lenny because I didn't want to be alone? Is it really sex that I want, or is it companionship and a warm body next to me?

Nah. Sex for sure.

I reach into my nightstand and pull out my vibrator.

TEN
Heath

It's two-something in the morning and I can't sleep. My pillow is warm; my sheets feel heavy on my skin. I flip my pillow over and push the blanket down to my waist with a huff.

My phone sits next to me. I pick it up with the hope that doom-scrolling will help lull me back to sleep. In my messages, the last one is from Teagan to schedule our next appointment. Even a quick thought of getting her naked makes my cock twitch against my leg. If I text her, she'll be pissed about me waking her, remind me about the schedule, and somehow manage to call me a dumbass six times. The thought makes me smile.

I swear the typing indicator shows up for a second, but when I blink, it's gone. A figment of my horny imagination. My thumb opens the text box, but as I stare at the letters, I change my mind. Teagan already gave me an extra day last Sunday. I can wait a few more hours.

Doesn't mean I like it, though.

~

Work always lifts my mood, which shows I chose the right profession, regardless of what my dad thinks. He wanted me to go into business, get my MBA, and join him in representing athletes going pro—a constant reminder of what my accident stole from me. Helping others recover from serious injuries, walk again, or accept their new physical normal, heals me too.

The hours fly by when I do what I love, especially when I get to work with great patients. I'm pretty fond of the one I'm with right now.

Her name is Shelley. Blond, athletic but still curvy, she's attractive for sure. She came to us after having surgery for a gnarly ACL tear, but she loves the exercises I give her, smiling through the whole session even when I'm trying to kick her ass. It's a nice smile, which is good considering how difficult it is not to look at her tits.

My hands hover below hers while she balances on the Bosu ball. Her left knee holds strong, but the injured one twitches medially. "Knees over toes," I say. Her knee moves back into the proper position. I'm great at my job, but it's easier when you have a patient willing to do the work.

The timer on my watch beeps. "That's it. Come on down." She takes my hands and carefully rocks herself off the ball. "You're doing great."

"Thank you." She smiles like I hit on her or something. "I'm feeling great."

"No other tenderness or pain?"

"Nope."

"That's good. Just keep up with the regimen from Dr. Bennett and don't slack. I'll know if you do, and I'll make you pay for it," I tease with a grin. Her cheeks redden when she looks away. *Yeah, I know. I'm hot.* "See you next week, Shelley."

She can barely look at me when she says, "See you next week, Heath."

She's into me, and I'm just a few hours from getting into someone else. I can't think about that right now.

When she leaves, I take her paperwork back to the office. Dr. Bennett, who lets us all call him by his first name, Dro, stands at his desk rapid-firing notes into the computer the way he always does. His fingers fly over the keys while his eyes stay fixed on his screen. He doesn't even glance my way when he says, "Looks like she's doing well."

The dude is a beast. Six foot six, built like the pro-level wide receiver he almost was. His beard is always edged up, fade always clean, with that bright, Hollywood-white smile. I want to be like him one day. Forty, still in great shape, still scoring twentysomethings.

"She's progressing quicker than expected," I say. "She has no trouble with her balancing exercises or flexion, and no visible swelling. Should we bump her up to the next phase?"

"Let's stay with the plan for now. The last thing we want is reinjury."

"Sounds good." I walk to my desk behind him and pull up her file to enter the notes.

My phone buzzes on the desk next to me. A reminder text from Teagan. She always acts like I'll forget, as if she thinks I don't want to be inside her as much as humanly possible. She's crazy, but she still turns me on. I move my hips to adjust my semi.

Just six hours left. Time can't fly by fast enough.

"What are you grinning about?" Dro asks. I swear he has eyes on the back of his head.

"Nothing."

"It doesn't look like nothing." He turns to face me, leaning an elbow on his desk. "It looks like you got away with murder."

I laugh. *I'm about to murder some pu—* "Nah, I just locked down some plans for tonight."

"Plans? You have a date?"

"Kind of."

"Ah, you have the fun part that usually comes *after* a date, huh?"

It's hard to tell where the line is drawn between us. I know the bra size of the woman he slept with last weekend, but I don't know where he grew up, if he has family, or anything else people would usually know about someone they're around fifty hours a week. I've worked for him since my internship started last fall. After nine months, I've given up trying to know him, and have accepted this is the only way we'll connect. He's no different than anyone else around me. "You get it."

"Who is it this time?" he asks.

I begin my practiced lie, but stop, realizing he is one of the few people I talk to who is outside my circle. I don't have to lie to him. "Her name's Teagan."

"And what's Teagan got goin' on?"

I feel my smile spread. "I'm not gonna lie. She's hot, man. She's got a 'Run This Town' body."

He looks confused. "A what?"

"You know." I recite the questionable genius's lyrics about G-strings and beestings until Dro cuts me off with a groan.

"Oh, hell no. Don't ever say that again," he says with a laugh. "But a white girl with a fat ass? That's a win."

"She's not white, her parents are," I explain. "She was adopted from an orphanage in Ethiopia when she was two, and her parents changed her name. Same with her brothers."

Dro lets out a *huh* like he's impressed. "You seem to know a lot about this girl."

"I do, yeah. She's my . . . mutual friend." I regret my unintentional pause. "She's planning everything for our friend's wedding that we're in together. Since I'm going to be stuck with her all summer, I convinced her to let me get *in* her all summer too."

Dro laughs. "Your sneaky link is your best friend's friend. Someone you'll be at public events with."

I don't get what he's saying. "Yeah?"

His grin tilts into a smirk. "Your sneaky link doesn't sound so sneaky."

"It is. Seriously, we have it locked down."

"Man, to be twenty-three again." He turns back around and resumes typing. "Go ahead and get out of here. I'm sure you need to shower and manscape or something."

"Really? I can go?"

"Yep." He holds out a fist. "Give her my best."

I bump his knuckles with mine. "I will after I give her mine."

~

I can't remember where I parked, making it that much harder to figure out which black BMW 4 Series is mine. It also makes it hard to tell if I'm surrounded by people just like me, or if I'm becoming like *them*.

My car chirps in the distance and I remember I parked behind the light this time. On my way, my phone buzzes again. Thinking it's Teagan asking to move up our time, my smile perks up, but when I see who it really is, I get nervous.

"Hey, Mom."

"Heath." She sounds upset, making my heart break. "I don't want to be here anymore. Can you please come get me?"

"Mom." I hate being powerless to help her. I'd rather drive my car into the Hudson while chained to the steering wheel than see her hurting, but I can't change things. My father is in control. "Dad said you were supposed to stay the full two weeks. Did you talk to him?"

"He's out of town again. I don't need to be here." At this point, I can tell she's crying. "Please, come get me."

I brace myself against my car with a hand. Dad has made it clear that the choice isn't up to me. I'm already on thin ice with him, but I would do anything for my mom.

"All right. I'm on my way. Just hang on, okay?"

I know how this will end. Badly. Very badly.

ELEVEN

Teagan

Sleeping for six hours last night, two hours longer than planned, really messed up my schedule. I didn't wake up until 8:00 a.m., which left me no time for studying before work. I *hate* starting my day already behind. But it's a sex day. I'm always in a better mood on a sex day.

I pick up my phone and scroll through my messages to find the last one he sent.

Me: Can we do 8:30 tonight?

Heath: Sounds good

The anticipation makes me want it even more. Warmth spreads through me and settles hot in my panties. I ache so bad to have him inside me I have to shift the way I'm sitting. I need to focus on something else. It's only 8:12.

Study time with Ryan has been hot and cold. The wedding is distracting—I get it—but unlike his attention span, deadlines don't move around like chipmunks on coke. I scour through my textbook for the millionth time. There's a case I've been trying to remember, one that aligns perfectly with what Ryan was getting at this afternoon, but I can't seem to figure it out. I'm not one to forget, but I have a lot on my mind right now.

"You're so boring," Levi grumbles, bringing me out of my head and back into my apartment.

"You are too," I say back.

Levi sits next to me on the sofa, resting his head on the back while he switches through Netflix previews. He has made himself comfortable under the throw blanket Jeremy bought to cover the red wine stain he left on the beige cushion. Levi's hair is half down, the top in his typical bun, the rest falling onto the top of his shoulders in a cascade of shiny, black tendrils. Most days I wish I had his stupid, perfect hair. But not on a sex day. I don't want anything but dick on a sex day.

It's 7:15 now. Levi leaves at 7:30 for practice and I need Jeremy out by 8:15 or there's a risk he'll run into Heath on his walk over. Jeremy locked himself in his room an hour ago and hasn't come out. I'm surprised he's home at all as he usually spends every weeknight at Chet's.

I don't necessarily *want* him home all the time. Sharing a six-hundred-square-foot apartment is cozy, to say the least. It's nice to have the place to myself, especially when I have my scheduled self-care time with Heath's penis. To be honest, I miss Jeremy when he only comes home on the weekends to eat, sleep, and leave a mess for me to clean up after. Less on that last one, though.

But it's fine. It's a sex day. I never feel lonely on a sex day.

Finally, Jeremy's door swings open. He walks out carrying a cardboard box, not looking my way even though our living room only has enough space for our sofa, coffee table, and my sunny disposition. "Hey, Levi," he says.

"Hey, Jer."

"What's in the box?" I ask just to be acknowledged.

"My business, nosy ass," he says without missing a beat.

"Got it." I appreciate his brashness, his *everyone and their mother can catch these hands* kind of attitude—until I'm on the receiving end. But it doesn't bother me today. Little bothers me on a sex day.

"If you must know, it's shoes," he says. "I'm trading some with Chet so we have enough for all the parties coming up." It must be nice to be the same size as your significant other. The joy of doubling your closet for free. "Ryan is doing too much. I just recovered from all of Brett's wedding shit last summer, and now Ryan is being just as extra. Just assuming we'd pay for last-minute, peak-time accommodations in Ibiza? Why can't any of our friends be normal and get married somewhere other than an island on the opposite side of the world?"

"All valid questions." He's venting, and he's not saying anything I haven't thought at some point in the last three months, but it's a frustrating reminder all the same. The timid knock on the door lifts my mood.

Jeremy opens the door for Chet and they exchange a quiet greeting and kiss.

"Hi, Chet," I say.

"Hi, Teagan! Oh, little brother is here too? Hi. You two are the cutest siblings." His warm smile brightens the dark cloud of Jeremy's mood. He comes over and leans down to give me a hug; his big arm is as hot and damp as the apartment. He must have walked. Maybe it's the heat making Jeremy extra pissy.

"Let's go," Jeremy says.

"Oh, okay." Chet rejoins Jeremy at the door. In and out, just like that. "Bye, Teagan! Bye, Levi!"

"Bye, Chet. Bye, Jere—" The door closes before I can finish his name. Oh well. It's 7:20.

"He is so tired of you," Levi says, snickering to himself.

"He loves me, he just loves Chet more." Even if we didn't have another nine months left on our lease, Jeremy does whatever Jeremy wants whenever Jeremy feels like it. To be fair, I would also prefer to stay in a shiny new high-rise apartment with central air if I had the chance.

"Are you going to move in?" I ask.

"With you?" he asks.

"Yeah. When Jeremy leaves me for Chet."

"Never."

"Why?"

"Because you're boring."

I lift my gaze to give him a look, but the TV has his attention. "If I'm so bad, why do you come here before practice?"

"Convenience."

"Mm-hmm." He has murderball practice a few times a month in Brooklyn. Even with traffic, it's not much shorter of a drive from here than it is from our parents' house, so I know it's an excuse to see me. It's Hargrove nature to hide our fondness for each other beneath a layer of criticism.

"You're really going to sit there and study the whole time I'm here?" he hassles me again. "You can't do that after I leave?"

I can't because I'll be doing *Heath* after he leaves. "I'm always busy, you know that." I avoid his question. "Summer-mester sucks, but it's less I have to do later. I want to graduate and pass the bar as soon as possible so Mom and Dad will get off my back."

Levi laughs. "Yeah, because they're totally going to let go of the marrying Lenny thing."

I close my eyes with a sigh. "Thanks for that."

"You're welcome."

My phone beeps from the coffee table. I don't need to look to know it's my reminder for my dick appointment. At least I know it's 7:30.

I shut my book and set it beside me. "You need to get to practice."

Levi's brow stitches with confusion. He looks at his watch and says, "It's *exactly* 7:30. You have a problem."

~

Heath is late because of course he is. My panties are already wet with anticipation. I thought about buzzing one out before he got here but knew it wouldn't be as good. Out of all the men I have been with, Heath is the only one who can beat a toy—and in the rare moment he can't, he's more than happy to collaborate with it. Remembering that makes me hornier.

I pick up my phone and huff when I see it's 8:50. The second I pull up his number to call him, there's a knock at the door. I drop my phone on the couch and sprint over.

It's barely open before I scold him. "You're late."

Heath gives me a look of contempt. "And the Browns haven't won a Super Bowl. Any other keen observations?"

He's such an asshole, but damn it, he's pretty. His gray eyes look darkened by his annoyance. His black work polo hangs untucked from matching pants, leaving him halfway between medical professional and catalog model. It reminds me I could have had him naked by now.

"Would it kill you to be on time for shit?"

"Leave me alone." He takes a step inside. "Something came up. I'm a few minutes late. Get over it."

"Be here when you say you'll be here, and I will."

"Teagan!" He slams the door closed and pushes me back against it. His hand grips my chin, keeping my face in place while he looks me in the eyes. "Shut. The. Fuck. Up." He steps closer to press his body against mine, making me tingle from head to toe. His expression is gentle yet insistent. "Please."

Something about that "please" really does it for me. I bite my lip to keep from moaning *Okay*.

His hand tilts up my chin and his mouth finds my neck. He sucks my sensitive skin while his hands lower to my chest. The surprise mixed with his fervor makes my body warm with desire. His fingers tickle under the sides of my shirt, then rip it up, exposing me. Warm lips circle my nipple, hands tear at my fly. I moan before I can stop myself.

It all happens so fast. I can barely focus beneath the heat washing over me. He seems to feel the same. It's as if he was as impatient as I had been feeling. He matches my energy, reads me so easily, and hating that he can do that only makes it hotter.

He rips my pants down to my thighs, then turns me around, pushing my chest against the door this time. I can't see him, but I feel him crouch down. A second later, his tongue is against me.

My body shivers with excitement. His tongue teases me, his hand massages my ass, his hum of pleasure vibrates against me when he finds my wet center. I lean my forehead against the door between my palms, giving in to his aggression. Every touch feels better than the last.

When his mouth leaves me I can't stop a whine from escaping, but the sound of a condom opening keeps me high. Only a few seconds of pause leave me cold before I feel him at my entrance. A gasp is my response.

He slides in easily and immediately gets to work. His hips pump against my ass while he strokes hard against my front wall. The position keeps him shallow enough to fuck up my G-spot like it's his job.

The moan that leaves me is louder than intended, but completely warranted.

"You want to keep talking shit?" He dares me.

"You're . . . ah! Fuck."

"That's right." He pulls my hips back, crashing them against his with every hard thrust.

I want to cry it feels so good. I smack my palm against the door instead of letting out the stream of curse words he makes me want to moan. We're either pissing off the neighbors or giving them quite a show.

"I fucking hate it when you're late." Over and over, he hits the perfect spot. Fucking hell.

"Yeah, I know." He smacks a hand hard against my ass. "Do you hate me too?"

"Yes," I whimper, unsure if it is an answer to his question or a response to the feeling he's drowning me in.

"Do you hate this?" A hand slides between my legs. His fingers circle against my clit and my legs shiver. I don't hate that at all.

He knows I'm close. He knows exactly what he's doing to me. He always does. "No," I admit against my better judgment.

"That's what I thought."

The pleasure settles in my head and rids me of all other thoughts. All the anticipation and frustration build inside me, blindingly hot, threatening to burst. Then— "Oh god!"

The orgasm hits me hard. My body sings while I clench around him over and over. I shake like an earthquake while I struggle to stay on my feet. He pushes deep and stills. Only when my moans taper off do I hear him.

"Fuck," he breathes, only an inch from my ear. His hips shudder while he eases himself in and out, making me clench around him each time. The feeling seems to flow through us in the same way. I look back at him, watching his eyes rise to mine, feeling the intensity of his gaze in my core.

With one last moan, he slips from me. His hands leave, taking my warmth and stability with them.

Out of breath, I turn to face him, steadying myself by leaning back against the door. He looks me up and down, his cocky smirk curling his lips when he sees what he has done to me.

The condom goes into the trash. We pull up our pants. I can't form words.

"Want to complain about me being late again?"

I leer at him, fighting the smile I feel on the inside, and swallow to rid the desire from my voice. "Just leave earlier than you think you should. It's not that hard."

With a shake of his head, he steps closer and slowly zips his fly. His eyes trace over my body, that smirk still tugging at the corner of his lips. I can't decide if he wants to laugh at me or take me again.

To my surprise, he leans in close, his lips hovering just a breath from mine. I stare at them while I wet my own.

"I'll see you tomorrow," he whispers. Leaning away, he pulls at the door. I move so he can open it. "My place, right?"

I nod. He slips through the door, leaving me alone.

With a sigh, the rest of my strength leaves me. I slide down the door to sit on the floor. My head is still spinning, my body still buzzing. I can still feel him inside me.

What the hell got into him?

TWELVE
Heath

My breath is quick, my heart rate up. The treadmill's belt whips beneath my feet but I keep up with it, no problem. I'm killing it today.

"Damn, Heath. Are you trying to make me look bad?" Brett looks at my screen. His pace is half of mine.

I lower my speed back to my normal jog and smile. "I have a lot of . . . energy today," I pant.

"Yeah, I can see that. What's up with you?"

Even if I could tell him, I wouldn't.

My time with Teagan last night was too short. I got what I wanted—what I needed—to clear my head of what happened with my mom right before. My stress and anxiety faded the second I tasted Teagan. Nothing else was on my mind while I was inside her, fucking her against that door. It was everything. Making Teagan, the catty control freak, bend to my will—just thinking about it makes my blood rush downward.

I should have stayed for a second round, but after seeing her look at me like I was some kind of sex god, my ego exploded. I'll let her get the snarky last word if it means I get to use it against her next time. The hours can't pass quickly enough.

"Nothing's up." I dodge Brett's question.

"Nothing's up?" He gives me a suspicious look. His eyes widen and his jaw drops when it clicks. "You're getting laid!"

Ugh. "Try to sound a *bit* less surprised."

"Sorry." He laughs. "This is big news! You were on, like, month six of no sex."

"Are you tracking my dry spells? Also, it was not that long."

"Sure it wasn't. Did you finally get with the girl you took home from the party?"

"No," I say, hoping he'll let it go.

"A new girl?"

He won't drop it. When he doesn't stop staring at me for an answer, I give in. "Sure. She's new. But we're not dating. It's just sex. Like, *great* sex."

Brett laughs. "No shit? Who is this girl?"

"No one you need to know. Stop asking."

Our treadmills beep to signal our twenty minutes is up. My screen reads *3.25 miles*. I haven't done that in a while. We slow to a cool-down pace, and as I catch my breath, I see Brett still staring at me.

"Stop looking at me like that. I'm not telling you shit."

"Why not?"

"Uh, because it's not your fucking business?"

"Come on," he whines. "This chick has you buzzing. Bring her out this weekend and let us meet her."

Just *imagining* how that would blow over makes me cackle. "Absolutely not." He looks down at his screen with a pout. Against my better judgment, I acknowledge it. "*What?*" I huff.

"Nothing, I guess."

"Oh really?"

"It's just that I always kind of hope you'll find someone." There it is.

Brett always acts like I've never been in a serious relationship. I can't tell if he wants me to be in another one because he thinks it would be good for me or if he wants me to be in one so he isn't alone in his misery.

We climb off and stretch. "You've been married too long, bro," I say. "Let me live."

He acknowledges the end of our conversation with a frown. "As long as you're happy and shit."

"I'm definitely happy and shit." I wipe my face with my towel. When I'm done, he's still staring at me. "Bro, if you don't stop—"

"I haven't seen you this way about a girl in forever. Since high school, forever," he says. My eyes narrow. "I think you're really into whoever this girl is."

"I'm not into her. Drop it."

"Whatever you say."

I'm so ready to be done with him. "I gotta go."

"Do you want to grab lunch?"

"I can't today, I need to go see my mom." I wait for him to ask why, but his attention stays on packing his bag.

"Next time, then. We have to try out that new tapas place on Eighty-Fifth. It's all over Instagram right now."

Brett never asks about anything important in my life, especially not my mom. It's just money and sex with him. He has his boats, his cars, and now his trophy wife to go with them. Everyone has problems, but I can't have mine wiped away with tapas and a yacht.

"Yeah, for sure."

~

Pulling up to my parents' house raises my blood pressure. I hit the gas and speed up the long driveway snaking through the trees.

The house comes into view and it still feels unreal. I haven't gotten used to this place, and I'm not sure I ever will. We lived in four different houses in Westchester between the time I was in sixth grade to when I graduated high school. Dad bought this one two years ago. Mom says it reminds her of home on the island, but I don't see how. As long as she's happy and still close enough for me to visit, I don't care which massive mansion my dad decides is the flavor of the year.

The house is a renovated mid-century bungalow. The split gable roofline defines the two wings, one a sprawling rectangular swath of glass seeming to float behind black metal posts, the other warm wooden slats and stone anchored to a towering chimney. It is the epitome of my dad's personality: two-faced, pretentious, and over-bearing. If it were *exactly* like him, it'd be full of shit.

My dad's red Audi R8 isn't out front, meaning he isn't here. He leaves too frequently to park his daily driver in the detached garage out back with the other seven collectibles. I pull up and park in his place right in front of the door.

Our estate manager, Silas, the silver fox, comes out, greeting me when I approach. He has been with us since I was eight, a more con-sistent male role model to me than my dad. His suit today matches the color of his hair. "Mr. Heath. Welcome home."

He knows how I feel about this house, but he'll keep saying it, hoping I'll change my mind. He's a well-meaning old man, stuck in a world long gone. "Did you miss me?" I ask, trying to hang on to the last of my good mood.

He grins at our inside joke. "Always."

We walk inside together. "Where's Mom?"

"The dining room, last I saw her."

"Cool." I take a step in that direction, but Silas stops me with a hand on my arm.

"She is doing well," he says. Deeper meaning lies behind his tone and tense expression.

"Good." Maybe I didn't make a mistake by picking her up.

Mom sits at a table, watching the gardeners tending to the weeping cherry tree in the atrium's garden, absentmindedly fingering the waves of her hair, which hangs to her hip. "*Mālō, tinā!*" Hey, Mom, I call to her in Samoan. I can't remember much, but it always makes her happy to hear me speak what I can.

She turns in my direction and her face lights up. "*Tālofa, si a'u tama!*" Hello, my son. She stands, inviting me into a hug. I wrap her in my arms, resting my head on her shoulder and squeezing her tight. "*Ou te alofa ia te oe.*" Another phrase she will always say to me: *I love you.*

"I love you too." I let her go and she pulls my face closer to kiss my cheek. My heart feels fuller when she smiles at me. I can do no wrong in my mother's eyes. "Dad's not here?"

"No. It's just us. Come, sit."

The chair's legs sputter against the floor as I pull it out. I watch every move she makes. She sits next to me, pulling her long hair over her shoulder to keep it from getting trapped beneath her. She wears a taupe cardigan, and underneath it a loose dress covered with tropical flowers. The red looks pretty against her brown skin. I know she dresses like she's back home to comfort herself.

I wish we could go back to the island again, but we haven't visited since my grandmother passed away. Mom still feels her loss immensely. They were very close and remarkably similar. My mom was the daughter of a model and a man who left the second he found out he was going to be a father. Then Mom also ended up becoming a model and marrying a man who didn't want a kid. History has a funny way of repeating itself.

I want to break the chain, but here I am, fucking up every relationship I have. It's hard to know you were never wanted, only tolerated, by your parent. I would never put another kid through that.

"How are you feeling?"

"I'm good now that you are here." The dimple on her left cheek deepens when her smile spreads. I want to believe her, so for the moment, I do. "Are you hungry?"

She doesn't wait for an answer before she waves over our housekeeper from the kitchen. Homa brings over juice, a plate of fruit, and traditional pani popo. Their sweet coconut scent calls to me. I lose the fight against my simple carbohydrate avoidance and take a large, sinful bite. Mom does the same before she pours our cups, putting me at ease.

"Tell me more about your plans this summer. Which of your friends are getting married? Ryan and then Ritchie, right?"

"Yeah, it's hard to keep track." After a sip, I add, "For now, it's just Ryan. I don't think Ritchie's thing is going to happen. He talks about proposing to his girlfriend, but their relationship is really toxic." I'm hoping he's close to figuring that out, but I won't hold my breath.

"Well, that isn't good." She pops a grape into her mouth. "Maybe you'll be the next to get married, then? Find someone before you start your physical therapy program."

I stop chewing and wait for her to look at me. It's a red flag when she gets forgetful or loses track of time, that cloudiness and disassociation that comes right before the worst hits. I'd hate to think Dad was right.

"Mom, you know I only have a year left of school, right?"

"Yes. I mean whatever your internship is called after you graduate."

"Oh. My residency." That's a relief. "Yeah, well, that leaves me this summer and I'm already working full-time. I'll have to find someone quick."

"I hope it won't be too hard on Teagan."

My muscles tense again. "Teagan? What do you mean?"

"All the wedding events," she says, and I relax. "All of you drag her around like she's one of the boys. You have to let her be a woman sometimes."

"It's not like we're *forcing* her to come with us. She prefers doing stuff with the guys more than the bridesmaids."

Because the bridesmaids prefer doing trips to wine country, and Teagan prefers doing girls. Strip clubs are her happy place, not Ryan's. He will probably sit there like a deer in headlights again.

"That doesn't matter. She is unique. She has needs and desires you and your friends can't understand. You should let her tell you what she needs, listen when she does. It will help get you in touch with your feminine side as well."

"My feminine side?"

"Yes. Your full range of emotions. The way they help you see the world around you. "

"That's feminine?"

"Not exactly, but it's different from you boys who never talk about how you're feeling," she says. "Not everything has to be a struggle. You shouldn't hang on to this anger. Letting yourself connect to your emotions is much healthier than being angry all the time."

"I have good reason to be angry."

"Heath." She grips my hand in hers. "You shouldn't have reasons. I'm sorry you had to come pick me up."

"I'll always be there for you, Mom. You know that. But I don't want you to keep doing this to yourself."

"You won't have to any longer. This is the last time it will happen, I swear." Her hand leaves mine and settles under her chin. The smile on her face makes me almost believe her. "Besides, I'll always be okay when I have my two boys to take care of me."

"Does he?" I ask. She tilts her head in confusion. "Does he take care of you? When he's gone ninety percent of the time, then dragging you around like an accessory whenever he's here."

"Yes, tama." She sighs and takes my hand again. "He is not perfect, but no one is. I know you and your father don't see eye to eye, but we love each other very much. He cares for me the best way he knows how."

If that's the best he knows how, it seems he has plenty left to learn.

They've been doing this same dance for years. Dad travels a lot during football season, and Mom gets worse. He comes home more often over the summers, finally notices something is wrong with her, and decides to "fix it" before he leaves on his next trip. But everything is fine because they love each other, and that is somehow enough.

I've only been in love once in my life—blind, stupid, crazy in love—and it fell apart so easily. I haven't seen the point of trying to have anything real since then. Letting someone in is as good as cracking open your chest and telling someone to take a swing. I have enough hurting me right now.

My arrangement with Teagan is everything I need and nothing I don't. No talking, no room for emotions, no space for me to fuck things up again. Pain free.

"No more frowning." Mom pulls me out of my head. "It's the weekend! Do you have fun plans for tonight?"

I chuckle. "You wouldn't believe me if I told you."

~

I left Mom feeling much better than I had when I dropped her off a couple of days ago, and for a moment, it feels like everything will be okay.

Inside my building, Teagan walks up to my apartment door at

the same time I do. Her heels tap against the wood floors. Those little shorts and thin blouse draw my eyes to her body like magnets. I don't care if she sees the smile on my face or not. She's my pain relief, even though it hurts to admit that.

She crosses her ankles and then her arms, and I can *see* the shitty words coming. "Looks like you're on time for once," she says.

If she only knew how bad I've wanted to hear her bitchy little comments all day. I unlock my door and open it for her. "Don't get used to it."

THIRTEEN

Teagan

I may not live at home anymore, but most of my closet does. As little as I enjoy making an extra visit to my parents' house, it's a good excuse to see Levi between Sundays. Even when he's being a brat.

"You look so stressed it's stressing me out," Levi complains from my bed.

"Sorry for the inconvenience," I joke.

I *am* stressed. As ready as I am to be done with my class, it also means I'm one step closer to being best ma'am full-time. Banquets, showers, parties—so many events with so many vague dress codes. A normal person would love the opportunity to dress up and go to fancy events, spotting celebrities, getting free food and alcohol, and staring at the skyline from the top floor of a luxury hotel, but not me—especially not the events I have to plan, coordinate, and clean up when it's over, all while wearing heels.

As if that's not enough to worry about, it's also a faux pas to wear the same dress twice in a season, so I rented four to complement the ones I didn't wear last year. I have too many choices and too little patience. Piles of classwork, a courtroom, and juggling a full-time job I can manage, but parties make my eye twitch.

"I have a lot to do," I tell Levi. "Mary's brother is in Spain for the summer, so he's handling the actual wedding part with the planner, but I'm in charge of everything stateside and groom related, including coordinating all the travel and deadlines."

"But why, though?" Levi always asks the real questions.

"You know how Ryan is. He doesn't realize how much work anything takes outside of school because he's always paid someone to do it."

"So, is he paying you?"

"Yes. With his undying gratitude."

Levi laughs. "Ryan would fall apart if you weren't by his side all the time."

"Believe me, I know."

My closet here is the size of my apartment's bedroom. Mom drops little surprises in it sometimes, heavy suggestions on what she would like me to wear to an upcoming event or a suggested replacement for what I had just worn. My perfectionism rarely serves me outside of a professional setting, and when it comes to attire, I will run myself in circles trying to figure it out. But luckily, I have a cheat code.

Everyone thinks Jeremy is my style guru because he's gay, but he's a bear who can barely dress himself. My secret weapon is straight as an arrow and lounging against my headboard in an Off-White hoodie.

Going back to the closet, I pull the fitted dress from the rack and grab my black stilettos. It's neutral enough for me to fade into the background while keeping everything organized. *I think.*

Holding them in the doorway for Levi to see, I ask, "This isn't too much, is it?"

"Too much for what? Your shift on the corner?"

I scowl. "What's that supposed to mean?"

He sets his phone beside his hip and leans forward, pressing his fingertips together like a CEO reprimanding an intern. "The dress is see-through, Teagan. You're going to a wedding."

"It's a *reception*, and only the exterior layer is transparent. It's solid underneath."

"It's giving Shein," he quips.

Begrudgingly, I let out a laugh. "Fine. What about the Marchesa? Is it too formal for black tie optional?" What even *is* black tie optional?

He rests his cheek on a fist. "You don't want me to answer that."

I have four other vetoed outfits laid out on the bed beside him. He's not being helpful at all. "You are the *only* other fashionable one in the family. Why can't you help me choose?"

He smirks. "I'm the only fashionable one in the family, but that's not saying much when this is what you're working with." He gestures to all the options.

I groan. "Help me!"

"Fine! Do the fluffy dress with the fluffy Jimmys for the reception, the Lhuillier with the strappy sandals for the rehearsal dinner, then save the Marchesa and Louboutins for Mom and Dad's black tie."

The "fluffy dress" is powder blue, floor length, and backless other than thin straps that cross back and forth. Light ruffles trace the vertical straps on the shoulder blades, looking like tiny angel wings, and the skirt consists of asymmetrical, scalloped layers of organza. The two elements stress the band at the waist, creating a dramatic A-line. I kind of love it.

"The fluffy Jimmys aren't overkill with the fluffy dress?"

"No, it looks good," he says as he picks up his phone, obviously done with me. Setting the shoes next to the hem of the dress, I see that he's right. But can I— "You have the body of a Dior model, don't ask me if you can pull it off."

"Okay. Damn." Levi can always read my mind.

I glance at the clock and see I have fifteen minutes left of the time I scheduled for this. I take a deep breath to calm myself—so much stress over what is ultimately just fabric. I'm lucky Levi is the way he is. I sit on the bed next to him and let my head fall onto his shoulder. He brushes his silky hair out of my way—silent acceptance of my affection.

I want to be low-maintenance like him, not needing a bimonthly trip to the salon for the bare minimum nail and hair upkeep. Rolling out of bed, sliding on a hoodie, looking presentable after brushing my fingers through my hair sounds like perfection . . . but his life isn't easy. It's just a different type of hard than mine. I admire every-thing about him, and I'm impressed by everything he does.

When I look up at him, he's smiling mischievously at his screen. I lean up from his shoulder and see the profile picture on his phone that is 75 percent boobs and 25 percent face.

"You're still on Tinder?" I ask.

"You're not?"

I feel the grin tug at my cheeks as I pull the phone from his hands. "No, actually. I'm taking a break for the summer."

He lets out a quiet gasp. "You're getting some."

"Maybe." I give him a side-eye, but my smile grows.

"Who is it?" he asks.

"No one."

"That means someone."

"Fuck off." I laugh. I swipe right on the boobs and go to his profile. "Your tagline is 'Yes, it still works'?"

He takes his phone away from me. "Yeah, so? Mind the business that *lays* you," he jokes. "At least I don't have Mom and Dad trying to marry me off for political gain."

My laugh becomes a cackle.

When I calm myself, my phone pings with what I assume is a calendar reminder. It's probably time to leave if I want to be at the library on time.

"Why is Heath texting you?"

Shit. Rather than lying, I deflect. "Why do any of the guys text me?" I turn and stand so he can't see any hidden information I might show on my face. "I have to go."

"Going to see your fuck buddy?"

"No, sadly. I'm going to prep for court with Ryan." *Then* I'm going to see my fuck buddy. The stress of the truth covers the stress of hiding my secret, but I keep my focus trained on packing the dresses into the garment bag just in case.

"You know he wants to be with you, right?" Levi prods again.

"Ryan? Are you out of your mind?"

"No. Heath."

I hesitate for a split second but cover my silence with the sound of a zip. "He doesn't, either, not that it matters."

"I think it does."

"It doesn't." Levi is biased. Fuck my feelings, he would love *any* excuse to hang out with Heath more often. "I'm running late. I'll see you at dinner this weekend."

"Bye. Love you."

I kiss his cheek. "Love you more."

Fleeing the room, I swing the garment bag over my shoulder and pull out my phone. Heath's message makes me roll my eyes.

Heath: What time are we getting it in tonight?

That was close.

He's such a fucking idiot. I praise myself for turning off my message previews.

When I pass by Rowan's room, I spot him inside, hunched

over his desk with headphones on. A book sits in front of him, and directly behind it, his laptop. Rowan never stops studying. He's like me in that aspect, but I don't know if he's having any fun to offset his stress.

I walk in and tap his shoulder lightly so as not to scare him. Still, he jumps and pulls off his headphones. "Oh. Hi." He looks at me with tired eyes, his voice lacking enthusiasm.

"Hi, I'm leaving, but I'll see you Sunday."

"Yeah, see you Sunday." He puts his headphones back on and returns to his book. I don't take it personally; I just kiss his cheek and leave him be.

When I'm safely down the hall, I text Heath back.

Me: At 8, dumbass

~

After hours of work and studying, doing something mindless feels amazing. *Heath* feels amazing.

My eyes are screwed shut as I ride him like my life depends on it. Buried deep, stroking him against a needy spot, the pleasure blooms hot and heady. I'm drunk on it, and right on the edge. Heath moans as I ride him faster and faster, his fingers digging into my hips so hard it hurts. "Ah!" I whimper. "I'm gonna come."

"Fuck, me too."

The pleasure floods through me. I open my eyes to look down at him in all his frustratingly gorgeous glory, my pace never changing. A string of curse words falls from my mouth while I watch the orgasm bleed through him. His veins rise, his skin reddens, muscles flexing as his face twists with torment. His mouth drops open when it hits him.

His moan makes me clench around him again. He's so hard as he comes, but I want more. My hips move ragged and desperate, taking everything I can before—"*Ah! Yes!*"

My head falls back, the orgasm flowing from my core to my brain in rush after rush. My body clenches and releases around his perfect dick.

His hands on my waist are all that keep me from falling backward. He leans up, his mouth feathering warm kisses across my breasts, then a few gentle tastes of my nipple as we come down. Out of breath and misted with sweat, I lean my head back up, stroking his hair while his mouth teases my soul back into my body. My mind settles from my high into a blissful calm. Then the clarity brings me back to the message I forgot to give him before I started ripping his pants off.

"You can't text me like that," I pant.

Heath chuckles. "Love the segue, babe."

He falls back to the mattress, his hand replacing his mouth to knead my breast. I pull it away. "Seriously. Levi almost saw your last one."

His face contorts. "Can we not talk about your brother while I'm inside you?"

With a sigh, I let him slip from me and tumble to lie beside him. "We agreed to keep this shit on lock. We have a contract and a schedule for a reason. Clause 3b. No unprofessional communication means you only need to text me if you're running late or giving notice, and you don't have to spell it out like an idiot."

"Sheesh, sorry. Won't happen again."

I pull down my shirt and straighten my panties. Apparently, I wanted it so badly I didn't wait long enough to take my clothes off. That won't get to happen anymore if he keeps being a dumbass.

"Don't ruin this for me, Heath. I'm serious."

"For you? Don't ruin it for me!"

"I'm not the one texting you about 'getting it in,' shithead."

"Okay, but—"

"I don't care. Thank you for your service, now please leave my apartment."

He grumbles and lifts himself from my pillow. "You know, you're lucky your pissy little attitude turns me on."

While he fumbles around with the condom and his clothes, I enjoy the view. He's smaller than Lenny—only where the sun shines, that is—but his muscles are more defined, and his ass is out of this world. I love a soft woman with plenty of curves to explore, but with men, I like them hard in every possible way.

I roll to my side to get a better view of him pulling on his underwear. He seems to move in slow motion when he stands, his abs flexing, his dark hair falling into his face. He settles the band at his hips and catches me watching. A smirk curls his lips.

As much as he annoys me, this has been great so far. All I want is to keep having meaningless sex every time I'm stressed. More undressing, less depressing. My summer mantra.

"Hey, I almost forgot," I remind myself. "I can't do Friday."

"What? Why not?"

The end of my two-day mock trial, aka my final and entire grade for the class, the bane of my existence, and the only stressor that has kept my focus away from the wedding events waiting in line behind it. Although I feel confident, my fear of failure won't allow me to admit it. The dinner after will either be for celebration or consolation. "None of your business. I have a thing."

"Well, do I get a rain check?"

"Is that in the contract?" I retort.

He groans with annoyance. His shirt goes back on and I settle back onto my pillow. He grabs his keys and wallet from my nightstand. "What time on Saturday?"

"I'll send you a calendar invite so you stop asking me."

He laughs, then catches himself. "Oh, you're serious?"

~

The next morning, I feel good. I took out a lot of my frustration on Heath last night, but it's impossible to rid myself of everything. So much rides on how well Ryan and I perform today and tomorrow. A poor grade will be another reason for my parents to be disappointed in me. A poor grade will make me disappointed in myself too.

"Do I look okay?" Ryan breaks me from my inner torment. Out of all the things he could worry about, he always picks the thing that matters least. It's court, not fashion week, and half his closet is coordinated suit separates. What did he think? That he would accidentally throw on his pink shorts and boat shoes?

"You look professional. It's perfect," I answer as I resituate his tie clip.

His frown turns up. "Okay, good. You look great too."

My dress is a plum-colored wool blend with half-sleeves and a pencil skirt. It's my power suit, second only to the white-on-white Olivia Pope special I have planned for tomorrow. I know what I look like. "Thanks."

Ryan lets out a nervous breath. "I need to pee again." He turns on his heel.

"Thanks for sharing."

He power walks away. Ryan and his nervous bladder. In some ways it's comforting to see someone like him nervous. He's like a well-trained attack dog: cuddly around family but zero restraint when it's time to win a case. It's a nice reminder that seemingly phlegmatic people also have weak spots. Even if it's just their bladders.

I turn back and find a security guard standing in front of me. I flinch.

"Hi, can I help you find where you're going?" he asks with a smile.

I look at him, and I already know what is about to happen. "Oh, no. I'm where I'm supposed to be. Thank you."

"It's just that the room numbers are the same between the floors. Only the letters change," he continues. "This room is reserved. Civil cases and jury selection are in the same place on the floor below us."

I give my best fuck you smile and repeat myself. "I'm in the right place."

"Could I see your letter or summons to verify?"

His smile is polite, just as I'm sure he believes he is being, but behind the aloof look in his blue eyes he doesn't see the layers of biases that tell him someone who looks like me doesn't belong in a place like this. "No. As I said before, I'm in the right place. Thanks."

"What's going on?" Ryan comes to stand beside me. My knight in white armor.

"This helpful person is insisting I'm in the wrong place for some reason."

The accusatory look on Ryan's face is the same one he gets in the courtroom. "There are six other students here. Why would you think she's in the wrong place and the others aren't?" he asks.

"That's not—" The guard's expression drops into a worried state. "I was simply checking to make sure she didn't need help. That was all."

"Okay," I say. "Maybe the third time I say it will suffice. I'm where I'm supposed to be. Thank you."

The worry on his face turns to offense, but he leaves anyway. This is not the brand of annoyance I need before our trial, but such is life.

While I'm over it in two seconds, I can feel Ryan stewing beside me. "He knows you belong here. Why would he single you out like that? In front of everyone." *Think about it, Ry.* "There's no way he . . . I thought people here were better than that."

"Well, they're not."

Our names get called. The prompter spots us and motions us inside. I turn back to Ryan, knowing I need him to focus if we're going to pull this off.

"Don't let it upset you." I pat him on the chest. "Let's go do this thing."

He nods, and yet again I coddle someone rather than have my discomfort addressed. Just two more days.

FOURTEEN
Teagan

Class is finally over, and after getting through twelve hours of court, *relief* barely begins to describe it.

As we walk to our favorite sushi restaurant, Ryan snakes his arm around my waist. "We fucking rocked it," he growls the reminder into my ear. He's right, we did. And he hasn't stopped celebrating since.

"Yep. Now, let's get drunk."

Ryan made this reservation the second we found out when our trial would be. This place has a two-year waiting list—if your dad isn't on retainer with the owner. Just like mine, Ryan's parents always know somebody who knows somebody, and it comes with major perks.

Inside, the black walls and floors of the lobby swallow the mood lighting from the geometric bamboo chandelier hanging overhead. In front of us, slender pendants hang like raindrops over the rest of the restaurant, every table and booth full of young, sexy people. The place has a type. Dressed in all white, losing my suit jacket, keeping the body-flattering dress beneath it, I know I fit the vibe, but after yesterday's run-in with the security guard, I'm feeling the spotlight again—the one that follows you everywhere, making you hyperaware of how different you are from everyone else in the room. In the back of my mind I worry other people will notice it too. That is typical for me, especially with my family, and especially during summer when I'm surrounded by the guys, but it's hitting a little harder right now.

We stalk up to the hostess. I look around for Jeremy, but when I see Ritchie instead, I get confused.

"Hey, Rich. What are you doing here?" I slip from Ryan's arm to move into Ritchie's instead. I hug him back, the added height from my heels making his head fall right beneath my chin.

"What do you mean?" He laughs with that goofy smile. "We're here to celebrate our boy!"

Our boy? When did this become a celebration for only Ryan? "What?"

Jeremy finally makes his appearance. I try to give him a *what the hell* face but he won't look at me. Beside him is Brett—the only other person invited—and behind him, Heath. My eyes widen.

He stops walking when he sees me. The same look of surprise graces his face. *Why is he here?*

"Hey, guys," I greet them as a group. "Nice of you to join us." I give Brett and Jeremy a quick side-hugs, but when it's Heath's turn, I don't know what to do. We didn't plan for this.

Awkwardly, we turn and wait for the hostess to gather our menus.

"This was the thing you had?" Heath whispers without looking at me.

I cross my arms. "Yeah, apparently you had a thing too."

"Brett invited me yesterday. I didn't know you'd be here."

"Yeah, well, fucking surprise, I guess."

Ryan turns around and frowns at us. "Can you two get along for one dinner, please? For me?"

~

Sandwiched between them, Ryan laughs it up with the guys to my right while Jeremy makes disparaging comments under his breath to my left. "Wasn't this supposed to be *your* celebration? Like, for your class, not wedding shit again?"

"Yep."

He takes an untouched piece of sashimi from my plate, and I don't stop him. "Love that for you."

Even though he's pissy about everything I do for the wedding, too, I love it when he shit talks the rest of the group with me. When Chet isn't there to balance the oppressive het-male vibes of our group, it's borderline intolerable for both of us. All I wanted tonight was some sushi and sake, not more bros bro-ing while I'm trying to drink my day away.

"Tell us what we're doing for the bachelor party, Best Ma'am," Brett prods.

I'm not amused. The guys are three drinks deep at least, and Brett is always two drinks away from pissing me off. This will be fun. "Considering I thought this dinner was about something else, I didn't bring the itinerary, but—"

"Are we going to that club?" Ritchie butts in.

That club is one of the most famous strip clubs in Vegas. Asking me if I want to see naked women dance for me is like asking if a golden retriever wants to play fetch. I snake my arm around Ryan's shoulders to spare his feelings and keep him inculpable. "We're going to have fun. It will be very *classy*," I say, then mouth *Filthy* where Ryan can't see.

Ritchie pumps his fist like the baby-eating-sand meme. It will be fun until Ritchie fucks it up, which he will. After his shenanigans with Brett last summer, I question whether I should go to Martha's Vineyard with Mary and the bridesmaids and send the guys off to

Vegas without me. Dealing with a wine migraine is more comfortable than dealing with Ritchie. We're basically family, but I would still enjoy watching him choke.

"You guys have to say congratulations to Teags too," Ryan says. "We rocked our class final today."

The others lift their glasses and murmur some sort of congratulations. "Oh, wow, the enthusiasm. Thanks, guys," I coo. *Where is my sake?*

"You wouldn't believe what happened, though," Ryan continues. "When we were waiting to go in yesterday, a rent-a-cop started giving her shit in front of our other classmates. The guy tried to tell her she was in the wrong place, like she was a litigant rather than a lawyer. *Teagan.*"

He means it as a compliment, but it's one I don't want. The server arrives with the next round and I have to fight myself not to snatch it. I give Ryan a look that says *Drop It*, but he's either not getting it or he's not paying attention. He continues, "Dude was a racist prick. It's crazy that shit is still happening."

"When did it look like it stopped?" Heath laughs.

I give him a sideways glance. Being the mama's boy he is, it doesn't take much for Heath to pop off about racial inequalities. It's one of his very, *very* few redeeming qualities.

"Well, I mean . . . you know what I'm saying."

"I don't," I say. Ryan looks at me with a frown. "Do you think it's rare for that to happen to me?"

"Is it not?"

I let out an exasperated breath. "It happened two weeks ago when I was going home. The woman in front of me closed the door in my face because she thought I was trying to sneak into my building. The one I've lived in for five years," I say. "Before that, when I was helping Mary with your registry, the Bloomingdale's associates reminded me where I was three times, and followed me around until Mary got there."

Ryan looks like he wants to cry. "Are you serious?"

"Oh stop. We've all had times when people think we're someone else," Brett pipes up for no reason other than to tempt me. "Not everything is about race."

"Oh, definitely not, babes," I say with a sea of sarcasm. Trying to explain my life experience to an apathetic cis-het white man in the 0.1 percent simply isn't worth my breath.

Heath turns to Brett. "Teagan is just as wealthy as we are, has gone to the same places we have, yet *she* is always the one who has her status and presence questioned. Why do you think that is?"

Brett rolls his eyes. "It could be for a million other reasons. The vast majority of people aren't racist, it's just a convenient card to play."

I snort.

"Getting harassed is convenient for her?" Heath asks.

"Bro, no. Teagan is like a sister to me, and I'm sure it's awful for that to happen, but I seriously doubt it was because of her skin color or sex. That's all I'm saying."

"You tokenize her all the time to explain away your ignorance, then you want to turn around and say none of it matters? The math ain't mathing, friend."

"I don't tokenize her."

"Oh yeah? Then tell me how you're not racist without mentioning her."

The guys awkwardly turn their attention, trying to carry on a different conversation while the bromance of the century has a lovers' quarrel. I'm oddly transfixed.

"Bro, I'm not racist at all. Tea—well, it wouldn't matter who it was. You know I don't see color."

"Wrong."

"I don't! Black, white, green, purple, there's no difference. We all—"

"Wrong again."

"Oh my god, dude," Brett groans. "What makes *you* not racist, then? You can't be racist when your mom is Polynesian or whatever?"

Or whatever is wild.

"I have my biases like everyone else, but I don't need to *know* someone to believe they deserve the same basic level of human rights as I do. When you use her as an excuse, you're showing you do."

Brett searches for a rebuttal but doesn't find one in time.

"Give it up, bro. You're wrong," Heath says. "Check yourself before you say dumb shit like that again."

Brett's brow wrinkles with anger. "Dude, shut the fuck up."

"I'm not the one talking out of my ass! Why don't *you* shut the fuck up?"

Brett shoves Heath with both hands. Heath falls back against Ritchie's shoulder, causing him to fling his drink onto the table, Jeremy's phone, and the front of my dress. I can't cuss them out before Heath stands up and shoves Brett back, toppling him onto the table, a plate falling to the floor with a loud crash.

"Hey, hey, hey!" Ryan gets up and stands between them, parrying Brett's next attack. They have most of the dining room's attention already.

Jeremy sighs beside me. "This is some hetero shit. I'm out."

"Please don't"—he's out of his chair before I finish—"leave me here . . ."

"Calm. Down," Ryan says quietly but insistently. The guys are still staring each other down, Ritchie pulling Brett away while Ryan massages Heath's arms to cool him off.

Some of the restaurant staff approach our booth. *Ugh.* "You all are so fucking embarrassing," I seethe, dabbing the worthless cloth napkin against the stain on my dress. "Tuck your dicks away and leave!"

Ritchie drags Brett by the arm, Ryan holds Heath until they've gained enough distance. "I'll stay," Ryan says to me.

There is shattered ceramic and food on the floor, liquor dripping from the tabletop because he decided to invite the whole chaotic crew without telling me. His "help" is the last thing I need right now.

"This was supposed to be a dinner to celebrate, Ry. Go. I'll pay and get this mess cleaned up." I kiss his cheek to send him on his way. His mouth twists but he follows my direction, as he always does.

The restaurant manager looks at me with a cocked eyebrow. "I'll take the check with hefty gratuity and whatever this mess will cost," I tell him.

~

With everything taken care of, I can finally leave. Jeremy is long gone, and with him, my ride home. Outside, it's dark, but the air is still hot. Only the occasional breeze wafting through the buildings provides any relief. It's not quite enough to cool me off when I see who's left.

Heath stands alone on the curb, casually looking at his phone as if nothing happened inside. There's no way he is waiting for me. Someone else has to be here. I walk over and stand a distance from him. While I dig in my purse for my phone, he looks at me.

"Are you the last one here?" I ask.

"Yeah. Mary just picked Ryan up."

"Awesome." It's not awesome. It's more or less the opposite of awesome.

"You need a lift?"

"No. I'm calling an Uber."

He chuckles. "You're that mad at me? We *do* live close to each other, you know."

I breathe in, trying to bide time while I think up an excuse. "I've had enough bullshit for one day. I'd really rather not."

The silence that extends makes it seem like he accepts my answer. But then, "I'm sorry for what happened in there."

"Why are *you* apologizing?"

"Because I made a mess. Again."

Returning my gaze to my phone, I brush it off. "You guys always fight when you drink too much. I'm sure you two will be back to being besties in the morning."

"I wasn't drinking."

What? "Since when?"

"It's summer. Gotta be swimsuit ready, and alcohol has a lot of sugar. That was soda water with lime."

"You were sober?"

"Yeah."

I shake my head with confusion. *Defending me? For what?* It won't make me hate him any less. "I don't know whether to thank you or smack you."

He smirks and takes a step closer. "Why not both?"

I stop him with a hand against his chest. "Don't pretend you're kinky."

"And don't pretend you're not."

Why is there no winning with him tonight? Dude must want it bad if he's willing to pull some shit against his homeboy *and* try to flirt with me. "What was this really about, Heath?"

"Huh?"

"All this. Tonight." I gesture at the restaurant with a flourish of my hand. "You know you get laid regardless of what happens. What do you get out of pretending to give a shit?"

"I *do* give a shit, Teags. You know that."

I watch his expression grow morose. If not for me, he would do it for his mom. He wouldn't let anyone say *anything* about her. Ever. As he should.

"How is your mom?" I soften. "I miss her."

His eyes snap to mine. He stares for a second before some levity returns to his face. "She's . . . good. She misses you too." It's a nice lie, and one I'm happy to believe. "And I'm still sorry about tonight."

"Well, I appreciate you standing up for me, but stop it. I'm a big girl. I can fight off preppy rich boys all by myself."

"I know you can. Maybe I wanted to get a hit in on Brett for once."

The way he stands with his hands in his pockets, the muscles in his chest and arms popping beneath his shirt, that little smirk painted on his face . . . he's annoying, but it's hard to remember when he looks like that.

"Take me home," I say.

His smirk widens to a smile. "Okay."

~

Heath snags a parking spot on the street behind my building. I can't remember the last time I've been able to park on my block without fighting someone for the space, but everyone but me seems to get a win tonight.

"Thanks for the ride." I try to sound less annoyed than I am.

"I'm walking you in."

"The fuck you are."

"It's eleven thirty and you look rich as hell, Teags. I'm not going to ruin your night *and* let you get mugged." He gets out of the car before I can protest. I yank the handle to keep him from opening the door for me.

He follows me around the corner and up to the entrance. I unlock the door, but even inside the safety of my foyer, he follows.

"Bye," I say, but he catches my hand. I know what he's going to say before I turn around. "Yes?"

He takes me by the waist and steps closer, his eyes heavy as he looks me up and down. "It's still our day."

"No. We canceled, and we didn't give proper notice to reschedule. Clause 1b."

"But I'm right here, and that dress . . ." His hands sink to my backside, pulling me against him and the growing erection he's hiding. I press my hands against his chest to keep a bit of space between us. "We can't break the rules one time?"

I look him in the eyes, scowling at his attempt. He's an idiot, obviously, to believe anything will happen, but I'd be an idiot if I ignored how much my body wants him. His core is hard under the pressure of my palms, and he's harder even lower. It's dark outside, and today was full of every type of frustration I could imagine. The way he looks at me, his gray eyes dark and heavy as he wets his lips, makes me warm. It's hard not to imagine him making the same face while he's naked and between my legs.

I look at his hands when his fingers flex and grip me again, spreading me in a way that makes me ache for the image in my mind to become real, my body begging me to just give in and let him inside me. I hide a heavy breath.

"The 'rules,'"—I slide his hands back up to my waist—"are a contract. We break it and the whole thing is over. Is that what you want?"

His smolder drops into a pout. "You know it's not."

"Then you'll just have to wait."

He hums a little groan of disapproval. The grip of his hands slides up to my ribs and back down to my waist, exciting my skin further. His penis throbs against my stomach. "What if I say please?"

I tilt my head with a sigh and run my hand over his cheek. *If only you knew how badly I want to say yes,* I think as I trace my thumb over his lips.

I lift my hand and lightly land it against his cheek again. "No."

He grumbles when I pry myself from his grasp. "I hate you so much right now."

"Good. Take it out on me tomorrow."

FIFTEEN
Heath

The day after the dinner debacle, I'm feeling good. I had been worked up for months over Brett's apathetic bullshit. He needed a wakeup call and I was happy to give it to him, but I know he won't learn. We'll be back to normal by the next time we go to the gym together, and if not, I have one less person to pry into my love life and question why my nights have been so enjoyable.

Working on a Saturday isn't my favorite thing in the world, but today is going to be a good day *and* a good night. Teagan turning me down last night is going to backfire in the hottest possible way. She'll see.

"Look at you and your energy," Dro comments while watching me finish my eighteenth pull-up.

The laugh that escapes me takes the rest of my stamina. With lackluster form, I pull out one more, then drop from the bar to my feet. "People need to stop telling me that," I say back.

Dro's white teeth flash between his lips. "You're doing pull-ups between patients. Something's got you going today. Your little friend still treating you well?"

Little friend? Teagan is pretty tall, but I guess *parts* of her are little. Her waist, ankles, wrists . . . all small enough to grip when I'm—nope. Can't think about that right now. "She is, but I'm a little pent up at the moment."

He passes me the mat and adjusts the rest of the therapy equipment between his arms. "Haven't been in it in a few days?"

My snicker is enough of an answer. As ridiculous as the contract is, it has me spoiled. Skipping one of our days only to have her show up unexpectedly and tease me left me so riled up and in my head that . . . let's just say my sheets needed a wash this morning.

Frustrated or not, I'm in a great mood, because even if I didn't have an appointment to fuck Teagan's brains out tonight, today is one of my favorite days at work. Levi is here.

He waves at me through the glass walls of the waiting room. I wave back, a huge smile on my face. I love that kid. He's here early—a Hargrove trait—but I'm not mad about it. It sucks to only see him for an hour a month, but I'll take what I can get.

He's the closest thing I have to a little brother. Few people have the type of unbreakable bond we do, which is good, considering it was made through the breaking of my femur and the separation of his spine. What we went through I wouldn't wish on my worst enemy, but I'm grateful for our connection in a morbid way.

"You got this, right?" Dro asks.

That's a surprise. He lets me fly solo often enough but never on a case as intensive as paraplegia. I'll never back down from a challenge. "Yeah, definitely."

"Do your thing. I'll be right behind you for support." He holds out his arm. I bump the side of my fist against his.

"Badass. Thanks, Dro." When I turn to go to my space, a thought makes me turn right back around. "Hey." I grab his attention again. "Can you keep my situation on the DL with this next client?"

He looks confused. "Yeah, but why? I thought this one was your bro."

"He is, but he's my sneaky link's *actual* brother too."

Dro stares at me for a second too long, then his deep laugh breaks the silence. "You are one crazy motherfucker, Heath."

I set the equipment down and go to the waiting room to grab Levi, and I'm excited as hell. It's stupid how happy his goofy ass makes me.

Levi was Teagan's shadow when we were kids, but when he met me, he became mine. Like it was with her, meeting my mom made me seem safer, I think. While most people can't discern my ethnicity until they see her, knowing I'm less white than the sea of white dudes around us provides a sense of comfort, in a way. Those who get it, get it, and those who don't never will.

Levi was always tagging along with me to practice, games, everything. When my injury ended my pro-ball prospects, I was depressed as hell. But when his accident happened not two months later—the fear I felt thinking we would lose him, it put the loss of a sports career into perspective. While it sounds self-centered, helping him through his recovery showed me what I really wanted to do with my life.

"Hey, Levi." We slap hands.

He smiles up at me. "Heath." He is in his typical wardrobe—a black hoodie and gray sweatpants, similar to what I wear on my days off—but he always has an extra flair. All designer, on-season color schemes, accessorized with a clean watch and chain. I would take credit for it all, but we've gotten to the point where I'm copying *his* style.

"Ready to get your ass kicked?"

"Might as well let you try here. We all know you can't beat me anywhere else."

"Oh, it's like that?"

"Hell yeah, it is."

Levi plays murderball—wheelchair rugby for those who haven't seen it. I've gone to a handful of games, and when I tell you I was shitting bricks the whole time, I'm not kidding. It's violent, full-contact nightmare fuel. Even thinking about it makes my ass clench.

Levi climbs out of his chair and gets into position on the exam table by himself.

"How's everything feeling?"

He pulls his shoulder-length hair up into a rubber band. "Well, I haven't miraculously regained my ability to walk yet, but other than that I'm doing great." Sarcastic ass.

"How about the hips and back?"

"Good and fine."

"Details, Levi. Tingles? Cramps? Spasms?"

"Nah. Everything's about the same. Lower back still gets sore after practice."

"I'm sure ramming yourself into solid metal has nothing to do with that."

"Definitely not. Ramming myself into my dates may be setting it off, though."

My laugh comes out like a cough. "Bro." He smiles with pride. "Not to sound like one of your lucky ladies, but it's time to take it off, man," I joke.

He laughs because he knows the protocol. He pulls his hoodie off to leave only his fitted tee on. The dude is ripped, but he hides it as much as possible. As electrifying as his personality is, he is humble in the weirdest ways. Always complimentary and caring, but hiding it behind wisecracks.

"Roll over for me."

Levi turns himself to lie on his stomach. His legs don't unlace. I unhook his shoe from his pant leg and lay them parallel. I roll up the end of his shirt and tug his pants down just a bit, then run through the steps while I clean my hands and grab the lotion.

"Heath, I need more foreplay before we jump into things."

"You *wish* you could hit this."

I start in on his back, running my thumbs along the sides of his lumbar spine, feeling his thoracolumbar fascia for any inflammation. He doesn't twitch or show anything on his face, but he rarely does. Next to it, his medial latissimus dorsi is in knots. When I add a little pressure, his face twists, though his smile holds.

"How often do they have you lifting during practice?" I ask.

"Only about half the time."

"What is that? Two, three times a week?"

"Two, yeah. I've been skipping leg days." His grin is sheepish with his dark joke.

I close my eyes with a sigh to avoid rewarding him with a laugh. I know I'll go to hell if I do, but the dude almost got me with that one. "I cannot stand you sometimes."

"At least you can stand."

"Levi, I swear to god." I toss him the harness as he laughs at his own joke. "Put this on before I kick your ass out of here."

It's a bitch to put on and get attached to the lift, but it's important for his mobility. Dro slides the equipment over for me and waits. This is the two-man part of Levi's session. The unweighting machine cost more than my car. It's more complicated than it looks, of course, but the arched metal apparatus dangles him from a rolling support, allowing us to control the amount of weight placed on his legs while we have him walk a few lengths of the track.

Levi gets into everything like a pro, which, after years of this shit, he basically is. There's always a doctor telling him that some people with his injury miraculously regain their ability to walk, as if that's the only thing keeping him going. It is frustrating people can look at someone like him and think there's something missing from his life.

When he's secure and on his feet between the parallel bars, Dro pats me on the back and leaves my side to shadow from a distance again. "Is it a good height?" I ask Levi.

"Yep. Let's get this shit over with."

He grips the bars and leans his weight forward. I spot him while walking backward, tracing the movement of his lower pelvic hip complex as he swings a leg forward and measures his balance atop it. After one step, I can tell why his muscles were wound so tight.

"Hey. I saw you messaged my sister the other day," he says casually, though his voice is strained by the effort he's putting in. "What was that about?"

I chuckle at his attempt. Looks like Teagan was right to be pissed at me for that text. "Probably Ryan's wedding shit. Why? What were you hoping it was about?"

"Nothing," he lies. "I mean, I found out she's hooking up with someone. Hoped it was you."

This is Levi's way of telling me he wants me to be with Teagan. Not just physically, but more. As if the contract wasn't clear enough, having something more with *me* is the last thing Teagan wants.

"Sorry to let you down," I say. Everything I do with Teagan is complicated on its own. There's no way I'm going to add any fuel to Levi's meddling fire.

Levi reaches the end of the rails and I'm not surprised by how quickly our session has gone. He is an athlete. He will push himself hard, every time, and deal with the consequences later. "Ready to go back?"

He nods. I watch him as he turns around, but he doesn't need my help.

"I'm just saying, you should shoot your shot. Summer's the perfect time."

"Give it up."

"You should ask Teagan to do that. I'm sure she would."

They have no problem talking about sex with each other. I don't know if that's a normal sibling thing or not, but with the two of their personalities, I'm sure there is little they don't talk about. Except me, it seems. That's also on brand for Teagan.

"Levi, please stop asking me to get it in with your sister." *I still have to wait a few hours before I get to do that.*

"Fine!" he says with that goofy smile. "Don't fuck her."

~

"*Yes!* Fuck me," Teagan moans.

She lies beneath me with her legs spread wide, letting me hit her deep. So deep. Her arms lie limp near her head, her face twisted in ecstasy as she takes everything I have to give her. Drowning in pleasure, I pump hard and fast. I'm finally buried in my soft, wet happy place, staring at her tits as they toss with every thrust.

"You're so fucking hot," I murmur under my breath.

Her gaze finds mine. The heaviness in her eyes and the breathless, pouty look of pleasure drive me crazy. Her hand grips one breast, and her teeth sink into her lip as she mewls.

"Don't look at me like that," I tell her.

Staring straight into my eyes, she dares me.

I don't stop, I can't. My hips slap against her thighs while I stroke myself in her tight grip. The head of my cock pushes against her with every stroke. I'm rock-hard, right on the verge, but I have a reputation to uphold.

The moan I attempt to hide comes out like a growl. "Do you want me to fuck you harder?"

She nods. "Yeah."

"Are you sure?"

"Yes. Do it."

I slow to a stop, and she looks like she wants to murder me. When I open my drawer and grab our best friend, her expression changes real quick. I flip the little switch and it comes alive in my palm. Her eyes stay glued to it, her chest heaving with anticipation.

The second the little flower touches her clit, she bucks.

Holding the toy against her, I stroke it deep, even. Her hands fist the sheets while her hips lift from the bed. She's sopping wet, shaking, and I can't tell if she is coming or if she has been coming the whole time.

With something between a moan and a scream, her back arches and her knees snap together. I drop the toy to hold her thighs against me and cradle her hips off the mattress. Her pussy squeezes me like a fist. I stroke it just a few more times before my eyes roll back and I spill.

Sense leaves me with every shot. Over and over, the feeling rushes through me, and for a few moments of pure bliss, I think—*hope*—it will never stop. My cock continues to pulse even after I'm empty.

My strength leaves me and I drop her hips onto the bed between my thighs. I slip from her and run my hands over the tops of her legs while I pant. When my vision returns, I find her with both arms draped over her face, her chest rising and lowering with heavy breaths. I stare until the sound of our friend gains my attention again. I flip it off and toss it beside us. Untangling myself from her legs, I leave her for the bathroom to take care of business.

When I'm cleaned up, I grab a towel and go back. She's already sitting up, hair back in place, cold demeanor trying to mask the desire still lingering behind her gaze when she looks at me.

Taking the towel from my hand, she says, "We need to talk."

I glare at her, my muscles tensing with anger. "You cannot be serious right now. I just fucked your brains out and now you want to—"

"About the schedule, chill."

I breathe out in a mix of relief and frustration. Giving me the classic breakup line? She had me thinking we were done for no reason. "Why did you phrase it like that?"

"If you'd let me finish my sentence before flipping out, I wouldn't have."

I flop back onto the bed. "I swear to god if I didn't just come inside you, I'd—"

"We're less than two months before the wedding, which means a ton of events with the guys are coming up, including the engagement party next weekend."

I'm still in my feelings. "'Kay."

"Dinner was already a whole thing. This has been easy to hide until now. We need to be careful going forward."

"We won't get caught."

"How do you know?"

Still lying on my back, I look up and give her a grin. "You think *I'm* a complete dumbass, but you have to admit I'm still smarter than half the group," I remind her. "If we're not holding hands or tonguing each other down, they're not going to notice."

Her lips twist to the side while she considers my words. She puts her shirt back on and combs her hair back into place. "You're too confident for your own good."

"Weird way to say I'm hot, but okay." I get the eye roll I've been looking for. "Teags, they know we hate each other. A small increase in your tolerance for me isn't gonna wave a flag. Keep being you and they'll never know anything has changed."

"Nothing *has* changed."

I reach up. "This wet spot you left on my sheets begs to differ." Her little groan of annoyance is cute. "This is good, Teags, whether you want to admit it or not. I'm not going to risk getting laid four times a week by having the guys find out. Trust."

"Three times a week. Four if you're lucky." She looks over her shoulder, eyeing me as if trying to find the lie. "But you mean it?"

"Every part."

She keeps looking at me and I have no idea what she's thinking. Not that I ever do. "Okay."

"Okay," I repeat, telling her the conversation is done.

Teagan stands up and limps to her pants, wobbling as she does. The girl can't walk straight. She squeaks when she reaches down to grab them.

"You good?" I ask with a laugh.

She straightens up with a wince. "I bet you're real proud of yourself right now."

"Yep."

SIXTEEN

Teagan

I don't want to be here.

With only six weeks until the wedding, the homestretch of events has begun. The reception started less than an hour ago and I'm already ready for it to be over. I shouldn't complain, but I will, because I can. I reserve the right to bitch about something I sacrificed my rare free time to plan.

Out of the options I found last minute, Mary and Ryan picked this banquet hall. It's a moderately sized room in SoHo that spills out onto a larger outdoor space, very similar to their wedding venue on the island. The interior space is maybe a *bit* too small for the two hundred attendees, but we will only be here for as long as the cocktail hour lasts. *Hour* is a loose term.

I stand at my hostess post near the entrance. Peonies, roses, streamers, and balloons, all in shades of pale pink and white. It looks like Barbie's wet dream, but the bride gets what the bride wants. The outdoor space has more classic wedding vibes—a white tent to block the glare from the sunset, white-clothed tables sitting beneath hanging flower chandeliers of white wisteria and the same pink peonies as inside, everything coordinating perfectly with the gold Chiavari chairs and place settings, and the pink rose petals scattered beneath mini bouquet centerpieces.

I outdid myself, as always, but it wasn't easy. Or cheap.

Fifty-eight thousand dollars, and I kept it *under* budget. This party is as big a celebration as any weddingless reception can be, but it is frustrating to know it costs just as much as most couples' entire wedding. We all come from money, but I am the only one who seems to care about how it's spent. It's not lingering trauma from the orphanage or any other reason my parents have come up with. I *choose* not to detach myself from the reality of life outside our overprivileged bubble, unlike the rest.

A couple walks in and looks lost in the sea of pink. I snap into hostess mode. "Hi, welcome! You can leave the gift here or I can take it for you." They smile and hand the box to me. Based on its shape and weight I can tell it's another piece of the china place settings. A dinner plate, specifically. "Hors d'oeuvres are on the tables across the room and the bar is in the corner next to it. Please help yourself and enjoy."

They thank me and head toward the food that cost $110 per head. I let my forced smile drop when I walk over to deliver the box.

Lingering by the gifts table, I gaze into the crowd as they mingle. The room is full of people I don't know. Mary's family consists of a thousand unidentifiable aunts, uncles, cousins, and who knows who else. Ryan's parents brought all of the business associates they pretend are friends. The "limited" guest list they gave me quickly expanded to almost three hundred names before I made them cut it down to meet the venue's maximum occupancy, but that's what they get for having their wedding in Ibiza.

Destination weddings limit the number of people who can go. It's an expensive flight from New York, and it's impossible to find affordable accommodations during peak season. Those who can't swing the cost get their feelings hurt and beg for another way to celebrate with them. Thus, this root canal of a party was born.

Glancing at the clock on the wall, I see only forty minutes have passed. Cocktail hour will likely go on for *another* hour, then dinner, dancing, and speeches will happen outside in the tent. Four hours and twenty minutes left. Shoot me.

"Having fun?" a voice asks beside me.

I know it's him without looking. "I did a lot of work for this thing, Heath. Let me have my pissy mood," I grumble. "Are *you* having fun?"

"Oh yeah, a blast." His matching sarcasm feels nice. He aggravates me, but compared to everything else in this room, he's not at the top of my shit list for once. "A cash bar? Seriously? They're fucking trust fund babies and can't pay for drinks?"

"The venue wouldn't allow it," I answer his rhetorical question. "I'd rather be drunk, too, believe me."

"If you hate these things so much, why did you agree to plan all of them?"

"Because that's what friends are for, or whatever." I finally turn my head to look at him. His black blazer, white shirt, and thin tie look delicious on him. Not that I would ever say that aloud. The perfect fit of his jacket definitely helps, but something about the monochrome makes his skin look bronzer and his mother's Polynesian features more noticeable in his face. "Ryan would have picked one of you to do it instead, if any of you had a smidge of taste or competence."

"I don't know about that."

"Why?"

He shrugs. "We pretend it's all equal in the squad, but you know how it really is," he says. We continue to stare ahead at the crowd as if we're not having a conversation. "We have less and less in common every summer. Ryan is your law bestie, but you both are busy as hell. Jeremy is basically just your roomie since we almost never see his ass." *Neither do I.* "Brett and Ryan are basically family, but I barely hang with Brett outside of the gym now that he's flown off to 'I'm married' land, and it's about to be the same with Ritchie."

"The same how?"

His gray gaze is full of exasperation. "He's gonna propose to his girlfriend. Bought the ring and everything."

"What?" The idea of another wedding in our group is horrifying enough, but *him*? This is just a dick slap in the face. "Is it . . . what's her name? Julia?"

"Giuliana. Gigi."

Not bothering to learn her name is a great example of how serious I thought they were. "I thought they broke up."

"Oh, they did. Two weeks ago."

I rub my temple with confusion. "What the actual fuck?"

"I *know.*"

"They break up every five seconds and that makes him think he should marry her?"

"I know."

I want to throw up. With the way my parents guilt me about my choice to break up with Lenny, it makes me wonder if they'd rather I act like Ritchie and just marry Lenny next week. Who cares how toxic it is if it's on their schedule?

"And here I was thinking I couldn't hate being here more."

Heath chuckles beside me.

My eyes dance through the crowd. Jeremy and Chet hover by the food, talking alone. Ritchie and his future bride bicker in the back of the room. Brett and his wife stand just a few steps away from Ryan and Mary, talking to their common acquaintances.

Maybe Heath is right. Everyone is in their own world, completely unaware of us or anything else around them. I'm lucky I have Heath to keep me sane while I run in circles doing everything for a group as aloof as our friends.

Still beside me, he licks the remnants of a mini quiche from his fingertips and catches my eyes. I look away to save myself. It's easy to pretend we aren't sneaking around when everyone is too wrapped up in their own shit to notice, but it *won't* be if someone catches me drooling.

"Hey." Heath grabs my attention again. He crumples his little plate and places it on the table beside me. I pick it up and throw it into the bin right next to us while shooting him a glare. "I know we're not scheduled until later, but . . . "

"But what?"

"Why not give this party the middle finger and go find a closet?"

"What? No."

"Why not?"

"Well, one, I left the closet a long time ago, and two, I don't want to get caught."

He laughs. "Caught by who? Someone's grandma?"

"Yes, because it would be *Ryan's or Mary's* grandmother. We have a twelve-hour notice clause for a reason."

He hums in question. "We didn't cancel for tonight, and if I recall correctly, clause 1a of the contract says our times are between seven and eleven." He stretches his arm out to expose his watch. "It's 7:18. Think of it as me being early."

Quoting the contract *and* tempting me with punctuality? He's really trying it. "Shut up."

"This thing won't be over until ten, guaranteed, and I'm assuming you'll have to stay after too. Would you rather stand here waiting to talk to a ton of strangers or go somewhere and let me give you an orgasm?"

Let him? That's technically correct, but *lord*. My body wakes up at the mere memory of the last time I *let* him.

It is infuriating how annoying Heath is. Moreso, how annoyingly difficult it is to turn him down. Does he know I was counting down the minutes until this would be over and I could convince him to fuck me in his car so I wouldn't have to wait until we got to his apartment?

Of course I'd rather have sex. I'd rather have sex than do 99 percent of this wedding shit.

My thoughts battle until the warmth in my panties is too difficult to ignore. "Fine."

"Fine?" He perks up as if he thought I'd turn him down.

"One condition. I'm running this shit on my own tonight. Jeremy and I got in a fight so he's avoiding me, Brett and Ritchie are worthless, and I need the happy couple to stay happy. If you can keep the guys from fucking shit up until after the toasts"—I turn my head to look him in the eyes—"you can have me. Wherever you want."

His stare tells me everything I need to know.

"Deal?" I ask to snap him out of it.

"Yeah," he says, sounding absolutely parched. "Deal."

"*Good luck,*" I sing.

He has no idea I am going to fuck him regardless, but now I get sex *and* less stress. I smirk over my win.

SEVENTEEN
Heath

Knowing I get sex soon, my mood is a million times better. I don't mind cleaning up after people and schmoozing grandmothers when it shaves a couple of hours off my countdown. Actually, the added tasks made the time fly by. Now I'm sitting at the long VIP table facing a crowd of faces I don't know, choking on the smell of flowers and house-brand sparkling wine. When I hear the signature tap of a glass, my mood sours.

Speech time. I'm not afraid of public speaking, but I'm not a fan either. Luckily, no one wants to hear a speech from all ten members of the wedding party. I get to sit this one out, but I still have to sit and listen.

Wedding toasts are stupid and predictable. Someone always cries, someone always tries to be a stand-up, someone always gets so nervous they stammer and look like they're going to piss their pants.

I zone out during the speeches, barely listening to Mary's brother's and the start of Teagan's.

"So, I guess I mostly want to thank you, Mary," she says. "Thank you for making my best friend the happiest he has ever been. And, from all of us, thank you for making him *significantly* less of a douchebag." The crowd laughs. "In all seriousness, congratulations. I can't wait to see where the future takes you. Cheers and *salud!*" The crowd repeats her final word. We all take a sip.

Teagan's speech is flawless. Of course it is.

She's on right now—professional, focused, unflappable. She told me I could get it, then she got back to business. Meanwhile I can barely keep my mind off it for more than a two-minute stretch. She has mastered the art of convincing people she is perfect, but I know her better than that.

If she asked for *my* help and *my* company, she's desperate. The stress has her close to cracking, and *fuck*, I want to be the one to break her open, not one of the dumbasses sitting between us.

When I pay attention again, Brett is choking up. I stare at my plate, fighting back my urge to roll my eyes.

"We've always done everything together, ever since"—he takes a breath to compose himself—"ever since we were little kids. And I'm so happy we get to move into this next stage of our lives together too. I love you, man." Ryan stands up and gives him a hug. The crowd *awws* and applauds.

He acts like *they're* the ones getting married. I clap, trying to keep my thoughts from reaching my face.

Finally, it's over. Teagan goes to get the mic but Ritchie stands and grabs it before she can. Her smile drops to a flat line. Going off script? That's going to piss her off.

"Mary, Ryan, congratulations to you both. You two are amazing together," Ritchie says slowly, his eyes squinted. The alcohol's effect on his judgment is glaringly obvious. "Your love is an inspiration, and I can't help myself from wanting the same. So, tonight, surrounded by all our friends and family, there's something I wanna do."

Oh shit. I look over and see Teagan's eyes widen at the same time as mine. *No, no, no, no, no.*

"Gigi, I love you so much," he starts, and I stand to grab the mic from him. I barely get my hand on it when he spills, "Will you m—"

I snatch it and cover with, "Will you all stand and join us in toasting the happy couple one last time?"

I lift my glass from the table. Chairs screech and people rise from them, the sound covering Ritchie's complaints. "Congratulations, *Mary and Ryan*. Here's to a lifetime of well-deserved happiness."

The crowd says whichever version of praise they prefer and sips their drinks. The music kicks up and I breathe a sigh of relief. Holy shit, that almost made *me* the person pissing my pants during the toasts.

People move around to exchange hugs and go to the dance floor. I switch off the mic, feeling secure in my win.

"Why'd you do that?" Ritchie whines.

"Because you're a fucking dumbass, Rich. Why would you think *this* is the time to propose to Gigi?" I ask rhetorically. "Sit down and don't say shit else the rest of the night, or I swear to god, I will kick your ass."

He looks at me and doesn't protest, knowing I've been *begging* for a reason to punch him. I go over to the venue coordinator standing next to Teagan and hand them the mic.

"Thank you," Teagan says.

"Wow, I finally did something worthy of your praise?"

"Don't push it." Teagan can't let me win for too long. She walks by me but stops, standing just close enough for me to hear her whisper, "I despise you, but right now, I want to suck your dick so hard you're going to worry it'll fall off. Find us a closet before I change my mind."

My not-so-little man thuds in my pants. She walks away and I have to take a seat.

~

I love how horny Teagan gets when she hates something. That's one reason she's such a good lay. She hates me plenty.

It only took me a minute to find a closet. Down the hall and around the corner, the room is full of coats, dresses, and jackets hanging on lines of racks, all of them looking abandoned beneath a layer of dust. Inside it's dim and windowless, the mood set by the muted sounds of the music wafting in from outside. My dick is in my pocket and I'm counting down the seconds until I get to free it.

Teagan finally appears at the end of the hall, checking over her shoulder five thousand times while she approaches. I hold the door open for her.

She's inside for half a second before she starts complaining. "It stinks in here."

"What? No it doesn't." I pull her around two racks of clothes to a little open space tucked behind a large concrete column. There's nothing but a bare wall back here, but that's all I need.

"It smells like mothballs."

Her complaints don't slow my eagerness. My belt is already unfastened and my fly is halfway down. "Stop bitching and take your panties off."

She purses her plump lips the way she does when I annoy her, but she can't think of a comeback. To no one's surprise, she reaches down to lift her skirt.

Her dress is a million layers of frilly shit. I pull out my not-so-little man and stroke it while she unburies that ass from beneath it all. The round perfection attracts my hand like a magnet. I squeeze it while my cock swells.

"There's no way we can do this. How am I supposed to—"

I shut her up with a hard spank. "We made a deal. Take your fucking panties off or I'll take them off myself." Finally, she does what

I tell her. The little string of fabric slides over her shoes. She holds them out to me on the tip of her finger. "Thank you."

"Mm-hmm." She can't hide the cute little grin on her lips. She drops to her knees and I hold my breath.

Her lips glide over my head, then she sucks until it hurts. She pushes me to the back of her throat and oxygen no longer exists. *Goddamn.* I have to brace myself with a hand against the wall to keep my knees from buckling.

The sound of her mouth sliding up and down drives me almost as crazy as the way it feels. Gentle, warm, then cruel and hot. She massages me gently, sucks me hard, and laps that soft tongue over my head. I look down and catch her eyes and her evil glint inside them. If I didn't know her better, I'd think *this* was my reward. But I know what she wants—what she expects. And I want to give it to her.

Pulling out the condom I hid in my jacket pocket for this exact occasion, I tear it open. She lets me slip from her lips and stands. "Seriously, how the fuck is this going to work?"

I push her back against the wall, pressing my body against hers. "Why don't you shut up and let me show you?"

She stares at me with those dark, doe eyes and I know she wants to tell me off, but it's already game over for her.

I reach down between her legs, and she shuts her mouth. Circling the little bud with my fingertips, I feel her breath grow heavier against my chest. My finger glides easily inside her, so I let another join it. She feels tight around them, barely enough room to rub my fingers against her special spot. It makes waiting to get in her feel harder than my cock.

When her breath quickens and she grows slick, I can't wait any longer. I lift her leg to wrap around my waist, rub myself against her entrance, then push my way in.

She gasps. I flex my hips to push in deeper, feeling her warmth grip me with every inch I give her. "*Oh!*" Her moan sounds like she's surprised. *That's right.*

Inside her, I'm in my happy place. So tight in this position, I breathe out with contentment and hide my smile against her neck.

As I stroke it nice and slow, she whimpers. Her hands move between us and pluck at my buttons. I grin and toss my tie over my shoulder, giving her access to anything she wants. She reaches up my shirt and runs her hand against my stomach and chest. Her hips flex toward mine to push me deeper. She can pretend she hates me all she wants, but she can't pretend she doesn't love my body or what I can do to hers.

"It's not so bad in here now, huh?" I tease her.

She looks at me with heavy eyes. Her teeth hold her bottom lip in their grasp. That version of a yes makes my blood go south.

Her hips move faster against mine. I hook my hand under her other leg and lift her up. She moans when I push deeper. "Oh, fuck." The rasp in her breathy whisper makes it hotter. Her arms wrap around my neck to put part of her weight on my shoulders. She acts like she's heavy, or that I don't plan to nail her to this fucking wall.

I roll my hips, changing my angle a little each time to feel all of her. Her nails claw down my chest. I pick up my pace, using the wall to help me fight my way into her tight grip over and over, making her legs shake in my hands.

"Oh god. Right there. Just like that," she says.

I do as she commands. She muffles her moans near my ear, her quick breaths matching the rhythmic thud of our hips against the wall. The feeling surges through me. My head falls back with a moan. "*Uhn.*"

"Someone's coming," she says.

"Yeah, I'm close."

"No, someone's here."

"Huh?"

The door opens and light shines under the line of coats. I freeze.

Two people scuttle in, giggling as they do. I hold my breath, trying to think of a way to explain how I ended up balls deep in Teagan while looking for a coat in the middle of summer.

"You're so bad!" a woman says.

"Why? Don't you remember doing this all the time when we were young?"

There's more giggling, then the sound of kissing.

I look at Teagan with a silent *What the fuck?*

She shrugs in confusion, her grimace screaming *I have no fucking idea!*

We stay where we are, afraid to make a sound. The door opens again. "Mom! Dad! What the hell are you doing?" another voice yells.

"Nothing! We're doing nothing!"

"Are you screwing around in a coat closet? You're seventy years old, not a couple of teenagers!"

"And what's wrong with that?" the older woman complains. The door opens again. "You'll wish you're half as frisky as we are when you're our age." The voices trail away, and the door closes behind them.

Teagan cackles. The laugh I've been holding in bursts from me.

I put her back on her feet and look at her; the carefree smile on her face is real. Rare too. "Should we stop?"

"And what? Violate the contract?" she quips.

I smirk, pick her up, and get back to work.

~

Teagan's mood matched mine the rest of the night. A little smile on her face at all times, even through the petty annoyances and lack of alcohol. I watch her from across the room while she dances with

Ryan and Chet, unable to let go of that warm, fuzzy bliss she gave me.

While she chats with a small group of Mary's relatives, her eyes find mine. She scowls, making me laugh. I don't care how much she pretends to hate me if it makes me feel like this.

"I was going to head out. Do you need any help?"

"I'm good, thanks."

"Cool." I turn on my heel to leave but she stops me.

"Hey. Twelve-hour notice for tomorrow."

I'm confident I went above and beyond in that closet, but her admitting it *and* asking for more is a surprise. "Oh yeah?"

"Don't get cocky."

EIGHTEEN
Teagan

It's Sunday dinner, and I'm significantly less annoyed than usual. Either the world is ending or Heath is *really* doing it for me. Not sure which I'd prefer, to be honest.

"How did the party go?" Mom asks to distract us from Dad's grumbling. Even though we have a rule of no business at the dinner table, that doesn't work when a big case gets tricky. When your clientele is mainly *Fortune* 500 companies on retainer, tricky is the name of the game. Corporate law is wild.

"It was fun," I say, and I mean it. *I had fun.* I enjoyed something at a wedding event. It was sex that I enjoyed, but still.

Dad comes in from the next room, exhaustion hanging from his face. He must be losing sleep over it too. He sits with a sigh and picks up his glass of scotch. It's a hard liquor kind of night.

"How's everything going with the case?" I ask.

"Not well," he answers, then takes a generous swig from his tumbler. "Always keep a client happy, and always keep them quiet. That's my advice."

Sounds like *my* contract with Heath.

Levi goes back and forth from the kitchen to the table, helping with the cleanup after our meal. Rowan has already left us to head back to his room to study yet again. I'm on my own with Mom and Dad, just waiting for an opportunity to excuse myself so I can drive back to the city and fulfill my contractual obligations.

"You were saying something about your class." Mom prompts me to continue an earlier conversation.

"Right. We got our grades back for the summer semester last night. Ryan and I got a high pass for our trial performance." The pride I feel must show on my face. My ego lies in wait for their rare praise.

"Very good, Teagan," Dad says.

"Yes, great work, darling," Mom agrees. She reaches forward and squeezes my hand in hers. "My perfect little girl. You always do well, and we know you always will."

"Thank you." My skin warms with their words. Inside, I'm bursting brighter than a sunrise. I live for their validation.

"And you received the top score, no doubt," he says.

My warmth cools. "One team scored higher, but that's out of ten teams. We both got a high pass, that's all that matters."

He hums as if he's trying to solve a riddle. "I figured you would be first. You always come in first. Ryan is dragging you down with him." Dad's snide remark slips out as smooth as butter while he returns to his phone.

That's not true. Ryan pulled me through half of the first day after the run-in with the security guard threw me off my game. "It wasn't his fault. Something happened right before we went in." I attempt to explain. "There was this security guard who—" Dad's ringtone ruins my sentence.

"Sorry, I have to take this." He rises from his seat. "Good job, Teagan. There's always room for improvement."

My smile twitches back up for his benefit, but faking it can't mask the immediate downhill slide of my mood. My mind wanders for a moment as I cross my arms over my middle, fighting the urge to nibble at my thumb. Heaven forbid either one of my parents let me feel accomplished for more than a second before reminding me how I fell short. Accepted into six Ivy League schools? *I wonder why the other two didn't like you.* Graduated valedictorian of my college? *Someone was valedictorian of the* university, *but you can try again in law school.* The joys of being the oldest child, the trial run for the appositeness of their lofty standards, losing a piece of myself every time they shape me to fit into their mold.

"Have you patched things up with Lenny?" my mother asks. My mood slips down the rest of the hill and drowns in a river as shitty as the Seine.

"Mom, no. I haven't even seen him," I respond in a tone much softer than I'd like. "He's busy, I'm busy. You know how our schedules are."

"Yes, but you must have spoken to him sometime in the last month."

"We really haven't, but that's fine. He's not mad and neither am I." She doesn't need to know how my last interaction with Lenny went, how hurt he was, or how hearing him slut-shame me made me want to drag his face across the pavement. My sex life is the only part of me I get to keep private.

"I don't mean to pressure you into anything with him." Yes, she does. "We just want to see you with someone who matches your ambition and won't hold you back. Someone who can make you happy."

"Really? You've hated everyone Teagan's dated before," Levi defends me as he comes back to the table.

"That is not true." Her lips scrunch to the side the way they do when she's upset with herself. Lawyers are rarely wrong. At least in their minds. While Levi takes the stack of plates to the kitchen, she adds, "That boy you were with in high school. He was a nice boy."

"High school? That's the last time you liked someone I was with?"

"I liked him a lot! We all did. Right, Levi?" she calls to him.

"Hm?" Levi comes to my side again, this time to grab the glasses.

"Can we please drop this?" I beg Mom not to continue the conversation in front of him.

She lets it go with a sigh, and I distract myself with my last sip of wine. "Well, the party will give you another chance to speak with Lenny if you can't catch him before then."

"The party? Which party?"

"The banquet. We'll be hosting most of our associates, potential clients. It's the perfect time to introduce him as a junior partner now that he's passed the bar."

"Oh." *Fucking fabulous.* "That's . . . great."

Levi looks at me and smirks. I smack his arm as he rolls away.

~

My eyes cross when the climax quakes through me. My thighs shake like butterfly wings in the wind, the same frantic fluttering as the vibrator Heath holds against my favorite spot. I push it away to save myself, enjoying the last of my orgasm on my own.

He's still hard inside me. I have to brace myself against his strong, tattooed thighs, and enjoy stroking him deep just a few more times until I hear the beautiful sound of him getting his too. Our pace tapers off, and the heat of my orgasm settles into a drunken warmth.

Reverse cowgirl isn't usually my thing, but I like the way Heath stares at my ass when he's inside me—positively mesmerized by its resplendence. It makes a girl feel pretty. He probably wishes he was *in* my ass instead, but I don't care. He knows how to get me there regardless of the position—propping himself up on a hand to give me a better angle, adding a little friend to the equation—and this time was no different. *Both* times. I switch off the wand beside me, dabbing the sweat from my upper lip.

Heath collapses onto his back behind me. I look at him over my shoulder and smirk at how depleted he is. His arms laid off to the side, his eyes closed, all semblance of emotion stricken by euphoria. The only indicator that he's alive is the movement of his chest as he breathes.

"You okay?" I ask.

"*Mm-hmm,*" he hums slowly.

Forget about my day, forget my parents' approval or lack thereof, forget my schedule of impending events and this newly added Lenny banquet. Riding Heath out of consciousness was just what I needed to clear my mind. I may hate him, but I don't hate his brand of validation.

Reluctantly, I let him slip from me, letting out an embarrassing whimper when he does. I cover it by clearing my throat. "I'm gonna go pee."

"Cool." His voice is raspy like I woke him up from a nap. "Pee quick, I gotta . . ."

I wait for him to finish his sentence. "Gotta what?"

"I forgot." His eyes close again. I already know he's going to fall asleep.

After I grab my clothes from the floor, I glance at his phone. The screen is full of calls and texts from *Mom.*

I love his mother. Truly. She is kind, comforting, and warm—beautiful inside and out, as they say. She never gives backhanded compliments or adds a "but" after saying she's proud of you. She is as lovely as her personality, with her gorgeous brown skin and waves of hair that fall to her hips like a waterfall. For a blond, his dad is fine too, but Heath won't hear a single good word about that man.

When it rings again, I look over at Sleeping Beauty and yell, "Heath!"

"What?"

"It's your mom calling. Answer it."

"Shit."

He darts up and fumbles with his phone. I leave him for the bathroom, do my business, wash my hands, put on my underwear, and hop into my pants. I still hear him talking through the door when I notice my shirt is missing. Not wanting to interrupt, I peek out and find it lying by his feet. So much for good intentions.

"I can't do that, Mom. I don't want to talk to him. You have to do it." He scrubs a hand over his face, letting his fingers tangle in his hair. Whatever they're talking about is *really* stressing him out. "Eventually. I don't know, but not today. I have to go. I love you." He ends the call and his hand joins the other to press against his forehead.

"Is everything okay?" I ask. He looks at me for a moment, as if he's surprised by my question. When his eyes drop to his feet, I decide not to press it further. "Sorry, forget I asked."

He grabs his pants from the floor and hands me my shirt. "It's fine. Parent drama again. You know how it is."

We may repulse each other now, but there was a time when we bonded over the tepid nature of our families. His dad is so much like my parents—the looming disappointment at every turn. In the love-hate relationship with his parents, his mom is all the love and his dad all the hate.

"Are they finally getting a divorce?" My joke doesn't land the way I wanted.

He lets out a weak laugh. "I wish."

We dress in silence. The air feels heavy with unspoken words, but what am I supposed to do? Talking isn't in our agreement. It's only coming and going—emphasis on the coming.

He stretches his shirt over his arms to pull it over his head. I frown when the clothes conceal his body from my view. He catches me, an eyebrow raising in question. "You good?"

"Yeah, I'm good. I'm leaving."

We awkwardly exit the room together. I grab my purse from the kitchen counter as I pass by. "See you Wednesday," I say as a reminder. "It's in the calendar."

"Oh, I know." A flirtatious grin returns to his face. There's the Heath we all know and tolerate.

"Bye, stupid." I leave him and his little smirk behind.

As I stroll down the sidewalk, the lightness in my step has returned. There's something about these extra days, the ability to fuck away the Sunday Scaries and get my mind off the bullshit of family dinner. After three days in a row, I'm not thinking about anything but the good sleep I'm about to get.

I consider my cuticle before sacrificing it to the violence of my nervous tic. It has almost fully healed since the damage I did leading up to the reception. The only time I manage to keep myself intact is on days with Heath. That was the goal, technically, but it worries me.

I'm not catching feelings—I *don't* catch feelings—but Heath is making it a little harder to hold on to the contempt I have for him.

As little as I want to remember it, there are times when the reason for my hatred pops into my mind. Always quick, never lingering, I push it down easier every time, but years still haven't been long enough to bleach it from my mind. Forgetting is as hard for me as forgiving. Maybe it's a character flaw, but it serves me well enough.

It's not that deep. My parents are a mess, Lenny continues to ruin my day, even when he's not in it, and the wedding saps the rest of my energy, so of course I enjoy being around Heath. Sex with him makes me feel good when little else does.

It's nothing more than that.

NINETEEN
Heath

Seeing my mom always puts me in a good mood. A Saturday afternoon, right before the sunset, the breeze is refreshing at the end of a long, hot day. With just a couple of hours before I get to see Teagan, the smile on my face is fueled by many things.

"You look so happy," my mom says. Her arm loops through mine while we stroll across the yard in the shade of the sycamore trees. "Did you have fun last weekend?"

Ryan's wedding reception was trash, but the rest of the night was not. My smile grows. "Yeah, I had a lot of fun."

"Oh, good. Tell me about it?"

I try to think of an explanation that doesn't involve closets and leaving with panties in my pocket, but nothing come to mind. Just a stupid grin on my stupid horny face.

"You're blushing!" she says.

"No, I'm not."

"Oh, yes, you are." She pats my cheek. "I know when my son is having a good time with a woman."

I gasp. "Mom!"

"What? Am I wrong?" Her dimple appears.

"No, but . . . it's not . . . it's just . . ."

"Complicated?" She finds the word for me.

"Well, yeah."

"Don't be embarrassed. You should enjoy summer. It's the best season."

My mom lives for the humidity and heat that summer brings. It reminds her of home on the island. It's a surprise she can stand the winters here at all. For her, it's not only cold, but lonely. My dad's busiest times are from the playoff season through the big game in February. He is gone almost every day, with a small break before the drafts. We used to go to the island in the winter when I was out of school, but that changed when my grandmother got sick. Mom moved her in with us so she could care for her in her last days, but it turned out that she didn't have many left.

Her death took a toll on Mom, making the winters colder, lonelier, and making her old coping habits return. I've always hoped she would leave Dad and move back to the island, let the sun heal her and free us of this endless cycle with her health, but that's a pipe dream.

When we walk inside the house, reality hits. My dad stands in the hallway, on his phone, and smiles when he sees Mom. She leaves my side for his, letting him pull her close. He doesn't acknowledge my presence—maybe he doesn't notice I'm here at all—but it doesn't matter. When he looks at me, I don't feel anything but his disappointment.

"I'm gonna head out, Mom." She returns to me for one last hug. "Ou te alofa ia te oe," I tell her again. She grips my hands in hers as I step away. The smile on her face is the opposite of my mood.

"Son. A word, please?"

Fuck. Apparently, he finished his call just in time to ruin my day. "Sure."

He motions for me to follow him. My blood pressure instantly goes up. Every moment we're together I count down the seconds until he says something that will make me feel like shit.

We have never gotten along. He has always been career driven, not family driven like my mom. A celebrity in the sports scene, he didn't have to pressure me into being an athlete, but he did anyway. He gave me the legacy for football, but my passion was soccer. That wasn't the first of my decisions to disappoint him, but it didn't help.

After my injury, he couldn't seem to understand why it was hard for me to return to the game I loved. My leg had bolts in it, I had to relearn how to walk, and yet he thought I would go right back to it after I healed. I couldn't have a defender sprint toward me without cowering in fear, but fuck my trauma, I guess.

If I couldn't play, he expected me to be a sports agent or accountant for one of his many companies. He didn't say anything the whole time I was getting my degree in sports medicine, then had the nerve to act shocked that I decided on a doctor of physical therapy rather than going into the family business. The DPT program was just as hard to get into, but he didn't care. That was the last connection we had other than Mom.

Following Dad into the foyer, I already know what he is going to say. He stops walking when the front door is in sight, and I consider running through it to avoid this conversation. "You shouldn't have come here."

"I shouldn't see my mom?"

"You shouldn't sneak around behind my back the way you did before." He knows I took her out of rehab again.

I won't say she called me and asked me to pick her up. If he wants to blame me, he will, and I'll let him. "I would have told you to your face if you were here. But you weren't. You never are when you send her away."

The wrinkles deepen between his eyebrows and his blue glower grows darker. "It wasn't your choice to make," he says.

"That treatment facility doesn't help her—it's a glorified spa retreat. She goes in, feels lonely and miserable, then comes out the same. She's better off at home where she has people around her and I can come visit."

"Better off? You don't know how bad it has gotten."

"And you do?"

"Heath—" He pinches the bridge of his nose in his frustration. The feeling is mutual. "You have no idea what she needs, and even if you did, these decisions are simply not up to you. I am her husband. You are the son she continues to coddle like a child."

He's always this way, making it clear that I am my mother's son, not his. He barely talks to me outside of holidays or when Mom makes him, and we butt heads constantly. People always say my dad and I are the same person—that we can't get along because we are too much alike—but I pray that isn't true. All I see in him are the parts of myself that I hate. The selfish parts. The mistakes I've made. The callous ways I've treated people I care about.

"Whatever," I say. "I will always do whatever she wants to do. You should try that sometime. You know, when you're not too busy to pay attention to your fucking wife."

I walk out the front door, not looking back.

~

The next morning, I wake up early after a fitful night's sleep and decide to grab some coffee to help me wake up. The line is long, and now the woman in front of me can't decide what she wants. My phone buzzes in my pocket. When I pull it out to look, I grin.

Teagan: 12-hour notice

Teagan: My plans were canceled. Are you free later?

Me: Definitely. My place at 3?

Teagan: Sure

The best news ever. I had a lot of frustration to work out last night. *A lot.* I wasn't sure her spine would still be in alignment after what I did to her, but here she is running back for seconds. Or thirds. I lost count.

I feel my not-so-little man swell. The woman in front of me moves away and I step up and back into the real world.

"Twelve-ounce Americano with room, please." I realize I never ask anymore. The please is just for flair.

The total comes up and I tap my watch against the machine to pay. An *X* shows on the screen along with an offensive beep.

"It didn't accept it. Here." The barista clears the screen. "Try again."

My watch must be broken because it fucks up again. I give up when the person behind me sighs. I pull out my wallet and try my card. Still, nothing. *What the fuck?*

"Is something wrong?"

"Sorry, I'm having issues." I pull out another. *Is this card linked to where my paychecks go?* Declined again.

"Sir, is there something I can help you with?"

Explain to me why I can't pay for a fucking six-dollar coffee? "No. Sorry, can you cancel my order? Thanks."

Embarrassed, I leave the café, avoiding the gaze of everyone in line behind me. Once outside, I climb back into my car and hang my head in my hand. That was fucking embarrassing. My bank app loads slowly, but once it's done, my jaw drops.

Savings Account: Current Balance - $0
Flex Account: Current Balance - $0

I pull up my credit card app and log in with my fingerprint. In the tab for my accounts, the only thing it shows is *Click HERE to Sign Up*. And in my statement history, a zero-dollar balance followed by *Account Closed*.

What. The. Fuck.

I fume the whole way back to my apartment, knowing damn well what is going on.

Dad. He's a piece of shit. I know this is some sort of punishment, but for what? Caring about my mother?

The door slams behind me. I lock it while I call him. He answers with a generic, "Reynolds."

"It's me." He says nothing back. "Why are all my cards cut off?"

"You know why, Heath. Why would I continue to support you when you go against me at every turn?"

A chill settles heavily on my skin. My anger forms words I know I'll regret. "You can't fucking do this shit, Dad!"

"Except I can. Either learn some respect or learn how to pay your own bills."

I hate him. I fucking hate him. "If you think I'm going to side with you over Mom, you're an idiot."

"You are so naïve," he says with a sigh. "I've made my decision."

Rage burns away my chill until I burst. "Cut me off then. I don't give a fuck. I don't want your blood money anyway!" I hang up on him and throw my phone against the wall.

Shit. I don't know if I can afford to fix that.

~

The fear of financial instability ruins my whole day. Hours of anger and worry leave me emotionally drained. But none of that matters while I'm lounging on my couch, having the hottest lazy sex of my life.

Teagan, naked on my lap, balances herself with her hands on my chest, her tits bouncing right in front of my face while she strokes that snug pussy up and down my cock.

Whatever shit *she* went through this morning, I'm glad for it. She hums her approval, but her eyes stay closed tight. She's in her own world, taking what she wants from me. I'm a dildo with a pulse and I am not complaining. It's good. So fucking good.

"*Uhn.*" I try to hang on, to savor every second I can have, but it's too much. She curls up, her hips shaking in my hands as she comes. I follow right after her, moaning while my soul pours from me and into the condom. Holy fucking shit.

I'm spent and I didn't have to do anything but drop trou. My thank-you is a weak spank and a grip of her ass.

"That was good," I say, sounding as spent as I feel.

With a happy sigh, she slides her hands down my chest. She won't compliment me back. Not for a while, at least. For some reason, she thinks not saying I rocked her world means I won't know.

Too soon, she lifts herself from me and I slip from her warmth. My cock instantly misses her. She sits beside me, that cute little post-orgasm look of stupor on her face. I take that as a win.

"Can we make Sundays an official part of our schedule yet?" I ask.

"Shut up," she says between labored breaths. She reaches for the throw blanket and covers herself with it. My fun is over. "Did you book your flight yet?" she asks.

"Are you serious?" I look at her with a laugh. "That's where your brain goes when we fuck?"

"No, I just remembered. It's the after-sex brain thing."

"Post-nut clarity?"

"Yeah, whatever."

That's where her brain goes when we fuck—to mush. That's a hand job's worth of stroking to my ego.

After another calming breath, she sits up. As I watch her pick her clothes up from the floor, I can tell she's in business mode again. "Did you book it or not?"

The blanket hangs low when she stands, exposing her again, teasing me until she lets it fall to raise her arms and slip her shirt back on. In profile, the smooth lines of her body move like falling silk. A path of perfection from her chest to the narrowness of her waist to the swell of her ass, and down those long, long legs. My eyes trace every inch of every curve.

She hops to help get her jeans over her ass and I have to appreciate the sight. She fastens them around her waist and looks down at me with a glare. "Heath!"

"Huh? Yeah, I paid for that after we decided which club to go to."

"Not the flight to Vegas. The flight to Valencia."

Oh shit. I haven't, and I already know how she'll react when I tell her. "Um."

She groans in a less enjoyable tone than she did a few moments ago. "I told everyone about this weeks ago."

"I thought Brett was flying us out on his plane."

"No. We're flying to Valencia and he's taking us from there to the island. He hasn't bragged to you about his new yacht five thousand times already? Because he has with me."

"No, he has. Sorry, I meant to do it this weekend."

"Well, do it now."

She lifts my phone from the table and tosses it to me. I don't know what to tell her. I don't know if I want to tell her at all. Not only am I lost over how to navigate this, I'm fucking embarrassed. When has anyone in our group not had money? We were born with silver spoons in our mouths and a drawer full of more right beside us. Paying for something as small as a commercial flight? That's nothing. When you have a working credit card, at least.

Teagan grabs her little purse from the table and slings the strap over her head. She looks ready to leave, and I'm holding my breath hoping she does. But, as always, she scowls at me, crossing her arms over her chest.

"The second I walk out you're going to fall asleep and forget again." When she's right, she's right. "I'm staying until you do it." *Then you better get comfortable, babe.*

I don't want to tell her what happened. I definitely don't want to tell her *why* it happened, either, but she will be pissed if she finds out I didn't book it. "I would, but . . ."

"But what?"

I take a deep breath for courage. Telling her the truth is going to suck. But here goes nothing.

"I can't afford it right now."

TWENTY
Teagan

Heath's eyes cast downward as if he's ashamed. Heath. Ashamed. He's sitting bare-assed on his couch, manspreading with only a throw pillow covering his dick, but whatever he's about to say is what embarrasses him?

"What do you mean you can't afford it?" I ask. "You've known about this for months. You—"

"I don't have the money."

I purse my lips at him. "You don't have money, Mr. BMW Manhattan Penthouse Apartment?"

He scowls. "My dad cut me off, okay?"

The air in the room goes flat and cold. His words take a second to make sense. "Cut you off?"

"Yeah. Canceled all my cards, cleared out our shared accounts."

"No shit?"

"No shit."

It's so difficult for me to have pity for him when he has lived his whole life never having to worry about money. Realizing 90 percent of the people on the planet pay their own bills and still manage to survive blows their minds. They are delusional in the most comical way.

I can't keep my laugh in any longer. "You must be so lost."

"Shut up, I'm not playing. I don't know what I'm supposed to do now."

"Doesn't your job pay you?"

"Yeah."

"Then use your big boy money from your next check to buy your ticket. Shit. You act like you're broke."

"I kind of am."

"I am *absolutely* certain you are not," I say. "Have you made a budget?"

"A budget?"

Jesus. "Yes. You know, figuring out how much you can spend each month," I explain. This should be common knowledge.

His gaze is vacant. Not a single thought lies behind those pretty eyes.

"Oh my god. Google *budgeting* and figure it out."

I turn around to leave, but remember my keys. When I slip them into my bag, I find Heath with the most pathetic look on his face. It's like someone kicked his puppy *and* stole it.

"You're really freaking out about this, aren't you?" I ask.

"Yeah," he says with another pout. "It's not just the flight. It's everything. I don't even know how I'm going to eat tonight."

I almost feel bad for him. Almost.

It's not my responsibility to help him, but a tiny piece of me feels I should. The life we live—the one our parents thrust us into—isn't normal. How many people can live alone in Manhattan on an intern's salary? They did not set us up to survive without needing their help, which was completely intentional. Whatever is going on between him and his dad has reached a new level of petty. I know Heath would rather lick a subway floor than grovel to that man, and I can't say I blame him. Heath's dad is a bigger douche than he is.

"Ugh. Fine," I give in. "Let me grab my stuff and I'll help you figure it out. Bring your bills and meet me at the café across the street from my apartment." He still has that stupid look on his face. "Yes, I'll pay for your coffee."

Finally, he smiles. "Okay!"

~

I pick a table tucked away in the back between some bookshelves, safe from view. The setting sun barely reaches us past the reclaimed wood tabletops full of people working on laptops and the line of mustachioed millennial baristas pouring steamed milk into leaf shapes while bopping to early-2000s hip-hop. This is *my* place. The way it attracts a contrast of ages, backgrounds, and cultures grounds me in the beauty of this city and pulls me from the lifestyle Heath will now struggle to maintain. None of our friends like this café. Even if someone was to stumble across us, all they would see is me torturing Heath in the least sexual way possible.

He is going to have a rough time. His spending will have to go from nearly eight grand per month to two. I doubt the man has ever looked at his monthly credit card statements before we looked at them together. I help him defer his loan payments and cancel a collection of subscriptions that were no longer on the table for him. He almost cried when I showed him how little seventy thousand per year gets you while living in the city.

I look over and find him with his head lying on the table. "You still alive?"

"Barely." He leans up and runs his fingers into his hair. "How am I supposed to live without all that?"

"You will survive, I promise."

"How do you know?"

"Believe it or not, entire families live on less than what you make. I also live on less than that."

"Your parents don't help you out?"

"They do, but I put it away and only use it for all the extra shit you guys want to do. I've paid my rent, utilities, and food on my own since we started college."

He looks shocked. "Seriously?"

"Yes, seriously. Trust me, I don't live with Jeremy for fun."

He looks at the budget again and sighs heavily. "I don't know how I'm going to do this."

"Well, your rent is paid until September. Your best option is to move to a smaller place, ask your boss for a raise, and start grocery shopping rather than ordering out for every meal. You still have a place to live, food, clean water . . ." I list, hoping he'll realize how obnoxious his situation would seem to the vast majority of the world. He stares ahead at the screen with a pitiful frown. "Good god. Do you want to keep crying over Netflix or do you wanna go have sex again?"

He perks up. "Sex, please."

"Look at that. A free subscription."

I pack up my things, but he doesn't move. I look at him in question.

"Thank you, Teags," he says.

"You don't have to thank me. I like getting laid too."

"No, for this. Thank you for the sex, too, but I mean the budget."

I eye him, looking for the facetiousness that would usually be there. But there's none. He actually appreciates someone doing something for him. "Don't mention it. Seeing you have to grow up will be very enjoyable for me."

He chuckles but stops with a gasp. "The bachelor party. Fuck, I completely forgot. Will I have enough for Vegas, plus the flight and hotel for the wedding?"

"You mean the *luxury ocean-side resort*? Definitely not."

"Then what do I do?"

I sigh and pull out my tablet to bring up his spreadsheet again. Looking over it, he's nowhere close to affording the rest of his accommodations for the wedding and is short for the flight. "You'll have to figure out a way to get your own credit card or ask one of the guys to spot you."

He scrubs his hands over his face. "There's no way."

"Well, you better find one. You are not bailing and leaving me to deal with Ritchie. I can handle Colorblind and Ryan, but I swear I'll turn my back for two seconds and Ritchie will pull a *Hangover* and roofie us or—"

"Could I room with you?" he asks.

His question makes me snort. "Be *so* for real."

"Please, Teags. The guys will freak if they find out what happened."

"But they won't freak out when they find out we're staying in a room together?"

"We've been sneaking around this long and they haven't figured it out. What's a night in Vegas and three nights in Ibiza?"

"Um. A lot?"

"Come on. We can split the costs, I'll be on time everywhere we go, and . . . I'll go down on you every night."

"As if you weren't going to already?"

"I can't do it if I'm not there," he rebuts.

We knew we'd sneak around in Vegas either way—one of the "public events" I planned for in the contract—but staying in a room together adds a level of difficulty I didn't plan for. Not that the guys ever do anything according to plan. Without Heath there, I'll be the fifth wheel of a testosterone clusterfuck.

I glare at him for a moment, but I can't think of an alternative that doesn't end with me in prison for choking one of the guys to death. "Ugh, whatever."

"Yes! Thank you."

"You owe me. Big-time."

"I'll do anything. Just name it."

I love when a man subjugates himself. The possibilities are endless, but anxiety keeps my mind transfixed on the looming storm cloud approaching. "I know what you can do for me."

He smirks. "Should I stretch beforehand?"

"No, goofy. My family is throwing a party for my ex."

"The weak dick ex?"

"Yeah."

"So, do you want me to pull the fire alarm, or do you want me to make him go missing?"

I laugh. "I was going to ask if you would go with me, but your ideas sound better."

Suspicion tilts his head. "Wait. You're asking for a *date*?"

"Not a date. A distraction. It's another public appearance, same as Vegas," I correct. "It's on a Saturday, so we're already scheduled."

"But *me*? Won't they think—"

"It doesn't matter." Only because I won't let it. "Levi can't go because he has a game that night, so it's just Rowan and my parents. I just need them to be distracted and have a reason for Lenny to avoid talking to me."

His eyes narrow as his lips curl into a mischievous grin. "You want me there to make him jealous."

"Stop." I huff. "He already knows Ryan, and most anyone else I could get to go with me last minute. You're the most logical option."

He leans his head on his fist, that stupid smirk still on his lips. "Yeah, but it's mostly because I'm hot."

Of course I think he's hot. Everyone with functioning eyes thinks he's attractive. "You're annoying," I scold him.

"And hot."

"Forget it."

"Say it. Say I'm hot and I'll go."

"You are such a prick."

"Say it."

I glare at him. I don't want to give in to his buffoonery, but I also don't want to go to that party alone. "You'd be a nine if you weren't such an astoundingly imbecilic douchebag."

He smiles like he won something. "I'm hotter than your ex."

"I wouldn't go that far." I give him a sideways glance. "Will you come with me and not make it a thing?"

"Me make it a thing? Never."

What did I just get myself into? "I'm regretting this already."

His chuckle sounds deep and suggestive. "Let's go back to my place and I'll give you something you won't regret at all."

The smolder behind his narrowed gray gaze makes me warm, but we've tested the limitations of my guidelines enough times tonight and my invitation made it even worse. "I will see you Wednesday." The snarl he gives me when I stand makes it worth it. "And I better get my money's worth."

"Bet."

TWENTY-ONE
Teagan

Three days later, it's hot. *I'm* hot, my skin misting with sweat and threatening more. My window unit barely keeps up with the ninety-degree weather outside, but that isn't the only reason the bedroom is steaming.

Each breath I take gives me half the air I need, bringing me in and out of reality. One moment I'm floating in a warm haze, as if my bed was the soft sand of the beach, and the next I'm back in my bed, gasping, shaking, my thighs tightening around my hand while I tangle Heath's hair between my fingers.

The pleasure rushes through me and I have to stop myself from leaving him bald. I move my hand to grip the sheets instead.

A moan slips slowly from my throat as my hips grind against him. "Come here," I beg. "I can't do it again like this. I need to feel you."

He hums a no against me. "I'm not done yet."

Talk about an upgrade. I dumped a man who thought oral sex was disgusting, and now I have one who whines if he doesn't get a taste. I let my head fall back and beckon orgasm number two.

The warm sand swallows me. My breathing grows quicker and quicker as I get closer. Suddenly he stops, leaving me on edge.

Heath rolls on the condom with impatient speed, then falls forward onto his palms, his hips settling between my thighs in one fluid movement. He looks down at me with a knowing expression. As if doing a dance we've practiced a million times, I lift my knees to tilt my hips toward him and he sinks inside me with no hands. When he starts to move, I'm lost again in the heat of summer—breathless, hot, and loving every second.

Every rough thrust slides me up my satin sheets until my head leaves the edge of the bed. Then my shoulders. "Heath," I moan. "I'm falling."

"I got you." I fear he has me in more ways than one.

My upper back dangles from the mattress while my hips stay firm in his grasp. In my arched position, he hits me in all the right places. Over and over, the pleasure shoots through me. His eager pace and his desperate grip make me so hot. I love when he takes me just how he wants me.

"Oh my god," I whine, gripping his wrists to hold on the best I can. My legs are tense, my pussy tight around him. "Oh my fucking god."

His hand moves from my thigh to my stomach. He rubs his thumb against me in time with his thrusts, making the pleasure burst inside me. I call out loudly, my body shaking with my impending climax. "Come on," he commands with impatience. "Let go."

My body melts for him, and then it hits me. "*Ah-ahh!*"

I come hard. My knees snap together, my body shakes. He goes harder, pulling my hips down to meet his. As it rolls through me, my eyes open to an upside-down world that quakes with every move he makes.

"Yes. *Yes,*" I moan as my orgasm continues to wash over me.

He lets out a deep groan and stops. His hips shudder between my thighs. I feel the relief radiate from him, and in it, I find my own.

Like clouds gathering over my imaginary beach, I welcome the cool calm of satiation.

Gravity brings me down from my high with each breath. But then I realize it's bringing me down *literally*.

"I'm falling." I try to call Heath's attention back to reality, and reach for his hand. "Heath, I'm—" I slip from him and fall to the floor, landing on my upper back, my knee smacking against my forehead. "*Ow!*"

He bursts into laughter.

I rub my head and glare at him. "You're an asshole."

His laughter calms, but that smile remains. "Don't act like I did you a disservice," he says. "Come here."

He extends a hand to me. I take it, crawling back onto the bed and onto his lap. I brush his hair back, tilting his head so he looks up at me. "You dropped me on my head, you prick," I tease him, making his smile widen. He's pretty and I'm still coming down from the hour-long high he just gave me. When he looks up at me and drags his fingers down my back, it's clear he feels the same. "Say you're sorry."

"I'm sorry," he says in a sexy, growly voice.

I drape my arms over his shoulders, laughing to myself over his willing compliance. "Thank you." His smile fades when I lean closer and pull his face to mine. Wait.

I catch myself, awkwardly hesitating with my lips a mere inch from his.

What am I doing? Our contract is very black-and-white, but this? Whatever *this* is feels very gray. But he doesn't care. His smile perks up in a little laugh before he pulls me closer to close the distance.

Our lips can't touch before the sound of a door catches my attention. We both look toward the sound. Jeremy's laugh carries from up the hall. "Shit. You have to go," I say in a frantic whisper.

"What?"

"Right now."

Heath rolls his eyes. "The condom's not even off yet."

"Well, take it off and get out." I scramble to gather our clothes, tossing his shirt against his chest. He groans in frustration.

Once I'm dressed, Heath's barely in his pants. "Go out the window."

His eyes widen. "Are you serious?"

"Yes." I start to open it.

"Oh my god, will you chill?" He pulls my hands away from the latch. "Jer barely talks to the guys anyway—it won't be the end of the world if he finds out. He's not a snitch, and even if he was, it's just sex."

"You know it will turn into a thing. And even if he doesn't snitch, he won't let me live it down." I smooth my hair and open the door. "Just stay here and shut up."

"Whatever."

I walk out of my room and up the hall, pretending everything is normal. Jeremy and Chet stand in the kitchen giggling about something. "Hey, guys," I greet them. "When did you get back?"

Jeremy looks at me with a sheepish grin. "A while ago. You were too busy getting your back blown out to hear us come in."

Shit.

"That man had you screaming," he says. "I'm jealous."

Chet waves to remind Jeremy of his presence. "Um, hello?"

"There's no way that's Lenny."

"Definitely not."

"Then who is it? I'd love to meet the sex god."

"It's no—" I stop short when Jeremy brushes past me. "What are you doing?"

"I'm just gonna say hi."

"What? No! Oh my god, stop!" I jump on his back, as if I could stop his burly mass with my body weight alone. "Jeremy, stop it. Don't—"

The door swings open, and there is Heath, caught halfway through putting his shirt back on. Jer's mouth drops open in shock. "*Heath?*"

He looks between the two of us. "Uh . . . hey, Jer."

I drop off Jeremy's back and wish every curse would fall upon them both. My mind races through what every person in our circle will say when he tells them. Jeremy might not be a snitch, but he's a gossipy bitch.

"Well, I gotta run but I'll see you at the bachelor party, right?" Heath asks while walking past him.

"Yeah."

"Cool. See you then. Bye, Chet!"

"Bye, Heath!"

The door closes behind him. Jeremy's eyes stay glued to me over a conniving smirk.

I press my palm against my forehead. "Don't say it."

"You and Heath are—"

"I said don't say it."

"Oh . . . *my* god," Jeremy gushes with a wide smile. Just as I expected, he's living for this.

"It's nothing. Just a one-night stand kind of thing."

"A one-night stand on a Wednesday. Cute."

"It's not a thing. Seriously, drop it."

"Wait until the guys hear about this. They are going to lose their shit." He grabs his phone. I yank it from his hands and smack it down against the countertop.

I know he's trying to rile me up, but part of me worries he'll actually do it. I have enough drama lined up this summer. "You're not going to tell anyone."

"I'm not?" He cracks a smile again. "Is that where you've been on weekends? Shacking up with your—"

"Don't even go there," I stop him.

"Honey, be nice," Chet defends me. "She's a busy girl. Let her get it where she can and leave her alone."

Jeremy's wicked smile shows all the ways he plans to blackmail me.

"What do you want?" I ask with a sigh.

"I want to break the lease."

The words take a moment register. My brow tenses in confusion. *"What?"*

"Do you want to tell her or should I?" Jeremy asks his man.

"Honey, I didn't want to do it like this."

Jeremy takes that as a green light and turns around with excitement. "Chet proposed. We're moving in together."

It's too much information for my brain to process at once. "Wait, what? You're moving—you're getting married? He proposed?"

"Yes."

"I mean, congratulations! But what the hell? When did this happen? Today?"

"Two weeks ago," Jeremy says, as if I'm the last person to know. *Am* I the last person to know?

"And you weren't going to tell me?"

He crosses his arms. "I was going to tell everyone at Ryan's dinner, but Heath and Brett had their fight. Then I was going to mention it after the reception, but Ritchie went and tried to make shit about him and I figured it wasn't a good time, so, between you running around a million places and our friends being rabid shitheads, I didn't get the chance."

"This is huge news. You should have told me."

"I'm telling you now."

The news mixed with the potential loss of my secret gives me whiplash. "I'm happy for you both, seriously, but you can't break the lease. Even if I wanted to live by myself, I can't afford this place on my own."

He snorts. "Yes, you can. You just have to kiss up to daddy dearest a little more."

Funny how I just had this conversation on Sunday with Heath and now I'm facing something similar. My family has money. A lot of money. My parents could buy this entire building tomorrow if they were so inclined, but that's not the point. It's one more thing they would get to hold over my head. One more thing I'd feel like I owe them.

I owe them for saving me from an orphanage I can't remember, providing me with safety, security, and all the support I would need to achieve their wildest dreams. But they don't see that. It's a line item in a ledger, another quid pro quo. But what do I have left to give them?

"When are you moving? *Where* are you moving?"

"Philadelphia. Next month."

"Phila—Philadelphia? Jeremy!"

"I'll be at the wedding, but you know I wasn't planning to go to that hetero-as-hell bachelor party."

"Well, yeah, but you have to tell the guys. This is major."

"Is it?" he asks. "Do you really think they care? We're friends of proximity, we always have been. By the time you graduate law school and we get married, we'll barely talk," he explains. "Why would I keep hanging out with passive homophobes like Brett and Ritchie longer than I have to? They don't even respect you and you're only half gay."

"Half? I'm bi not—what? Ugh, rewind." I press my palms into my eyelids, hoping it will help me make sense of what's happening.

"It's time for us all to grow up, Teags. This is how life works."

My body is warring between anger and anxiety. "Just like that, you're going to leave me on my own?"

"You'll have Heath."

His facetious comment earns him my glare. "That's supposed to be a compromise?"

"This is what I want, Teags. To be happy and start the next chapter of my life." I want that *for* him, but it doesn't stop it from hurting. "I'll pay the remainder of the lease so it doesn't fall to you, but I'll be out after Ryan's wedding."

"Okay." That's all I can say.

He walks away, leaving me with a guilty-looking Chet. "I'm sorry," he whispers.

The swirl of uncomfortable emotions churns in my stomach. I watch the two of them grab cardboard boxes from Jeremy's room. I wonder how long the boxes have been there. Had Jeremy been moving out piece by piece for weeks and I didn't notice that either? They slip by me, Chet tossing another look of remorse my way.

Once they're gone, I don't know what to do with myself. *Fuck, fuck, fuck.* I wince and pull my bloody fingertip from between my teeth. The only respite I get from drama is when I'm with Heath. The fuckboy of my nightmares has become my only source of calm.

Guess the world is ending *and* I'm looking for a new roommate. *Damn it.*

TWENTY-TWO
Heath

Did I fuck up?

I was in my happy place, giving Teagan the time of her fucking life, then *Jeremy* came in and she went right back to hating me. The only thing I did wrong was not crawl half naked through her window. Maybe Jeremy is the one who fucked up. He definitely fucked it up for me.

After I left her apartment, my dick felt bruised and my balls were empty as hell, but I still had a semi in the shower when I got home. It's impossible to watch her unravel for me and not spend the rest of my time wanting to do it again.

No. I need to focus.

I put another fork of my microwave meal into my mouth, pretending it's takeout from the hotel restaurant up the street. Sitting cross-legged on the floor by my coffee table, I stare at my laptop screen. Just a few minutes with Teagan's spreadsheet and I know how much I'll be able to swing for the rest of the month. She might be a little batty, but no one can say she isn't smart as hell.

This budget situation will not work out well for me, especially during the summer when the guys want to act like high rollers everywhere we go. I remember the last time we went *ham* at the club. The receipt in my pocket the next morning was something around eight grand. I doubt Vegas will be any different. At least I have my back pay and some savings in my personal account, and my next paycheck will add to it. This will teach me how *not* to blow eight grand in the meantime, seeing as I won't be able to afford a shitty microwave meal when we get back if I do.

As I close the spreadsheet tab, my calendar stays up. The next thing on it is my extra shift on Friday, but nothing afterward.

I stare at it, hoping I missed something from Teagan or accidentally deleted her invite. But there's nothing. "Oh no. Please, no."

I whip out my phone and start typing a message, but stop myself. No phrasing other than *Are we not fucking this weekend?* comes to my mind, so I delete the text and call her instead.

It rings a few times while I hold my breath. Finally, she answers. "Why are you calling me?"

Lovely. "I don't have a calendar invite from you. Are we not meeting up tonight?"

"Wow, you actually looked at your calendar?"

"Look at me. I'm learning. Are we fucking or not?"

"Yeah. Sorry, I've been wrapped up in this shit with Jeremy."

"Is he going to snitch?"

"Not if I give in to his demands."

"We're negotiating with terrorists now?" I say with a chuckle.

"He's moving in with Chet. And now he doesn't want to go to any of Ryan's events."

"Breaking a lease *and* bailing on you? I'm surprised your head hasn't popped off."

"If you fuck anything else up for me, it might."

"Well . . . I've been meaning to talk to you."

There's a short pause, then the call ends. I cackle and call her back. She answers without a word.

"I was kidding! Calm down," I assure her.

She growls in frustration. "I'm obviously not in the mood for jokes right now, asshole. I'll be over at ten." She hangs up again before I can say okay.

My smile pulls at my cheeks and my not-so-little man rubs against my fly. Just a few more hours. I can find a way to distract myself until then.

~

Work is good, but Teagan, as always, haunts my thoughts. The spreadsheet is clear. Without help from my dad, I can't afford any apartment I've looked at in the city unless I get a raise. When classes start up in September, I have to have my shit together. I can't pick up a second job when all my time outside of class goes to my internship.

Dro stands in the office at his desk the way he always does this time of day. I can ask him, right? Our conversations are always casual and easy. There's not a way to get close to him in a traditional sense, but we have a good time, and I relate to him in any way I can. It's worth a try.

"What's up?" Dro says to me without looking my way.

"Hey, Dro. Could I talk to you real quick?"

"Sure."

When I close the door behind me, Dro cocks an eyebrow with confusion. "I've been looking at my bills and a lot of them are going up next year. I was wondering if there was any way to increase my pay."

He stares for a moment then bursts into laughter. "Heath, no." He shakes his head, still laughing like I told a joke.

I realize I have never negotiated my pay, and it has me questioning everything. Is this not the way to do it? "Um, why?"

"Because you're an intern." He turns to face me, crossing his arms. His huge biceps make him more intimidating as I wait for his explanation to ruin my day. "Interns do not make money—that's the way the world works. You're learning, working under *my* license. When you are qualified on your own, then you can ask for more. Right now you're making as much as anyone else in your position should expect."

Fuck. In my head, the size of my next apartment gets even smaller. "Okay."

"I'm gonna be real with you, Heath. You're a rich kid, so you probably don't know this, but this is the phase of life where you're *supposed* to struggle, learn how to hustle. Not everyone gets to grow up with the safety net you have, and most people don't even land on their feet when they fall. Be thankful for what you have and stay humble."

I assume he means himself, just like I assume he doesn't want to talk more about it. "Thanks, Dro."

"Get back to work. We're not paying you pennies to slack off." His smirk is a balm for the reality he slapped me with, but I'm still bleeding after my fall from financial grace.

"Will do."

~

It's the end of my shift before I know it. Dro was right. Sinking into work was exactly what I needed to keep my mind off my bank account, but I will have *hours* between work and the next dose of pain relief I'll get between Teagan's thighs. I won't worry about that yet.

"Six more. You got this."

Shelley's face scrunches but she pushes through with a groan. The sound barely distracts me. Her tight pink workout set makes it hard not to stare, but I manage with ease. Work is the *only* place I keep myself from being a pig.

"Three . . . two . . . last one." She stands up, finishing the set. "Great job!" I hold out my hand and she slaps it. The beaming smile on her face makes me happy. "And that's the end of your last session! How do you feel?"

"Good. Strong. As close to normal as I'm going to get, I think."

"You came back from a serious injury. I'm proud of you," I say. "If you keep wearing your brace and continue those exercises, you'll never have to come back and let me torture you again."

She looks away with that little laugh, her face turning pink. I pick up the Bosu ball and bands from the floor.

"I'm going to miss seeing you every week," she says.

"Nah, there are plenty of better ways to spend an hour than looking at my ugly mug." I smirk and her face reddens again.

"Um, Heath?" she squeaks from behind me. I look at her over my shoulder. "Now that I'm not your patient anymore, would you want to go out with me sometime?"

Her boldness surprises me. For someone who seems shy, she really came right out with it. I turn to face her again. Her cheeks are bright red but she looks me in the eyes, waiting for me to answer.

"Um."

For a second, I try to think of a nice way to say no. But why should I? She's hot, athletic, knows nothing about my circle or my family drama. It's not a violation of the contract Teagan uses to keep me at arm's length. She likes me. So, why the hell not?

"Yeah. That'd be cool."

Her smile widens. "Would you want to get dinner tonight?"

Her sudden confidence is kind of hot. Without thinking, I say, "Sure. Let's do it."

~

It's weird having to move money around to make sure I can pay for something as small as dinner, but that's my life now. I'm still surprised this is even happening. It's kind of cool. I can't remember the last time a girl asked me out, or the last time I went on a date without hoping to get laid when it was over.

I should probably feel bad that I'm going out with Shelley, knowing in three hours I'll be fucking someone else. But I don't. The only requirement in the contract is to pause if we sleep with someone else, which I won't be doing. Teagan planned for this to happen. This is *way* better than some of the shit I've done before, but something feels off. I can't figure out what it is.

Shelley sits across the small table from me, grinning while she sips her twelve-dollar drink. It's the first time I've seen her with her hair down. The three shades of blond hang in loose waves onto her shoulders, directing me to the cleavage she barely hides behind two struggling buttons. She doesn't wear much makeup, at least not that I notice. All I see is tan skin, wide blue eyes, and blushing cheeks.

She picked a restaurant in SoHo. A little sushi place with good vibes. The dim lights make it feel like a date, but being outdoors near the bar makes it casual and chill. Sitting off in the corner, it's fairly quiet. It makes it easy to talk, if only I knew what to say.

"It's weird, isn't it?" Shelley asks.

"What's weird?"

"You know my body, my medical history, and all the personal information I've blabbed about for six months, but I don't even know if you like sushi."

"It's not that weird, I promise. And I do like sushi."

"Okay, good," she says with a shy smile. We both take a sip to ease the awkwardness. She perks up and leans her arms on the table. "You should give me your elevator pitch."

"My what?"

"Your elevator pitch. Sell yourself to me in thirty seconds."

"I'll gladly sell myself to you, but you should know I'm expensive," I say with a smirk, though I *could* use the additional income.

"You know what I mean." She giggles. "Tell me what makes Heath, Heath, and why I should snatch him up before someone else does."

Usually, taking my clothes off or pulling out my black card accomplishes that, but Shelley is a *nice girl*. She's an elementary school teacher from Jersey, the only daughter in a happy family of six. The kind of girl who doesn't want a sly line or a bow for blow. She wants something real from me. Or at least she thinks she does.

My mind flashes through all the shit that people say when they introduce me—my namesake, D-list celebrity parents, my social status. None of that defines *me*, and it isn't something I'm proud of right now.

What makes me who I am isn't any of the pretty, shiny shit. It's the stuff nice girls don't want to hear. We'll skip to the good parts instead.

"Do you want to know why I became a physical therapist?" I ask.

"Yeah, I'd love that."

"Back in high school, I got scouted for the soccer team. A group of big-name recruiters came out to watch one of my games, and halfway through the game, in a freak accident, I took a cleat to the thigh and snapped my femur."

Her mouth drops open. "Oh my god. Your *femur?*"

"Yeah, it was pretty gnarly." My fingers trace the outline of the scars most people don't notice beneath my *pe'a*. The tattoo came before the scars, but both were important, though extremely painful, gifts. "I had to kiss my soccer career prospects goodbye, and I had to relearn how to walk."

"Wow. That must have been devastating," she says. "Is that when you decided?"

"Not quite." I pause for a second, thinking through how I can dodge the parts that aren't so *wow*. "After losing my chance to be in the pros, I was deep in my feelings about it. But then—" What are the right words to explain this? "My best friend's little brother got into a bad car accident and almost died."

"Oh god."

"He separated his spine and the doctors said he would most likely end up with quadriplegia. My friend and I were really close back then, so it felt like he was my little brother too. His rehab started right after mine, but it was obviously a million times harder for him. He didn't want to do it—but I knew how the shock of getting news like that made it easy to want to give up. So, I did what no one else wanted to do."

"What was that?"

"I didn't let him say no."

Shelley stares at me, her chin resting in her palm as she waits for me to tell her more. That's a first for me.

"I went to rehab with him every day, made sure he did everything the doctors said. Once I recovered, I was there with him even more, taking him to PT, watching every inch he progressed. He beat the odds and regained a lot of his mobility and strength. Being there to witness it was the best feeling."

She shakes her head, a smile spreads across her face. "Wow," she whispers this time.

I've never been able to tell the story that way. Everyone else either knows what happened or they're not interested in hearing about it. Levi changed me, and I don't think anyone knows that except Teagan.

"Do you still see him?" she asks.

"Yeah, but not as much anymore. His sister and I aren't close like we were back then."

"Why not?"

I shrug for her benefit, but I know the answer. Any happy feelings that story brings me fade fast when I think about what happened right after. So, I don't think about it. Ever. Unlike her. "People just grow apart sometimes," is all I say.

"You're amazing, Heath. I mean that."

I love a woman who can stroke my ego, but for some reason, I'm not here for it right now. In a rare moment, I change the subject away from me. "It's your turn. Tell me what makes Shelley, Shelley."

~

"Are you sure I can't give you a lift?" she offers again.

Shelley is cool. She's much better than I expected. Much better than I deserve, if we're being real. "No, seriously. I live close."

"All right. Well, I had a great time tonight."

"I did too."

As I start to say I'll call her, she leans up and presses her lips against mine.

Her kiss is soft and timid like she is. My hand floats over her cheek, not knowing whether to pull her closer or push her away. I let it drop without doing either.

It feels nice. Kissing. Being desired for more than contractual sex.

She pulls away. Her eyes cast down, cheeks bright red. "Call me, okay?" Her eyes flutter up.

"Okay."

Her little smile returns. "Bye, Heath."

"Bye, Shelley."

She shuffles away and I laugh to myself. *What the hell just happened?*

Wait. What the hell just happened?

~

My unease grows the closer I get to home. I still feel Shelley's lips on mine, and with that feeling comes guilt. It's not like this is new for me. My past track record with relationships isn't exactly stellar, so I don't know why I feel so thrown for a loop. There's a lot of *past* on my mind tonight.

Teagan is leaning against the wall by my front door, staring down at her phone. "Hey," I greet her. Her eyes find mine, and somehow, she doesn't look pissed. "Am I late again?"

She smirks. "Of course you are."

I unlock my door and we go inside. Without talking, we drop the contents of our pockets onto the island countertop and head to the bedroom. She pushes me to sit on the edge of the bed, then climbs onto her knees, one on each side of my thighs. I hold her hips when she sits; my dick swells with every heartbeat.

She pulls at the buttons of my shirt, unfastening them lower and lower. Is she going to wonder why I'm dressed up?

"Hey," I start to tell her, but the second the word leaves my mouth, I regret it.

She glances up for a second but returns her attention to my shirt. "What?"

I hesitate. I'm dying to get inside her, but I also don't want her to flip out on me if I wait until after to tell her. "Um, so . . . I kind of went on a date."

She rips my belt from the loops, an unamused look on her face. "Congratulations."

"No, like . . ." I trail off when she pulls her shirt off over her head, her nipples visible under thin red lace. Why am I still talking? "I went on a date *tonight*."

"Okay?" Her eyes narrow with suspicion.

"That's cool with you, right?"

She sits up straighter, glaring down at me. "Did you fuck her?"

"No."

"Then why are you telling me about it?"

I've been asking myself the same question. "I don't know."

"Great. Now stop talking." She pushes me to my back and unfastens my fly. A smile pulls at my lips.

Fuck the past; I'll take whatever I can get right now.

TWENTY-THREE
Teagan

At the airport, I make it to the gate two hours before boarding time, like always, and find the closest bar. In my last moments of douche-free solitude this weekend, I try everything I can to boost my mood. Jeremy isn't coming, everyone is late, and Ryan is being rather sus. I hate surprises, I abhor last-minute changes to my plans, and my drink isn't strong enough to help me with either. A chat with my brother usually helps, but maybe not in this case.

"Please, Levi," I beg him over the phone. "You know you don't want to live with Mom and Dad anymore. Jeremy will be out by the end of next month. It's the perfect time for you to move in."

"Teags, no. Seriously." The sound of clinking metal explains his grunt. He's at the gym twenty minutes from my apartment, but yet he still doesn't realize how much I was thinking about him when looking for places with Jeremy.

The location is within walking distance from campus, yes, but it is also close to a good portion of his home games, and I begged Jeremy for the unit on the ground floor closest to the accessible entrance. All that was to make sure Levi would be comfortable every time he visited, and to let him move in if the opportunity arose. In a way, I knew Jeremy wouldn't be with me forever, but I expected more forewarning than this.

"Why would you want to live a few feet away from me when I spend half my time trying to get laid?" Levi asks. "Why would I want to live down the hall from you when *you're* trying to get laid? Imagine that for a second."

"I'll pass, thanks."

"Exactly. Stop asking me."

My lips twist. I don't necessarily *want* to live with my brothers, I just miss them. "I'm going to lose the apartment if I don't find a roommate."

"No, you're not! Oh my god. You will do anything to keep from asking Mom and Dad for money."

"Obviously."

"They're going to be fine with it."

"Yeah, but what are they going to expect as nonmonetary repayment?"

He grunts again with his next movement. "Probably force you to get back with Lenny."

"Bare minimum."

"It's not a big deal. It's rent, not a Bugatti." He laughs at his own joke. "Do you want me to ask them for you?"

"Yeah, when you tell them you're moving in."

I can't tell if his heavy sigh is because of me or his workout. "I'm not moving in with you."

"Please?"

"You're stupid. Love you, bye." He ends the call, giving me my answer. So much for my mood booster. I gesture to the bartender, hoping to climb out of my feelings with the help of a second vodka tonic.

On my way to call Rowan, my phone rings instead. I hope it's

Levi calling to say he changed his mind, but to my disappointment, it's the groom. "Hey."

"Hey, I'm running late," Ryan states the obvious.

"Yeah, I noticed. How are you going to be late for your own bachelor party?"

"I know! We're going as fast as we can. It's traffic."

I can't stand it when people use traffic in the city as an excuse. It's New York. When is there not traffic? "Okay. See you whenever."

"I'm *sorry*. I'll be punctual the rest of the weekend, I promise," he teases me, knowing I will be the one *forcing* everyone to be on time.

"Boy, bye." I put my phone back in my pocket and sigh. Maybe I should use the weekend to get shit-faced and let the guys bail themselves out of jail this time.

"Teags!"

I turn to find Brett walking closer. Oh good. Pregaming with Brett. Maybe if I'm lucky he'll explain to me how the patriarchy doesn't exist. "Hey, babes." I greet him.

"Where's Jer?"

"He's not coming. Something came up with Chet and he can't make it."

He smiles wide. "I'm the first one here?" The news means nothing to him.

"You are."

"Badass!" *How? How is that badass, Brett?* He is not who I wanted to see first, second, or third today. I'm still miffed about my ruined celebration dinner, but that's not much different from how I feel about him most days. He's my best friend's best friend, an inescapable cohort. I don't have to like him—I *don't* like him—but he's family all the same.

He grabs the bartender's attention and orders a whiskey. We're both starting with the hard stuff, likely for the same reason. "What's the plan for the weekend?"

"That's for me to know and for you to do as I say."

He thanks the bartender and takes a hefty swig of his drink. "God, I am so excited for this weekend."

"Oh yeah?"

"Yeah. Don't get me wrong, I love being married, but I do miss being free with you guys sometimes. Weekends like this remind me of the old days, you know?"

"The old days? You mean when *you* used to be the one who got to get their dick wet on vacation?" He laughs, but I know I'm right. "You can still have fun, you'll just have to be a good boy and keep it in your pants from now on. I'm sure Felicity will forgive you for everything else you do this weekend."

"Everything she'll find out about." He winks at me and takes a sip.

Brett never should have gotten married. I would have sworn he didn't know what the word *monogamy* meant before he got engaged—and I'm not completely sure he knows it now—but he jumped into his marriage with both feet like he was happily flinging himself into the ocean off the side of his yacht. Liss must have a black hole for a mouth and a boa constrictor for a snatch.

"Yo, I've been meaning to ask you," he starts his gossip. "Did you hear Heath's been dating some chick? Can you believe that shit?"

One sentence sinks me back into my feelings. "I know, right?"

"You know about it?"

In some ways, I wish I didn't. The relationship clause was in the contract for a reason, but I didn't expect him to be the one to use it first. He puts his dick wherever someone lets him, but Heath doesn't *date*. Not in the traditional sense. But he's been "hanging out" with this girl for two weeks. I would let it bother me, but when he shows up and fucks me on every surface of his apartment, my stupid post-orgasm brain turns into complicitous mush.

I don't care that Heath is trying to get it wherever he can. That's basically his MO. What I care about is the fact that he chose to do it now, when I'm relying on him most. But therein lies the problem. He's as unreliable as Ryan's ability to plan for traffic.

The guys are like a playpen full of kittens, getting distracted by anything that moves. When they drink, they're hive minded and moronic. If one of them jumps off a bridge, the rest hold hands and follow. Jeremy would usually be the soberest one, making him somewhat qualified to help me keep the guys in line, but those days are over, it seems. Brett has no off switch when he's turned up, Ryan goes from brainiac to idiot the second alcohol touches his lips, and Ritchie is always, *always* on his bullshit.

How did we get to a place where Heath is the most reliable one? I'll have to check hell for signs of frost.

I shrug and take a sip. "I don't know any details, but I'm not surprised. When does he not have a roster of hotties ready to go?"

Brett laughs. "He says they're not dating, but I'm not convinced. He's been way too happy the last couple of months for him to not be into this girl."

Months? Knowing that's *me* and not his new squeeze, I'm not sure how to feel. I tap my teeth against the edge of my glass to save my manicure. With this stress, it's just a matter of time before my cuticles will suffer.

"Sorry, do you not want to talk about it?" he asks.

"What? No, it's fine." I shamelessly stroke my ego. "You think he's happy, though? He's seemed kind of out of it lately, like something else is going on."

"Nah. All I've gotten from him is a bunch of smiles and bragging about how often he's getting laid. He probably just doesn't want to tell you since—"

"Hey, fuckers."

I turn to find Heath. Ritchie tags along behind him having what looks to be an angry conversation over the phone. Heath is in his expensive athleisure wear, looking like a tasty plate of monochrome deliciousness. His gray joggers fit just tight enough to show a tempting outline between his legs, and the matching color-block hoodie flatters his slender core and broad shoulders. I hate him so much right now but *zamn*.

"Look at you being on time," I coo.

"I've been practicing," he says, the slightest smirk on his lips. He nudges his head over his shoulder. "That will probably be happening all weekend."

Brett looks concerned. "What's his deal?"

"Girlfriend—fiancé?—drama again." He pulls out the stool next to me and sits. His thigh lies against mine when he lounges back and manspreads. "Where's the ineligible bachelor?" he asks.

"He's late."

Heath laughs. "Your punctual Ry Ry? No way."

"He says he's in traffic, but I think he's lying. I don't know how thrilled Mary was about this trip. She kept asking me to go with her and the bridesmaids instead of coming here with you guys."

Brett laughs. "Doesn't she know you love strippers more than wine?"

"Apparently not."

Ritchie sits next to Brett, hunching over his phone with a scowl as his thumbs rapid fire what I assume is a novel-length text message that starts with *I just think it's funny that* . . .

Brett and I exchange a look, then return our attention to our drinks. Beside me, Heath sighs. He stares down at his phone, too, his head hanging in a hand. It's the same way he's been since we started this mess. When we're fucking, he's fine, but leave him alone long enough and he's all heavy sighs and irritated looks. Relatable, but it's still odd to see his sunshine turn sulky so quickly.

"You okay?" I whisper.

He looks at me with tired eyes. "Yeah. I'm fine."

Beneath the shield of the bar top, Heath's hand slides between my legs and gives my inner thigh a squeeze. It leaves as quickly as it came. I stare into my glass, trying not to slap him.

"How's your girl?" Brett teases Heath.

"My what?"

"Your girl. Your budding beau. Whatever you want to call her."

Heath looks back down at his phone. "Shelley is cool, but she's not my girl."

Brett gasps. "She has a name?" He cracks a smile and takes a sip. I want to crawl into my glass and drown in booze so I can't hear Brett's voice anymore. "Does that mean you're ready to admit she's more than a serial hookup?"

Heath stares at him with a look of confusion until it seems to click. "Oh. No, definitely not."

As expected, they seem back to normal. What it must be like to have a testosterone-dominated brain. Just punch each other until the disagreement is resolved, forgiven, and forgotten. Maybe I should try it sometime.

"Just wondering if I need to watch you this weekend. Make sure you're on your best behavior." Brett snickers. I consider picking a fight just so I can watch Heath beat his ass again.

"Why don't you spend your energy making sure you're on your best behavior, Brett?" I snip. "I'm not going to bail your ass out of jail or the doghouse this time."

"Whatever."

"Yeah, whatever," I mock him.

"Hey!" Brett's yell makes me jump. "You made it!"

Ryan walks up with his hands in the air. "Let's get the fucking party started!"

Looks like someone else has been pregaming too. I glance around at the strangers sneering in our direction. *Let the chaos begin.*

~

The long flight was my last bit of quiet before what I expect to be a shit show of an evening. Once we make it to the hotel, I'm careful to let the guys check in before I do. Heath lingers behind us on his phone.

"We're meeting down here at eight. Not eight thirty, not nine. Eight," I warn them, knowing full well our dinner reservation is at nine. I'll be lucky if I get them together before nine fifteen.

"Yes, ma'am."

As I wait at the counter for the attendant, Heath waits for the guys to disappear into the elevator lobby before joining me. He leans his elbows on the counter, getting a bit too comfortable while being so close to me. I shoot him a look.

"Checking in as well?" The front desk assistant looks thrilled for a person who probably gets yelled at 50 percent of their day. Their smile is bright and genuine while their brown eyes shift between Heath and me, unsure whom to address.

"Yes. Reservation for Teagan Hargrove," I answer.

A nod and some keyboard tapping happens. "All right. I have you two on the twelfth floor, city view, king room."

The fuck? "Oh, no. We're supposed to be booked for a doub—"

"Yeah, that's perfect," Heath cuts me off. I cast him a confused look that he doesn't see.

"No, it's not perfect." *Idiot.* "Can you move us to a double, please?"

Watching our back and forth, the assistant's smile gains an edge of humor, but they drop it. "I'm sorry, it looks like our doubles are all booked, but we can set you up in the king with a rollaway bed, if that works."

"The king works for us. Thank you," Heath answers.

"The rollaway will be better for you, I promise," I say, narrowing my eyes at him. The assistant tucks in their lips to keep from laughing at the bickering spectacle we've become. I hold in the rest of my snarky comments to keep from providing more entertainment.

After more typing, they say, "You are all set. We just need a card on file for incidentals."

Heath hands one over without hesitation and I'm even more confused than before.

"Did you make up with your dad?" I ask just above a whisper.

"Hell no. But this baddie I know gave me a cool spreadsheet to balance my shit, so I have it covered." He looks over and gives me a smile. I don't know whether to feel proud or smack him for calling me a *baddie*.

"Here are your keys. Enjoy your stay!"

I walk with Heath to the elevators, still trying to figure out where his head is at. He seems eager to follow through with our little plan, but something else tempers his mood. The doors open and we step inside. He presses the button for our floor and leans back against the rail, looking at me expectantly.

"Is Kelly going to be cool with you sharing a bed with someone else?" I ask what he already knew was coming.

"Her name is Shelley. And it doesn't matter."

"What does that mean?"

"We haven't had sex."

"Okay. But you're together."

"We're not together, and we're not *dating*. We've hung out, like, twice," he says. "We're friends. I told her I'm not looking for anything serious right now."

"Why not?"

He shrugs and looks away from me as if to mask the real answer hiding in his expression. "Because I knew we were coming here?"

There it is.

I laugh at his expense. "You're such a fuckboy."

He smiles while his eyes trace me up and down. The doors open. "Come on," he says. "We have a weekend of debauchery to enjoy."

TWENTY-FOUR
Heath

Nothing cures depression like tits in your face.

The stripper shakes her chest an inch from my nose. I grip my cash, wishing I could grip her instead. She tugs on the side of her G-string to remind me why she's here. My fingers drag over her mound when I tuck the bill into it.

"Thank you," she says and slowly climbs off me. I hate to see her go but . . . you get it.

Vegas is always a good time, but it's hard for me to stay present when my mind's going in circles about what's happening at home. Something is going on with my mom—at least, I *suspect* something is. The telltale signs are back, but she has been quiet since Dad came home. If he sees what I see, I'm sure he will send her back to the treatment center, and she won't be happy about that. I can't know anything for certain unless she tells me or I go see her and find out for myself. All I can do until we go home is worry, and that's not what I want to do while I'm supposed to be celebrating. It gave me a reason to turn my phone off and make the absolute most of this weekend.

Ryan looks like a virgin at an orgy. His eyes are a mile wide, his face red as a beet. He stares at every girl who walks by and looks flustered each time one stops for him. I constantly find myself wondering if he saved himself for his wedding night.

I smack the back of my hand against his chest and yell over the music. "Bro! Loosen up, this is supposed to be your night!"

"Yeah?"

"Yeah! What's up with you?"

"Nothing! Well . . ." He stares at me for a moment too long, his face twisted like someone told him his dog in middle school didn't actually run away. "Do you think I'm making a mistake?"

"It's a strip club, not a brothel. Here." I hand him my next shot. "Drink this. It'll help."

He takes it with a nod. The first taste makes him grimace. A good sign.

Beside us, Brett is getting his life, blowing all his money, and gaining the attention of half the girls in the club. I'd take advantage of that if I wasn't counting down my last fifty dollars.

I throw back my beer and glance over at Teagan, who is going up for the strippers the way she always does. She moves her little body to the beat, tossing cash onto a stripper's ass as she twerks in front of her. My tongue traces the rim of my bottle while I stare. The stripper turns around and climbs onto Teagan's lap, saying something that makes Teagan give that *shut up and fuck me* smile. Flipping her hair over her shoulder, the stripper slides her hands over Teagan's breasts, teasing her nipples with her thumbs while whispering something in her ear. Girls always get to have more fun in here.

Teagan puts a bill between her teeth; the fold down the middle brings the stripper's lips just an inch from hers when she takes it. The wicked smirk on her face afterward makes me smile. She's wild.

It's fucking hot.

"Heath!" I look at Ritchie, who has two girls in his arms. "Come get a dance with me."

"Are you paying?"

He punches my arm. "Yes, cheap-ass. Come on!"

The private room is quieter and calmer than the excitement of the main floor. The bouncer in the corner watches us like a hawk. It's uncomfortable, but it's not enough to keep my dick down.

"Do you think Ryan's a virgin?" Ritchie asks.

I laugh. "I have no fucking idea."

My girl grinds against my lap and leans back onto my shoulder. Her hands grip her tits and then side between her legs. Everything I'd like to do.

"I think I'm gonna break up with Gigi."

That's not surprising when it comes to their relationship, but random to bring up now. I guess staring at someone else's ass might make you remember how little you want the one you're allowed to touch. "Why?"

"She's been on my case about this trip all week. She wouldn't even talk to me yesterday before we left."

Why does he think I care? Everyone has been praying for their toxic asses to break up for good. "That sucks."

"That's not even all of it."

I roll my eyes. My girl smirks when she climbs up to straddle me and moves her hips over my lap, her pussy barely shielded by a sparkly thong. My not-so-little man reaches for it.

"She's done nothing but cry and bitch and cry for the last month. And now she got sick and is taking it all out on me."

"Sick?"

"Yeah, caught the flu or a stomach bug or something. Been throwing up, asking me to hold her hair and shit. I don't wanna see that!"

The air gets colder. My mind creeps to places I don't want it to go. The reminder of what I've been pushing down sinks my mood into the floor. It seems so obvious to me, but not to Ritchie.

"Could she be pregnant?" I ask.

His face wrinkles with confusion. "What?"

"She's sick, upset, suddenly doesn't want you to leave . . . when was the last time she had her period?" I watch Ritchie stare off into space.

"Oh shit."

Drunk or not, he's a fucking idiot. "Maybe you should call her, bro."

"Yeah." He lifts the girl from his lap and leaves the room.

The two women look annoyed while they watch him leave. The room suddenly feels more awkward than before.

"Um . . . I should probably go too," I tell the one on my lap. "He paid you, right?"

She looks unamused when she turns around. "Yes, sweetheart. We get paid up front for a reason. You'd be surprised how often your little conversation happens in here."

Yikes. I apologize for the both of us and awkwardly slink out of the room.

Back on the floor, Ritchie is crying to Brett. Ryan, confused out of his drunken mind, tugs at them, leading them away from the stage to the bar at the back of the room. Let them go. I have enough drama going on to want to be part of theirs.

Teagan sits curled up in a booth alone, scrolling on her phone. I slide in next to her and fight the urge to wrap her in my arms. Ritchie's shit really fucked with my head. I feel like I need a cuddle. A little hug at least. But I'll chew glass before I tell Teagan that.

"What's wrong with *you?*" she asks without looking at me.

Telling her what happened would ruin the night, so I lie. "I hate strip clubs."

"No you don't."

"They frustrate me."

"Sexually or otherwise?"

I prop my elbow on the back of the booth, leaning my head on my hand while I look at her. "Both."

With a sigh, she sets down her phone and lifts her arms to place them behind her head. Between the frame of her long, straightened hair, her tits threaten to spill out of her top. The edge of her shirt lifts just enough to show the arch of her lower back and the curve of her amazing ass. It's honestly disrespectful that she sits on such perfection at all.

When I look back up, her eyes narrow the way they do when she's about to read me for filth. "Everyone likes boobs, Heath. If you're mad you can't touch them, just say that."

With her body looking the way it does, all I want to touch is her. "You caught me."

I can tell she doesn't believe me, but I can't tell if she cares.

She drops an arm and tugs at the collar of my shirt. "Want to get out of here?" she asks.

"Yeah. I really do."

~

As worried as we were about getting caught on this trip, we've had zero problems. We left separately, but the guys were too busy commiserating with Ritchie at the bar to notice us. We made it back to the room and immediately, our clothes came off.

The room is dark, but a yellow glow from the city coming through the windows traces over her brown skin like a river of gold. Her head leans onto the back of the chair, her chest rising and falling with every circle of my tongue. The thankful brush of her hand over my hair and the shudder of her thigh in my grasp gets me high. Her warm, honey-sweet taste has me rock-hard in my hand, but I want to savor every moment, every wet kiss, every pull of her little bud between my lips.

"How are you so fucking good at this?" she breathes.

I smile against her. She only compliments me when I have her as fucked up as I am right now. After one more taste, I know I can't take it much longer.

I dry my face with kisses against her thigh, hip bone, and waist. Leaning up higher, I drag my tongue over her nipple before catching it with my lips. Her legs curl up against my sides and her hand wraps around me.

She nibbles her lips when she feels how hard I am. Half stroking me, half pulling me closer, she stares down at me, her eyes heavy with a look of desperation.

"Do you want me inside you?" I ask. With a little whimper, she nods. "Come sit on it," I tell her, pulling her hips from the chair.

She doesn't fight me. In a quick move, we switch places. I lounge back and push my hips toward her. Looking at me over her shoulder, she places me against her and slowly sinks onto my lap.

My eyes roll back when I feel her heat envelop me.

This is everything I've wanted since I saw her in the airport. I hold her hips, guiding her into the angle we both want while she moves up and down. She cries out that beautiful sound, holding on to the arms of the chair for support while her body melts around mine. It's too much, the way she grips me, the image of her, the sounds she makes. My blood rushes south, and my cock swells against her plush walls.

It's good. *So* good. It always is.

"Mmm, *fuck*," I say as quietly as I can manage, but all I want to do is thank everything in the universe for giving me this gift.

I move my hips forward in time with her drops. Each time, my head presses deep against her. Teagan's cries turn into a throaty moans, then quiet into desperate humming. The mere thought of giving her what she wants shreds the last of my stamina as easily as tissue paper in the rain. I let myself go.

A blinding rush flows through me. My head drops back against the chair. My soul feels like it leaves me with every shot into the condom. *"Fu-uck."*

I reach around and slide my hand between her thighs. Teagan's legs shake, and her pussy tightens around me. As I continue to spill, I thrust my hips up, stroking with everything I have left, circling my fingers against her until her body curls up with a wail.

While her body grips me, her hand reaches down to hold mine in place, her fingers tracing mine to continue their circle, both of us shuddering with our orgasms.

The calm settles over me little by little. This feeling is better than being drunk, better than being high—better than both at the same time. Nothing melts my stress away like Teagan's pussy melting for me. Pussy in general, but Teagan's . . . hers is hard to compete with.

I slide my hand down between her legs again. Feeling how slick she is everywhere, tracing her lips stretched around me.

She lets me slip from her, then leans against my chest. Still sitting on my lap, she drops her head onto my shoulder. Draped over me like this, the way the shadows trace the curved lines of her perfect body is a work of art. I wrap my arms around her waist, feeling her ribs heave under my palm with her breaths.

For the first time this week, I feel relieved. The gnaw of anxiety is replaced with the quiet buzz of bliss.

"I'm glad we did this," I say, my brain not yet functioning at full capacity.

"When are you not happy about getting laid?" She chuckles.

"No, I mean the contract. Everything. I would have gone crazy this summer if we didn't decide to do this."

"Yeah, no." She sits up and looks back at me with a sneer. "Sharing a room is already pushing it. Keep killing my buzz with this reflective shit and I'll make your ass sleep on the floor." Her smirk displays the humor behind her words.

"My bad." I laugh, pushing her off my lap. I smack a hand against her ass when she walks away. We don't need to talk. That's the whole point. I want her—need her, in a way—and I'm not willing to scare her off by asking for more.

More of anything but this, that is. "Round two?"

TWENTY-FIVE
Teagan

The sunlight burns my eyes when I finally wake up. *Did I sleep in?* A frantic peek at my phone shows it's just past eight o'clock.

I didn't expect to be this worn out after last night. I also didn't plan for last night to be that . . . eventful. Luckily, I *did* plan for the guys to need some recovery time. We have another two hours before we have to be anywhere.

Rolling over, I find Heath at the other side of the bed, rubbing the sleep from his eyes. The sheets hang low on his hips, showing off *most* of why I tolerate him. I want to run my tongue over every ridge of his scrumptious six-pack and the deep seam of his chest, but more than that, I want to know why he's lying next to me.

"Why are you in the bed?" I ask.

He looks my way. His dark hair hangs in his face, the natural waves loose with the lack of product. "After what I did to you last night, I think I deserve more than a cot." He smirks. "Want to fit in round four?"

I give him the side-eye. Sitting up, I realize I'm naked. I never sleep naked, but our third time around was a bit of a surprise. After our second go, I had enough wherewithal to wrap whatever remained of my blowout after he had been fully intent on making me sweat it out like Beyoncé. But then he bent me over the mattress and took me again, *hard*, leaving me brainless and without the energy to dress or make sure he stuck to the agreement and stayed out of the fucking bed. He's so annoying. Sexy as fuck, but so, *so* annoying.

Even if I wasn't sore and exhausted from lack of sleep, I wasn't going to let him break another rule. "You need to shower and get out of here before the guys get up."

"Is that a no, or . . . ?" He rolls closer and gives me that sexy look that makes my brain stop braining or whatever.

I stare him down, not wanting to tell him no or give him the benefit of a yes. "My bonnet really does it for you, huh?"

"Not gonna lie, it kind of does." His tongue traces his bottom lip while his smile widens. "I probably should have worn one too."

"I wasn't going to say it, but . . ." I reach over and brush his hair into his face. He laughs and lies back to run his fingers through it. "Get up."

"Oh, I'm up." He glances down, making me do the same, finding the tent he's pitching beneath the thin sheet.

"You need to stop," I say. "You're breaking *so* many rules right now."

"Oh yeah? Which ones?"

"No sleepovers, no pillow talk—"

"This isn't a sleepover. You knew what you signed up for when you agreed to share a room."

"I expected to save money, not share a bed. Sleepover or not, this is still pillow talk."

He chuckles. "We're talking while we're on pillows. It's not pillow talk."

"That's literally the same thing."

"Okay, then let's stop talking." He crawls closer and peers down at me with a conniving grin.

I sigh with frustration. "I'm too tired for your shit right now, Heath."

"Too tired? Who said you had to do anything?" He reaches down and takes me by the back of my knee, pulling it up. His hand slides up and down my thigh, sending tingles across my skin and a rush of warmth to my core. "I got this."

I consider giving in until someone bangs on the door. "*Teags!*"

Heath and I look at each other with the same face. *Shit.*

We fly out of the bed. While I rip off my bonnet and put on a robe, he gathers his clothes and other items from the floor and runs into the bathroom. The lock clicks behind him, and I open the door.

Brett's and Ryan's stupid faces peer at me. They are in last night's clothes, their eyes bloodshot and glassy, both looking panicked. *Goddamn it, Brett.* I know whatever drama comes next is his fault. "What the hell did you do?"

"Ritchie and Heath are gone," Brett says.

He means *Ritchie* is gone but I won't correct him. "What do you mean by 'gone'?"

"Gone as in they're not here and we can't reach them."

I press my palm to my forehead. "Not again."

Heath's dumb ass knocks something over in the bathroom, making it crash loudly on the floor. I pretend I don't hear it, but it makes no difference. "Do you have someone else in there?" Brett asks, looking past me in various directions.

"Priorities much?" I say with a glare. "Let me get ready and I'll meet you in your room. Keep calling them." I shut the door in their faces and lean back against it. Listening to their voices trail away, I sigh. "They're gone."

The bathroom lock clicks and Heath slides the door open. He's still naked, and seems to have no intention of changing that. It takes everything I have not to look down when he leans his arms on the door frame. "I should have answered my phone, I guess."

"You think?"

He laughs and walks back to the bed, not acknowledging how lucky he is our tweaked-out friends didn't consider why someone else is staying in the random room number he gave them.

"Do you have any idea where Ritchie could be?"

I can see the gears in his mind slowly start to turn. "I think I might."

~

"Tell me why Ritchie is at the fucking airport," I say to Heath when I return from my investigation. "Actually, don't. That would make what I'm about to do premeditated rather than a crime of passion."

The hotel manager was happy to be an accomplice, letting me know they called Ritchie a cab just like Heath suspected. Back in the guys' suite, Ryan and Brett pace in the next room, pretending they aren't tweaking out.

"He's having issues with Gigi again. I told him he should talk to her, not fly his ass back to New York." Before I can tell him to handle it, he offers. "Let me call him. Maybe he'll answer if he doesn't see your name pop up."

"Thank you." I trust him to speak Ritchie's language better than I can. He walks away while spewing angry words at a quieter volume than I can manage right now.

In the living space, I avert my eyes from the remnants of a white substance powdered on the coffee table, entertainment I'm certain Brett procured last night without my knowledge. One of the *many* problems with him is that he knows too many people and has too much money. Whatever he wants, he gets, and when he parties, he parties with very few restrictions—legal or otherwise. Judging by

Heath's angry whispers, Ritchie is probably in the same condition, but at least he got a hold of him.

The dank air of spoiled fuckboy shenanigans is enough to choke me. I open the balcony doors, inhaling gulps of fresh air to calm my blood pressure. Ryan appears from nowhere, looking a damn mess. His sunken eyes are wide with fear and a lack of sleep.

"Oh my god. What's wrong with *you* now?"

He looks at me and his brow furrows. "I'm freaking out, Teags."

"Yeah, I can see that."

"Ritchie just made me think—"

"Don't let Ritchie make you think about anything. He doesn't even think for himself."

"But . . ." he says in a quivering voice. "I'm starting to think that, maybe, like, what if—"

"Oh my god, spit it out!"

He looks me in the eyes. His are wet with tears. I sigh, knowing this is about to be melodramatic as hell. "How can you know for sure?" he asks.

This is like talking to a fucking toddler. "Know *what* for sure?"

"How do you know you're with the right person? Like, you look around at all these happy couples who are breaking up, couples married for twenty years getting a divorce. It's like you can be madly in love one minute and then suddenly your relationship is crumbling. How?" He fidgets while he breathes away tears. "Is it better to be alone than to waste your time with someone who will make you never want to be in love again? To let someone ruin you for everyone else?"

He's not asking a hypothetical. He's asking because that's what he thinks happened to *me*.

He reads my thoughts on my face. "I'm sorry. I didn't mean it like that."

"No, you definitely did."

He goes back to his bullshit. "But, I mean. You seemed so happy. And now you're—"

"Bitter and broken?" I finish for him.

"No! I mean, whatever happened, happened, and now you think you don't want to be in a relationship with *anyone*, even if—"

I raise a hand to keep him from finishing his sentence. "Please stop before I push you off this balcony." I wish I was kidding. "If you want to have a cold-footed freak-out, go ahead, but leave me out of it."

"But how do you know if you're with the wrong person?"

With a deep breath, I let the memories peek into my thoughts. "You can't know that," I tell him truthfully. A flicker of emotion twists in my stomach and grips my throat, but I shake it off. "You can love everything about someone, then life shows up and changes them in ways you can't predict. If you get married and five years from now everything falls apart, that's not time wasted, it's time you spent trying to be happy. That's all life really is. *Trying* to be happy while surviving the bullshit."

His brow crumples. "Really?"

I stare at him, fighting the angry tears I've cried too many times. "I don't know. Probably."

"Teags." He comes closer and wraps me in a hug. "What would I do without you?"

I wish I could find out, I answer in my head. Still annoyed, I return his unsolicited embrace with a few pats on the back. He leans away and looks at me for a moment, his hand finding my cheek. Not knowing where that hand has been, I try to pull it away. It doesn't work.

"How do I . . . how do I know it's not you?" he asks.

"What's not me?"

He gives me a pitiful look. His other hand joins his first, holding my face between them. His thumbs trace my cheekbones while I can *feel* how ugly the grimace on my face looks. "How do I know you're not the one?"

My brow scrunches with confusion. *"Huh?"*

"I love you, Teagan. You're the best friend I've ever had," he says. "Thinking about getting married is freaking me out, and I think maybe it's because I'm not marrying you."

What?

I stare at him, trying to hold it in, but I fail. The laugh I'm fighting comes out of my nose. I cover my mouth with a hand, but it bursts out. My head falls back as I cackle.

I have to hold on to him in fear of falling over. I laugh until my abs hurt and my eyes are watering. "You think you want to be with *me?* You think I'd ever want to be with you? Oh my god, I'm gonna pee my pants." I cackle again, gripping my stomach when it cramps. "Ryan, you cannot be serious. You must be high out of your damn mind."

His eyes stay wide while he contemplates my words. "Oh. I think you're right."

"Yeah, no shit." I wipe my eyes while my cheeks and stomach ache. As fucked up as he must be for that to ever cross his mind, at least he made me laugh. "Come on, you can sober up over breakfast."

"Yeah, I'm sorry, I don't know what I was thinking," Ryan says.

"You *weren't* thinking. Go drink some water."

Ryan stumbles away to join Brett when Heath wanders back, his conversation done.

"The cab is bringing him back," he says, his tone lackluster. The humor evaporates.

"Good. Thank you."

"Yeah, don't mention it." He tosses his eyes at Ryan, then walks away, scrubbing his hands over his face with an exasperated exhale.

Same.

~

The second we land at LaGuardia, reality creeps back in, and with it, my feelings. Heath is immediately on his phone again, his thumbs flying over the keys. The post-Vegas grovel text, I'm sure. He left his good mood back at the hotel. In the seat between us, Ryan is still asleep, his beanie pulled down over his eyes, his expensive head-phones on, blasting his shitty EDM mix. I won't wake him until we reach the gate. Less time to talk to him after the awkwardness of before.

He threw me. Geeked or not, he reminded me why I don't leave my heart open anymore. I no longer have the desire to let someone get close to me again.

When you're a kid, you think nothing can hurt you if you build your walls thick enough. Then you let someone in. No matter how deeply you love someone, there is always the chance of life showing up out of nowhere, crumbling every wall you've built, leaving you broken and raw. When the damage is too great, there is no point in trying to put the pieces back together. You move on and start anew, letting the shell of the person you were before lie beneath the rubble.

My eyes lift to Heath. Our contract is perfect. It keeps it black-and-white, clearly delineated, emotionless. There's no chance of gray if we stick to it.

"Back to business, I see," I say to him. He doesn't look at me, but rather continues to scowl at his phone. "When do you plan to confront her?"

He finally looks up at me with a surprised expression. "Confront her?"

"Confront her. Tell her. Whatever you want to call it." He looks even more confused than before. I don't know why I give him the benefit of the doubt when it comes to his mental capabilities. He thinks with his dick. "How long do you think you can go before she cares about you spending your evenings with her and your nights with someone else?"

It finally clicks with him. He looks away and shakes his head. "You're talking about Shelley. Again. I'm getting real sick of having to tell you she isn't my girlfriend."

"Yet."

He closes his eyes with an angry inhale. "I don't have time for this right now, Teags."

"Chill. I'm not trying to scold you. I just think it's best to be open with her. And with me," I try to reassure him. "If you're considering *more* with her, tell me. I just don't want any more surprises this summer. That's all."

His vexation burns into anger. He leans in to whisper, his glare intent and threatening. "I am not fucking Shelley. I do not *plan* to fuck Shelley. But if you'd like that to change, keep this shit up."

I rear back with surprise. "Excuse me?" The seat belt sign dings and the clacking sound of unbuckling interrupts me. I hadn't noticed us arriving at the gate. "I said everything is fine, Heath. I just want you to talk to me if—"

"There is nothing I want to talk to *you* about." The anger on his face is drastically out of context. "Fucking drop it."

Now I'm bothered. "Okay, so what you're doing right now is the definition of fuckshit. Don't come at me because you're in your feelings."

"Teagan. Respectfully, you have no *fucking* idea what you're talking about right now, so how about you shut the hell up."

My jaw drops.

"Why can't you guys go more than a day without fighting?" Ryan says in a gravelly voice. Caught up in whatever *that* just was, I didn't notice he'd woken up. "You're so dramatic."

"Yeah, you're one to talk," I snip, still riled up.

I look back up and see Heath pushing past people on his way down the aisle. He's gone.

I expected this weekend to be fucked, but not when it came to Heath. He's pissed at me, and I don't know why. To think I could be the one to fracture my contract's integrity bothers me to the core. If he's right—if *I'm* the one pushing things too far, crossing the lines set forth in our agreement—he has every right to call it. And if he does, then what? I don't have space for the unpredictable right now. So maybe it's best if I give *him* space.

I taste blood before I realize my finger is in my mouth.

TWENTY-SIX
Heath

My heart is still pounding when I drive up to my parents' house. Mom's last text message threw me, and she hasn't responded since. I haven't been able to calm down since I first saw it on the plane.

The fucking plane. I shouldn't have popped off on Teagan like that, but I didn't want to tell her the truth. That I'm worried about my mom, not someone else. Sex aside, she doesn't know what the weekend meant to me—how much it helped me separate myself from my mom's problem and my dad's shitty choices. But sometimes Teagan is just like the guys, self-interested and unbothered. The minute I think she gives a shit about me, she makes it clear she doesn't. Open to listening one minute, then shutting me down the next like some kind of game. I never known which version of her I'm going to get, and I'm not in a place to play with her.

She has her limits and I understand that. We've known each other too long for me not to know why she acts the way she does. She *loves* to remind me there's nothing between us but sex, and I'll respect that, but I just want . . .

I don't know what I want exactly. I'm spinning around in feelings I shouldn't have because I'd rather feel anything but this.

When I pull up at the front door, Silas approaches. "Is Dad here?" I ask when I climb out.

"He's away for a moment," he answers.

He reaches for my keys but I stop him. "Then I won't be long."

The wrinkled corners of his mouth turn down even more than usual, but he nods in acknowledgment. He knows he'll never see a day when my dad and I willingly spend time together.

Mom has been quiet since Dad came back, returning my texts a bit slower, not asking me to come visit before leaving for Vegas. They were busy making social appearances at his fundraisers, playing the role of Famous Baller and Trophy Wife, but her texts . . . something was off. I couldn't tell if she was talking about an upcoming event or one that just happened, mixing up words and dates again.

I tried to convince myself it was a typo. When she wouldn't text me back, I couldn't take it. Turning off my phone was the only way I could clear my mind. The second we landed, she confirmed it.

Mom: *I'm sorry. I think it's best I go back to the facility*

She hadn't been giving me the full truth. She is struggling again. But going back to the place she hates—the place she knows has never helped her? This was Dad's doing.

Inside the house, I find Mom standing in the atrium, rearranging the stones at the base of her weeping cherry tree. I watch her for a moment, wanting to believe that everything is okay.

She flinches with surprise when she sees me. Her face splits into a smile. It takes her no time to slide open the door and come to me. "Heath!" She raises her arms to welcome me into them.

I run to her and hug her tight. "Are you okay?"

"Yes. Of course I am." She pulls away to look at me. "What is wrong, son?"

"Your message."

"Message?" Her head tilts with confusion, making me worry whether she remembers telling me or not.

"You're going back to rehab?"

Her eyes drop from mine. "Yes."

"And is that what you want? To go back to a place you hate?"

"Yes." The shortness of the word hides piles of guilt behind it.

"Why?" She still won't look at me. I take her face in my hands to make her. "Mom, tell me the truth. Are you taking pills again?"

When she doesn't respond, that's the only answer I need. I drop my hands and she takes them in hers. "I'm sorry."

The truth hits me in the gut like a fist. I hide the swell of emotion behind a clenched jaw, not wanting to add to her guilt by crying in front of her. Hearing her apologize hurts worse than anything I could do to myself.

"I am going back. Your father thinks it's best if I have time away to relax and think."

"Relax and think? Because that's what you need, not support or help."

She pulls away and I realize my words came out more harshly than I meant.

"I want you to go if you want to, but you can't keep changing your mind after you're there. Every time you ask me to get you out, you put me in a position where I have to choose between you and Dad. And you know I will always choose you."

"It is not your job to take care of me. I am supposed to take care of *you*, la'u tama tama." The guilt on her face makes me want to stop talking. "I don't like it when you and your father argue. You're too alike sometimes—so strong-willed."

That pisses me off. "Yeah, well, we did argue. He cut me off this time."

Her eyes widen. "He didn't tell me."

Of course he didn't. They rarely talk about money, the same way they don't talk about the root of her issue. "I don't care about the money. I'm mad that he punished me for trying to help you."

A voice sounds behind me. "Is that what I did?"

My skin crawls when I turn around. Dad.

His icy glare warms when his eyes shift to my mom. "Say good-bye, Mea. He's not staying."

"Couldn't he—?"

"Say goodbye," he says again. It's a power move, telling her I'm leaving rather than asking me to go. I'm nothing to him, and when he ignores the way Mom feels, it makes it hard to believe she means much to him either.

With *that* as my example of love, it's no wonder I'm such a fuckup in relationships.

I kiss my mom on the cheek then shoulder check him on my way to the door. He follows, stoking my urge to tell him off once and for all.

"She is going back on Wednesday," he says to my back. I stop walking. "You can come with me to drop her off if you'd like."

"If I'd like?" I turn around. "I'd like it if you helped her, not treat her struggle like an inconvenience. But you won't. Because how the fuck does that serve you?"

He cocks his head to the side, amusedly watching me blow up.

"She's not getting better because you're not listening to her."

"To her?" he asks. "Or to you?"

The way he gets in my head makes it hard to piece together my thoughts. "You don't respect what I do, but I know what I'm talking about. I help people by treating the root cause, not masking it with superficial treatments. Rehab is superficial. She needs—"

"You don't know what you're talking about."

"Except I do. I talked to professionals, I've researched treatments.

I *want* her to get better. Unlike you." I fight the shaking of my voice. "I wish you would stop being a stubborn piece of shit."

"And I wish you were less of a disappointment." His tone is calm and even. That hurts worse than if he'd yelled. "We don't always get what we want."

His words stab me in the chest. It makes my eyes burn with tears, but I won't give him the satisfaction of crying. "Yeah, well, the apple doesn't fall far from the tree." I make my way to the door, not looking back. "Fuck you, Dad."

I climb into my car and peel out of the driveway. Speeding down the narrow drive feels dangerous and good. The trees flying by faster and faster, the winding road engaging my car's suspension. When I reach the street, I whip out before I see the oncoming car.

I slam on the brakes, screeching to a stop just a foot before I T-bone them. They blare their horn as they drive by.

My heart pounds for a different reason. The fear pulls me back into my body.

It hurts. All of it hurts.

I dig my fingernails into my steering wheel and scream.

~

After sleeping like shit, I can't shake myself out of my exhaustion. The stress keeps piling on, leaving me incensed and on edge, one spark away from exploding.

I'm not okay. As much as I want to pretend everything is fine, that I don't care what my dad says, I do. On top of it, I took it out on Teagan after she was the only person who would be able to understand. The person who can keep my mind off it better than anyone.

I look at my phone, hoping I missed a message from her, but my last two sit on Read.

Me: I have to cancel for Wednesday

Me: Sorry

With my messages being short and anything but sweet, there are five hundred ways she could read that and think I'm in the same shitty mood as I was on the plane. I want to apologize to her and make up for what happened, but I don't have an excuse for what I did unless I tell her the full truth. Days later, I still haven't heard from her.

Staring at the messages won't change anything. I don't want to respond to Brett's *crazy weekend, right?* or Ritchie's celebratory *guess who's not a daddy* texts. Remembering the weekend makes me regret what I said to Teagan even more.

I drape my arm over my eyes, hoping the pressure will keep them from watering. Just as I take in a shaking breath, my phone rings.

Hoping it's her, I snatch it from my covers, but when I see who it is, my hopefulness wanes. "Hey, Shelley."

"Hey!" She always has so much enthusiasm for life. I'm jealous. "How was Vegas?"

I sigh. "It was a mess."

"Oh no, what happened? Do you want to FaceTime?"

"I'm still in bed."

She giggles. "You say that like it's a bad thing."

A smile pulls on my cheeks. I sit up and lean back against my headboard, running my fingers through my hair as if that will help. Her face appears with a cute look of concern. She has her glasses on and her hair up in a little bun on top of her head. Big letters hang with cartoon palm trees on the wall behind her. Summer school aesthetic. "Are you at work?" I ask.

"Yes, but I'm done for the day."

"Did the rug rats behave this time?"

She rolls her eyes and deflates. "No. Oh my god, today was crazy! It's like they all had handfuls of sugar for breakfast, then got angry rather than tired when they crashed."

"Sounds like my weekend."

"Tell me what happened. The parts that *didn't* stay in Vegas, at least," she jokes.

I hang my head in a hand. My mind is in a negative place, but with all the bullshit that happened, there *were* times I was happy. The times I was with Teagan. "My friends always bring the drama. Breakups, bad decisions, a case of cold feet . . . I had a good time in the five minutes I wasn't dealing with all that."

"Your friends almost sound worse than my first graders."

"No one went to the hospital or got sent to prison, so I guess that's a win."

She giggles again. Her smile is infectious, but with my mood, I've developed partial immunity. "I'm sorry, but I am calling with ulterior motives."

"Oh yeah?"

"Yeah." She grimaces. "Friday is career day, and one of the parents we had lined up had to cancel last minute. Is there anything I could do to convince you to fill in?"

There are plenty of ideas on my list, but unless she has a homicide kink, I don't think she'll be into any of them. "I'm sure we can figure something out. When do you need me to be there?"

She gives me all the details. A school about half an hour away, right after my shift ends. It all works out. I wish I could muster more enthusiasm.

"We should do something afterward," she says.

I can read between the lines on occasion. "Something like a date, you mean?"

"Something like that. Let's hang out. I have no ulterior motives for anything but career day, I promise."

She knows this is casual, and I don't want to make it seem otherwise, but I could use some time away from the group—time away from their drama and stress. A compromise comes to mind. "I've been dying to go back to this cool café a friend took me to recently. They're open late and have coffee *and* cocktails. Would you want to go there?"

I can see her cheeks change color. "Yeah, I'd love to!"

"It's a date. In the calendar at least." I mean to joke, but when the words leave my mouth, I realize I should check. I open my calendar app to see when—*if*—I'm scheduled with Teagan. Just as I thought, we don't have an appointment scheduled, but there is a different event that day. Her parents' party.

Shit. I completely forgot.

"Is something wrong?" Shelley asks, making me remember I'm still on video.

The "do better" part of my brain tingles, but I'm still trying to learn how to listen to it. "I was supposed to go with a friend to a company party thing. I forgot."

"Was? Are you still going?"

After ignoring my texts, it's pretty clear Teagan doesn't want to talk to me, and I don't blame her. But does that mean I should stop trying? "Good question."

TWENTY-SEVEN
Teagan

I am at my limit.

The wedding events are still going according to plan, but the guys keep throwing me curveballs that remind me why I don't talk to them outside of the summer. They're messy and predictably unpredictable. No matter what I do, I know *one* of them will go off the rails, and I will be the only one responsible enough to get them back on track. I can handle one of them having a complete meltdown, not all fucking five of them at the same time.

Mary was already worried about Ryan going to Vegas, but I knew planning the trip weeks before the wedding would give them time to sort out any insecurities that their separate celebrations might create. Ryan getting blitzed out of his mind and thinking I would entertain the idea of ever being more to him was insanity. If I had a choice, I would spend the rest of the summer working only with Mary and let the guys fumble all the remaining groomsmen responsibilities on their own. I'm tired, and after whatever happened with Heath on the plane, I've lost my main outlet for stress. I blame that on Ryan too. I didn't need a reminder of the past, or another reason to get in my head and doubt my choices.

I'm not sure where I went wrong in my attempt to tell Heath all is well with our arrangement as long as he sticks to it, and I don't know what I did to get my head bit off, but when he canceled on Wednesday, I got the message. He's no different than the rest of our friends—showing up for me when it's convenient, never there for me when I need support—and I've known that for years. I'd rather go to the party alone than create more mess I'd have to clean up.

This party was a gray area, even before a potential girlfriend got involved. He hasn't canceled on me for tonight, at least not yet, so I'm holding on to my 10 p.m. calendar reminder, letting it be the glimmer of light at the end of the tunnel that will get me through this party.

I don't want to go without a date, but at least I won't be alone. Rowan will be there. Keeping him comfortable while in a crowd will be my focus.

This is fine. I will be fine.

My false lashes take forever to put on with my hands shaking this bad. My anxiety *and* my lack of sleep, no doubt. The Marchesa gown is the only thing lifting my mood. I lean back and check myself in the mirror. The rigid bodice creates a snatched waist, the black taffeta tracing the sweetheart neckline into an off-the-shoulder detail and down into an elegantly draped skirt. The gathered side balances the high slit and provides the blessing of hidden pockets. It's beautiful and perfect for the event, but beneath it is *me*—a listless shell, less alive than the hanger it was on before.

I stab a crystal hairpin into the side of up updo, hoping it will distract people from noticing it is the remnant of a failed attempt at a different style. So much effort goes into my hair for these events. My paranoia that I will play with it too much and reveal the fickleness of my natural texture, yet another detail proving to my parents' peers that I'm Not Like Them.

My finger catches on a pin when I pull it out. I hiss and look at it, realizing I've been gnawing my cuticle raw all day, even chipping the edge of my gel manicure. *Fuck it*. This is the best I can do.

I slip on my shoes and slide my clutch into my pocket.

Leaving my room for Rowan's, I take a calming breath, knowing my discomfort will only make him more anxious about the party. When I lean through his doorway, I find him sitting on the edge of his bed, his head hanging in his hands and his tux still laid out next to him.

"Rowie," I say. "You're not dressed yet?"

He turns his head to me, and I flinch when I see his face. His eyes are red with tears, cheeks blotchy and raw.

"What's wrong?"

He sniffles and looks away. "I got a thirteen fifty on my SAT."

While that is a great score for most people, under the fourteen hundred mark will not make an Ivy League college *or* our parents happy. "That's okay. You can retake it."

I reach for him, and he turns away and wipes his eye. "You got a fifteen ninety on your first try."

"That doesn't matter."

"How? How does it not matter?"

He's upset. I know how it feels to do well, then have your parents scold you for not doing better. "It doesn't matter because you can retake it. And even if you get the same score, it is one of multiple things colleges consider during admissions."

"Oh my god," he grumbles in frustration. "You don't get it!"

"Of course I get it. I've been right where you are."

"No! You haven't! *Nothing* is hard for you!"

It's a shock to hear my quiet Rowan yell. And directed at me? "What?"

"You do everything Mom and Dad want, exactly how they want it, all the time."

"And you think that isn't hard for me?" I reply to him in disbelief. "I'm stressed out all the time. Anxious as hell trying to live up to their expectations."

"But you meet them every time! You have no idea what it feels like to try to follow in your footsteps, to constantly fail in their eyes because Teagan did it first or Teagan did it better," he says. "You make it harder for us every single day and you don't even see it!"

"It isn't—"

"You may have to live up to their expectations, but so do we! And while you're succeeding, winning, never making a mistake, I'm the one left to fail at everything! Try living while feeling like that!"

I'm speechless. Rowan never shows emotion like this. It's painful to know he has this much animosity toward me and has never said anything before now.

My heart aches. "Rowie, I didn't know you felt this way."

"Well, I do. I hate you so much sometimes."

"Rowan!" Levi says from the doorway. "Stop it. It's not Teagan's fault."

"Yes it is! You know it is!" Rowan screams. Hugging myself, I cower from his anger. "I'm tired of it! I'm tired of *you*. I'm not going to this stupid party."

He storms out of the room, leaving me with Levi and a broken heart.

I love Rowan. I would never do *anything* to hurt him or make him go through the stress I do. To know he feels this way, that I have been causing him pain . . . My chest hurts so much my hand clutches it. In trying to make everything easier for him, I've made it so much worse. Nothing I do is right, not for my parents, and not for my brothers, the two people I love the most in the world.

"He's just mad," Levi tries to comfort me. "It's teenage shit. He doesn't mean it."

"But is it true? What he said?" I ask. Tears blur my vision. "Do you feel that way?"

He hesitates with a breath. "Well. . ."

I turn away in shame while my entire body wrenches with guilt.

"It's not your fault, Teags. It's Mom and Dad. They're hard on all of us, but you are their obvious favorite," he says. "At every party it's always them bragging about you and your accomplishments, all the new things you've done well and all the things you'll do soon. It sucks for you, I know it does, but to Rowan and me, it's just . . . different. We're never the ones they will brag about, but that's their shit, not yours."

Fuck. I've been so wrapped up in my life, surviving year after year while trying to match the image of me my parents show to their friends and associates, thinking it would leave space for Levi and Rowan to be free of it. And all this time, it was torturing them too.

"Do you resent me?" I turn back to face Levi. "Tell me the truth."

"No, Teags. I swear. I mean, yeah, I had some serious middle-child syndrome before the accident, but now they've lowered the bar to the floor for me."

That's practically the same thing. "I'm sorry," I say, my tears pinching my voice in a way I haven't heard in years. "I didn't know I was hurting you. I thought I was saving both of you by taking it all upon myself. If I knew, I would have never—"

"I know, Teags." He pulls me to him. I drop to my knees and let my head fall against his shoulder. "Don't let it get to you."

How can I not? What is the point of everything I've done if it still hurts the people I love?

"Darlings! It's time to go!" my mother calls from up the hall. I curse under my breath.

"Go. It'll be worse if Mom and Dad know what happened," he says.

I nod and dab the corners of my eyes to keep the tears from falling. Crying will have to happen later.

"I'll tell them Rowan is sick," Levi offers.

Sweep it under the rug. That'll make it all go away.

~

I grab my clutch for the millionth time, thinking my phone is vibrating inside it, but it's not. I put it back into my pocket and clench my hand into a fist to get it to stop shaking. Only a few more hours.

The banquet hall is set up like an awards ceremony. Round tables with white tablecloths and crystal flatware that shimmers like the chandeliers hanging above. A stage with a podium for speeches and open floor space in front, where some guests who've already finished their meals gather to mingle.

Sitting at a table nearest the stage, I am lucky to be at the table with some of my parents' most expensive clients, not Lenny and his family. Their table is far enough away that I can't see him. I've been so busy battling an army of my inner demons, I'm not sure he's here at all. If I let myself feel anything else, it will be the crack in my stone façade that sends me crumbling to the floor.

"Have we never told you about how Teagan came into our lives?" my father asks our tablemates. His mention of my name gains my attention. I look up and steel myself into a polite smile. With Heath and Rowan missing, I am stuck between my parents, no shield or way to distract from what they will say. But, energy or not, I know my role.

"We came across an orphanage while traveling through Ethiopia. She was so small, malnourished, but those big, beautiful eyes staring back at us had so much desire for life." He places a hand on my cheek, and I mimic his smile. "We knew we couldn't leave her in that place. Just like her brothers, the moment we met her, we knew she was meant to be with us."

"It's amazing to watch her succeed after all she has been through," my mother continues, not knowing the impact of her words. "To think of how different her life would have been, how her brilliance could have been wasted . . . It's been a gift to see her be able to shine."

I fight to maintain my smile when Rowan's words clench my throat again. They always tell this story, not knowing how small it makes me feel, how demoralizing it is to be reminded that you could be dead or in misery had your parents not *saved* you. A prized possession, not a person. Feeling like I owe it to them to live in the compact, rigid box they've placed me into, yet my acceptance of it— my fear of leaving it—forced Rowan into a box that was even smaller.

Why did I do any of this?

"Teagan?" My dad looks at me as if expecting an answer.

"Sorry, what?"

"Did you want to join us?" He gestures to the crowd of fraternizing strangers behind him, most of which he'll want to introduce me to.

The shaking of my hands has turned into anxious shivers. "I'll join you in a second."

He nods. "Eat something. You've barely touched your plate." He turns with his companions, and everyone leaves the table.

I'm finally alone to drown in my deep, dark pool of self-hatred. Anxiety makes me want to cry, scream, tear the hair out of my head chunk by chunk, but I can't do any of it. I never can. *Don't make a scene.*

My stomach twists while I look at the pile of potatoes and slab of meat on my plate. Heavy cream and butter galore, no doubt. Lactose intolerance aside, the salt and calories would have me swelling out of my ill-fitted dress. I take a big spoonful and put it in my mouth. It takes me a moment to force myself to swallow it, and the moment I do, I regret it.

The spoonful of nothing hits my twisted stomach like a rock, making it hurt worse. I force myself to take another bite. The physical and emotional discomfort double. My heart pounds, my hands refuse to stay still. When my skin turns from cold to clammy, I know what is about to happen.

No one sees me leave the table, no one watches as I go up the hall. When I reach the bathroom, I almost bump into someone as I go in.

"Excuse me," I apologize, slipping past her and into the stall. I can barely wait for her to close the door before I sink to the floor, and lose the contents of my stomach into the toilet.

I hadn't eaten much today, my nerves too high to allow much of anything past my daily coffee. My stomach aches from heaving, my throat burns from the acid. When my retching stops, I sob for what feels like minutes, every tear filled with regret over how I've lived my life, all the painful sacrifices I've made to maintain my guise of perfection.

When I hear the door open, I quiet myself and stand. I stare into space, letting my last tear fall while I wait for the other person to flush, wash up, and leave. By the time they do, I'm back to being numb.

I leave the stall and go to the sink and check myself in the mirror. Mouthwash sits next to fancy disposable cups in the array of lotions, perfumes, and sanitary products. I swish and rinse my mouth twice, the burning mint hiding what I've just done, then check myself in the mirror. The circles under my eyes look darker, the luster in my skin—or whatever is left of it—dulled by a hollowed gaze and running mascara. I wipe my eyes and lips with a hand towel and focus on my numbness. When I look put back together, I smooth out my dress and leave the room.

My anxiety isn't something I try to hide from everyone—it just goes unnoticed under the pile of accolades and achievements that mask my inner torture. Perfection is painful, they say, and so is being under a spotlight when all I want is to be invisible.

Only two steps out, I stop in my tracks and find him waiting for me in his perfectly fitted tux. "Heath."

"Hey," he says.

I let the door close behind me. "What are you doing here? I thought you weren't coming."

He tilts his head in confusion. "I thought you wanted to meet me here." His brow furrows with concern. "Are you okay?"

"Huh? Yeah."

"You look like you're about to cry." I would feel touched if I could feel anything right now. "Are you okay?"

"What? Yeah, I'm fine."

He looks at me like he sees through all my lies to the anxiety and pure emotional chaos I'm barely keeping inside. "Did you just throw up? Teags, what is wrong?"

My chest tightens and I feel like I can't breathe, like if I try to take another breath all my tears will come out too. I try to say something to hide it, but I can't manage a word. He can't see me break down. I refuse.

Turning away from him, I look for a way to run away from this, from everything that has happened today, even though it means going back to the party. I barely feel his hand on mine when he pulls me back to face him. "Teagan, you're shaking. Tell me what's going on."

"Stop it!" I snatch my hand from his. His eyes widen. "Stop acting like you give a shit. We don't talk, remember? We're having sex. That's it. We are not friends who talk about our feelings or admit that—" My throat tightens again. The tears burn my eyes. "—admit that everything in our life is falling apart."

He looks at me as if he's surprised. "We're not?"

His words hit me hard. I silently plead with him not to make me cry again.

"Do you want to leave?" he asks.

"I can't, I have to—"

"No, Teags. You don't have to do anything you don't want to." The fervor in his expression almost makes me believe him. "If you want to leave, the door is right there. I will happily drag you through it."

I look away, not knowing what to do.

"We're going. Come on." He tugs at my hand.

I follow him.

TWENTY-EIGHT
Teagan

Heath pulls me through the crowd by the hand, weaving through the amalgam of black dresses and tuxes, no one seeming to notice. It seems easy. Too easy.

We run into a group talking to my parents and he stops. My heart jumps into my throat. Mom spots him and her eyes go wide.

"Heath! Darling!" He snakes an arm around my waist, turning me to him and away from her. She can't see I've been crying if she can't see me. "It feels like forever. How have you been? How's the family?"

"Everyone is doing great, Mrs. H. Thank you for asking."

I place my hand on his shoulder and rest my chin on top of it. As they continue to talk, I close my eyes and take a deep breath to slow the pounding of my heart. It works, however briefly. When I open them again, I lock eyes with Lenny.

He stands with some of our dads' associates. They talk, but all he does is stare at me. His expression is unreadable, but Heath's hand on my hip and my smudged lipstick paint quite a picture, I assume.

I turn my head back to look at Heath and find him already looking at me. He pulls me with him when he takes a step and my hope returns.

"Tell your parents I said hello, won't you?" my mom adds.

"Absolutely."

He shields me from Lenny's view until we slip through the front doors of the banquet hall. When my heels sink into the hallway's carpet, I can't believe it.

Just like that, I'm free.

Heath pushes the button for the elevator, and we wait. The crowd visible through the open doors keeps the last of my fear from subsiding, but next to him, I feel safe. His hand strokes up and down my back as if to say, *You're okay*. I realize I'm clinging to him, holding on for dear life.

The elevator chimes and we step on with some others from the party. When the doors close, a sense of relief hits me like a tsunami. I breathe away the tears that come to my eyes, not wanting to cry with witnesses.

Without saying a word, Heath pulls me against his chest. I wrap my arms around his waist and rest my head on his shoulder. My tears fade. His touch calms me like nothing else can, as scary as that is to admit.

"I'm sorry I was late," he says beneath the volume of the elevator's crooning jazz. His expression is apologetic. Morose, in a way. It surprises me.

"It's okay."

The shadow of a smirk twitches on his lips. "Really?"

I rub my hand up and down his chest. After today, the harsh words, regrets, and disappointment I've felt in myself, the pain of admitting I want Heath close to me pales in comparison. "Really."

The elevator stops and the couple next to us gets off. Heath keeps looking at me with those gray eyes.

I don't know what I'm thinking—if I'm thinking at all—but when the doors close, I lean closer. He doesn't move away. My eyes drop to his lips. With his hand at the nape of my neck, he pulls me to him. I close my eyes and hold my breath, waiting, wanting to feel his kiss. His lips brush lightly against mine right as the elevator slows.

We step away from each other, and our eyes catch. The look of reluctance on his face leaves my body buzzing with a confusing mix of sensations. In a way, I'm glad we were interrupted. Kissing isn't part of the contract, but neither is piecing me back together when I'm lying broken on the ground.

He takes my hand again, leading me out of the elevator, and I know exactly where we're going.

~

In Heath's bed, the lights are low and the passion is high. I can't remember the last time I felt this way. Uninhibited, unafraid to be open and raw with someone, but for the first time in years, I feel like I can trust him.

Maybe it wouldn't hurt to finally let him in. Just a little bit.

Heath inhales a sharp breath when my lips crest his head. The salty taste of his excitement coats the tip of my tongue. His hand settles against my cheek, appreciating me rather than urging me to continue. I can't take it any longer.

I push myself up and crawl onto his lap. In his seated position, he reaches for the little packet beside him, but I don't let him finish tearing it open before I have him straddled and placed at my entrance.

He stops me from sinking onto him. "Babe, wait. I don't have—"

"I don't care," I breathe.

"Yes, you do." But I don't. Right now, all I care about is quelling my urge. I wrap my arms around his neck and widen my knees.

"Teagan." His breath trembles as he fights himself. Still, he stops me. With more sense than I can possibly muster, he rolls on the condom and pulls me back into position. Pushing my hips down, I finally feel him, stretching me, filling me, relieving me of my anxiety inch by delicious inch.

His hand grips my ass while I slide myself up and down his length. Bracing myself with both hands behind his neck, I watch his face twist when his head falls back with a moan. I drop harder onto his lap, my body numb to everything but the heat building inside me. His eyes look into mine with insistence, but the pleasure is too deep. I tangle my fingers in his hair while my body shudders with the feeling rushing through me, and I don't fight him when he rolls me onto my back beneath him.

He strokes it slow and deep, his perfect body on full display as he pulls himself out to the tip and plunges back inside me. Fast and deliberate, his hips pump between my thighs while he stares down at me. Sweat glistens against his skin as he pants.

"Yes." I sigh when the pleasure blooms inside me. "Just like that." Heath moans as if in acknowledgment.

"Fuck," he whispers, never stopping his pace, his thumb doing lazy circles against my favorite spot. The feeling makes me quiver around him. I'm close and he knows it.

Falling forward, he lies on me and buries his head in my neck. He pulls my legs up by the back of my thighs and fucks me, hard and fast.

My moan comes out like a gasp. As basic as the position is, his intensity makes it so hot. His breathy moans in my ear, his muscular body rolling on top of mine while our hips clash violently. He's hard, deep, hitting all the right places. My eyes roll back and my legs shake.

"Oh my god," I groan. "Heath, baby, yes. Yes!" I barely recognize the voice spewing from my mouth. His arm wraps around me and a hand cradles my head. His grip on my nape makes me feel dominated, supported. Touching me like this, I'll let him have me any way he wants me. I'll let him have all of me. "Oh god. Yes."

It's too much. I'm so close but I don't want to let go just yet. His lips claim my neck, his teeth soon after. My nails claw the skin of his back and his ass. His moan sets off a spark inside me and I clench around him. Then I lose myself to him completely.

I cry out when the orgasm tears through me. He keeps stroking as my body grips and releases him, each wave blinding me and drowning me in intoxicating, consuming ecstasy.

My limbs fall limp as he continues to take me, the orgasm still rolling through me. With a groan, his hips shudder and ruin his rhythm. His pace slows, and after a few more delicious thrusts, stops.

With my head still cradled in his hand, his other wrapped around my thigh, I lie swimming underneath him. I trail my palms over the scratches I left on his back, ready to apologize and compliment him when I can form words again. But when his shoulders shake, I go cold.

"Are you okay?" I ask.

He leaves me, hiding his face as he moves to the edge of the bed. He fiddles with the condom, but I can tell he's crying.

With my head still floating from my orgasm, I barely manage to cover myself and crawl over to sit beside him. As I watch him cry, I try to make sense of what is happening. "Heath. What's going on?"

"It's nothing," he says.

"It's obviously something." I grip the sheet to my chest and lean over to get a better view of his face. "You're freaking me out. Tell me what's going on."

He looks up at the ceiling, wiping a tear from his eye. "Seeing you hurting tonight, it set me off because—" He exhales, avoiding the words he knows he will say next. "I've been going through some shit with my mom lately. I can't help her, and it is killing me."

"Your mom?" I ask, still trying to comprehend the scene happening before me. "Is she okay?"

"No." I wait for him to elaborate. "When I snapped at you after

Vegas, it had nothing to do with you. I was fighting with my dad because he keeps putting my mom in rehab."

"Wait. What?"

"It's not what you're thinking. I mean, it is, but . . . can I tell you without you judging her?"

"Why would I—? Of course you can. Is she all right?"

"She's—" He takes a moment to collect his thoughts. "She has been abusing pills. But she's not addicted to *them* she's addicted to being thin."

Shock makes it difficult to process his words. How did I not know this was happening?

He continues. "She's been on and off diet pills for forever, ever since she was in pageants. Since my grandma died, she's been in a dark place, and her old coping mechanisms came back." The look of shame on his face breaks my heart. "The pills are just unregulated amphetamines. When she takes them for long enough, she loses track of reality, what year it is, everything. Doctors think it's drug-induced psychosis, and that the cycle will continue unless she gets help for the eating disorder she's struggled with for decades, but Dad finds the pills and instantly sends her away to rehab. Then when he leaves town, she begs me to get her out, and I have to decide if I want her to be miserable or want Dad to be pissed at me for going against him."

Jesus. "Is that why he cut you off?"

"Yeah." He wipes his cheek, but still can't look at me.

"I'm sorry I laughed about you getting cut off. Had I known why . . ." I want to apologize for not knowing what was going on, how serious it was, but we weren't supposed to be talking this way. We weren't supposed to be talking in *any* way.

"No, you were right to laugh. It was past time for me to grow up, and it has been good for me. I just wish he had done it for other reasons, you know?"

"I'm sorry about what is happening with your mom too."

Heath looks at me and his brow crumples again. "Teags, what were you doing in the bathroom at the party?" His eyes stare into mine, pleading for the truth.

My muscles tense. After everything he told me about his mom, I know what he must assume about me. "It's not what you think," I say. "I threw up, but it wasn't intentional. Tonight stressed me out and I just . . . couldn't keep it down."

"But what about the rest of the time? Are you eating enough? Do you feel guilty or anxious when you do?"

I can't answer his questions, because I'd have to admit it to myself first.

My eyes well with tears. It's not pity behind his words, it's the understanding no one else seems to have. I feel seen for the first time in a while. It hurts, but in the way it hurts to remove a bandage to clean the wound beneath it. A helpful sort of pain.

I stare at him but don't know what to say. I don't want to lie to him after he told me so much truth. "Sometimes, yeah," I admit past the lump in my throat. "Please don't be upset. I'm fine, I promise."

"But I want you to be better than fine, Teags. It's not okay for you to get so anxious you can't eat."

"I know. Usually I can deal with it, but today—" I want to cry again. "It was a lot."

"What happened?"

I shake my head, looking through the air to gather all the pieces into a single sentence. "I'm still cleaning up the mess from Vegas, my parents are the way they usually are, and Rowan . . . he hates me."

"Hates you?"

"Yeah. He thinks I'm perfect, that I've never made a mistake. But you know that's not true."

"No one is perfect, but you're pretty damn close."

"It makes me feel like shit," I admit. "The whole time I've been killing myself to make my parents happy, they've been turning it around to put more pressure on him."

"Your parents have always been on your asses. You shouldn't have to feel you're not enough if you don't do everything they want," he says. "Did you tell him that?"

I shake my head. "He wasn't in a place to listen to me. And even if that was true, I thought I was helping him by being the perfect kid they wanted. I can't remember the last time I did something I wanted to do until . . ." I hesitate to admit it. "Until I did this. With you."

He gives a weak laugh. "Yeah, well . . . me either."

Tears cloud my eyes until I can no longer make out the features of his face. I wipe them away before they fall.

Heath's hand strokes against my back. "I know we have our shit, but I don't want you to feel like you have to struggle on your own." Tears choke him again. He breathes them away, then looks me in the eye. "I love what we're doing and I love the contract. The sex is amazing, Teags. Seriously. But sometimes, I just . . . I fucking miss having you as my best friend."

I twist my lips to keep them from quivering. His words hurt me as much as they heal me. It is difficult to think about how close we were and be able to separate it from the pain that tore us apart. So much happened that we can't fix, so much we can't erase, but part of me misses him too.

Moving closer, I wrap my arm around him. He hugs me back. "I'm still here," I say into his shoulder. His grip tightens.

We let go and look away from each other. I dry my face and Heath clears his throat. The silence lingers.

"Now that we've made that awkward as fuck, do you want to have sex again?" he asks.

"Yeah."

TWENTY-NINE
Heath

I wake up in a bush. Not the fun kind.

Teagan's hair is halfway up my nose. I push it from my face and settle back onto the pillow. Somehow, we're spooning. My eyes trace over her body laid against me. One arm folded against her bare chest, the other outstretched, her fingers woven between mine. How we ended up this way, I don't remember, but she looks comfortable. I am too.

Inching forward, I brush my lips against her nape, smelling her cocoa butter–sweet scent. With a kiss, I taste her skin as I continue to breathe her in.

Last night was a trip. The last thing I expected to do was cry like a bitch, but here we are. I didn't know she was dealing with the shit she was. I guess she didn't know what I was dealing with either. Mortifying or not, it felt good to let it out. I'm happy last night is behind us, and even happier that Teagan is still here. Another violation of the contract, but right now, I couldn't care less.

My phone buzzes loudly against my nightstand. Careful not to wake her, I roll to my side and reach to grab it. Shelley's message glares on my screen.

Shelley: I can wait to see you tonight :)

I look at Teagan, then back at my phone. So much went down last night, I completely forgot about my rain check with Shelley.

"Why is your apartment so cold?" Teagan grumbles.

I didn't know she was awake. "Hey."

Her hand squeezes mine before her fingers slip away. She rolls to her back, still in my arm, and stretches with a cute little squeak. I try not to stare at her tits as she does.

Her eyes blink open and look up at me. "Sorry, I didn't mean to fall asleep."

"It's fine. I know I wore you out."

"He's so meek in the morning." She brushes her hands over her forehead, her eyes going wide when she reaches her hairline. "Damn it."

She sits up to mess with it, taking her chest from my view but replacing it with her perfect ass. She looks like a Greek muse when she pulls the white sheet over her chest, holding it there with a propped up knee, her hair tumbling into her face as she unravels it pin by pin.

I lean up beside her, and she glances at me. Her hesitation mimics mine. I don't know if she expects me to kick her out or take her again. I'm not sure which I want to do either.

"Do you want breakfast?" I ask.

"Um." She thinks for an insulting length of time. "Yeah, sure. From where?"

"Here."

"There's a restaurant downstairs?"

I chuckle. "No, *here*. I'll make some."

She continues to stare at me. "Make breakfast? *You?*"

"Cut me some slack. I turn your uptight ass out like it's nothing. You think I can't figure out how to make avocado toast?"

"Well . . ."

"Shut up." I laugh.

I climb out of the bed and grab some pants from my drawer, watching as she takes the sheet with her when she follows me. She curses when she finds only her dress and heels on the floor.

"You can borrow some of my clothes."

She grins. "Thanks."

I leave her for the kitchen, grabbing what I need and getting to work. As I'm sorting pans, lighting burners, splitting avocados, my phone buzzes on the counter again. I ignore it and crack the first egg, listening to the perfect sizzle as it hits the pan.

"This is actually happening?" Teagan says when she finally emerges from my bedroom. She swims in my favorite Nike jogger set, her hair parted in the middle and braided down either side, two little curls escaping by each ear. "You're cooking. In a kitchen. And nothing is on fire."

"Yeah. Look, I can even do this." I concentrate on my flip, lifting the pan at the right time and catching the egg in the perfect place.

She looks impressed, pulling out a stool to watch from the kitchen island behind me. "I'm not gonna lie. This is kind of turning me on."

Good.

I give the eggs a dash of this and a sprinkle of that before sliding them onto the plate in front of her. "Cracked black pepper *and* paprika? Heath, if you want to bend me over the counter again, just say that."

A smirk tugs at my cheeks. "Don't give me suggestions."

While wiping the pan, I watch her eye her plate. No hesitation crosses her face when she picks up her fork, or when she takes a bite. I exhale with relief. She's okay, relatively speaking, like she said. I lean forward and press a kiss to her cheek. She returns my smile when I leave her for the range. Poaching is still a little out of my realm, but me and a runny yolk have an understanding.

When I turn back around, she looks pissed. "What?"

She glares at me with those big eyes, but a little smile perks at her lips. "How are these eggs so fucking good?"

"You're lying."

"No! I'm legit mad at you right now."

Inside, I'm beaming. "Funny how being forced to be self-sufficient makes you grow up. Don't tell my dad."

"Your secret is safe with me."

I know it is. At this point, most of my secrets are *only* safe with her. "Do you want some orange juice? Coffee?"

"Yes."

"Which one?"

"Yes."

With a laugh, I set a mug and a kettle next to her, then pour her a glass of juice. Sliding onto the stool next to her, I notice her plate is almost empty when she takes the juice from me. I'm glad she told me what was really happening with her. Worrying that she was struggling in the same way as Mom almost broke me. Not that having her parents fucking with her head is much better, but at least there's a way I can help her.

"Hey, uh . . ." I trail off. It's still awkward. "Thanks for last night."

"I should thank you too. Having four orgasms was cool or whatever."

"Damn. If I knew cooking was all it took to get you to be nice to me, I would have done it sooner."

She grins at me. "I hate you, but maybe not *everything* about you."

A smirk pulls at my cheek. "I'll take it."

"I should tell you." She puts her hand on my knee and gives me the human version of puppy dog eyes. Bad news. "You're likely stuck when it comes to your mom's treatment. As far as I know, a spouse is the default decision maker unless a health care proxy is modified to designate someone else. And that would still only come into effect if they deem her incapacitated or not sound of mind."

My brain swirls while attempting to translate her words into English. "What does that mean?"

"Legally, your dad is the default person who gets to make decisions for her when she can't. She could change that if she wanted, or if she felt she needed to."

That I understood, but I wish I didn't. My mom is making her own decisions. She doesn't want my help. Maybe it's her way of protecting me, or *coddling* me, like Dad says.

Teagan gives me a hesitant look, but I appreciate her straight answer. I let my eyes fall to my plate, nodding instead of replying with words. Her hand squeezes my knee. "I can get you a legal consult to verify, but it's ultimately her decision in what treatment she gets, if any. I'm sorry."

Even if my dad is convincing her to go to rehab rather than a psychiatrist, it's still her choice. She'll go to rehab like he wants, call me to get her out, I'll do it, Dad will be pissed, we won't talk, and I'll get blamed while Mom doesn't get better. And we'll do it over and over until *she* wants it to change.

I shake my head. "Don't be sorry. I figured as much."

The kettle clicks. She turns her attention from me to the French press. I watch her absentmindedly chew on her lip while she focuses on pouring the water and putting the plunger into place. She's so goddamn beautiful when she's just *existing*. If there wasn't scalding water between us, I'd happily toss her onto the countertop and convince her to let me take her right now.

I slide my hand down her back, letting it linger on her hip. "What about you?"

"Me?"

"I can't get your parents to fuck off, but there has to be something I can do. What's the next item on your list of stressors?"

She stares at me for a moment, then looks down. "The wedding. Honestly, I can handle the event coordination and vendor shit, it's just the guys."

"Well, shit. I know I need to save on rent, but a quadruple homicide is gonna put me in a small apartment for a *while*."

"Stop it." She laughs.

"Did you tell Mary about what Ryan said to you in Vegas?"

"What did he say?"

"That he should marry you instead of her."

Her eyes study me to find the motive behind my question. "You heard that?"

"Yeah." I'm usually not territorial, but I would have dislocated Ryan's jaw if she hadn't started laughing right after he said it.

"I didn't and I won't. Ryan loves Mary more than anything. He got in his own head about having to be a big boy now, then got fucked up and made it my problem. Brett is the worst influence ever."

"How was that his fault?"

"His secret party favors." She taps the side of her nose. "I'm honestly shocked it wasn't Ritchie."

Same, but he brought a different type of drama to that weekend. "I can help keep the guys in check from now through the wedding, no problem."

"Seriously?"

"Seriously. You have no idea how much I've been wanting an excuse." I crack my knuckles. "You won't hear a peep from Brett or Ritchie until we get back. But what should I do about Jeremy?"

"I don't know if we can do anything about that. He's so done with us, and at this point, I can't even be mad."

"Why?"

"The things he said weren't wrong. Have we—" She turns to me, her knees settling between mine. I can't keep my hand from her thigh. "Have we been dealing with their shit so long that we've given up on expecting them to be better? I know they're problematic in a global sense, but . . . are we the ones tolerating *their* bullshit, or are *we* the shitty friends and haven't realized it yet?"

I snort. "Babe, be for real. Look at us. We're fucking amazing."

She chuckles. "Right. And so humble."

"We have shitty friends, for sure."

"*For sure.*"

We share a laugh, finally. Her smile does things to me. It makes me want to burn everything to the ground to make it stay, and at the same time, I want to wipe it off her face by kissing her until her lips bleed.

When I inch forward, she turns away. "I am running *so* late. I need to grab my shit and get out of here," she says.

"Oh. Yeah. My bad." I move out of her way. She disappears into my bedroom again.

What is wrong with me? We have a little cry sesh and great sex and now I'm tripping. Teagan being a little friendlier with me—still only a fraction of what we used to have—doesn't change anything. She made an entire contract just to make sure our situationship didn't turn into anything more, and I agreed to it.

At the time.

I try to find something to ground myself and bring me back to reality. The best I can manage is to scald my mouth with my coffee.

Teagan comes back out with that massive dress thrown over her arm. Her shoes dangle from her fingers somewhere beneath it. "I'll meet you back here tonight," she says. "Seven?" Only then do I remember.

"Um . . . I kind of have another date tonight." I say the words and instantly want them back.

"Kind of?" She looks at me. Her eyebrow lifts in understanding. "You're getting serious."

"Well, no. But I promised her we would go, and it would be shitty to cancel on her. Right?"

I want her to give me a reason not to go. Say anything to show me I'm not making all this shit up in my mind. I like Shelley. A lot. But she doesn't make me feel like *this*.

Saying what's on my mind—especially before I have it figured out for myself—will ruin everything. It's in the contract, all thanks to me. Catching feelings is a full stop. If we end it now, it's all over, and she disappears from my life like last summer. I don't know what I want exactly, but I know I don't want to lose her two seconds after getting her back.

"Don't do that thing," she stops me.

"What thing?"

She sets her heavy clothes on the stool with a sigh. "That thing where you get in your head about how you feel and then turn into a self-sabotaging dumbass."

I can't help but smile. "Your assessments of me are always spot-on."

She steps closer, coming to stand right in front of me. My hands find her waist as I stare up at her. The look in her eyes makes my next breath a struggle.

"Tell me the truth." She crosses her arms and tilts her head to the side. "Are you catching feelings?"

I gape at her in surprise, wondering how she sees through me so well. It scares me, but the answer is right there, hanging in the tension between us.

"Yeah," I admit. "I think I am."

Her mouth twitches into a little smirk. "Then we pause."

Reality slaps me across the face.

"Pause?"

"That's what's in the contract, isn't it?"

That's what we agreed to do if I caught feelings for someone else. Not if I caught feelings for *her*.

She doesn't see it.

Who was I kidding? Teagan hates me. There's not a world where she would ever let herself have feelings for me that are greater than her contempt.

"Give it a chance, Heath. A real one. You deserve a nice girl who makes you happy." Her chuckle is a punch in the gut. A nail in the coffin of my dead hopes and unrequited desires. She turns away to grab her things, slipping from my grasp. "And, if you accidentally scare her off when your inner fuckboy slips out, you know where to find me."

I don't know what to say, so I default to dumbass, just like she said. "Cool. I'll, um, call you if something changes, I guess?"

"Don't call me." Her smile shows the kind intent behind her words. She swings the folded dress over one arm and hugs me with the other. I grip her back, still confused by what's happening. "Have fun with Shelley. I mean it." She kisses my cheek and pulls away.

"Okay."

With that, she leaves. And for some reason, I let her.

THIRTY

Teagan

Why does it hurt?

Heath and I got carried away after the party, breaking rules we put in place for a reason. Any more crossed lines and we'd be back in that place again, reliving the shit we went through, ripping each other to shreds all over again. I do not want to be with Heath—most days, I don't even *like* Heath—but sex does stupid things to your brain, and the more sex you have, the more logic goes out the window. He called it at the right time.

The whole point of the contract was to keep feelings from happening. There was supposed to be nothing between us except text and sex, but that's hard when we have so much history. Bit by bit, he crept in. And I let him. It scares me to think part of me wanted him to be there the whole time.

A step back is better. It's room to breathe and regain some sense while I'm not grasping at everything in reach just to feel some sort of comfort. It's time to recenter myself and focus on what will heal me rather than hurt me.

But why do both of those lead back to Heath?

"Teagan." My mother grabs my attention.

I lift the phone back to my ear. "Sorry, I was reaching for something. What did you say?"

At work, it's late, and the room is empty except for me and the intern scanning documents in the opposite corner. The dark office is quiet other than the scanner's unending whirring sound while stacks of boxes slowly make their way off my desk and into the cloud. I wish I could evaporate too. Picking up extra hours at work before my week off was supposed to keep my mind busy and avoid opportunities to disappoint my parents again, especially if I end up having to ask them for money to cover my rent. Unfortunately, Mom is too familiar with my job and my schedule to think she can't call me on the office line.

"You left. Without telling us." She nags me about the party again.

"I told you I wasn't feeling well."

"You missed the announcement and Lenny's speech. We went to introduce you to an important client, and you were gone. That was unprofessional and very out of character for you."

"I'm sorry. I wasn't feeling well." I repeat the phrase as if it's a record, spinning around with no end. "Can I call you back? I need to work."

She sighs. "We'll talk more at our dinner."

"Okay." I hang up the phone with a groan.

Sunday dinner is going to be a shit show. I don't have the strength to argue or to tell them the truth about why I left the party. For a week they've been on me about it, taking turns calling me as if they don't work in the same office and live in the same house. It's another coordinated attack and I have no defense. Rowan hasn't spoken to me. Levi is out of state for a game. I'm an easy target, and all I want is to have an excuse to disappear. All I want is everything I can't have.

My phone rings again with a call from the front desk. "Hey, Brooke," I answer with a sigh. "Is it my dad this time?"

"No, baby." She lowers her voice to a whisper. "One of your white boys is here."

"What? Which one?" I hate that I have to clarify.

"He's tall. Has muscles. Looks *real* good."

Heath? My heart races against my will. "Be right there."

I scurry out of the office but force myself back to a normal walking pace before I am in view from the lobby. Brooke makes eyes with me, then tosses them in the direction of my guest waiting in the conference room. When I see him, my heartbeat slows with disappointment.

"Hey, Teagan," Lenny says.

I look side to side, trying to find the distortion in the universe that put him in front of me in Heath's place. His familiar broad shoulders and puppy dog eyes no longer "look good" to me. They remind me of the shitty things he said, and how nice it felt to avoid him for the last two months. "What are you doing here?"

He stares down at his feet. "Um." He shifts his weight, tucking his hands into his pockets before finally looking up. "I owe you an apology."

Surprise steals the words right out of my mouth, and I can't snatch them back before he continues.

"When we broke up, I shouldn't have said those things or called you names," he says. "You're a good person, and you have the right to live your life the way you want. It's not my place to judge you."

There's a glitch in the matrix for sure. "I'm sorry, I'm confused. Do you no longer think I'm a slut, or are you no longer *judging* me for being a slut?"

"No! I didn't mean that, I—" He fidgets again, dodging eye contact. Watching him squirm is oddly satisfying. "I thought we had something special. When you told me you didn't want me, I was heartbroken, and I said a lot of stupid things to get back at you. I'm really sorry."

"Well, thank you for saying that." I watch his mouth turn up in a weak grin. Surely, he isn't expecting an apology in return. "I was frustrated, but I didn't mean to hurt you. I hope you know that."

"I do." He seems sincere, but I can't trust it yet. "I tried to catch you at the party last weekend, but . . ." *I was with Heath*, I fill in his blank. "Is that guy your boyfriend?"

"No," I say a bit too quickly. "He's just a friend."

"Cool," he says. "I came here to ask if you would ever consider taking me back."

Without meaning to, a laugh escapes. I choke it back when I see the expression on Lenny's face. "Wait, really?"

"Yeah. There are a lot of changes that will need to happen, but I'm open to those—to listening and learning—whatever you need. I still love you, and I really want a chance to start over."

My mouth is hanging open, but I close it as soon as I notice. I love a man who can grovel. But I don't love Lenny. That doesn't mean I *can't* love him one day. Probably. To be completely honest, I'm not sure it matters if I ever do. My life is working overtime to show me love doesn't exist, and I'm finding little evidence to suggest the contrary.

"It's a lot to drop on you at once." Lenny breaks me from my mental circles. "Will you think about it?"

"I will, yeah."

He steps closer, his eyes tracing me up and down. "Would you want to think about it over dinner? And . . . after dinner too?"

"After—? Oh." I catch his meaning right as I ask.

"I want to—" He looks around, verifying we're out of earshot. Knowing Brooke, we aren't. "I want to try some of the things we talked about."

Mr. Nice Guy shows up with a two-month redemption arc and tells me he wants to eat me out? What the fuck is happening?

"Are you serious?"

He nods. "My family is going out to the Berkshires after the weekend. How about the weekend after next?"

"I can't. I'll be in Spain for Ryan's wedding."

"Oh." He looks as surprised as I feel. "The summer's almost over already?"

"Right?"

He steps even closer. His hand runs down my arm, leaving a painful chill in its wake. "Then maybe call me tomorrow instead?"

People place love on a pedestal, but ultimately, does love matter more than the ability to commit to a lifetime of partnership, just like a successful business? It's my parents' story all over again, and everything they've wanted for me.

As perfect as it would be to fulfill my parents' wishes and connect the dots of my future with a nice, crisp line, if I'm real with myself, is that even worth it?

Still confused, I agree. "I'll think about it."

"Great." He looks at me, then his eyes drop to my lips. With a hand on my cheek, he leans in.

I don't fight it when he kisses me. It's over as soon as it started. Looking at him, I feel defeated.

"See you soon," he says, and leaves.

I wait until the elevator arrives to go back to my desk, but catch the look on Brooke's face. "He's not the white boy you wanted to see, was he?" She already knows the answer to that. "It's none of my business."

"But?"

She acknowledges her transparency with a sigh. "*But* . . . you work hard, all the time, and sometimes on the wrong things. You don't have to make everyone around you comfortable all the time. You deserve to be comfortable too."

Do I?

~

It's four in the afternoon the next day, but caffeine is warranted. I slept like shit last night, wondering what to do about Lenny, trying to figure out how much of myself I can sacrifice before I'm in pieces on the dinner table tomorrow, letting my parents pick apart what's left like the emotional vultures they are.

The café is busy enough to distract me, the music loud enough to drown out my thoughts. I order my iced almond milk latte and watch the baristas dance to the music while they prepare it. My brain focuses on the banality of the beat and the strangers' lack of rhythm rather than worrying about getting scolded by my parents and possibly getting back together with my ex. The toxic voice in my brain imagines a world where *Hey, Lenny decided he'd eat my pussy now, so I took him back. Are you happy?* is both an appropriate statement to make to my parents and one that will satisfy them enough to leave me alone.

I need to touch all of the fucking grass.

"Here you go." The barista slides the compostable cup over to me.

"Thank you so much." I shake off my thoughts, snap on my lid, and stab my straw into the hole with a bit too much enthusiasm. Ready to go home and resume my existential crisis, I turn around and freeze when I see him.

Heath.

And a blond woman standing next to him.

I look around, trying to find a route to avoid them or a place to hide, but it's too late. He spots me and his eyes widen, his stupid, handsome face looking like he got caught in the act. "Hey, Teags," he says.

"Hey."

He pulls me into a hug with one arm, as friends do. I try to smile at him, but I can't. He looks good. His dark hair falls in perfect waves above a fresh fade. Body tight. Smelling nice. *Ugh.*

"What are you doing here?" he asks.

"What am I doing in *my* coffee shop?" I say, lifting my straw to my mouth. "I wonder."

He smirks. "Got it."

I turn to his companion. "Hi. You must be Shelley."

"Yes! Hi!" She's a smiley one. Short, curvy. Pretty too.

"It's great to meet you finally. I've heard so much about you."

"You have?"

We both look at Heath. He stares at me while an awkward silence settles. I raise an eyebrow.

"I'll go order for us," Shelley says to him. "What do you want?"

"Just an Americano. Thanks."

"No problem!"

She leaves us, and in a rare moment, I'm at a loss for words. "She's cute," is the best I can come up with. "*Great* tits too."

Heath laughs. The awkwardness breaks a little. "How are you?" he asks. "Everything good? We haven't talked since—" *We paused.*

Barely a week has passed, and it feels like a month. What can I say to him? That I fucking miss him? That standing next to him right now is the first time I've felt alive in days, even though it's killing me that I can't touch him? That he shouldn't try to be happy with someone else, he should be miserable with me instead?

"I'm fine," I lie. "Life is a smidge above mid right now."

Rather than giving me the laugh I expected, he stares at me with those gray eyes and waits for me to tell him the truth. But I can't. Not the full truth, at least.

"Okay, fine. My parents are pissed about me leaving the party. They keep calling me about it and I don't know what to tell them at dinner tomorrow."

"Blame it on me," he says. "Tell them I got bored and made you leave with me. It'll be believable. I *am* a douchebag, right?"

I want to laugh but it doesn't come out. "True."

"Or—and this is going to sound crazy—don't go to dinner."

Now the laughter comes out. "You're right. That is crazy."

"Like I told you before, you don't have to do anything you don't want to. Blame it on me, focus on getting through the wedding, then you can figure it out when you get back."

"Really?"

"Really." He gives me a lopsided grin. "I've got you, remember?"

I swallow away the emotion climbing up my throat. I'm still too raw to have him look at me like that, saying all the right things at exactly the wrong time. "I remember."

His little girlfriend comes back over. She's not someone I'd expect him to go for, but that's probably a good thing. He looks lighter, at ease—nothing like our last night together. I picture them together, Shelley making his smile as wide as she does, her taking my place in his bed. My body burns with jealousy.

I should be happy for him, but my heart hurts too much. "You two have fun. I'll see you on the floating city Brett calls a boat."

Heath's sarcastic laugh sounds more like a hum. "Yeah, can't wait."

I place my hand behind his head and press my lips to his cheek. I pull away and look at him, regretting what I did, yet wishing I could do more. "Bye."

His eyes never leave mine. "Bye."

I wave to Smiley to diffuse any tension. "Bye, Shelley."

She waves back. "Bye! Nice to meet you!"

"Nice to meet you too."

~

I didn't make it home before I started crying.

Sitting on the floor beside my bed like the definitively sane person I am, I sequester myself from the sights and sounds of Jeremy packing in the next room. I wipe my face, listening to the traffic and sipping my coffee, waiting to go numb again.

This is how summers always are. The sun feels amazing at first, but the longer I try to stay in it, the more I get burned. Life isn't full of sunshine and happy times, and it's not supposed to be, but I wish I could have more than three months a year to pretend it is.

I curl my knees up and stare down at my phone sitting beside me. When I tap the screen, the light adds a soft glow to the shadow I'm in. Lenny wants me to call him—he's giving me a way to smooth things over with him and my parents—a surefire way to reduce the stress my parents will pile onto me at dinner tomorrow, and still, I hesitate.

Make the call. I try to convince myself, but I only get as far as opening my contacts. I nibble at my nail while I shift my gaze to the ceiling. *Make the call, make the call, make the call.*

I tap the Call button but tap to end it just as quickly. My hesitancy isn't because of Heath. I won't let it be. But seeing him with someone else was an unexpectedly painful source of encouragement.

Still, I don't want to hear Lenny's voice or have to debate someone over the validity of the feelings I still can't discern. A text is the best I can do.

> **Me**: Hey, Lenny. I've given it some thought, and I think it's best if we try to be friends. You are a good guy, and you are going to be a great business partner one day, but we don't have to be in a relationship to make that work. Can you be okay with that?

At the end of the day, I can keep crying, wishing I could have something I knew wasn't mine in the first place, or I can move forward. I can be the friend I said I would be.

I hit Send, not waiting for Lenny's response before making a different call instead.

It rings three times. I decide to hang up just as I hear, "Hello?"

"Hi, Mrs. Reynolds." I'm not sure what to call Heath's mom now. Her name is Manamea, but I used to call her *mama*. "It's Teagan."

She gasps. "Teagan! Sweetheart! How have you been?"

I haven't heard her voice in so long. I forget how comforting it is. "I've been . . . I've been okay. How have you been?"

Her slight hesitation speaks volumes. "I've been okay too."

"There's something I wanted to talk to you about. If that's all right?"

"Of course! You can talk to me about anything. Always."

I take a breath to calm my emotions. "It's about something Heath said. How much time do you have?"

THIRTY-ONE
Heath

At lunch, Teagan's calendar reminder buzzes on my phone. It's been almost two weeks since we paused, but I still haven't canceled them. I can't stop thinking about the last time I saw her—I can't stop thinking about her *most* of the time. Was I trying to run into her? No. Did I come up with the stupid idea to take Shelley to the café Teagan introduced me to because of the slim chance I would run into her again? Yeah. I need to let it go.

Teagan doesn't want me, and she's made that perfectly clear for *years*. She reconfirmed that the minute she assumed my desire to be with Shelley, not her. So why can't I accept that? Why don't I *want* to accept that?

"Hey." Shelley nudges my arm. "What are you thinking about so hard?" She leans her cheek on her fist and gives me that cute smile.

Hanging out with Shelley is a nice break from the guys right before the wedding, but I can barely pull my mind away from Teagan long enough to give Shelley the attention she deserves. Telling her the truth would probably hurt her, so I go with the typical, "It's nothing."

"It didn't look like nothing."

"It's just shit with my friends again. Drama always peaks this time of year."

"The heat makes everyone crazy," she says.

"It does." I dismiss the calendar reminder and turn off my screen. "Ready to go?"

"Yeah."

Lunch is much less expensive than dinner. One of the new tricks I've learned while being an ex–rich kid. There's not a great way to hang out in this city without spending money, unless they come over to your place to hang out. I still haven't had a girl in my apartment without the intention of getting her naked, so cheap lunches and happy hours it is.

Shelley lives close to the restaurant, so we walk. It's hot but not hot enough to warrant a cab ride for a few blocks. Another way to save. I have mastered this budgeting shit.

"I wish I could go with you to the wedding," she says. I'm not sure if she is hinting at something or not. "Ibiza? That sounds amazing."

"It's just another island."

"Well, it sounds fun. I've never been to Europe. It's in Europe, right?"

I smile. "Yeah, Spain. I would take you with me if I had a plus-one. And if my friends weren't a bunch of assholes." I wouldn't, even if I had money to afford my own—

Shit.

Everything happened so fast, I didn't even think about sharing a room with Teagan again. Surely, she secured a double-occupancy one again, but that's semantics. We'll be together in a small space. Alone.

The thought does something funny in my chest, but I can't think about that right now.

"It's really stressing you out, huh?"

I shake my thoughts away. There's no point in worrying about the future. "It's over the top for no reason. I think they're trying to one-up our other friend's wedding from last summer."

Last summer. Memories of Teagan's sweat-glistened skin and moans flash through my head. Ugh, I'm thinking about her again. I should give up on thinking altogether. Insert joke about being a dumbass here, I guess.

"Okay, so explain your friends to me again. The one getting married is . . . ?"

"Ryan."

"Yes, Ryan. I remember that. He's the whiny one." Her correctness makes me laugh. I'm glad she enjoys trash talking my friends as much as I do. "Who got married last year?"

"Brett."

"And the others are—there's six of you, right?"

"Right. It's Ryan and Brett, Jeremy, who is about to move to Philly with his fiancé, Ritchie the toxic one, and—" I stop. Shelley looks at me expectantly. "And Teagan."

"Teagan is the one I met at the café?"

"Yeah."

"Oh my god, she is so pretty. And *tall.* Is she a model?"

"Not that I know of."

"She's really nice," she remarks. I snort with laughter. "What?"

Teagan and *nice* don't go in the same sentence unless we're discussing her ass. "Not if you know her well enough. She can be a little mean, and she's *very* bossy, but both are needed in a group like ours."

"Sounds like it. The way you describe your friends reminds me of my last class. A lot of big personalities in those eight-year-olds. It's like preparing for a battle every morning."

"Yeah, that's about right."

My phone vibrates in my pocket again. When it keeps going, I pull it out and see it's Mom. *Why is she calling me?* When I miss it, I see the text she sent first.

Mom: You should come over this afternoon!

She is back from her little "spa visit," and this is the first time she has invited me over since before Vegas. I'd be more worried if she hadn't put in the exclamation mark.

Shelley turns to me and I realize we're already at her house. "Thanks for hanging out with me today," she says.

"Thanks for letting me."

Her smile lingers, and her eyes drift over me like I'm a work of art she enjoys but doesn't quite understand. She steps forward and wraps her arms around my waist. "Come upstairs with me," she whispers. Her tone does not suggest that she wants to have a beer and watch the game.

I hesitate. "Oh, um. . ."

"I know we're just friends, but that doesn't mean we can't have some fun, right?" She runs her hands up and down my chest.

The hesitancy chokes me again. Am I considering saying no? When have I ever turned down sex? Her lips are on mine before I can finish my thoughts.

I can feel the eagerness behind her lips, the heaviness of her breath while she takes control. She moves her arms to drape them over my shoulders. Reflexively, I move mine to her waist.

She ends the kiss but doesn't lean away. "Let's go upstairs."

"Okay," I agree.

Inside, it's a quick walk down a hall. Shelley's apartment is old and small, but it has some charm and a bedroom. The second the door closes, her mouth is on mine again. The velocity of her kiss pushes me back against the wall. Her hands tug at my fly. Damn.

My body wakes up, my blood going to the places it should. My pocket vibrates again. I break the kiss and put my hand inside to silence it. "Sorry."

"It's okay." She takes my hands and pulls me with her into the next room. Her bedroom.

Things move quickly. Shirts come off, my fly goes down.

My newly gained sense of decency screams at me. "I have to tell you something." This is new for me, and so uncomfortable. She looks at me. "I've had sex with someone recently. It was protected, but it was less than two weeks ago."

A beat passes before she says, "I appreciate you telling me that." Her smile widens when she sits on the edge of her bed. "I have some condoms in my drawer."

That went a million times better than expected.

I empty my pockets onto her nightstand and open the drawer. An unopened box sits inside. I rip it open and tear off a single packet. She lies back and I crawl on top of her.

We're kissing, I'm unfastening her shorts, she's pushing mine down, and it happens again. I think about Teagan.

My mind harps on the way *she* feels when she's beneath me, the way I can't calm down when I even think about getting *her* naked. But here I am, limp while trying to get with someone else, acting like a fuckboy because I can't have *her*.

I pull away. Shelley frowns. "Is something wrong?"

"I'm sorry. I don't think I can do this right now."

She looks surprised when I get up. "Right now? You're leaving for Ibiza tomorrow," she reminds me.

"I am, yeah. But it's only for a long weekend. I'll be back Tuesday."

"Right." She sounds disappointed.

"I'm really sorry."

"Don't be." She waves her disappointment away. "We're definitely not doing this if you don't want to."

"Thanks, Shell. I am sorry, though."

After I put my shirt back on and gather my things, Shelley suddenly asks, "Teagan is the friend, isn't she?"

I turn back to her. "What?"

"She's *the* friend. The one whose brother you helped—the one you said you grew apart from."

"She is." I'm not sure why it took me a moment to say that. "How did you know?"

"The way you look at her. It's like you're afraid she'll run away if you blink." She looks me in the eye. "She's more than a friend to you."

Shelley doesn't sound accusing, just curious. What is it with women and their ability to know what I'm thinking before I do? What shows on my face that gives away half of my secrets? "I'm not really sure," I admit.

"But do you want her to be?" she asks.

My silence says everything. I don't know how to answer that.

"Shelley, I'm sorry. I didn't go into this knowing I had feelings for her."

A little giggle leaves her. "Believe me, I can tell," she says, with a dimmer version of her usual smile.

"I'll see you when I get back from the wedding?"

She nods. "Right." She leans up to press her lips against my cheek. "Bye, Heath."

That didn't sound like a *See you later.* "Bye, Shelley."

~

By the time I made it to the house, Mom still hadn't returned any of my calls. She said to come over but never said why. Silas doesn't look concerned when I drive up and park. That calms my nerves a bit.

"Mom is here, right?" I ask.

"Yes, she's in the parlor."

"With Dad?"

"No." He draws out the word, and there's something quirky about his grin. He's not telling me something. Everyone's having a great time while I'm turning down sex and feeling confused as hell.

Inside, I hear Mom laughing with someone. I round the corner and find her at the table near the kitchen where we usually sit. And next to her is Teagan.

My heart jumps. *Why is she here?*

"Hi," I interrupt.

They turn to me. Teagan's face drops but my mom's lights up. "Heath, you came to visit!" She stands to hug me.

I wrap her in my arms, relieved she seems good but curious about what's going on. "You kept calling me. I was worried."

"Oh, that must have been a butt dial."

"Did you butt text me too?" I whisper. I know what she's doing. She doesn't answer. "Teagan is here."

"Yeah, I see that. Why?"

Teagan looks at me, her doe eyes sending sparks over my skin. Her hair is already done for the trip. The abundance of tiny braids twist into a looser one that hangs over her shoulder. The audacity she has, showing up looking that goddamn beautiful when I'm in peak fuckup mode.

"We just got back from shopping and doing some other things in the city," Mom says, but I don't believe her.

"Other things?"

"Oh, I completely forgot," Mom says. "I need to go call your dad. You two should sit and talk."

She kisses Teagan's cheek and whispers something to her. Teagan looks at her as if Mom just said every compliment her parents never gave her as a kid. "Thank you," she says.

Mom scurries away and Teagan and I laugh at her poorly veiled attempt to get us together. She stands up and takes a few timid strides toward me. "Hi."

"Hi."

"Why are you here?"

"We were hanging out."

"Hanging out?"

"Yes."

"You're trying to steal my mom, aren't you?"

"It's not fair to keep her all to yourself." We joke, but she avoids looking at me like she's hiding something. When she lets her eyes find me again, I swear I see tears in them. "She said I could tell you, but I wasn't sure how. I told her that you were worried about me at the party. It worried her, too, and when she wanted to help me the way *you* had been trying to help *her*, I think it clicked."

The words take a second to make sense. "You got her to see the psychiatrist?"

"Yeah."

My jaw drops. "You got her to go? Just like that?"

She grins. "I've been told I can formulate a pretty convincing argument."

I smile at her joke, but inside I'm so fucking happy I could cry. Months of fighting with my dad, trying to convince my mom to listen to me, and the second Teagan shows up in my corner, all my struggle turns into success. "You should think about becoming a lawyer or something," I say to cover my true feelings.

"I should." She chuckles.

Without another thought, I grab her hand and pull her to me. She lands against my chest. I wrap her up in my arms and whisper, "Thank you."

"You did this, not me. I'm just trying to be a good friend."

Friend isn't what I want to call her anymore, that much I know, but I don't have the balls or the words to explain that to her. Instead, I hold her tighter, savoring the way she nuzzles her head against my neck before she releases me.

"I better go," she says. "I hear there's a wedding happening this weekend."

"Right."

I let her slip from my arms, watching her as she walks away. Instant regret.

"Teags, wait."

She turns back to me with a curious expression. All the things I want to say—all the thoughts I wish I could piece together to explain how I feel—crumple beneath my fear.

"I, um . . . I'll see you tomorrow," I say.

She smirks. "Don't be late."

Watching her leave has me wanting to run after her. I can't tear my eyes from her, even when Silas appears in my peripheral.

"I believe the phrase you were looking for is 'I love you,'" he says, then strolls away.

THIRTY-TWO
Teagan

Wedding weekend has arrived. If I can make it through the next three days, I can . . . relax? No, never that, especially with all the shit I'll have to clean up with my parents when I get home, but at least my schedule will go back to normal when school starts again. I will be busy doing something I'm good at rather than disappointing myself along with everyone else—too busy to allow myself to fall for the same old trick of getting my hopes up just to have them dashed at the end of the summer.

Hiding behind my responsibilities for the weekend keeps me at a distance from everyone else's cheerfulness. Seeing their excitement only reminds me of my gloom.

All I need to do is make sure everyone is in the right place at the right time. A harrowing task for a party of fourteen. I scramble to keep everyone together during our short layover in London, and still barely keep Ritchie from missing the flight. Filling first class on both flights, there were only two hours where everyone decided to stay quiet enough to sleep. Tucking myself in the farthest corner, I still managed to make eye contact with Heath again and again. I couldn't tell if he wanted to talk to me or if I only *wished* he did—the same way I couldn't tell if he meant to say more than he did at his mom's house or if that's what *I* wanted.

But what else is there to say? A week left of summer and all this will be over. No more having time to connect without fully connecting, letting ourselves grow closer beneath the guise of meaningless sex. We can go back to our separate lives, living in two incompatible realities, and giving us space to remember why we are mutual friends and nothing more.

We arrive in Valencia at 6:00 a.m. New York time, but a second wind fueled by excitement and the midday sun shining over the crystal blue waters reconfirmed the judiciousness of my schedule. I didn't book a hotel in Valencia, instead opting to spend the night on Brett's yacht to force away the jet lag, and then arrive on the island at the hotel's check-in time.

With Felicity present, Brett is playing the role of Good Husband, leaving the bridesmaids with Ritchie, who is temporarily single after another apparent breakup with Gigi, and Heath, who is . . . Heath. Cocky, delicious, and off-limits. Two of the bridesmaids have been trying to paw at him since the jet.

In a way, I wish he *would* sleep with one of them to remind me of how much of a fuckboy he can be, but all he has done is ignore their advances. I'm pissed that I've become a person who gets mad when Heath acts like a good person. I know why, but it's difficult to get out of your feelings when the person who put you in them is being very *feelable*.

On our long walk up the pier, the wheels of my suitcase clack a droning rhythm over the wood planks, reminding me of my lack of sleep, but I have one last message to send. I grip my phone tighter, not wanting to drop it into the ocean.

E.M. WILSON

To my misfortune, I bump into Brett, who nearly knocks it out of my hands. "There she is," he says with a beaming smile. "Isn't she beautiful?"

I look up and see the behemoth he calls a boat. The sun glares off the white sides of its two-hundred-foot length and three-story height. It looks to be the size of a boutique hotel.

"That thing is fucking huge, Brett," I say. "A sentence Liss has never said before."

He bats my arm playfully but Felicity's expression doesn't disagree. She hugs his arm tighter with a smile as big as his. She loves a shiny new toy just as much as he does. I can't begin to imagine how many millions this boat costs, but he swears renting it out turns a profit. That could never be me, literally or figuratively.

I tag along, going through the motions of climbing on and handing over my bags while I put together the last of the day-of schedule. I lean against the railing beneath the shade and scan through it again. With the hairdresser showing up later and now needing to style the mother-in-law, I have to shift the start time and photo window for the guys to avoid—

"Teags."

I look up and find Heath. He's in his element. Bronze skin popping beneath a white linen shirt, his hair in perfect sea-salt waves, the length of his shorts displaying an alluring majority of his thigh tattoos. You can take the boy off the island, but . . . "Hi."

"I grabbed you this." He holds out a little paper takeaway box. "It's an egg soufflé. Balanced macros—proteins, fats, carbs. Perfect fuel for the marathon your thumbs are running right now," he says with a smirk.

He hands it to me, and I realize I forgot to eat breakfast. It's comforting the way he doesn't scold me for it or point it out; he just notices and helps. He's doing that Good Friend thing again, and I need him to stop.

"Thank you. I'll be done with this in a hot five, then I'll be better, I swear."

"The wedding is still going to happen whether things are in fifteen-minute increments or not," he teases me. "You're on a yacht in the Mediterranean. Can you let yourself enjoy it a little?"

Right now, I'd enjoy running my tongue over the muscles peeking out between his shirt's buttons, but that's illegal. "I'll try."

His gray eyes give me a once-over before I return to my phone. He's right, though. My schedule is clean enough to review with Mary, which she won't be able to do until she's sober. I have hours until that happens.

Heath leans back against the railing beside me. "You're hovering," I say.

"We're on a boat. Where else am I supposed to go?"

"It's the size of a mansion. I'm sure you can find somewhere."

He laughs. I smile at the sound until his hand grazes my arm. The light touch makes my entire body tingle. "Can I talk to you about something?"

The sincerity of his tone is concerning. "Sure. What's up?"

He looks hesitant before Ritchie flies into view like a capuchin monkey, nearly tackling Heath to the deck by his neck. Heath doesn't look amused, but Ritchie's too drunk to notice. He pulls him away by the arm, Heath grumbling as he does. He tosses a look my way that says *Sorry*.

The boat vibrates beneath my feet when we start our journey into the water. I sit down on a couch and open the little box, finding the perfectly baked pastry, a tiny fork, and two strawberries tucked in the corner. It's perfect.

A lump builds in my throat, but I push it back down and take my first bite.

~

At dinner, the full party sits together in the open-air dining room, enjoying the sunset with paella and sangria. All I want to do is go to bed, but I refuse to miss out on time with Mary or throw off my sleep schedule. My body protests. I blink and it feels like ten minutes have passed. Only the shouts of drunk boys horseplaying brings me back to consciousness.

The guys are on the deck causing havoc, as per usual. I leave them to their own devices, opting to enjoy the company of multiple women for the first time in *months*. The summer is almost over. I will have more moments like this again soon, but I need this right now.

Mary's bridesmaids are so much like her—beautiful and sociable—but have an intimidating homogeneity. Some friends, some cousins, their matching black hair falls in matching waves onto matching white resort wear. My outfit fits in, at least.

The loudest of the bunch, Zara, pours me another glass of rosé. I would be lying if I said I haven't scoped her for sapphic vibes since we arrived, but she, like the rest of their group, hasn't included me enough for me to get much of a chance. Wedding party hookups are always messy, but I'm frustrated about sharing a room with Heath when he's off-limits. Adding wine to that situation makes me inconveniently horny. I try to ignore the heat between my legs when my mind drifts to pictures of the hotel room, images of what could happen inside it, and focus only on the conversation that flows between Spanish and English, relying on Mary to keep me included.

While taking a sip, Mary reads it on my face and her eyes widen. "Oh my god. I just realized this is the first time you've met our Best Ma'am in person. Isn't she wonderful?"

The olive-skinned beauties turn to me with the same smile, like Spanish Stepford wives.

"Teagan is always stuck with Ryan and their *chicos locos*." Mary explains away my standoffish behavior. "Be gentle with her, she's not used to civility."

I love her.

"It is great to finally meet all of Ryan's friends," Zara says. The first part of her next sentence is in Spanish, then, ". . . it is odd that you are the only girl in a group of *boys*." Her tone is suspicious, implying a friendship between sexes is inherently untrustworthy.

The thought of Ryan's tweaked-out confession weighs on me, but Mary has nothing to worry about. "It's not odd. We've all been friends since we were kids," I explain. Mary's smile settles my mood. "If you want dirt on any of them, I have it."

"One of your friends—the handsome one," Zara says, ruining my hopes and my mood. "What is his name?"

"Heath." Who needs to clarify when it's either him or the gremlin, Ritchie?

"He's *muy guapo*," another says. She is one of the two who have been ogling him since we arrived. "What is his situation?" she asks.

Me, I want to say, but refrain. That's not the truth anymore. "He's seeing someone."

"Oh. Is it serious?"

My laugh is more awkward than intended. "Knowing him, probably not."

"Yes! You should go for it!" Zara encourages the other one.

My heart drops when she stands to approach him. I force myself to look away, which is stupid. No matter how intertwined we are, it changes nothing. He's with Shelley, and that's a good thing. For him at least.

"I can tell her to back off," Mary whispers to me.

"Why?"

"If you don't want her to flirt with Heath."

I study her, wondering how much she knows. When I open my mouth to speak, someone else's voice comes out instead. "Tea-*gan!*" Brett bellows, adding extra emphasis to the last syllable. He's drunk as hell, my nightmare. "It's groomsman time in the hot tub!"

"It's what time where?"

"Come on," he complains, as if I have any idea what he is talking about. He stumbles over and pulls out my chair.

"Brett, what—" He scoops me into his arms, grunting when he lifts me. Flattering. "Well." I grab my glass on the way up, knowing I will need it to get through whatever mess he's about to pull me into. "It was nice meeting you!"

The girls giggle to themselves as Brett carries me away.

He carries me—somehow maintaining his footing—over to a hot tub embedded in the deck near a bar, the water glowing with lights that fade from green to blue to purple. Ryan and Ritchie are in the water already. Brett walks into it, flopping as he lets me go. I manage to keep my glass above the water. Priorities.

"Guys, come on! We have shots!" Brett calls to the rest.

I set my glass on the side of the tub, remove my drenched swim cover, then secure my braids into a bun on the top of my head. I didn't spend eight hours in a chair just to soak them in unshowered-ass-and-ball juice.

Jeremy climbs in next to me. He gives me a snarky look, then pulls me to his side. I hug him and lay my head against his hairy chest, a quiet *I forgive you* for the past few days.

Ritchie lifts the tray of twelve shot glasses into the middle. I take one and sniff it, smelling the floral scent of expensive brandy. Brown liquor? This is going to go downhill quickly.

Brett raises his glass. "To Ryan on his special weekend! Welcome to the married club, bro!"

We clink then drink. The liquid slides down like water but makes my next breath come out like fire. As I fight for less flammable air, I succumb to the peer pressure and take the next glass.

"And to Jer! The next in line to join the club!"

I swear I hear a record scratch. Eyes shift around in silence as we decipher who knew before Brett snitched.

"What?" Ryan asks. "You're getting married?"

"We were going to wait until after the wedding to tell everyone," Jeremy says, giving Brett *a look*. "I don't want to take any attention away from your special day."

"No! This is great news!" Ryan is intoxicated but his happiness is genuine. Crisis averted. "Congratulations! Oh my god, cheers to that!"

Clink. Drink.

The minute I swallow, it tries to come back up, but I don't let it. We sit down, and I attempt to chase the taste away with my rosé. Bad idea, but not worse than anything else happening in this tub.

"Where's Chet?" Brett asks. "Chet!"

"You said this was groomsmen only," Jeremy says.

"Eh, he's a dude too. This can be all the guys."

I wave to Brett. "Hello?" He ignores me.

Chet comes over and climbs into the tub as well. Six bodies is a lot, even for a hot tub this luxuriously sized, and seven is a squeeze, but no one can be upset when Chet is the exception. That's like getting mad a puppy showed up in a playpen of kittens.

"Hey, guys," he says in his honeyed tone. "I guess you heard the news."

We exchange congratulatory sentiments, then the conversation devolves into engagement parties and wedding planning. With a yawn I rest my head against the edge of the tub, letting a jet massage my lower back, and stare up at the sky.

The last bit of orange slips away over horizon, dragging darkness in behind it. The waning crescent adds little moonlight to the equation, but it's better that way. The night sky is full of stars I've never seen before, multitudes more than what you can see beyond the city lights of home. Open bodies of water usually freak me out—a vast depth filled with the unknown, the possibility of the boat sinking and no one finding us before the hungry sea creatures do—but it's easy to forget that when I'm in a glowing hot tub with the warmth of liquor settling in.

Ryan leaves my side to go after Ritchie, splashing water into my ear. They laugh about something, but I have been out of the conversation for too long. I turn my head and find Heath moving out of the way of the aggressive bromance.

He sits beside me. "Feeling good?"

It must show on my face. My warmth gains a happy blur, my brain floating like my body in the water. It erases every other feeling except the ache I have for him. "Sure. You?"

He shrugs, then sinks deeper into the water, matching my position. His thigh slides against mine and his hand appears on my leg. The little bit of touch he allows teases in my core. I would think he was pulling fuckboy shit again, but the timid grin he gives me makes it seem like he has a deeper intention hidden away.

"What did you want to talk about earlier?"

He stares for a moment and then shakes his head. "Later."

His mood doesn't sit right with me. "Okay."

Heath stares up at the sky the way I had before, but I can't look away from him. I don't want to. His fingers trace absent-minded circles on my inner thigh, and I despise how quickly it makes my body hotter than the water.

Jeremy grumbles beside me. When I see him, he is red and fuming. I imagine steam rising from his head while he glares at Brett. Chet's arm is around his shoulders attempting to keep him calm.

"I'm just saying. Making us travel to a wedding in *Philly?* You might as well get married in Jersey." Brett's laugh is as smug as his sentence. He means to tease, but Jeremy is going to pop off if Brett says anything else. Lucky for no one, he continues, "If you don't want us to go, just say that."

"You are oblivious to everything, aren't you?" Jeremy says.

"What?"

"Nothing." Jeremy drowns his snarky comment in a heavy swig of his drink. "You know what? No. It's not nothing."

Heath sits up at the same time I do. We both know what's coming.

"Why would I want you at my wedding, Brett? With your shitty little comments and judgments."

"Because we're family," Brett says.

"Family? We've been friends for a long time. That doesn't mean we need to *keep* being friends." Jeremy didn't come to play.

"Honey." Chet's attempt to calm him is obscenely futile.

"What?" Brett looks shocked. "Why would we ever stop being friends?"

"You say borderline homophobic and racist shit all the time. 'No homo-ing' with Ritchie, talking about Teagan like she's not even a person." Not sure why I'm getting pulled into this, but here we are. "You voted for a guy who said he'd take away my right to get married."

"Oh, come on. You know that's not what I believe. We have different politics, but that doesn't change anything."

"It's not 'just politics' when it affects someone's humanity," Jeremy corrects him. Politics isn't a taboo subject to him: it's his profession. "You always make jokes then laugh off my feelings about them, not caring that it makes me feel subhuman. And you do it all the time."

"Why are you blaming me for everything?"

"I'm not blaming you. I'm telling you," Jeremy says.

"But I do love you, Jer. And I respect the hell out of you."

"You can love someone and still dislike everything about them."

The wide-eyed look of shock on Ryan's face gains my attention. "Hey, so maybe this isn't the best time for this conversation," I say. "How about we do this later. Like not—"

"I'm not a bad person, Jer." Brett sets his glass on the deck, but his slurred speech proves it's too late for me to stop him. "I don't dislike anything about people like you or Teagan."

That hits me in exactly the wrong place. "People like me?" I feel my face twist in confusion but try to give Brett a chance to fix his mistake.

"I'm just saying."

"Saying *what?*" I ask.

"You know exactly what. The same shit he always does," Jeremy says.

"Yo, why are you causing drama when we're supposed to be celebrating?" Ritchie butts in.

"Shut up, Ritchie," Jeremy snips. "You are just as bad. Always starting shit and causing drama for no reason other than to be just like your idol, Brett."

The confusion makes Ritchie squint. His lack of self-awareness will baffle me until the end of time. "Don't act like you don't know this. Look what you did in Vegas, if you even remember," I say.

"Well, you're not perfect either. You can be really bitchy some-times, but we all take it on the chin because 'That's Teagan.'"

Even with my lack of sobriety, Ritchie's words sting. It reminds me of what Rowan said, *Teagan did it first or Teagan did it better,* and the wound reopens again. It's painful to be the villain in everyone else's story when I'm not even the hero in my own.

"Shut up, Rich. You're literally starting shit right now," Heath says.

"Don't defend her! You act like she doesn't treat you like shit all the time."

"She doesn't," Heath says, his voice low, his tone defensive. Once again, he protects me when I should be protecting myself.

"Ritchie's right," Brett says.

"Oh, is he?" I dare him to grow balls and double down. He doesn't answer, just takes another sip of his courage juice. "What? Do you expect me to apologize?"

"No, we definitely don't," Brett says with a roll of his eyes.

Ryan tries to pacify the situation. "Guys, let's just calm—"

"You call me the problem when Teagan is the drama queen. Always pissed off at someone about something." Ritchie reinserts himself in a conversation he has no place in.

"Are you saying I'm *angry*?" I ask.

"Pretty much."

"Rich, stop. You don't even know what you're talking about right now," Heath warns. They never hear what they're saying, never see how it could affect me worse than what my words can do to them. They don't see me at all. Only Heath does. "Shut the fuck up before I make you."

"Even if I was the stereotype you want to paint me, I have plenty of reasons to be angry, especially when I'm surrounded by 'friends' like you."

"Have you ever stopped to think maybe *you're* the reason everything sucks for you?" Brett asks me. "Always mad about life being unfair when *you're* the one making it hard for yourself by always being a fucking bitch."

His words land on me like an anchor, and I can't keep it in any longer.

"As if there's any other way I could hold my own in a group like this? A bunch of overprivileged, cishet white dudes, thinking that my life is *exactly* like yours. I don't tell you half the shit I deal with on the daily because you wouldn't listen or believe me even if I did!" I'm so mad I'm shaking, my *anger* spilling out. "I'm a bitch to protect myself. You're a willfully ignorant bigot for fun."

Brett's eyes narrow. With a deep swipe of his arm, he splashes water in my face. I gasp.

Before I can react, Heath shoves him down, looking like he wants to start swinging. I grab him and pull him back, not needing him to fight my battle for me yet again. The scene devolves into chaos, Jeremy and Heath exchanging more choice words with Brett and Ritchie, but I'm too focused on keeping my angry tears from spilling to take in anything else they have to say.

The girls finally come over, Mary leading the way, their faces blanched by our bullshit. "What is happening?"

Shit. I deflate, remembering how I had tried to keep the peace two minutes ago, just to let the guys weasel their way under my skin and put me right back in my feelings. But I'm tired. The last thing I should have to do is defend myself against the people who call themselves my friends.

"This was my point," Jeremy says. "We're not friends. We're just a bunch of people who have been in the same places for a long time, and it's about time we admit it. Relationships are a choice, not a default."

A painfully awkward silence settles between us. It's the quiet that falls when a debate is over, when the perfect point is made and there's no counterargument to be had. For what feels like a minute the only sounds are the bubbling jets and my heart pounding in my ears.

Finally, Felicity pulls Brett from the water. Mary is by her side, doing the same with Ryan who looks like he's crying. I feel guiltier than ever.

Brett sees Ryan's face, too, and turns back. "This is your fucking fault, Jer!"

"Fuck you, too, Brett."

My skin aches and my stomach turns. Everything is shattering under my feet. But frankly, I'd rather drown with the sea monsters than feel like this any longer.

THIRTY-THREE
Heath

The chaos calms when Brett and Ritchie disappear down the hall and Chet takes Jeremy away from the battlefield he scattered with bodies. Ryan's drunk crying makes it more dramatic than it needs to be, but it is what it is. I didn't expect vitriol like that from a group like ours—a group so used to each other's bullshit, it's habit—but no lies were told. We've all had it.

With distance between us, I let out a breath to calm myself down and sit next to Teagan. Her hand covers her face, and she has her knees curled up a little too tight. "Well, hot tubs used to be fun," I joke.

Teagan laughs from behind her hand. She moves it and wipes a tear from her eye.

"Babe, no. Come on." I pull her into a hug, resting my cheek against hers. "Crying because of Brett? Are you drunk?"

Her laugh sounds like a sob. "Yeah." She hugs me tighter, not allowing me to let her go. As if I would anyway. Holding her calms me.

I run a hand up and down her back and my finger gets stuck in the tie of her bikini top, accidentally tugging it a little looser. Her leg floats against my side, threatening to wrap around my waist. My blood is rushing too much to focus on that right now.

"You gonna be okay?" I ask.

"I'm just embarrassed." She cries again. "Mary is going to be so mad at me."

"She won't. You didn't start this shit."

"But I made it worse."

"We're all drunk and delirious. Everyone just needs to sleep it off and we'll be fine in the morning."

"*Shit*," she groans. "I'm supposed to share a room with Mary and the bridesmaids."

"Yeah, well, I'm supposed to share a room with Ryan and Ritchie. Wanna trade?" A sniffle interrupts her laugh. Such a cute, pathetic sound. It's not even ten o'clock yet, but after a red-eye flight and hours of drinking, it's only a matter of time. "Give it another thirty and everyone will be passed out."

She nods, but I'm not sure if that's what she wants to hear right now. I want to fix everything for her, make up for the stress she just went through, especially when I know she was stressed before any of us were even *thinking* about the wedding. She wipes her eye again and keeps staring down into the water. The LED glow of the hot tub dances mesmerizing lines over her body and the tearful look on her face.

"Teags," I whisper. "What's going on?"

She doesn't look my way. "Is Jeremy right?"

"Which part?"

"That we should stop being friends," she says. "I've said it, you've said it. We're friends of proximity. But Jeremy is leaving, Ryan is making me reevaluate how close we can be without threatening his marriage, and I fucking hate Brett."

"And Ritchie."

"And Ritchie," she agrees. "We're all starting to live different lives, overlapping less and less. I know it's natural. It's happened with every new school we went to, but . . . am I the only one who can't seem to keep other friends?"

"No," I admit. "I don't know how to meet people who can tolerate my bullshit. I couldn't even keep Shelley around for a month before I ruined it."

"What? You broke up with Shelley?"

I wouldn't call it a breakup. You can't end what never started. "Yeah. It's over. Like, *really* over."

"What did you do this time?" She pouts.

I hesitate to tell her, knowing it's not the right time to explain. "The usual dumbassery."

"Why can't you let yourself have a nice girl for once?"

There is so much on my mind that I want to tell her. How I feel about her, how much I want her, how scared I am to lose her if I admit it. She had to have known I was talking about her before we paused. As oblivious as she has been acting, she's the smartest person I know and she sees through me like I'm glass. It has to be a ruse.

"You know why," I say.

Her eyes stare into mine, but I can't tell what she's thinking.

She loops her arms around my neck and leans in closer. "You really broke it off with her?"

"Yeah."

Her plump lips curl into a smirk. I'm not sure if she wants to laugh at me or kiss me, but when she crawls onto my lap, I figure it out.

Her hips come to rest on mine. I instinctively grip them, my fingers sliding into the side of her bottoms, but I force myself not to pull on them. The pounding in my chest returns.

"Does that mean we can resume the contract?" she asks. My heart is beating too hard to put words together. Instead, I nod. Her arms tighten around me with a chuckle. "You have impeccable timing."

"Yeah. Something like that." My eyes drop to her lips, and I pull her closer.

"Sorry," a staff member interrupts us. My eyes snap open and I remember where we are. "We need to close up the tub before we turn in." He hands us towels, not giving me a chance to protest.

We leave the water and dry off. I keep Teagan from tumbling over when she grabs her clothes. She's even drunker than I thought. "It hasn't been thirty minutes," she says.

"Fuck. Yeah." I look around for an alternative and remember the lounge on the second level. "Let's go up there."

It's difficult to get her up the stairs, but it pays off. A set of couches sit around a coffee table, overlooking the balcony. Each is as big as a twin-sized bed, but she pulls me onto one with her. The dark look in her eyes and teeth digging into her lip scream *fuck me*. I hate that she's drunk right now.

"Let me grab us a blanket," I say.

It takes me a second to find one, and by the time I turn back, Teagan is out cold.

Deep, even breaths slip between her lips, squashed against the pillow. Considering how hard I am and how hard it is to turn her down even when she's sober, this is for the best. I shake open the blanket and lay it over her. When I settle under it, she rolls onto my chest, hugging my waist with an arm and nuzzling her head into my neck. I hope she can't hear how hard my heart is pounding.

This is the best feeling. Not better than sex, but maybe a close second. If she wasn't drunk I'd be between her thighs in a heartbeat, but have no problem waiting until tomorrow if *this* is how I will spend my night instead.

I breathe her in to slow my heart rate, and I'm asleep before I know it. When the sunlight wakes me, she's already gone.

~

I was right. The minute everyone woke up we were back to smiling and laughing again as if the fight never happened. The buffet-style breakfast and numerous lounge areas provided enough space for the most upset of us to keep from crossing paths, just in case. We can't un-ring the bell, but sobriety makes it easier to maintain civility. We'll get through the wedding, have fun while we do, and we'll handle it later. Or never.

When we arrive at the island in the early afternoon, the resort is a great distraction. Everyone goes their separate ways, getting massages, jumping into the pool, or disappearing onto the beach. Teagan and I move into our room separately, our only exchange her slipping me a key while walking past me to the pool. I can't read her mood, but the room changed mine for the better.

It's cool as shit. Separated from the main building, the only way to get to it is through an outdoor pathway that snakes through a bamboo garden, or to swim up. There are only three rooms like this, all opening onto the same semiprivate pool, and so far, the others are empty. The room is small, only big enough for a bathroom, a coat closet, and a single queen bed. Nowhere to run.

We'll be alone soon, and when we are, I'll tell her. I have to.

Our contract ends with the summer, just a few days after we get back home. That's what I agreed to, what I thought I wanted. I was lying to myself then and I'm lying to myself now.

Convincing her to do this with me wasn't my way to get laid or avoid commitment, it was my way of getting Teagan close to me again, even if all we would have was sex. For years I convinced myself I didn't want a relationship with *anyone*, but the last few months made me realize the truth. The reason I didn't want to give my heart away was because it wasn't mine to give. It has always belonged to Teagan. It always will. I will ruin every relationship I have as long as there's a whisper of a chance to be with her.

I love her. The only thing I hate about Teagan is that she hates me.

I practice ways to tell her, how I'll pull her aside and what I'll say when I do. Words jumble in my head on my way to find her, none piecing together into something coherent before I arrive at the hotel pool. Everyone is here, some floating on inflatable unicorns, the others sunbathing beside it, everyone basking in the Mediterranean sunshine softened by a few clouds. With the company of about fifty other guests, it's loud but chill, full of all the laughter we should have had last night.

I find Teagan standing with Brett at a drink stand. She wears tall sandals that defy physics, the added height making her legs look impossibly long. Her potato-sack shirt hangs from her like a sexy rag—yeah, I don't know how that makes sense either—the thin white fabric displaying the strappy black swimsuit she has on underneath.

She wears her braids in a big bun on top of her head like a crown, looking like a queen. All I want to do is drag her off her throne and into bed with me.

When I calm the thudding in my shorts, I see how rigid *she* is. Arms and ankles crossed, she isn't thrilled to be next to Brett again, but she's not intimidated either. While he talks, she gives that practiced, polite smile she does when talking to a stranger. As I go to save her from his bullshit, Brett brushes his hand down her arm and walks away. She deflates with relief, closing her eyes when she drinks from the straw sticking out of a young coconut.

I make her jump when I say, "Tell me he's behaving."

She clutches her chest, then moves her hand to grip my arm. "Do not sneak up on me right now, Heath. I almost peed."

I laugh and slide her coconut my way to steal a drink. "Is he being good, though?"

"Mostly."

"So, I don't need to murder?"

"I didn't say that." She smirks. "Whatever he does tonight, I'm blaming it on you."

"Fuck. What is he doing now?"

"Not completely sure. Sounds like he plans to start his apology tour after the rehearsal dinner."

"Are you for real?"

"Sadly. Fuck my schedule, I guess."

"Sorry, babe." I chuckle. "Weddings are the worst."

"They're trash," she agrees. We share sheepish smiles.

A loud rumble of thunder sounds in the distance. I look up at the sky, swearing it was sunny a few seconds ago. "Jesus. It sounds like it's going to—" I can't finish my sentence before it starts pouring.

People scramble from the pool. I cover her with a towel and we run toward our room.

The winding wooden planks are a bitch to navigate in the rain. I slip a few times, she does the same, and we're cursing and laughing at the absurdity the whole way.

Under the cover of an awning, we stop to catch our breath. The rain comes down in sheets. We can barely see the door to our room, even though it can only be a few steps away.

Teagan is still laughing. "You could walk better if you weren't holding a towel. My hair would have been fine, and look at you." She runs her hands over my hair to squeeze out the water. "You're sopping wet."

While she tries in vain to dry me off, I'm captivated by her effortless beauty and the carefree look in her eyes. I want that smile to stay there forever. I want her to stay. "Teags."

"What? I can't help that you look like a wet dog."

She wipes my cheeks. I grab her wrists, not wanting her hands to leave me. Her smile dims. Those big eyes look into mine.

I stare back for a moment, mesmerized, longing for more. Then without another thought, I do what I've wanted to do for weeks. I pull her into my kiss.

In the warm rain, alone in a garden, I lose myself in her. Her plump lips fit perfectly with mine, and when I coax them apart, her tongue is smooth and delicious. It's everything I've craved for weeks, maybe even months. She melts into me, her hands pulling me closer, her breath heavy against my cheek when I press her back against the wall.

I don't want to stop, but when I try, she pulls me back in for more, the electricity rumbling through me like the clouds above us. When our lips slowly part, I lick mine to taste what lingers. The look of desire on her face is more than lust. There's something else hidden behind her heavy gaze.

Maybe she feels it too. Maybe I'm only seeing what I want to see. Either way, I have to tell her.

"Teags," I whisper. "Please don't hate me for saying this."

Her brow stitches. "For saying what?"

It feels like the rain is drowning me, stealing the last of my oxygen. "When you asked me if I was catching feelings . . . I wasn't talking about someone else." My heart pounds hard in my chest. "I meant I was catching feelings for *you*."

THIRTY-FOUR

Teagan

The look in Heath's eyes makes my heart stutter in my chest.

I can't tear my eyes away from him while his words echo in my head. *He has feelings for me?* Hearing him say it, I didn't think it would affect me this deeply, frighten me and enrapture me at the same time, but it did. He flipped my world upside down with a single sentence.

I swallow, though my mouth is dry. "Really?" I ask, the only word I can get out.

He nods, seemingly unable to form words himself. My mind shuts off when he grips the nape of my neck and pulls me into him again.

His kiss is everything. Calming and thrilling. Comforting and painful. My rationale fades the longer his lips are on mine. The contract, my fear, my inability to forget the past—none of it matters in this moment. I relax into the feeling of his body against mine, melting beneath his touch, my mind quiet for the first time since we were last together. I cup his face in my hands, deepen the kiss, and let him wash every thought away.

When our lips part, he whispers, "Don't run, Teags. Please." He holds me tight against him, as if keeping me from betraying his request. I feel his heartbeat racing against my chest, and wonder if he can feel mine doing the same.

"I'm not."

We kiss again, more passionately than before. Suddenly, a blinding flash and a cracking boom make us jump. We wrap around each other in fear, then laugh.

"Okay, no. I'm running now," I say. He chuckles and takes my hand.

Our room is dry and safe. The rain pelts loudly into the pool right outside, thunder rumbling in the distance. Beautiful weather for a wedding.

Heath laughs while wiping the water from his face. His white shirt clings to him, showing every hard muscle beneath it. His swim trunks do much of the same. My body warms at the sight.

He watches me as I step closer and pull on the hem of his shirt, raising his arms to let me remove it from him. He returns the favor, stripping my dress over my head, careful to keep it from dragging over my face or hair. His ridiculous body makes me long to feel it against me again. *In* me again.

I want him, yes, but in what way, I can't begin to define. Letting him in while I feel this raw might destroy me, but the heat building between my legs tries to convince me it's worth the risk.

"Heath." I run my hands down his torso, his smooth, damp skin teasing my palms. "I don't know what you want me to say right now."

"I don't want you to say anything," he says, pulling me closer by my waist. "Right now, I want to do something much better than talking." He tilts up my chin and steals my lips again.

The passion behind his kiss burns my desire into need. I wrap my arms around his neck. His hands run over my ass before he lifts me by the backs of my legs.

The kiss breaks when he crawls onto the bed. Rather than lying me down, he keeps me with him, letting me drop onto his lap. Chest to chest, his tongue licking mine, my lips sucking his, I want him closer. My hand slides between his legs, stroking over his erection. His breath grows heavier against my cheek.

I'm too lost in my desire for him to notice him untie my top. It tickles over my breasts when it falls away. His mouth circles my nipple, sucking it hard, then following with a gentle tease of his tongue. It sets my body on fire, and I grind my hips hungrily against his lap. He cups my ass, encouraging me to go harder.

We are on the same page. Hot, ready, full of angst. All I want is to savor this feeling, to ignore the gravity of the situation and the words he said right before. Ignore the fear that we have ruined what we had, that we won't have moments like this in the future. The way his hands slow my hips while increasing their intensity, one sliding up to the nape of my neck to pull me back in, he makes it easy to forget.

My body craves him so much it hurts. The layers of fabric between his erection and my wet center feel like a prison. I pull at his trunks until I can reach in. He's rock-hard and I'm tired of waiting.

"I need you," I whisper as I stroke him.

"You have me." He kisses me, humming against my lips. "However you want me."

I fall to my back and slip my bottoms from my hips. "Come here."

He takes my ankle in his hand and lifts it higher. I stare up at him, watching his look of longing while he unzips the back of my shoe and pulls it from me. He sets it beside us and lifts my other leg to remove its twin. Looping his fingers into the sides of my bottoms, he slides them up and off my legs. His unhurried pace is tantalizing torture.

Easing my thighs apart, he lowers himself to the mattress, and I am panting with desire. His mouth is on me not a second later.

My eyes roll back. His tongue slides over me languidly, skillfully, stimulating me further. When I moan, he hums his enjoyment with my clit between his lips.

"Oh my god," I whimper. His tongue flickers over my most sensitive spot in a perfect rhythm. I grip my pillow, the sheets, fist his hair as the heat builds and builds, leaving me teetering on the edge of climax. I can't bear him taking his time any longer.

I pull him toward me and rip his shorts down his hips. Furiously, he tears open a condom, staring down at me while he rolls it on. He falls forward onto his palms and when he pushes into me, my back arches and my legs fall to the sides.

He fills me perfectly, as if I was made just for him, stretching my sensitive walls around him. It has been too long since I've felt him. Reading it on my face, he gives me a moment to revel in it before he starts to move.

His hips pump perfectly between my thighs, stroking against every aching spot inside me. The feeling is all-consuming. Taking everything from me, he trades me for all of him. My body clenches around him with the mere thought.

"Heath!" I gasp. He moans in response.

He pulls my arm from his neck and pins it to the mattress, his hand sliding up my wrist, his fingers lacing between mine. I look up at him, watching the way he unravels while shattering me into pieces. He kicks up my leg to gain the perfect angle. The veins pop from his tensed muscles. He moves faster, his desperation palpable, his brow tensing in ecstasy. It's too much.

I melt around him. He hits that deep spot over and over, his hips clashing hard against mine. He doesn't look away, those gray eyes growing darker, his breath becoming ragged.

After weeks of wishing I could have this moment with him, I'm not ready for it to end, but my body betrays me.

The pleasure floods through me, blinding me until—*"Ah-ahh! Fuck!"*

His moans grow louder while the orgasm tears me apart. He fucks me faster, harder, his hand squeezing mine until it hurts. Then, with a deep moan, he stills, his penis twitching inside me.

When I open my eyes, I catch his smile. That drunken look of bliss on his face makes me tremble with delight. My body still grips him hungrily, the pleasure still flooding my brain with every chemical that makes me want to say and do stupid shit. I let myself drown in them.

"I fucking missed you," I whisper through my heavy breaths.

"I fucking missed you more." He lays his body on mine. With a kiss, he keeps me breathless.

I wrap myself around him, looking him in the eye when I tell him, "I'm not done with you yet."

He smiles and kisses me again.

~

The first time left me weak, but the second round took me out. I don't realize I've fallen asleep until I wake up. The rain is lighter than before but still falling, tapping against the water and the glass. I can't tell if it's dark because of the clouds or because it's getting late.

My head rests on Heath's arm, our fingers twisting together beside my head. I roll to my back and find him awake.

"Hey," he says with a grin.

"How long have I been sleeping?"

"A while. It's almost nine."

I dart up. "What?!"

"I'm fucking with you." He laughs. "You know you're too high-strung for naps. It's been, like, twenty minutes."

"You are such an ass."

He laughs harder and sits up. Pulls me to him. When his lips catch mine, my anger fades. "I put that ass to sleep," he jokes.

I hold his face in my hands. "God, it's so sexy when you compliment yourself." He acknowledges my sarcasm with a grin and kisses me again. I glance at the clock behind him and see the time. "Fuck, Heath! You said I wasn't late!"

I scramble out of the bed and run to the bathroom, snatching my outfit from the closet and checking my hair. *Shit, shit, shit.*

After I'm dressed and have an acceptable amount of makeup smashed onto my face, I rush out. "Have you seen my shoes?" I ask. Heath pushes the sheets beside him and lifts one up.

I sit on the edge of the bed to put it on. He hands me the second shoe, and I pretend to ignore the tickle of his fingers stroking up and down my back. I turn to tell him goodbye but stop.

The look in his eyes begs me to admit I know what he's thinking, what he's feeling, but I don't want to admit it to myself. "I missed this," he says. "I missed us."

"Heath." My anxiety kicks up. "I missed this, too, but . . ."

"But what?"

"What does this change? Anything?" I ask, genuinely wanting to know. "When we made the contract, we agreed on everything for a reason. We didn't want to end up in a place where feelings would obscure reality, make us believe we want to be together when we know we can't be."

"We didn't? Or *you* didn't?"

I give him a confused look. My phone vibrates against the side table. I glance at it, but he pulls my face back to look at him. The intensity behind his eyes makes my brow furrow.

"You know how I feel about you, Teags. The contract is over," he says. My heart drops with his words. "What do you want to do now?"

My phone vibrates again. *Damn it.* Ryan's name and antagonizing smile light up my screen. "I have to answer. It's Ryan."

Heath lies back with a frustrated sigh.

I answer it. "Yes, groom?"

"Where are you at? You're late!" He laughs while I grimace. Shitty timing all around.

"Yeah, I know. I'll be there in a sec." We end the call and I curse. "I really have to go."

"Teags."

I look at him over my shoulder. His expression begs me to stay. "I'm not running," I assure him. "We can talk after dinner, okay?"

His eyes leave mine, and his fingers trail down the end of my spine and drop to the sheets. "Yeah. Go."

Outside the room, I try to shake my thoughts away and focus on the responsibilities I have tonight and tomorrow. Anything to distract from my desire to run back to Heath.

THIRTY-FIVE
Heath

A rehearsal dinner after-party. Who the hell thought this was a good idea?

The run-through of the wedding processional and the two hours of dinner with close family and friends dragged on forever, people trickling out slowly until only the wedding party remained. The company of spouses eases the awkwardness of the group, but it's still there. It feels like everyone is holding it together for the sake of Mary and Ryan, waiting to pick it back up later on, but I don't care about that right now. The only thing on my mind is the conversation Teagan and I will have when this dinner is over. Time crawls when I'm anxiously waiting for her answer.

She was buzzing around during the rehearsal, coordinating the guests, dinner, toasts, photos, everything. I did my job, keeping the guys out of her way. Only when dinner was over did she get to sit down and relax.

She's so hard to read. Directly across the table from me, she doesn't avoid eye contact or look afraid to let me down. She just looks tired.

Fourteen of us sit around the oval table made of carved driftwood, the remnants of our meal and rounds of champagne scattered across its surface. Brett leaves my side, but my eyes are glued to Teagan. She grins at Ryan's banter with Mary, her chin resting on her fist, and I can't stop staring.

I swear this hour has felt like five.

Brett gains my attention when he places a projector at the end of the table. He turns it on, shooting a beam of light onto the opposite wall. I let out a heavy sigh, remembering the apology tour Teagan said would come after dinner. How long is this bullshit going to take?

He excuses the bridesmaids and wives, leaving only the guys, Mary, and Teagan. It's too late for however he plans to apologize, but here we go.

"I wanted to do something special tonight," Brett says. His tone and cadence sound like he's pitching an idea to a table of venture capitalists rather than talking to friends. "First, I want to apologize to everyone, especially you, Jer. And you, Teags. Last night we were a little too lit, and we said some things we didn't mean. We are a family, and while we fight like siblings sometimes, there is so much love between us."

So much effort to grovel when he could just say *I'm sorry for . . .* and list anything and everything he has ever said or done.

"I want to focus on that love, and a reminder of all the life we've lived together. And Mary, since you're marrying into this crazy bunch, it's time for you to see it too," Brett says. "I'm sorry for what I'm about to show you."

My brow tenses in confusion, but when Ryan's preschool picture shows up, I catch onto what's happening.

He wore glasses back then, the thin wire-framed ones with the nose pads. He had the same goofy smile and bright blue eyes, but his cheeks were at least three times as plump. It's a picture we used to tease him with constantly, even though he was one of the cutest kids ever.

"We go back. Way back. And that means we know a lot of shit about your man," Brett continues. "For instance, he was a cute kid. That clearly went awry."

We all laugh. Even while looking nervous, Ryan's smile is wide. The image changes to our class photo from second or third grade. I give in and start to let myself enjoy it.

"The squad met when we were practically babies. We had a small class, and the six of us were the coolest by far."

An embarrassing picture of our third-grade play, which, of course, was *Peter Pan*—a core memory for sure. Ryan was the lead, Teagan was Tinker Bell, Brett and Ritchie were Lost Boys, Jeremy a pirate. And I was a fucking tree.

"Heath really carried the show in this performance, I must say," Brett jokes.

I allow myself to laugh with everyone else. The picture changes to one taken in middle school, Ritchie, Brett, me, and Jeremy on the soccer field with the rest of our team, all of us swimming in uniforms we wouldn't grow into for months. Well, three of us at least. Ritchie's short ass stayed about the same size.

"The four of us tried to make up for that by establishing ourselves as hot jocks, but that only worked for Heath." He clicks to a slide of some pictures of me right before high school. The typical motion shots from games that make my leg ache. "Such a babe, right?"

Ritchie whistles to keep everyone laughing.

He switches to a picture of middle school. Teagan, Ryan, Jeremy, and some of the other debate club nerds are holding up a trophy.

"Sadly, our Ry guy went to the dark side." He sighs dramatically. "He fit in well with the geeks, especially Teagan and Jeremy. And that is when their beautiful love of all things boring began."

Next is a picture of Ryan and Teagan cheek to cheek, hugging at one of their speech competitions, I assume. I look back at Ryan and catch the nervous glance he throws at Teagan. She may have thought he was out of his mind when he confessed his desire to be with her in Vegas, but it had to come from somewhere. He never had a chance with her, but maybe he always hoped he did—the longing to have the unattainable. Or maybe that's just the effect Teagan has on people.

"Your man may not be a model, but we can't ignore the glow-up." He flips through Ryan's class photos. I forgot how nerdy he was before he gave up the glasses, the acne cleared up, and he lost his baby fat. Eleventh grade was very kind to him. "He's not Heath-level hot, but it's something."

"Bro, are you okay?" I ask with a laugh. "Do we need to go make out somewhere?"

"Don't tease me when my wife isn't present," he jokes. With practiced comedic timing, he waits for his lull. "Ry went from nerd to wannabe ladies' man overnight. Do you know how girl-crazy he was?"

Mary giggles nervously. "No."

"He was chasing everyone. Half the cheer team, my sister, two of Ritchie's girlfriends . . ." *Now Teagan.* "But, of course,"—he presses his palms together like a prayer—"he saved himself for you."

Mary and Ryan laugh, but I still can't tell if it's true or not.

"As much as I tease, high school was a big time for our friend-ship." He flips through pictures of all of us in pairs. Ryan and Ritchie in their exchange semester in Italy. Me and Brett at a soccer tour-nament. Jeremy and Teags at Pride. Then all of us together in those places as well, visiting, cheering each other on, laughing.

We point to the pictures, exchanging inside jokes, sharing memories of the shenanigans we pulled. A thousand words is an understatement when it comes to those pictures. The friend group, as forced together as we have been, still comes with as many good memories as bad. I laugh until my stomach cramps.

"We relied on each other for everything. Ritchie would have gone missing in Europe if he didn't have Ryan to keep him from getting lost. I would have failed every math class and half of science if I didn't have Jeremy's tests to copy from." Our laughter interrupts him. "And none of us would have known what true love looked like if we didn't have the power couple, Heath and Teags."

My smile fades. I look over at Teagan and watch hers do the same. She shifts uncomfortably in her chair.

I look at the screen and there's our picture from the seventh grade. Two babies holding hands and staring at each other as if we had everything figured out. The next one is from junior year, my arms wrapped around her like she was mine, my mouth on hers, Teagan smiling beneath my kiss.

"The OG couple," Brett says. Everyone joins in, aww-ing. "Seventh grade and all through high school. They were goals for real."

He clicks through more photos, and each one feels like another punch in the gut. Holding hands, kissing, posing for junior prom, senior prom. The two of us smiling in the hospital bed after my accident, my leg in that massive cast, her head resting on my shoulder. At the time, my dreams were as shattered as my femur, but I was still smiling because she was with me.

I've blocked out the memories, haven't thought about all these small moments in years. After all this time, it still hurts to see.

We were inseparable. Until we weren't.

"You two were *the* couple."

"Bro, don't." I warn him with a shake of my head.

Brett looks back up at Ryan. "We thought Ryan was going to be single forever. At least the last of us to get married for sure." I hope the conversation moves on, but it doesn't. "But everyone thought

Heath and Teags would be the first ones down the aisle. Then college started and it was . . ." He traces a hand across his throat. "Dead on arrival, out of the blue."

As the guys continue to laugh and pile on, I look at Teagan while she stares down at the table. The guilt hits me hard in the chest.

"You two went from love to hate like that." He snaps his fingers. "It must have been something bad."

I know she doesn't want to show it, but Teagan's brow twitches with sadness. The truth isn't something either of us will talk about, especially not with them, and definitely not like this. "It was forever ago. It doesn't matter," I say.

"No, come on!" Ryan says. "We've been wondering about this for years. Tell us, finally!"

Teagan looks away, obviously losing the battle with her tears. Seeing her in pain hurts but it also pisses me off. She has been through enough. I'll do anything to make them fucking drop it.

"I cheated," I lie. The laughter tapers. "Now let it go."

The words tastes bitter. Teagan may have believed that was true back then, but it wasn't. She just wanted a reason to leave me and all the memories behind.

"That's fucked up, man," Brett says, that stupid smile on his face. Teagan's chair screeches against the floor when she gets up to walk away. "Teags! We were just teasing!" Brett laughs.

I glare at him. "You are such an asshole." I leave the table and go after her.

She's already outside the restaurant and halfway down the pathway to our room when I spot her.

"Teags!" I catch up. She covers her face with a hand. She sniffles and that sick feeling creeps up and settles in my throat. The last thing I want to do is cry in front of her again. "I'm sorry they brought it up. I didn't think you wanted them to know the truth."

"You told them the truth!" she cries.

"No, I didn't."

"Oh, so you didn't run off and fuck the first girl who would put out?"

Her words piss me off. "No!"

"Then why did you just say you did?!"

"What did you want me to say?! Did you want me to tell them you—" My last words don't want to come out. "Did you want me to tell them you were pregnant?"

THIRTY-SIX

Teagan

"Fuck you, Heath," I seethe through my tears.

I turn and keep going toward the room. The sound of blood rushing in my ears drowns out his pleas for me to stay. When I make it to the room, I have to pause to unlock it, and he catches up again.

"Stop following me! I don't want you in here!" I yell.

"It's my room too!"

I try to slam the door closed but he stops it with his shoulder and comes in.

"I got pregnant? That's why we broke up?" I yell at him. "Don't you dare put this all on me! As if *you* didn't get me pregnant. As if *you* didn't make the decision with me, then turn around and cheated two seconds later!"

"I didn't cheat on you! Oh my fucking god, Teagan!" he yells right back, his volume high to match mine. We're lucky there are no neighbors to hear us. "How many times do I have to tell you before you believe me? I never even *thought* about being with anyone else. I was there with you the whole time!"

"Bullshit!" I throw the pillow at him and he blocks it. "You were there, then you left. I was wrecked, and you moved on like nothing happened."

His eyes go wide. "I moved on? You think I moved on?"

"What do you call it when it took you less than a week to go fuck someone else?"

"Jesus fucking Christ, Teagan! I swear on my mother's life I never cheated on you!"

He would never play with a phrase as serious as that—never play with *anything* related to his mom or her well-being. I don't want to believe him, and my glare holds strong.

"The night you think I was with someone else, I slept over at Ritchie's to keep him from asking questions about our trip to the clinic. At some point I passed out and his dumb ass invited girls over. I didn't even *meet* them."

He stares me down with the truth behind his eyes. I can't find words to say back.

"*You* were the one who left, Teagan. *You* were the one who went cold and wanted nothing to do with me!"

"I went cold?" I feel angry tears run down my cheeks. "You didn't think that was because I was depressed? That I was so fucked up about what happened I could barely get out of bed—barely hold it together while having to hide it from everyone else?"

"You don't think I was feeling the same way?"

"It was *not* the same for you. Fuck! I couldn't even go pee without being reminded of what happened. I had to hold it all in, crying in private, because the only person I could talk to about it was you!"

"Then why didn't you?" he asks in a quieter, calmer voice, staring me in the eyes while tears fill his own. "Why didn't you talk to me?"

My mind stutters. I pushed down the memories so hard it takes a moment to remember. I hid everything beneath the pain, the fear, the inherent remorse of ever being seventeen and stupid.

"I couldn't," I say, my voice husky with tears. "I just . . . couldn't."

It had been the best summer of my life until that point. Valedictorian with a perfect SAT and my pick of more than half the Ivy Leagues in the country. When Heath got accepted into Columbia, that's where I went, no second thoughts. Being close to him made me happy in ways I still haven't found a way to replicate, and I knew whatever struggle college or our families presented, we would still be okay if we were by each other's side. However briefly, I was free from stress, excited for the future, and so in love. Then everything changed.

Six weeks.

We knew we fucked up and we tried what we could to fix it, but still, I missed a period, took the test, and saw the two blue lines. I was throwing up, having panic attacks, mostly because I was petrified of what my parents would do if they found out. It was killing me, and in some ways, I was letting it.

The decision was barely a choice.

Heath looks away as he processes his thoughts, my words, something. His face crumples more with emotion. "I know you blame me, and you should. If I hadn't been lazy and just gotten the condom like you asked . . . I wouldn't have ruined everything. I wouldn't have ruined *us*."

I stare at him, his words sinking in, and it feels like I'm losing him all over again. The abortion was hard, but the procedure itself wasn't even a fraction of the pain I felt when I realized I had lost him.

"I'm sorry, Teags," he says, losing the fight with his tears. "I'm so sorry."

Watching him cry hurts. It reminds me of who he was, what he meant to me when we went through it. What we had been before it happened.

He was my world. I loved him more than anyone and anything in the universe. Somehow, I lost the ability to remember that. When he left, I went cold. It was easier to hate him than to miss how it felt when I loved him.

"I didn't blame you," I admit. He finally looks at me again. "It was the worst thing I've ever had to go through, but I didn't blame you. I was angry because it hurt to watch you move on while I was still reeling."

"But I didn't move on," he says. "I'm still in that place. Still hating myself, still knowing I'm a fuckup who ruins everything for everyone I love. You were the one who seemed okay."

"Well, I wasn't. I was the complete opposite of okay." I sob and cover my face with my hands.

I crumple, my back sliding down the end of the bed as I sink to the floor. He sits beside me and hugs me close. I cry onto his shoulder.

It was too much for me to process back then. Too many adult decisions needing to be made by two kids. I saw how he behaved and made my assumptions like a stupid teenager. And why?

I have no regret about our decision. I thought we would try again one day, years down the line when I had gotten through school, passed the bar, achieved everything my parents wanted of me. The picture I always had was the two of us together when we were older. Little brown, curly-haired dumbasses running around our Manhattan condo, Heath chasing them while I laughed over a mug of coffee and the work I'd brought home for the weekend.

The animosity didn't come from what happened. It came from losing that perfect picture.

But now, I realize I never asked what that picture looked like to him.

"Do you regret it?" I ask.

He takes another shaky breath. "No," he says wistfully. "Sometimes I wonder what our lives would have been like if we'd had a kid, but you have achieved so much and come so far in your life, and I know that wouldn't have been possible if we did. It wouldn't have been the same, at least."

"Yeah." I sniffle.

He holds me for a moment, letting my tears calm. When I finally look up at him, I find an intent expression on his face.

"You know I love you, right?" he says. My brow tenses even harder. "I've always loved you. I probably always will. I just get mad sometimes because . . ." He trails off.

"Because what?"

His mouth twists with a sad frown. "Because it's hard to see you being amazing on your own when I had my heart set on you being amazing with me."

Those words rip me to shreds. I lose myself to my tears again. I wrap my arms around his neck, hugging him while hiding the pain that is clearly drawn on my face.

There is so much I want to say but I can't stop crying enough to get it out. He holds me and the words go unsaid again.

We can't go back to how we were. As much as we wish we could, all we have is this.

Our tears, our company, and five days left of summer.

~

We barely slept last night, but we didn't talk anymore either. We held each other until we woke up, then rushed off to get ready for the big event.

As the bridal party walks to the altar, I try to stay present and take it all in. Months of planning, all for this, and yet I want to be anywhere but here.

It's the perfect beach wedding. White and pink flowers hang from the sides of the gold Chiavari chairs, fluttering in the wind while their scent mixes with the smell of saltwater. The dusty-rose color of my dress compliments the ecru suit Mary's brother wears, and looks perfect with the other shades of pink Mary picked for the bridesmaids. Organza ribbons drape across the trellis that creates the altar. Petals of soft pink roses and peonies dangle from translucent strings behind the priest, dancing as the wind passes through them.

It's beautiful. Just as they had imagined, just as they deserve.

Smiles light up people's faces as they watch us walk down the aisle. Happy. That's how weddings should feel.

We part ways at the end, and I take my place on the raised platform, smiling at Ryan and ignoring the ache in my chest while I wait for Heath.

He appears, and I feel my heart stop. While his bridesmaid cheers and wriggles with glee, he can't hide his sadness, no matter how much he tries to smile at the family and friends seated around us.

His eyes find mine when he lets her go. They flicker away, and he takes his place behind Brett.

The music changes. Mary comes into view. A bride in all white, her arm around her father's, just like in the movies. She looks beautiful with tears in her eyes and a wide smile on her face. I'm happy for her, but I can't say I'm happy.

I feel nothing as I go through the motions, pretending to hear the vows, handing Ryan the ring. It goes by quickly, and for that I'm glad. When the priest begins his speech, I count the seconds until it's over.

"True partnership stems from love and is bound by trust," he says in his Spanish accent. "The trust we will always have for the one we love, the one we promise to love forever, for better or for worse. I hope you always revel in the good times, when the sun shines, when laughter fills the day. But even more, I hope you hold each other and rely on each other when the bad times come—and there will be many bad times. We say 'better and worse' because there will always be both. And for that, we thank God, for it is the better that helps us through the worst, and the worst that makes us thankful for the better."

I glance over and find Heath looking at me. He makes no move to look away, and neither do I.

"For richer or for poorer is straightforward, so we will skip past that," the priest continues, gaining a laugh from the crowd. "In sickness and in health, love means we never have to go through anything alone. The worst times of our lives, the moments we feel the weakest and the furthest from God's light, you will survive because you will have each other, always. And how blessed you will feel to have each other after you survive it all as well."

The words make a lump form in my throat. I feel my brow tense and I see Heath's do the same. What we went through, it was scary, and it was painful, but I had him. Through it all, he held my hand, told me it would be all right. But then it wasn't.

We were young. Stupid. If we had one more day alone with each other to talk things out, to keep grieving, to keep going through the worst *together*, how different things could have been. How different *we* could have been.

The crowd cheers, pulling me back into the present. I blink, a tear falling from my eye, and clap as the two of them kiss. I wipe my cheek, relieved to know my tears won't seem out of place.

As everyone else watches the happy couple, all I can see is Heath.

I love him. I miss him. And it hurts so fucking much.

THIRTY-SEVEN
Heath

I hate weddings.

The priest's words hit me hard, and I could tell they did the same to Teagan. But since the moment the ceremony was over, I haven't been able to catch her. She has been running around, coordinating with vendors, organizing things, keeping people in place. All I can do is watch and wait, knowing I'm leaving in a few hours and she's staying through tomorrow.

Our conversation feels unfinished. Everything between us always feels unfinished.

I catch a glimpse of her standing at the end of the hall, but when I take a step, Brett gets in my way.

"Hey!" he greets me, but I'm beyond disinterested. "Great reception, huh? And that ceremony."

I leer at him and say nothing.

"What? You didn't like it?"

"It's not about the wedding, it's about you," I say. "I'll keep things copacetic today. But tomorrow, when we land, we're done."

"Done? Don't tell me this is because of Teagan."

"It's because of everything, Brett. You hurt people—especially her—all the time. I'm over it."

I walk past him, but he stops me. "The fuck? Just like that? You're my brother, Heath. She's just your ex."

The laugh that leaves me is as condescending as I intended. She's "just my ex" as much as breathing is "just a thing I do."

Anger twitches on his face. He crosses his arms defensively. "You're really going to let her come between *us*? She's not worth it, bro."

"She's not?" I ask, matching his stance. "You say we're close, but what do you know about my life right now? Do you know how work is going? And how is my mom? Do you know? Do you care?"

"Of course I care, Heath. You just don't talk about that stuff."

"I don't talk about it, or do you not listen?" His mouth opens to answer my rhetorical question, but I don't let him finish. "Oh, here's one you should know. Why did I switch to physical therapy rather than stay in business with you and Ritchie?"

I know he doesn't know the real reason. "Because you love soccer and everything."

I shake my head with a smile. "It's because of Teagan's brother," I correct him. "I was at the hospital for months with him. Those cute pictures you showed of us in the hospital when I broke my leg, you weren't in them. Teagan was."

"Bro, why are you doing this?"

"Because you don't get it. Teagan is an integral part of my life— the parts that make me a better person. Yeah, we've broken each other down, but she will always help build me back up, and I will always do the same for her. She is the best friend I have. And you?" I don't know how to finish that sentence, not that it matters. "I love her, Brett. And I hate what you do to her. It's not even a choice."

He looks away from me. "So it's like that?"

There's nothing else he can say, because there's no changing him. There's no changing anyone. We grow the way we grow, and sometimes that means we outgrow each other.

"Yeah. It's like that."

~

With the cake eaten and the alcohol running low, the party settles down to a murmur of what it was before. The dance floor spills from the banquet room onto the patio outside. The sun starts its descent over the ocean, casting a golden glow over everything. It's almost time to leave.

In the corner of the room, Teagan sits at an empty table, slumped in her chair, absentmindedly tracing her lips across the top of her champagne flute.

I don't want the summer to end like this. All I want is to hold her one more time. To apologize, to tell her how much I wish I could go back and stop hurting her over and over. What's stopping me?

She only snaps out of her trance when I'm two steps away from her. She looks at me with surprise.

"Dance with me?"

I expect a glare—a look of annoyance at least—but all she does is stare. "Okay."

She takes my hand and we go onto the floor, staying to the edge of the crowd. I pull her against me, my hand resting on her bare back while my other takes her hand. We sway back and forth to the slow jazz, neither of us saying a thing.

A thousand words fly through my mind but I can't piece any of them together. All I know is it feels better to have her close to me, to know I still have her for one more dance at least.

Teagan's arm wraps around my shoulder and she lays her chin next to it. Her hand leaves mine, her arm lifting and wrapping around my neck.

Maybe, just maybe, she doesn't hate me anymore. But I wouldn't blame her if she did.

I run my hands up and down her back in silent penance.

"I'm sorry," I whisper into her neck. The emotion blindsides me, almost choking me. "I'm sorry for everything I did to hurt you."

Her hand holds the back of my neck. "I'm sorry for everything I did too."

So much is left unsaid beneath the swoon of the music, so much hidden in our embrace and the slow swaying of our bodies. Surrounded by the crowd, it feels like we're alone. But even with her against me, it feels like the universe is pulling her away.

"I'm gonna miss this," I whisper rather than saying what I truly want.

"Miss what?"

"We'll get busy again like we always do. School, work, family shit. We won't see each other 'three times per week, guaranteed, with the possibility of four,'" I quote her, getting a little tearful laugh in return. The stupid contract, the forced proximity that our group always requires, all of it is slipping away. "I'm gonna miss having time with you."

She nuzzles her head against my neck.

"This doesn't have to end," I say. My heart swells with hope, longing, the combination threatening to make it jump out of my chest. "We could go back to how we were before. Start over."

"But we can't." Her voice is a painful whisper while she speaks the truth neither of us want to face. Voiceless, I stare off into space, my heart shattering to pieces. "We're not those kids anymore. And I don't want to be."

It hurts. But she's right.

"I don't want to lose you."

"You won't," she says. "There's always next summer, right?"

Her words calm me and make me want to cry all at the same time. "Right."

"Best Ma'am!"

I look up and Teagan turns to face Mary's brother. My hands don't want to leave her skin. I don't want to let her go.

"We need you," he says with a smile.

"Be right there."

Teagan turns back to me, the tears still visible in her eyes.

"I love you," I say, only loud enough for her to hear, because she is the only person in the world who will ever make me say it. She looks like she wants to say something, but she doesn't. Her hand finds my cheek, her thumb strokes back and forth.

She presses her lips against mine. I breathe her in, hoping time will stop and the universe will give me the words to make her stay. She leans away, and when she looks into my eyes, I imagine she feels what I'm feeling too.

"See you next summer?" she asks.

"Yeah."

When she turns to leave, my hand slides down her arm to her hand. She gives it a squeeze as she walks away. I feel my heart break when her fingertips slip from my grasp.

I slide my hands into my pockets and watch her give me one last look over her shoulder.

She leaves me again. Alone on the dance floor.

THIRTY-EIGHT

Teagan

Back home and almost a week later, my wound still feels fresh. I didn't see this coming. I thought that chapter with Heath had ended and that I could hide my heart behind sex and vitriol. What I didn't see was that the resentment only existed because the love did too.

I had nowhere to put my sadness but inside myself until it came out as anger. It takes time to learn that, and to be able to recognize it when it's happening in real time. I'm almost there.

Back at my parents' house for Sunday dinner, I walk past the library. My graduation pictures hang in the largest frames, my decade-old trophies line the top of the mantel and cast shadows over Levi's hard-earned medals. Had I seen it earlier, maybe I could have said something—pointed out how fucked up it all was. But, deep down, I know my fear would have stopped me like it always has. I couldn't even choose my own way in life without feeling like their disappointment would be the death of me.

"There you are." My father's voice sends a shiver up my spine. "Dinner is ready, sweetheart. Come on."

I sit in my place next to Levi. Mom passes me the dish of steamed vegetables I promised myself I would eat.

When I hand it to Levi, he quirks an eyebrow. "You look like shit."

"Thanks."

Levi laughs but stops when I don't return it. His brow creases with concern. "Is everything okay?"

"I'm still trying to figure that out," I answer.

I return my focus to my plate and my glass of wine, letting myself zone out while the table conversation goes along its monotonous trail. My mind is elsewhere, back on the island, going through every word I said—every word I *didn't* say. Did I protect my heart? Or did I run away again?

"I'm sorry," I hear Rowan say. The slight tremble in his voice matches the emotion I'm trying to suppress.

"You must do better than that! A thirteen fifty is nowhere near where you need to be," Mom chides.

"Leave him alone, Mom. It's just a test," Levi says.

"It's a *very important* test. Rowan can do better—he *should* do better."

Rowan looks down, but I can still see his chin quiver. The scolding continues, and I watch him edge closer to tears—closer to the breakdown I've had too many times. Anger burns in my chest.

"We'll have to get you into classes again. Or maybe Teagan can help you. If she got a perfect score, surely she can raise yours to an acceptable level. You just need to try harder."

"Oh my god, leave him alone!" I don't realize I've yelled the words until they are out of my mouth. My parents' eyes on me rein me back in but embolden me at the same time. "Rowan is going to be fine. It's just a test."

"Teagan, please. You know this test sets the foundation for the next. If he doesn't do better—"

"Shut up, Mom. Seriously. Shut up."

"Teagan! Do not speak to your mother that way!"

"I will when you both accept the fact that we're not perfect. We'll never be exactly how you want us to be. Rowan is a good person—a rare, genuinely good person. He's kind, gentle, and so smart. He'll be just fine whether he does everything to your standards or not."

"What has gotten into you?" my mother asks. "We only want the best for all of you."

"No, you want what *you* think is best for us," I correct her. She leans back in her chair in offense. "So what if he doesn't get into an Ivy League school? And what if he doesn't want to go to college at all?"

"*Teagan,*" my father scolds me.

"You can't see what you're doing. Reminding us how you gave us this privileged life of comfort most of the world will never experience—comfort *we* wouldn't have unless you *saved* us—it makes me feel like I have to make my life seem worthwhile to you." Even thinking about it makes my stomach twist. Saying it aloud is even worse. "The fear that I'll disappoint you has seeped so deep into me I've accepted living in a constant state of anxiety. But I wasn't born like this. You raised me to be this way."

My mother looks concerned, but my message clearly doesn't click. "Maybe we were hard on you, but only because we want you to succeed. Look at all you've accomplished in your life!"

"All I've accomplished?" I repeat with disdain. "You want to know what I've accomplished? I've been unable to eat—starving myself off and on since I was eleven. I've mastered the art of having panic attacks in closets or bathrooms so I don't make a scene. I—" The fearful pounding in my chest stops me.

After all the courage I built up to confront them, admitting it is terrifying. But it has to come out. I can't have Rowan go through something even worse.

With a quivering breath, I say it. "I had an abortion because I knew you would never forgive me if I compromised my college career."

My parents' expressions fade from anger to shock. "What? When?"

"The summer before freshman year of college," I answer. "I told you we were going on a graduation trip with our class, but we didn't go. I went upstate to a clinic so you wouldn't find out." I can barely look at my mother's face.

"But why? Why didn't you tell us about this?"

"I was scared! If I had told you—if I had ruined the perfect image you had of me—tell me the truth. Tell me you wouldn't have been disappointed in me."

Their eyes fall from me. They don't deny my claim, and it doesn't surprise me at all.

"That's what my fear of your disappointment has done to me. It was easier to get lost in school, to keep slowly killing myself while pretending I was still the kid who never made a mistake." The tears in my eyes are angry, not sad. "I have done *everything* you wanted me to do, and it came with sacrifices I never should have had to make. Do not do to Rowan what you did to me."

The gaping look of shock remains on their faces. A tear rolls down my mother's cheek. "Teagan, I am so sorry. I didn't know we were making you feel that way."

"We are so proud of you. Of all of you," Dad says. "We love you more than anything in the world. No matter what you do."

Their words choke me. They are what I have wanted to hear them say all my life, and in this moment, I can't accept them. "If that's really how you feel, you have a messed-up way of showing it."

I leave the table before they can see me cry.

My brain doesn't reconnect to my body until I'm outside the

front door. Too many emotions crash together in my head, leaving me with my heart feeling like it's trapped inside a fist. I want to flee to my car and drive away, avoid it all, but my bag and keys are still inside. I sit on the front steps and hang my head in my hands.

After a pitiful minute of crying, I hear someone behind me. I know it's my brothers without looking. Rowan sits next to me on the step. I take his hand in mine, knowing he isn't capable of expressing more. I made it awkward and painful for everyone.

"I'm sorry for what I said to you when I was mad." His voice is just a whisper.

"It's okay, Rowie."

"I didn't mean any of it." I understand how his emotion made him think the worst and made him use all the wrong words to explain it. I did the same. He'll have to process being seventeen in his own time, just like I had to.

"I know." I squeeze his hand and give him a teary smile. "Now go back inside. Mom and Dad are the ones who need to apologize."

He gives me a little nod, then gets up to follow my direction. Levi climbs down from his chair and takes Rowan's place. "Are you gonna be okay?" he asks.

"I'll be fine. I always am."

He wraps his arm around me. "I had no idea you went through all that. I'm sorry I was too wrapped up in my own shit to see it."

"You have no reason to apologize. You were busy staying alive. That's the most important thing you could do for me."

We sit quietly for a moment. I'm thankful for his company.

"It was Heath's, right?" he asks timidly.

"Of course it was."

"Is that why you broke up?"

My breath comes out in a pained sigh. I wipe my eyes with the backs of my hands. "It wasn't like that. We made the decision together and he was there with me through everything. We were just stupid teenagers and let it all fall apart afterward."

"You still love him."

"Yeah," I say through my tears. "I do."

"You should tell him that."

"It doesn't matter."

"Why not?"

Fuck, this hurts. I sniffle. "There's no going back to what we had before."

"Who says you're supposed to go back?" he asks. I look at him questioningly. "Before my accident, I had a whole plan for my life. Not once did I see this coming." He gestures to his legs and his chair. "But that's how it is. You can't go back to before everything happened, but you learn to accept it, and move forward."

The broken pieces of my heart swell with pride. "I'm the big sister. I'm supposed to be teaching you shit about life, not the other way around."

"You *did* teach me this, Teags." He grips my hand. "You and Heath were the only ones who made me look ahead at what my life could be rather than thinking it was over. Now stop being a couple of dumbasses and do that for yourselves. Go talk to him before he leaves tonight."

"Before he leaves?"

"He's moving out of the city. He didn't tell you?"

"No!"

"You might be able to catch him if you leave now."

"But—"

"Go!"

"My keys and phone are—"

He reaches up to his chair and plops my bag into my lap. "Come up with one more excuse and I will throw your ass across the lawn. Go!"

I hug him as tight as I can, then I race to my car.

~

It's official. I've lost my goddamn mind, and it is time for grippy socks.

I couldn't find parking on his block, so I resorted to parking at my place and running down the sidewalk in five-inch heels. A moving truck sits just outside, so I run up to find him. My pounding heart drops when I find his door open and his apartment empty. Just then, I spot him through a window, walking up the sidewalk.

I fly down the stairs, wondering how I've managed not to fall yet. "Heath!"

He turns and looks surprised to see me. I come closer and realize I'm completely out of breath.

"Did you just run here?" he asks with a chuckle.

"Yes. Shut up." I lean my hands on my knees and try to gain enough oxygen to speak in full sentences. *Say the thing. Just say the thing.*

"Would you—" "Do you—" we say at the same time. We look at each other.

"What?" I ask.

"What were you going to say?"

"Nothing," I lie. "What were you saying?"

"Nothing."

Still flustered and not quite knowing what to say, I spot an iced latte from my café, a *T* written on the side, dripping in his hand. "What is that?"

He glances down at it and stammers, "It's an almond milk latte. I, um, I got it—"

"For me?" I finish for him.

He looks at me with hesitance in his gray eyes. "Yeah."

Caffeine *is* my love language. I lean up, smiling when I see we're in the same grippy-sock boat. "Were you coming to say goodbye to me before you left?"

"Kind of the opposite." Nerves stitch his face and make him fidget. He straightens up with a breath and finally says everything I've needed to hear. "I was going to tell you I don't want the summer to end, that I don't want to wait and see if next year life won't pull you away from me again. I was going to tell you I want you back—I want *us* back. And I guess I was hoping your favorite drink would make you tell me you feel the same way."

As I look at him, my heart calms, and breathing seems optional. He is everything to me, and I have no intention of running away again. "Heath . . ."

I step closer to him and pull his face to mine, savoring the feel of his lips as if it would be the last time I'd taste them. His arms wrapping around me are the only things keeping me standing.

My lips leave his slowly. When my eyes open, I look into his and say, "I love you."

THIRTY-NINE
Heath

"I love you."

Teagan's words hit me right in the chest, knocking the wind out of my lungs and the latte out of my hand. "I love you too."

Teagan holds my face in her hands as she kisses me. Her breath is still quick from whatever she did to get here. The desperation behind her lips surprises me, but I'm thankful for it. Thinking I had kissed her for the last time has been killing me.

Her lips slip from mine too soon. She looks at me with intensity. Her eyes are wide and wet with tears. "Don't move away," she says.

As I hold her in my arms, I can't think straight. "Don't move? I just sold my car. I have a new lease and—" Her mouth crashes onto mine again. *Mmm.* Yeah, I'll shut up.

She grabs the front of my shirt with both hands. "This doesn't have to end. No, we can't go back to what we had before, but that's the point. We can start something new. *Now.* Not wait to see if we'll get another chance next summer."

I open my mouth to give a reason why I can't, but nothing comes out. There is nothing good enough to make me want to walk away from her. "You love me?"

"Yes, dumbass." She smiles through her tears. She pulls me close and we kiss again. I can feel the passion behind her lips, the warmth and comfort I've missed. A sense of being exactly where I'm meant to be, with the only person I want to be with.

"Yo!" We both turn to the driver. "This is a sweet moment or whateva, but I ain't got all day. Are we goin' or not?" His heavy Bronx accent cuts the tension.

"Move in with me," Teagan says.

"Move—? *What?*"

"Jeremy is gone, I need a roommate anyway, and . . . I don't know, just move in with me. We can figure it out later."

I don't know if I want to laugh or celebrate. "You want to live with me? I just learned how to clean a toilet, like, two weeks ago."

Luckily, that makes her laugh instead of cringe. "I didn't say it was a good idea. But let's do it anyway."

That's more than enough reason for me. "Okay. Let's fucking do it."

~

Moving up the street is a hell of a lot easier—and cheaper—than moving out of the city. The movers have all my shit inside her place in less than an hour. My furniture looks ridiculous in her—*our*—apartment. Three sofas piled on top of each other in the living room, bags of bedding on the floor beside them, boxes stacked taller than me in the kitchen. But, as she said, we'll figure it out later.

The movers take their tip and leave. We're finally alone. Teagan stands in the doorway with me, appraising the mess we'll have to sort out over the next few weeks. I watch her lips twist to the side while she takes it in.

"Regretting your decision yet?" I ask.

Her sneer melts into a grin. "Not yet." She wraps her arms around my neck, pressing herself against me. "Are you?"

When her body is against mine, it reminds me how perfectly we fit together. She is mine, the way she always has been, and now there are no contracts or secrets forcing us to deny it. The only regret I can have is being clothed. "Not yet."

We kiss again, more passionately than before. I pull her in for another, then another, poised and ready to show her just how happy I am to be here with her. She tries to pull away but I'm already feral for her, and have missed her too long to hold myself back.

"So, what's the first thing you want to do as room—*eek!*" She shrieks when I pick her up by the back of her legs and toss her onto my shoulder. I kick the door closed behind us. "Heath! I need to lock—"

She stops when I drop her onto her couch and lie on top of her. Finally, she gets the message.

"This is what you want to do first?"

"It is," I tease her, then lower myself between her legs.

I push up her knees and rip her panties up her thighs. Breathless, she smiles down at me as she waits for more. When I finally taste her, it doesn't take long for her giggles of amusement to melt into sighs of pleasure. She's sweet and wet already. Clearly, she has wanted this as long as I have.

She blossoms for me and I can't take it anymore. I pull up my shirt and rip it over my head. She tugs at my fly, but not quickly enough. I take over, ripping it open and pushing my pants down my hips. She lets out a little gasp when I yank her hips to me and, with barely a pause, push my way in.

Her body welcomes me, wrapping me in her snug heat, melting away every worry and regret I've ever felt. Finally inside her, skin against skin, I inhale my first calm breath in days. I could lose myself right now—fill her with everything I've been holding back since she walked away—but I want more. I want all of her. Forever.

I start to move, slow, long, and deep at first, listening to her body as it tells me everything she needs. In the right spot, with the perfect pace, I unravel her piece by piece until she's moaning, shaking, and begging for more. Her legs still tied together by the panties on her thighs, she's trapped, powerless, *mine*.

She arches back with a moan, gripping the arm of the couch above her head, her perfect body on display just for me. My dick strains in response. *"Fucking hell, babe."*

The rest of my self-control leaves me. I fall forward, pressing her legs onto my shoulders. Her hips curl up off the couch and she lets out a loud moan. I drop my hips down harder, stroking deep, still drowning in her and the incomparable pleasure she gives me.

We linger together in that blur of ecstasy, both of us holding on to a feeling we thought we lost, neither of us wanting to let go. My vision darkens. My desire to come is all consuming. The air fills with our heavy breaths and the sounds of our colliding bodies.

"Don't stop," she begs.

"I won't. Don't worry." There's nothing I wouldn't give her, and I will do anything it takes to show her that.

Her back arches, her fingers dig into my skin. *"Ahh!"*

My pace slows as I watch her come apart for me, feeling her body grip me as tight as a fist. I shrug her legs from my shoulders, letting them drop to my waist. She looks up at me, speechless and panting, and I know I've done my job right. Lowering myself onto her, chest against chest, my face hovering just an inch above hers, I take her how I want. Fast. Hard. Unrelenting.

Her eyes find mine. I can tell she's in shreds, still lost in the feeling I give her. With a moan, I pull out just before I lose myself too.

As my soul leaves my body and spills onto her stomach between us, I thank every particle of stardust in the universe for bringing her back to me. It was meant to be this way. The pleasure, the pain, the time needed for us to grow before we came back to each other. We can't change the past, but we have this moment and every moment we choose to be together from now on.

She pulls my face to hers and places a luscious kiss on my lips. "I love you," she whispers.

I smile against her lips. The words make me feel higher than my orgasm. "Say it again."

The front door clicks. I sit up and pull up my pants a second before Jeremy and Chet walk in. Chet's little "Oh" lessens the blow.

"Hey . . . " I awkwardly greet them, my fly still unbuttoned, Teagan doing the best she can to hide the evidence of our fuck from their view, and covering the embarrassment on her face with a hand.

Jeremy's eyes shift between the two of us. "Just leaving my keys, don't mind us. Wouldn't want to interrupt your 'one-night stand.'"

Teagan lets out a little laugh when she sits up. Resting her chin on the couch's back, she sighs. "I'll miss you, Jer."

"No, you won't," Jeremy jokes. On their way out, he stops and looks over his shoulder. "I'm really happy for you two. Seriously," he says, then closes the door.

"One-night stand?" I ask.

She drapes an arm over her eyes and laughs.

~

Feeling thirsty after round three, I pop the bottle of champagne I stole from the wedding, and pour it into one of my glasses I'm sure Teagan will have in the recycle bin tomorrow. The sun went down an hour ago, but we still haven't unpacked a single box. Lying together in bed is enough for us right now. I hand her the glass and curl up next to her beneath the blankets.

She looks exhausted and so goddamn beautiful. The dim light of some candles mixes with the halogen glow from the streetlights outside. It's some dreamy, romantic shit I hope I never wake up from.

"I know it's the first day," I muse, "but this roomie thing is pretty lit."

"Give it time." With a smirk she turns to face me, her hand on my chest, her nose brushing against mine when I wrap her in my arm. "So, about our situationship . . . "

"Yeah?"

"My contract was immaculate, obviously, but it's void now."

"What are you saying?" I let out a sarcastic gasp. "Am I your boyfriend?"

She gives me a weak shove and lies back down.

"We should go over some house rules," she says.

Of course. "Should have seen this coming. Hit me."

"No outside shoes in the house."

"Duh, that's gross."

"Clean up after yourself."

"Yep."

"Toilet seat down, every time. No unwashed dishes in the sink. No dirty underwear on the floor."

"Unless we fall asleep after you take them off me?" I smirk but she doesn't look amused. "Okay, fine. What else?"

After a moment of pondering, she adds, "Cook breakfast for me on the weekends? Those eggs you made?"

"I can do that."

She gnaws her lip to pin her smile. "What about you?"

"I get to make rules too?"

"Two parties doing life together should agree on the terms, right?"

Agreeing on terms we'll likely break almost instantaneously will be our inside joke from now on. "Right." I run my hands along her waist, ignoring the movement happening against my leg. "When you come home from studying at 2 a.m., only wake me up if it's for sex."

"Okay." She laughs.

"Clothing should be kept to the bare minimum while we're home. Bras are for outside use, not indoor. Pants too—except when we have guests."

"Seriously?"

"Uh-huh."

"Are *all* of your rules sex related?"

"No."

"Okay, then. What else?"

I wrap my arms tighter around her, pulling her as close as possible. "Kiss me when you get home and every time you leave, whether you're mad at me or not. And talk to me. About everything. All the time. Even when it hurts."

She gives me a knowing grin. "Deal."

As I brush my fingers against her cheek, my eyes trace every captivating detail of her face. "No breaks, no pauses. Just you and me, forever. We can make it work this time."

She nods. Her smile and soft kiss fill me with bliss. "Should I draft up the new contract?"

EPILOGUE
Teagan

Yet another engagement party.

Practically everyone I know will be there, including the guys. I haven't seen most of them in a year, not since Ryan's wedding, and it has been for the best. Taking a step back from them, even Ryan, was the easiest way to protect my peace through what was by far my most difficult year of school. But we will be together tonight to celebrate another milestone, the same way we always have and possibly always will. Maybe distance makes the heart less prone to homicidal thoughts.

I can't decide on a dress. It's as if I'm going through a checklist of stressors just so I can be upset with *something*. Hate my hair? Check. Wait until the last minute to pick a dress? Check. Get pissed about having to go at all? Check-ity fucking check. Finally, I snatch one from the hanger and step into it.

"If you're putting on the green dress, we are going to fight," Levi yells from my bedroom.

I stare at the green silk in my hands. "I'm not!"

"Oh my god, Teagan. Put on the one I got you!"

I roll my eyes and hang the dress back up. The green one is beautiful and subtle. The one Levi got me screams *Look at me!* at a four-thousand-dollar volume. At least he listened to me and rented it for a somewhat tolerable price, but it's still ridiculous. I'm looking forward to the day when everyone I know is in the *divorce* stage of life so I no longer have to stress over the shape and color of overpriced cloth in my parents' house. But it doesn't seem like that will happen anytime soon.

The silk feels cold when it slides up my legs. Your girl loves a backless, floor-length gown with sleeves, but the color and little train are doing a little too much. It says *I'm excited to be here* when, really, I'm *not*.

I hold the front of the dress against my chest while I walk out. Levi nods with a sheepish smile—so proud of himself—while Rowan sits next to him on my bed, silent but grinning. My nose scrunches into a sneer.

"Don't start, Teags. You look amazing."

"Ugh."

"I said don't start!"

Rowan covers his laugh with a hand. He is thriving—glowing, even—his joy coming easier with every new month of his gap year. Out of the shadow of his overachieving sister and medal-winning Paralympian brother, he is taking his time, finding himself, and it looks amazing on him.

"Levi's right. You look beautiful, sis."

The smile plastered on his face makes my lips twitch up, but I won't give Levi the satisfaction.

Levi slides a crystal bracelet onto my wrist and sets some heels in front of me. As annoying as he is, I trust him.

"You know, I really didn't think Heath would ever do it," Levi says.

"Do what?"

"Want to get married. And so soon." It's as if he is *trying* to give me another reason not to go.

"Yeah, well . . . he's always full of surprises. Fix this, please."

He finishes buckling the strap of the second shoe around my ankle. I take another look at myself in the mirror.

"You don't think it's too much?" I ask again.

"I *know* it's not too much. Now, let's go."

~

I don't want to be here, I complain in my head.

Slipping inside unnoticed, I duck into the back hallway and make my way upstairs. The empty art gallery looks small at first, but the lofted space and balcony provide more than enough room for however many people were invited to this gaudy bullshit. They dimmed the lighting to calming levels, but the fans of red uplighting against the walls adds unnecessary drama.

When I look over, I see him.

Heath laughs with his small circle of family and friends, looking exceptionally dapper in his tux. My body aches for him as I stand awkwardly, not wanting to call attention or interrupt. When he spots me, his expression melts and he comes over.

"There you are."

"Here I am."

With a delicate touch, he pulls my face closer. His warm, lingering kiss calms me.

He pulls away and gives me a dreamy grin. His eyebrows rise when he steps back and looks me over. "You look *hot*."

"Shut up. I knew this dress was ridiculous."

"Levi picked it?"

"Of course."

He laughs at my expense. "What's with the mood?" I kiss him again rather than answering. He pulls away with a chuckle. "You can't shit all over your own engagement party."

I give him the side-eye. "Watch me."

"Babe, your parents are excited and want to celebrate you."

"But I didn't do anything! The one thing that took me zero effort is the thing they decide to make the biggest deal about. Graduating, passing the bar—"

"They're trying," he cuts in. "This is the best they could do and that's more than they've ever done before. Just let it happen."

That's true. Whether they listened to me or Heath's reemergence into our lives finally pushed them over the edge, they've been better. They are being cognizant of the words they say, acknowledging their harmful actions from the past, and have let Rowan make choices for himself while withholding whatever opinions they may have. It's an improvement, however small.

Tonight is the first time they've pressured me into doing something since I blew up on them last summer, and all they were asking was for me to let them throw us this party. They still haven't figured me out, but to be fair, it took me a while to do the same.

I'm still seeing a therapist alongside Heath's mom. She is doing much better, no slipups or regression since starting her regular sessions, and it's been so healthy for their whole family. Even Heath's dad has been softer on him. With Mama healthy again, it gives them fewer reasons to butt heads. Nothing with either of our families is perfect, but it doesn't need to be.

I hug Heath close again. "You know I'm happy, right? Under all the complaining."

There's a dreamy look in his gray eyes when he says, "Of course I do."

"And you know I would marry you tomorrow—I would have married you yesterday, today, a year ago. So *why* do we have to have all these fucking parties?"

"It's a few hours, Teags. Let people have their fun. All you have to do is hold my hand, get drunk, and show people your ring."

I give it another glance. The sapphire-cut diamond with filigree flowers connecting it to the band sparkles in the low lighting. In all honesty, it is hard not to stare at it constantly. It's just so damn shiny. I would be mad about how big it is, but it is his mother's ring. Seeing how happy it made her to pass it to me made it that much more special.

"Can we discuss eloping again?" I ask. His eye-squinting laugh brightens my mood.

"I love you," he says.

"I love you more."

"Impossible."

He kisses me passionately. I melt when he hums against my lips, and we get a little too carried away.

"Do you want to find a closet somewhere?" he asks with a mischievous smile. "For old time's sake?"

"Are you offering me sex at an engagement party?" He nods slowly, that goofy smile plastered on his face. I chuckle, feeling lighter than I have all day. "Let's fucking go."

Looking down at the crowd who has yet to see us, Heath laces his fingers through mine and pulls me with him. Around the corner, we go down a hall and find an off-limits storage room.

We wrap ourselves up in one another, my body heating with every taste of his tongue, every movement of his erection growing against my stomach. His hand reaches up my skirt to pull down my panties. I lick my lips as I unfasten his belt.

"Teags? Teags!" Levi swings open the door. "Dad says the champagne toasts are—" He stops when he sees what's happening, looking back and forth between us. "Y'all are nasty."

He leaves. Heath laughs against my lips, and we get back to business.

~

The next morning, I'm hungover as hell, hiding it the best I can be-hind a pair of shades and a bottle of electrolyte water. I swear the cab hits every bump and pothole in Manhattan.

"Feeling good?" Heath teases me.

"Shut up."

"You can stop here," he tells the driver. He pulls to the curb two blocks from the building. We climb out and the chill of an early-fall breeze instantly helps.

We hold hands while walking up the sidewalk. People give us discerning looks as we pass by. Our accidentally coordinating outfits, his effortlessly handsome existence, my remnants of yesterday's pro-fessional hairstyle—I can admit we give power couple vibes. We're cute or whatever.

The building checks boxes right away. Doorman, elevator, quiet neighbors.

"Welcome in." The Realtor greets us, handing us a flier with the apartment's details. "Let me show you around."

We follow, and I'm half listening, half willing my headache to go away. It's beautiful, just like the three we visited last weekend, but something feels different about this one.

"It's three bedrooms, two baths, with an en suite for the primary bedroom. The previous owner put in new appliances, floors . . ." They continue on but my mind drifts. As we walk around, I get a sense of déjà vu.

The single-line kitchen and island right off the entryway, the straight path through to the living space, the wall of picture windows behind it overlooking the city—finally, it clicks.

I pull Heath's hand, keeping him in the kitchen with me. "This is it," I tell him.

He snakes his arms around my waist. "You like it?"

"It's more than that. This is the place I always pictured we'd be."

I look around the space again, the image filling my mind as if it's happening right in front of me. "This is the table I sit at when I bring work home over the weekends. That's the living room where you chase the kids around." My eyes well with tears. "This is the kitchen where I remember how long I've loved you, then kiss you when no one's looking."

His brow furrows over his smile. "Babe, that was romantic as hell. Are you still drunk?"

I smack a weak hand against his chest.

His playful tease melts into a smile. "I want all of those things too," he says. "This place is ours. I'll make sure of that."

I run my fingers against the back of his neck, staring into his gray eyes. "I know you will."

"Hey." He nudges me. "No one's looking right now."

I smile and pull him into a kiss.

It's funny to think how much difference twelve months can make. It took six years for us to come back to each other, six years to grow and heal from the past, six years we will never get back. But now I know it happened for a reason.

It gave us time to become the people we needed to be for ourselves and for each other. Better versions of those lost kids, newly assured in our identities, more understanding of our shortcomings and our fears—emotionally prepared to be together through it all.

With Heath, the hard times hurt half as much and the good times feel twice as nice. I look at him now and all I can think is, *Holy shit, we are never breaking up.*

ACKNOWLEDGMENTS

Situationship came about seven years ago. A little story outside of my usual subgenre, I lacked the confidence to write it but couldn't get the characters and their backstory out of my head.

Teagan was the embodiment of the "not nice" parts of the strong women I look up to, and the times when I am most proud of myself. Like her, I had to grow up as the odd one out, the unintentional mom of the group, going into a profession where few people looked like me—all while struggling with perfectionism and the damaging coping mechanisms that resulted.

Heath was the uncommon in-betweener, not always accepted as what we know we are but always in love with our culture. He is caught at that defining point in life when you realize you don't have to be like the people around you, and that you get to choose who does or doesn't stay in your life. Losing friends may hurt at first, but gaining the space needed to be your healthiest self is worth it.

This story was meant to be a long example of how growing up is the point. If the person you were five years ago doesn't embarrass you at least a little bit, you haven't grown. This debut of mine will definitely embarrass me five years from now, and that is okay, because this experience has shaped me in ways I never expected. Future me, how we doin'? We good?

To the beautiful humans who saw the teaser all the way back in 2018 and didn't let me know a day of peace until I finally finished it, you are my little bunch of real ones. I wouldn't be here without you. Thank you.

To my council of internet friends who turned into my real friends, thank you for being my messties, my mini PR team, my long-distance therapists.

To Deanna, my editor, thank you for holding my hand and giving me constant pep talks through this amazing journey. You had my back every step of the way, and I am and forever will be grateful for you.

To Anna and the team at Frayed Pages x Wattpad Books, thank you for seeing something I may never see for myself. I will forever be shocked, amazed, and grateful you took a chance on me. Thank you, thank you for this gift of an opportunity.

Finally, and most importantly, thank you to my husband. Thank you for being by my side as we grew from being seventeen and stupid to the weird adultish people we are today. Thank you for sticking with me through all our highs and my lowest of lows. You are my favorite person in the universe, you inspire me every day, and I am so, so proud of you. This book would not exist without your support. I would not exist without you. I like you a lot and you're pretty cute or whatever.

ABOUT THE AUTHOR

E.M. Wilson spends her days designing apartment buildings across the US and her nights immersing herself in the world of contemporary romance. Her passion lies in crafting diverse casts and unapologetically sassy, sex-positive leads. Through plenty of humor, spice, and modern subject matter, her novels provide a humanistic spin to the genre. Based in Seattle, Washington, she continues to expand her horizons alongside her high school sweetheart, ticking off countries on their travel bucket list.

READING GROUP GUIDE

1. Heath and Teagan begin their relationship with no-strings-attached—do you think situationships can stay casual, or are romantic feelings always inevitable?

2. How important is sex to a romantic relationship? And in what ways do Teagan and Heath use their physical relationship to mask intimacy issues?

3. If you have been in your own situationship, how similar was the experience to the one portrayed in the book?

4. In your opinion, which scene was the most romantic? Which scene was the spiciest?

5. Like Teagan, would you end a relationship if your partner wasn't satisfying you sexually? And when Teagan fights with herself about wanting sex versus wanting companionship, do you think she is being honest about her desires? How do you feel female sexuality is portrayed?

6. Teagan writes up a formal written agreement for the situationship—what stipulations do you think would be important to add to the contract?

7. When do you think Teagan and Heath cross over from frenemies to friends? And how does their relationship evolve in terms of their past?

8. Both main characters are using sex as a release and to avoid the hardships of their own personal lives, and we start to see their situationship crumble as their lives become more tense. Do relationships truly help people de-stress, or do they just bring more drama?

9. Teagan and Heath are both very sexually driven and stubborn people—if they never agreed to start their situationship, would they still have ended up together?

10. Can situationships lead to long-lasting romantic relationships, or do you think there are factors that could make the attempt at real companionship difficult?

COMING SOON FROM
FRAYED PAGES x WATTPAD BOOKS

Break Up for Two

BY E.M. WILSON